Praise for Alyssa Maxwell and her
Lady and Lady's Maid Mysteries!

A Devious Death

"Well-crafted . . . Maxwell artfully portrays the personal
dynamics of English society at the time, and readers will
hope to see more of the endearing Phoebe and Eva."
—*Publishers Weekly*

"Tailor-made for fans of Phryne Fisher mysteries
or anyone who misses *Downton Abbey.*"
—*VOYA*

A Pinch of Poison

"Colorful information on the postwar period is combined
with plenty of suspects, all neatly wrapped up in
the style of a classic mystery."
—*Kirkus Reviews*

"A sweet, delightful mystery, which is sure to appeal to
historical-fiction and mystery readers alike."
—*Foreword Reviews*

"Along with a bracing mystery, Maxwell explores
compelling themes. Although this is from a slightly
earlier time period, it's a good match with Rhys
Bowen's Her Royal Spyness series."
—*Booklist*

Murder Most Malicious

"Entertaining . . . some of the characters and scenes
are highly reminiscent of TV's *Downton Abbey,*
but Maxwell makes Phoebe and Eva distinctive
personalities in their own right."
—*Publishers Weekly*

Please turn the page for more rave reviews!

More Outstanding Praise for *Murder Most Malicious*!

"Maxwell provides a neat little mystery and a
heavily atmospheric look at life in a great house
after the trials of the war."
—*Kirkus Reviews*

"Details of the lives of the nobility and their servants,
and the aftermath of the war, are woven throughout
the story, and the forward-thinking Phoebe is
a charming main character."
—*Booklist*

"The story is so good, you don't want it to end."
—*Suspense Magazine*

"*Downton Abbey* fans will enjoy Maxwell's evocative
descriptions of a particular society as it transitions
from the Edwardian Age to modern times."
—*Library Journal*

A DEVIOUS
DEATH

Books by Alyssa Maxwell

Gilded Newport Mysteries

MURDER AT THE BREAKERS

MURDER AT MARBLE HOUSE

MURDER AT BEECHWOOD

MURDER AT ROUGH POINT

MURDER AT CHATEAU SUR MER

MURDER AT OCHRE COURT

Lady and Lady's Maid Mysteries

MURDER MOST MALICIOUS

A PINCH OF POISON

A DEVIOUS DEATH

A MURDEROUS MARRIAGE

Published by Kensington Publishing Corporation

A DEVIOUS DEATH

ALYSSA MAXWELL

KENSINGTON BOOKS
http://www.kensingtonbooks.com

KENSINGTON BOOKS are published by

Kensington Publishing Corp.
119 West 40th Street
New York, NY 10018

All Kensington titles, imprints, and distributed lines are available at special quantity discounts for bulk purchases for sales promotion, premiums, fund-raising, educational, or institutional use.

Special book excerpts or customized printings can also be created to fit specific needs. For details, write or phone the office of the Kensington Sales Manager: Attn. Sales Department. Kensington Publishing Corp, 119 West 40th Street, New York, NY 10018. Phone: 1-800-221-2647.

Kensington and the K logo Reg. U.S. Pat. & TM Off.

First Kensington Hardcover Edition: January 2018

ISBN-13: 978-1-61773-839-5 (ebook)
ISBN-10: 1-61773-839-5 (ebook)

ISBN-13: 978-1-61773-840-1
ISBN-10: 1-61773-840-9
First Kensington Trade Paperback Edition: December 2018

10 9 8 7 6 5 4 3 2 1

Printed in the United States of America

CHAPTER 1

August 1919

"Well, it certainly isn't Foxwood Hall."

Phoebe Renshaw regarded her elder sister, Julia, as she leaned to peer out the open window of their grandfather's Rolls-Royce. A gravel driveway snaked out before the motor-car, rising to meet the open forecourt of their destination, a Jacobean manor house whose gables and chimneys stood proud against an unblemished morning sky.

As Fulton, their chauffeur, negotiated a bend shaded by a sweet chestnut no longer in flower, Phoebe hunched lower in the seat to gaze out the windscreen. She admired the graceful lines of the twin bowed windows that spanned the ground and first floors on either side of an arched front doorway. "I'll grant you Foxwood Hall would dwarf it, but I think it's lovely. I do wonder, though, how Regina was able to afford the place."

"One imagines her father made generous arrangements for her in his will."

"Perhaps, but surely Hastings, as the heir, oversees her

accounts. I have a difficult time imagining him allowing his sister this much financial freedom."

"Yes, well, what Regina wants, Regina usually manages to get." Julia sat back with a sigh. "Besides, you misunderstand me. The house could be a tent for all I care. I'm just so thrilled to be away from Foxwood—I cannot even tell you. No restrictions, no little brother to contend with. When *does* Fox go back to school?" Her eyebrows converged above her midnight-blue eyes. She had taken to darkening her brows from their natural blond, and they stood out boldly against her flawless skin.

"Fox returns to Eton in a couple of weeks." Phoebe looked forward to it. As much as she loved her fifteen-year-old brother, she found she didn't particularly like him these days. He'd developed a defiant streak that reminded her of . . . well . . . of Julia. "Perhaps if you hadn't disappeared without a word in London, Grams wouldn't have kept you at home these past several weeks."

Julia compressed her lips and skewed them to one side in a show of bitterness. "What choice did I have? But it wasn't so much my disappearing that vexed her, as my having turned down Arthur Radbourne." She breathed in heavily and let it out slowly. "Grams and her eligible bachelors. I don't care how many millions he's got. He has an underbite and he's flatulent."

Phoebe chuckled. "Oh, Julia."

"The underbite I could overlook, but the other? Thank you, no. I had no choice but to disappear for a few days so he'd finally take no for an answer."

"Still, you might have telephoned home to let them know where you were. Grams and Grampapa were worried. Where *did* you go, by the way? You've never told me."

"Never you mind; it's best you don't know." To Phoebe's disappointment, Julia's face became shuttered, indicating an end to the conversation. She gazed out at the edifice fast filling the motorcar's windscreen. "I cannot for the life of me understand why anyone—especially Cousin Regina—would *want* to buy a relic like this nowadays. It's positively medieval. Not to mention tucked away where nothing exciting ever happens." Before Phoebe could get a word in, Julia laughed. "The events of last spring and Christmas aside, of course."

Yes, those events could hardly be considered unexciting.

"I'm sure Regina wanted a place where she could quietly grieve for her father." Phoebe frowned. Regina's father, Basil Brockhurst, was her mother's cousin, making Regina and her brother, Hastings, second cousins to Phoebe and her siblings. Basil, Lord Mandeville, had expired of heart failure not quite a month ago, at the relatively young age of sixty. Regina must surely be wretched. Phoebe and Julia's own grandfather suffered ailments of the heart as well. Cousin Basil's passing, tragic in itself, had been a stark reminder of life's all too precarious nature. If anything happened to darling Grampapa . . . First Mama, years ago when they were young, then Papa during the war . . . Phoebe didn't think she could bear another loss any time soon.

"I can't think why she invited us." Julia assumed a bored expression. "It's not as though we're her dearest friends. One supposes she did so out of convenience, seeing how close Foxwood Hall is to here. Once she tires of us, she can send us packing readily enough."

"Really, Julia, must you always be so cynical? I'm sure Regina had no such thought." When Julia offered one of her cavalier shrugs, Phoebe shook her head and allowed herself a small smile. At least they weren't sniping at each other, as they had in the past.

These several years since Papa died had been contentious ones, with Phoebe often feeling as though she had to justify her very existence to her beautiful, accomplished elder sister. The worst of it was, she never could figure out why her sister seemed to abhor her so thoroughly. But last April brought events at which even Julia couldn't shrug; they'd very nearly lost their younger sister, Amelia, and that had brought about a miraculous mellowing of Julia's acerbic self-importance. Phoebe still wouldn't term their relationship a close one, but a cordial one, yes, and she counted that as a huge improvement and quite a relief.

The motorcar rolled to a stop in front of the manor's entrance, arched in the gothic fashion and framed in thick granite casing. A second motorcar carrying their two lady's maids and their luggage had turned onto the service driveway that took them around back to the servants' entrance.

Fulton opened the rear passenger door, but Phoebe hesitated before sliding out. "Anyway, we'll find out why Regina invited us soon enough. Here she is now."

The front door had opened and Regina Brockhurst stepped out wearing stunning pink-and-purple crepe de chine with gold metallic trim. The garment rippled with the breeze like the petals of an exotic flower while the gold shimmered warmly in the sun. Her abundant, inky black hair was swept up in an arrangement of loose curls framed by a silk headband, and an amethyst and marcasite necklace glittered just below the hollow of her neck.

"She certainly doesn't appear to be much in mourning, does she?" With a grin, Julia slid over and nudged Phoebe to exit the vehicle.

"Julia, Phoebe, *darlings*." Regina came toward them, all five feet, eleven inches of her sleek form swaying gracefully. A beringed hand reached out to them. "I'm so pleased you could come."

Phoebe returned the greeting and rose up on her toes to kiss her cousin's cheek. "Dearest Regina, I'm so very sorry about your father."

"Yes, thank you, Phoebe. Poor Father, expiring so suddenly that way." Her lips formed a little ball of a pout, before she smiled again and reached to embrace Julia. "Do, *do* come inside and make yourselves utterly at home. I've been simply dying for you to see my newest acquisition. It's charming, isn't it, though admittedly rather gloomy inside. But that shall be remedied soon enough. And it's all mine, free and clear. What *do* you think?"

Phoebe might have imagined it, or perhaps it was the sigh of the breeze, but she could have sworn Julia groaned behind her.

Eva Huntford, lady's maid to the Earl of Wroxly's two younger granddaughters, couldn't exit the motorcar fast enough for her liking. Though the trip had only been a few miles from home, the distance had been interminable thanks to Eva's fellow passenger. Initially, she had welcomed the hiring of a new lady's maid for the eldest Renshaw sibling, Julia, for it meant a lightening of Eva's own duties. Now she had only two ladies to look after instead of three, and with youngest sister Amelia away at school most of the year, Eva could focus the lion's share of her efforts on middle sister, Phoebe.

Of course, the addition to Foxwood Hall's staff hadn't been for Eva's benefit. After a quiet spring following some disturbing events at the nearby Haverleigh School for Young Ladies, the Countess of Wroxly had decided it was time to center her attentions on her eldest granddaughter. After all, Lady Wroxly had declared, Julia wasn't getting any younger. What she needed was a husband—a wealthy one—and that meant venturing into society on a more regular basis. Hence she needed a lady's maid of her own.

But *this* woman! As the motorcar carrying the two maids followed the drive to the servants' entrance at the side of the house, Myra Stanley craned her neck to gaze out the back window. "Do you see that," she said in a voice that rasped as if with heavy doses of smoke and whiskey. Her stockings—silk, if Eva wasn't mistaken—made a shushing sound as she crossed one leg over the other beneath her calf-length skirt. "Not a single servant lined up to greet our ladies. What kind of welcome is that when the lady of the house steps out alone?"

"Perhaps Miss Brockhurst hasn't had time to hire a full house staff," Eva suggested. Indeed, the farther they drove off the main drive, the more unkempt the greenery became. Box hedges needed a good straightening, while hydrangea and tangled roses reached beyond their beds. Obviously, Miss Brockhurst was in need of a gardener.

"Then she has no business entertaining guests, does she?" The woman's green eyes sparked and her thin lips pursed.

"She is a cousin of the Renshaws and needn't stand on ceremony. Besides, it's hardly our place to judge."

"Bah." A terse shake of her head sent a lock of brown hair slipping from beneath Myra Stanley's hat, a felt, bowler-type affair that sported a blue rosette along the band. She rubbed the tip of her decidedly hawkish nose and sniffed. "What is anything without ceremony? Without the proper dignity?"

Eva was spared having to answer when the motorcar jerked to a stop. They had entered a circular courtyard enclosed by a ragged excuse for tall laurel hedges. Double oaken doors appeared to lead into the basement level of the house. She stepped out onto the drive, curious as to why no one appeared to greet them, and went to the doors to knock, having to tread over fallen leaves and twigs in the process.

After several moments of no response she called out, "Hello, is anyone there? Hello?"

Their driver, one of the footmen from home, set their bags, along with those of Lady Julia and Lady Phoebe, on the pavement, tipped his hat, and bade them good day, leaving Eva and Miss Stanley very much alone in the abandoned courtyard. A warm breeze sifted through unruly holes in the hedge, and somewhere beyond Eva's vision, a bird warbled. She knocked again.

"This is ridiculous," Miss Stanley said behind her. "No one out front, no one manning the service entrance. What kind of place is this? I tell you, Lady Diana would never countenance such a slapdash running of a household."

"Then perhaps you should have stayed in Lady Diana's employ," Eva murmured. She couldn't help herself. Avoiding eye contact with Miss Stanley, she sidestepped to peer in through a window. A black-and-white-tiled hallway stretched away into shadow.

"What was that?" Miss Stanley's heels clicked as she sauntered closer. "What did you say?"

"Nothing."

Eva moved away from the window and took several strides into the center of the driveway. She shielded her eyes from the midday sun and glanced up at the house. Abandonment seemed to define High Head Lodge, reminding her of when the Haverleigh School had been forced to close, the students sent home or farmed out to nearby families. A killer had prowled the halls and intruded on the most hallowed of the school's grounds. The dreadful memory sent a shiver through Eva despite the summer heat. A sudden step behind her sent her flinching out of Myra Stanley's reach.

Not that Miss Stanley had raised a hand to her. But the woman towered over her, glowering. "I heard very well what you said. As you know, Miss Huntford, it was through no fault of my own that I could not remain in Lady Diana's employ."

"Yes, yes. Honestly, what does it matter at the moment?" Eva dismissed Miss Stanley's pique with an impatient wave. An uneasy sensation that started at the base of her spine slithered up to her nape, a feeling that told her something wasn't right. It was an instinct born of necessity, and one she had learned to trust. Suddenly she longed to lay eyes on her young mistress, and Lady Julia as well, to reassure herself that High Head Lodge harbored no threats to their well-being.

"It matters to me," Myra Stanley persisted. "I will not have my reputation as a lady's maid maligned by you or anyone else, Miss Huntford. When Lady Diana married Mr. Cooper last month, she took on a new home with its own full staff. She was loath to let me go, I can tell you that."

Eva leveled a skeptical stare on Miss Stanley. She had never heard of a gentlewoman *not* taking her trusted lady's maid with her to a new home, fully staffed or not. No, there was more to the story of why Miss Stanley no longer worked for Lady Diana Manners Cooper, but at this precise moment Eva didn't give a fig about whatever secrets had sent Myra Stanley seeking new employment, or how she had bamboozled the Countess of Wroxly into taking her on without a proper inquiry into her background.

At present, Eva knew two things: She didn't care at all for Myra Stanley, and she needed to find entry into High Head Lodge.

As if someone read her thoughts, the service door opened with a rustle of the old leaves scattering on the walkway. A woman wearing a serviceable tweed suit in the military style that had become popular during the war beckoned to them. A mere slip of a woman, she reached Eva's chin at best and sported a slender physique and an almost girlish, elfin chin. Her eyes, however, held a steady confidence that spoke of someone well past her youth. "Come with me, please."

Past her youth, perhaps, but still far too young to be the housekeeper. And she was certainly not dressed as a maid, nor any other house staff Eva could think of. Even a lady's maid wouldn't wear brown tweed, nor would she sport anything approaching fashionable lines—even fashion two or three years behind the times—while on duty. Eva's gaze dropped to the woman's low-heeled boots, brown to match the suit, sturdy and sensible, but of fine leather and obviously new. Curious.

"High time you showed up to let us in." Miss Stanley's grating voice jarred Eva from her speculations, but daunted their mystery woman not in the least. Miss Stanley hefted her bag and held it out. "I am Lady Julia Renshaw's personal maid. Kindly call someone to carry the bags and escort us to our rooms. We have a lot of work to do settling our ladies in."

Eva winced. Even if this person were the scullery maid, she would not have taken that tone with her. This woman appeared unfazed. She merely chuckled and said, "Follow me." She turned about to lead the way.

"I beg your pardon." Miss Stanley hurried to catch up to her. "The bags, if you please."

"I'm afraid you'll have to carry them up yourselves. Or ask your mistresses to help you."

"What? Of all the impertinence. Do you know who the Renshaws *are?*"

Despite her own rising curiosity as to whom they were presently following into the house, Eva chuckled as well, content to observe how this would play out. She found herself hoping the woman *was* the housekeeper, for if so, Myra Stanley would find herself short of linens, hot water, and timely breakfasts for the duration of their stay. She hoisted Lady Phoebe's valises, one in each hand. With a great show of indignant reluctance, Miss Stanley did the same with Lady Julia's bags.

Without another word they were led past silent store-rooms, larders, and work areas. A pervasive stillness weighted the atmosphere, almost oppressive and so un-like the bustling servants' domain at Foxwood Hall. Miss Brockhurst did indeed need to people her new estate with workers and maintenance staff.

Soon they came to the main kitchen where two women, one barely out of her teens and the other middle-aged, stood quietly working at the center table. They barely glanced up as Eva and the others strode past, but the elder said to them, "Breakfast is at six thirty sharp. Be here or you're welcome to make your own."

Despite the terse message, the voice was not an unamiable one, but of course that did not stop Miss Stanley har-rumphing again. Finally, they climbed a narrow flight of stairs up three levels to a utilitarian corridor with numer-ous rooms opening onto either side. Their footsteps were loud on the wide-plank flooring. Panting to catch her breath, Eva peered into simply furnished bedrooms, some with two iron bedsteads, others with one. The rooms were spacious for servants' quarters, with large windows af-fording generous views of the surrounding treetops. What these quarters lacked, however, were any signs of habita-tion. There were no garments hanging on the wall pegs, no personal effects neatly arranged on the dresser tops, and not a single scuff mark on the buffed wooden floors. Miss Brockhurst appeared to be living in her newly acquired es-tate with merely a cook, a cook's assistant, and whatever role this woman happened to play.

"Here you are." The woman raised both tweed-clad arms, pointing to two rooms across from each other. "You may select whichever you prefer. These are the closest to the washroom and water closet." She stepped into the bedroom on her right. "See here." She waved Eva and Miss Stanley inside and pointed to a contraption with buttons, a tube, and a cone that sat on a hook much like that on a telephone. "Have you used one of these before?"

Both Eva and Miss Stanley shook their heads. Foxwood Hall still used the original system of bell pulls to alert the staff to the family's needs, but vocal communications were achieved through the more modern intra-house telephones that connected several of the main rooms to the house-keeper's office and butler's pantry. Eva had never had occasion to use a system like this.

"These speaking tubes connect you to the rooms below. When one of your employers pushes the button for a certain room, the bell will sound, letting you know she wishes to speak with you. Rather archaic, but efficient."

With that she exited the room with a quick step that spoke of the same efficiency as the speaking tubes—simple but direct. Miss Stanley followed her out to the corridor. "Excuse me."

The woman turned, one eyebrow raised in expectation. She waited in silence.

"We would like some tea, if you please."

"Then I suggest you return to the kitchen and make some."

With a huff, Miss Stanley drew up short. "How dare you? I'll have you know I intend to see that Miss Brockhurst learns of your boorish behavior. Miss Huntford and I are lady's maids, not common servants. Clearly you do not understand protocol, nor do you have the slightest grasp of basic common decency." Several seconds passed. When no response seemed imminent, Miss Stanley raised her chin to a haughty angle. "Well, what do you have to say for yourself?"

The woman smiled, but only briefly. "Clearly there has been a misunderstanding. I am no servant, common or otherwise. My name is Olive Asquith, and I am the very good friend of Miss Brockhurst. I received you below as a cour-

tesy to Miss Brockhurst and her guests, and if you must
know, I believe lady's maids—and butlers, footmen, and
all the rest—are a good lot of balderdash that have no
place in modern society. You had best realize that if you
intend to survive in a world that is fast losing its patience
with oppressive and outdated traditions.

"Now, in this house," she went on briskly and without
giving Miss Stanley a chance to deliver the retort so obviously sizzling on her tongue, "you'll find only the cook
and her assistant, for neither Miss Brockhurst nor I know
our way around a kitchen."

"But who cleans?" Miss Stanley demanded. "Who does
the laundry?"

"A married couple comes every other day or so to clean
and perform any labor that needs doing. The laundry is
sent out, and Miss Brockhurst intends to engage a gardener, since again, neither of us have any aptitude for hor-
ticulture. Other than that, we see no use for servants. Our
meals are served buffet style; we serve ourselves and stack
our own used dishes on the sideboard for the cook's assistant to collect. Now, I'll leave you to settle in, and if you
need anything, there is a linen cupboard at the end of the
hall. It's kept unlocked. Anything else you'll most likely
find belowstairs."

She strode away, her boots again loud on the floor-
boards, her small hips barely swaying beneath her narrow
skirt. Eva rather enjoyed the moment; for the first time
that day, Miss Myra Stanley had been rendered not only
silent, but utterly dumbfounded, as indicated by the drop
of her chin and her gaping mouth.

"Everything goes." Cousin Regina stood in the center of
the drawing room and swept her arms in wide circles. "All
of it."

Phoebe exchanged a glance of surprise with Julia. She

had just finished complimenting the lovely balance of the room's heavy brocades with lighter, airy florals. Regina had immediately turned up her nose.

"It's awful," she sang out. "So utterly last century. I bought the place lock, stock, and barrel, as you can see, but I had no intention of keeping any of the furnishings. We are marching into the modern era, and this house shall march with us."

"So you intend to gradually replace what's here," Phoebe ventured as she mentally began adding up the expense of such an undertaking.

Regina shook her ebony curls and wrinkled her nose. "No, silly. I want it gone as soon as humanly possible. That's why you're here."

Julia sat across from Phoebe on one of several settees in the long room, one leg crossed over the other and swinging with restless energy. "A rather ambitious endeavor in a house of this size, not to mention the expense."

Phoebe shot her sister another glance. Never mind that they rarely agreed on anything; it was uncharacteristic of Julia to ever mention money, or frugality in particular.

Regina chose to ignore the observation. "There is a particular style I want. I saw it in France before the war, promoted by *La Société des Artistes Décorateurs*. My instincts tell me it is going to be all the rage once the rest of Europe settles down. It's divinely innovative and so very modern. The best way I can describe it is clean, flowing, curving lines, very geometric, very . . ." Her expression became animated. "Daring and unencumbered."

"Rather like you," Phoebe remarked.

"Yes," Regina exclaimed. "Like me. I suppose spending the first few years of my life in India, during Father's posting on the viceroy's executive council, taught me to appreciate the exotic and the unexpected."

"Undoubtedly," Julia said with a slight roll of her eyes. "And how can we be of help?"

"I need your keen eyes to help me design a concept for each room of the house," Regina replied. "I wish to begin placing orders at the first opportunity."

"Shouldn't you seek out a professional? Julia can be of help, of course, but I'm afraid I'm not much for design of any kind." Phoebe took in the room again, experiencing a vague sense of mourning for the lovely furnishings, carved and gilded, that would soon be cast off. The paintings, many of them portraits of the family who once owned the estate, would undoubtedly be among the first to go. And the two matching silk fire screens, the heavy curtains with their sweeping, tasseled valances, and the adorable courting sofa in the far corner, with its seats that curved around to face each other—all relics of a bygone era.

Then, suddenly, she had an idea . . .

"Are you interested in donating some of the house's contents?" Hopefulness filled her. "Of course you'll wish to sell the larger pieces and anything of true value, but the organization I started last spring for the Relief and Comfort of Veterans and their Families, or the RCVF, as we call it, could truly benefit from household items—linens, draperies, bedding, things of that sort. It's for the—"

"Perhaps you should concentrate on a room at a time," Julia interrupted. "Not merely with expense in mind, but due to the rather overwhelming nature of such an undertaking. We're talking about an entire house."

Not to be overshadowed by her sister, Phoebe tried again. "Yes, but the RCVF—"

"I see your point," Regina said to Julia as if Phoebe hadn't spoken, "but I wish to accomplish one overall look for the place, rather than make a disjointed, higgledy-piggledy job of it. That's the old way. I want unity. Uni*form*ity. A sense of order throughout."

"Well, all right then . . ." Julia trailed off as a figure appeared in the doorway. She and Phoebe both regarded the woman, dressed in dreary country tweeds of a color that matched the severe and simple arrangement of her hair. The housekeeper, Phoebe guessed, possibly just arrived home from a trip to town. Regina's attention was focused on a collection of porcelain figurines in the gold-leafed curio cabinet. Julia whispered her name to capture her attention. "Regina, dear, this creature seems to want to speak to you."

"Creature?" Regina repeated far too loudly for Phoebe's comfort. She inwardly cringed at the discourtesy and was sorely tempted to kick Julia's ankle. Regina glanced over her shoulder, then straightened and turned. "Olive, don't be a goose. Come in and meet my cousins. Phoebe, Julia, this is my dear friend, Olive Asquith. Olive, these are my Renshaw cousins, whom I have told you so much about."

Julia's eyebrows went up, her interest obviously piqued. "Asquith, as in our former prime minister?"

"Indeed not. How d'you do?" Miss Asquith ran her gaze over Phoebe and Julia, leaving Phoebe with the distinct sense of having been judged and found wanting. It was something in the tilt of the woman's head, the twitch of her eyebrow that reminded Phoebe of her grandmother when she disapproved of something. She instinctively sat up straighter. "I've shown your maids to rooms on the third floor. Though honestly, Regina," she added, shifting her attention as she walked several steps into the room, "isn't relegating them to the attic rather an affront to our ideals?"

"What"—Julia spoke out of the side of her mouth, for Phoebe's hearing only—"is she talking about?"

As Phoebe shrugged, Miss Asquith's slight form whipped about in Julia's direction. "I am talking about the ridiculous notion that someone can be born better than anyone else."

If Regina's friend thought she could take Julia aback, she was in for disappointment. Phoebe compressed her lips to hide a smile as Julia met Miss Asquith's obvious disdain with an innocent expression. "But what has that got to do with where Eva and Myra sleep? Surely there are no ghosts in the attic, or bats or squirrels to bite them in their sleep?"

Phoebe suppressed a chuckle.

"Olive, be nice." Regina moved to her friend's side and wrapped an arm about her waist. "My cousins are used to doing things in a certain way. People don't change overnight, you know."

Miss Asquith shrugged, and her features eased from their stern expression of a moment ago. "If you say so, Regina."

"I do. We were discussing the refurbishment of the house, so you've arrived just in time." Regina said to Phoebe and Julia, "Olive has quite a few ideas herself."

"Exactly how do you believe people should change?" Julia persisted, apparently enjoying the discussion. Phoebe detected the mockery in her tone that would be lost on someone who didn't know her well.

"Oh, let's not talk about such things," Regina said quickly. "We're here to have a little fun. Come, let's all walk through the downstairs rooms. Julia, I'd especially like your opinion on the dining room. Come along, ladies. You, too, Olive," she added when the woman seemed disinclined to follow.

Regina and Julia led the way across the hall, charmingly oval in design with several rooms opening onto it from three sides of the house, and presided over by a curving staircase. Phoebe let her pace lag so Miss Asquith would have no choice but to remain alone in the drawing room, contrary to Regina's request, or fall into step with Phoebe, which she apparently chose to do. She seemed an unlikely companion for Regina, for the two women couldn't be more opposite in manner, looks, and, if Phoebe guessed correctly, circumstances. Surely Miss Asquith hailed from modest means—not that she personally found that a deterrent to friendship with Regina. But Regina had always struck her as someone who believed in choosing one's friends from one's own social circle. What could two such apparently different individuals possibly have in common?

A small suspicion sneaked into Phoebe's mind. She hoped it wasn't Regina's money that drew Olive Asquith to her side.

"How long have you and my cousin known each other?" she asked as she and Miss Asquith followed several paces behind Regina and Julia.

"About a year now, I suppose."

"And how did you meet?"

"At a meeting."

Phoebe waited for more to this cryptic answer, but nothing else seemed forthcoming. "Oh? What sort of meeting was that?"

"A social meeting," she said evasively. "Of the sort that are rather common in London nowadays, especially since the war ended."

"I see." Phoebe did not see, really, but she supposed direct questions would glean little from the reticent Miss Asquith. "Perhaps one of your social groups would be interested in the charity I run. We provide aid to veterans of the Great War who reside in the Cotswolds. Now that Regina owns a home here—"

"You'll have to speak to her."

The terse interruption felt rather like a slap on the hand. Phoebe flinched but quickly recovered. "Yes, I suppose that would be best. Will you be staying on here for a while?"

To her complete astonishment, Miss Asquith sped up to

join the others before Phoebe had finished asking the question. When she entered the dining room, Miss Asquith had once more taken up position at Regina's side. They linked arms. With her free hand Regina gestured to the tapestries, depicting hunting scenes, covering the north wall above the massive stone-and-marble hearth. "Those dismal things must come down, of course, and I intend to reface the fireplace in something sleek and—"

"Modern, yes." Julia went to the fireplace and ran her hand over the surround and mantle. "It's quite good craftsmanship, Regina, and I can see this has been carved from a single block. What a shame if it were to crack while being uninstalled. Are you certain you wish to take the chance?"

"Oh, pish posh. So what if it cracks into a million pieces. I don't want it, and so it must go."

With a sigh, Julia glanced up at the tapestries. "Are these very old, do you know? They look to me to be Flemish, which would mean they'll fetch a good price at auction."

"I suppose, but I won't wait for them or anything else to sell before I began making changes. I want this house renovated before Christmas at the latest. If I have to, I'll give them away. Do you think a museum might want them?"

Phoebe rounded on her cousin. "Surely you can't mean to simply dispose of a fortune's worth of treasures, Regina. There is no sense in that."

With laughter, Regina said, "Darlings, rest assured, I do not need the money. I've got heaps. Father saw to that."

Phoebe and Julia exchanged a thoroughly puzzled look. Julia cleared her throat. "I'm sure your father was very generous to you in his will, but what you're proposing for this house is—"

"You don't understand." Regina let go another peal of

laughter. Miss Asquith sniggered into her hand. "Father left me nearly everything."

Phoebe frowned, her expression mirrored by Julia. "But the entail . . . your brother . . ."

"Oh, yes, Hastings has inherited Father's title and honors. He's now Lord Mandeville, and long may he relish it. The entail, you see, is for all practical purposes bankrupt. Has been for nearly two generations before Father. But Father had a knack for finance and built up a fortune of his own, with which he was free to do as he pleased. And it pleased him to leave his riches to me."

"But . . ." Feeling slightly disoriented, Phebe pressed a hand to her breastbone. "What about your mother? And the London house? Without resources, how will Hastings manage?"

"That's Hastings's problem, isn't it? And Mother has a decent dower portion, if she can learn to live within her means."

"Surely you'll supplement her income." Even Julia, usually uninterested in the fortunes of others, seemed shocked by this development. "And you won't allow Hastings to lose Mandeville House."

Regina's only response was to turn a beaming smile on Olive Asquith. The two linked arms again, and Regina turned with her to face the windows. "Those diamond mullions obstruct the view, don't you think? I find them depressing."

"They certainly are," Miss Asquith readily agreed. "I think replacing them with wide-paned French doors would be a vast improvement. They would let in more light and give easier access to the veranda."

With a nod, Regina once more appealed to Julia. "Come, cousin, and give me your ideas on how to arrange this room to its best advantage."

Julia stayed where she was. "Perhaps if you gave us a hint as to your intentions for the house, I'd be better able to advise you. Will it be house parties, hunting, or perhaps your personal retreat?"

A school, Phoebe thought with a ray of hope, but knew better than to suggest such a thing.

"House parties, now there's a thought." Regina tipped back her head and laughed once more. "I assure you, I'm quite finished with house parties. Such a bore."

Phoebe tended to agree, but her cousin had yet to answer the question. "Then what? You're being terribly mysterious, Regina."

After seeking and receiving an encouraging nod from Miss Asquith, Regina grinned. "High Head Lodge is to be a place of study, discussion, and debate. A gathering place for today's enlightened individuals, where they can explore new ideas without fear of harassment. A place where the—"

"Perhaps that's enough said, Regina." Miss Asquith gave Regina's sleeve a tug. She also, Phoebe noticed, clenched her jaw before continuing. "You don't wish to overwhelm your cousins. And first things first. The house must be made ready before it can be used for anything."

"You're so right, Olive, dear." She regarded Phoebe and Julia like a society hostess greeting her guests. "Come. Let's have a little fun redesigning these rooms, and then we'll see what Cook has concocted for lunch. She's no Parisian chef, but for a local woman she's delightfully talented."

Over the next forty or so minutes, Julia threw herself into the task assigned her, while Phoebe continued to wonder about Regina's plans, the reasons behind them, and the role she herself was expected to play in the coming days. She knew little about interior design and, other than an appreciation for the artistic value of paintings and furniture, could not have cared less. To her knowledge, Foxwood Hall had looked much the same for generations, with any changes having been so gradual as to hardly be noticed. She couldn't fathom why it was so important to Regina to refurbish so quickly and completely.

Could Olive Asquith have anything to do with this re-decorating frenzy? Taking in the woman's less than flattering attire, Phoebe could hardly imagine the woman giving two figs about her surroundings. Then again, Miss Asquith's suit spoke of a no-nonsense, utilitarian approach to life. Had she impressed the same outlook on Regina? Hence her talk of clean, flowing lines?

It was all very confusing, but of one thing Phoebe felt fairly certain. Something wasn't quite right at High Head Lodge.

CHAPTER 2

Eva banged on Myra Stanley's bedroom door with the side of her fist. "What are you doing? We're needed downstairs. Now." Lady Phoebe had called up a few minutes ago on the speaking tubes that connected their rooms to those below. The ladies were going shopping this morning and they wished to leave within the half hour.

"Yes, I know. I'll come in a moment. I'm just . . ."

Her patience at its end, Eva tried the knob, only to find the door locked. She pounded again. "I'm going down without you, then. If Lady Julia asks—" The lock clicked and the door opened. Eva stepped back to let Miss Stanley out of the room, then took another backward lurch when she got a good look at her. "What have you done to yourself?" She leaned in closer. "Are you wearing cosmetics? Did you cut your hair?"

In the hour since they'd had their breakfast, Miss Stanley had transformed herself. The front of her hair, usually smoothed back in the same nondescript bun Eva wore, had been clipped into bangs that fell nearly into her eyes and heat-curled into frazzled spirals. Her lips were brighter, her eyes lined in black, and her cheeks each bore a splotch of rouge. Unless, of course, the other cosmetics had brought on a rash.

"You can't go out like that." Eva folded her arms in front of her. "What on earth are you thinking?"

"Are there laws against lady's maids wanting to look their best on a trip into town?"

"Laws, perhaps not. But general rules of proper behavior and decorum, most certainly." Eva dropped her arms to her sides and sighed. "And I'm sorry to have to tell you, but you don't exactly look your best. Now, if you value your position in the Renshaw household, you'll go scrub your face clean." She reached out, fingering one of the curls that grazed Miss Stanley's upper eyelids. "I don't suppose there's anything to be done about your hair for now. Perhaps Lady Julia won't notice. But go on, take off that makeup and be quick about it."

Miss Stanley reemerged five minutes later, her face freshly scrubbed. Eva hurried her at a run along the corridor and down the stairs to make up the time. They reached the first floor service landing, and as Eva opened the door, Miss Stanley came to an abrupt halt.

"Why doesn't this house have a guest wing? Foxwood Hall has a guest wing. It seems rather untoward to accommodate the guests along the same corridor as the lady of the house."

Eva suppressed a groan of frustration. "Untoward? In what way? What has come over you all of a sudden?" She seized Miss Stanley's hand and tugged her along. "We're late enough as it is."

Miss Stanley brushed past her, hurried down the corridor, and disappeared into Lady Julia's bedroom. As the door closed, Eva heard Lady Julia comment, "You look different, Stanley. Have you changed in some way?"

With a shake of her head, Eva continued to Lady Phoebe's room at a more sedate, and dignified, pace. She had fixed Lady Phoebe's hair earlier, and now Eva found her mistress nearly dressed as well. Lady Phoebe wore her silk chiffon today, with its layered hem, three-quarter sleeves, and high, ruched waistband. Eva buttoned the buttons down her back and helped her on with her jewelry, hat, and light summer gloves. Clear azure skies framed the trees outside the window, promising a lovely day with no threat of rain or chilly breezes—the perfect day for Phoebe's newest ensemble from Selfridge's.

"I'm sorry to keep you waiting, my lady," Eva said as she secured Phoebe's hat, a sporty little affair with a narrow brim and a wide band, with a simple pearl stick pin.

"Not at all." Phoebe turned toward the full-length mirror while Eva draped a nearly translucent wrap around her shoulders. "You did seem a bit out of breath when you arrived, though. Was there a problem?"

"No, everything is fine."

Phoebe eyed her while Eva attempted to avoid her gaze. It was no good, however; she never could hide anything from Lady Phoebe. "Eva, what?"

She didn't know whether to chuckle or frown as she confessed, "Miss Stanley was acting rather peculiar this morning."

"Peculiar how?"

"Suffice it to say, you'll understand when you see her. Although I've already intervened somewhat, much to her chagrin, I fear."

With a little grin of speculation, Lady Phoebe narrowed her gaze on Eva. A knock sounded at the door and, holding a wide-brimmed hat in her hand, Miss Brockhurst poked her head in. "Are you ready, Phoebe?"

"Yes, all ready to go."

"You, Julia, and Olive and I shall go in my car. I'll drive.

I've arranged for another car from the village for your maids." She gestured at Eva with her chin. "I'll go and see if Julia is ready. See you downstairs."

Lady Phoebe stopped her with a question. "Aren't you bringing your own maid?"

Regina scoffed, but good-naturedly. "I haven't got one, goose, not anymore. I do for myself, and I have Olive to help me if I need her. Come along, then." With that she sprang away with a light step. Phoebe turned to Eva.

"That's rather peculiar, too, don't you think?" She fingered the gold-encircled pearl hanging around her neck. "My cousin is planning to spend wildly to refurbish this house in the coming weeks, yet she no longer employs a lady's maid?"

"Perhaps she's economizing in some areas in order to afford her renovations."

"Perhaps, but she assured Julia and me that she's got, as she put it, 'heaps' of money. The bulk of her father's fortune wasn't part of the entail, and he left most of it to Regina."

"I suppose she simply doesn't want a maid, then." Eva widened the bedroom door. "After you, my lady."

They found Lady Julia and Myra Stanley waiting in the downstairs hall. Lady Julia appeared eager to go, her foot tapping with impatience. Miss Stanley, on the other hand, fidgeted and repeatedly darted her gaze at the staircase.

"We'll wait outside," Eva said to Phoebe, and walked past Miss Stanley to the front door. Miss Stanley hurried to follow her.

A four-door motorcar in shiny burgundy with a cream canvas roof sat on the drive, its sleek lines gleaming in the morning sunlight. Behind it, an ordinary sedan waited with its motor running. Eva went to stand beside the costly-looking convertible, undoubtedly Miss Brockhurst's vehicle.

"Let's wait in the other motorcar," Miss Stanley suggested and pointed her feet in that direction.

"No," Eva replied with a twinge of impatience, "we wait here in case the ladies need help getting into *this* motor."

"Oh, yes, I suppose . . ."

Eva rounded on the woman. "What is wrong with you today that I must explain your job to you? Is there something on your mind? Anything you'd like to tell me?"

"No, everything is—"

Miss Stanley broke off as the front door opened. Her chin disappeared into the collar of her light cotton coat. The four ladies strolled out onto the drive, three of them chatting and laughing at something that had apparently been said inside. Only Miss Asquith remained silent, looking, in Eva's opinion, rather surly in her gray felt hat and another utilitarian suit. This one had a pleated skirt that swayed when Miss Asquith walked and sported smart black braid on the shoulders and cuffs of the jacket.

Lady Phoebe was the first to reach the motorcar. "Goodness, Regina, is this a Daimler?"

Her sister answered for their cousin. "It most certainly is, and the latest model unless my eyes deceive me. The automobile of kings," Julia added with an appreciative lift of her eyebrows.

"It is pretty, isn't it? I needed a mode of transportation living out here in the country, didn't I? Why not the best?" Miss Brockhurst slipped an arm across Miss Asquith's shoulders. The elaborate pin holding her wide hat in place glittered in the sunlight. "Shall we have the hood down today, Olive?"

"I nearly sprained my wrist the other day trying to help you fold the dratted thing down."

"We'll lose our hats with the hood down. Let's just be off." As Lady Julia approached the vehicle with a decisive stride, Eva opened the rear passenger door for her since Miss Stanley made no move to do so. Over her shoulder Lady Julia asked her cousin, "Where's your driver?"

"You're looking at her, of course." Miss Brockhurst opened the driver's door, but just before she slipped in, she stopped short, her gaze pinned on Miss Stanley, whose chin continued to seek refuge within her collar. She stared for a good long moment, until even Eva felt the urge to squirm. Finally, her eyes narrowed and she said, "You look familiar. Do I know you?"

Miss Stanley flinched, then shook her head. "I don't believe so, miss."

Eva would have sworn she spoke a half octave lower than her usual register.

"I think I do . . ." Miss Brockhurst compressed her lips, obviously searching her memory. Miss Stanley's complexion drained of color, and suddenly Miss Brockhurst's eyes widened and her nose flared. She drew back as if Miss Stanley had struck her. After a second or two her genteel mask fell back into place. "No, I must be mistaken. Never mind." She slipped into the driver's seat. "Shall we, ladies? Phoebe, Olive, are you coming or not?"

Miss Asquith circled the long, lustrous nose of the vehicle to the passenger side. Miss Stanley hurried over the second motor and all but dove in. Before Lady Phoebe climbed into the rear seat of the Daimler, she whispered to Eva, "What was that just about? If I didn't know better, I'd think Miss Stanley attempted to don a disguise this morning so my cousin wouldn't recognize her. *Most* peculiar."

"Most," Eva agreed.

Phoebe's feet ached and her head throbbed. Beside her in the rear seat of Regina's Daimler, Julia didn't look as if she'd fared any better during their shopping trip to Bristol. Between them sat several parcels wrapped in brown paper

and secured with twine: new shoes and a matching handbag for Phoebe; a silk shirtwaist, several pairs of stockings, a set of lace-edged handkerchiefs, and three pairs of
gloves for Julia. Regina and Miss Asquith had a similar as-
sortment of items between them in the front seat, the ma-
jority of them for Regina. They had also visited at least a
half dozen drapers' shops and furniture import stores.

It wasn't so much the shopping that had brought on the
ache behind Phoebe's temples. It had been the bickering
between Regina and Miss Asquith. Every time Regina had
chosen an item for her new home, Miss Asquith raised an
argument about why it was a bad choice. Too elaborate,
too excessive, too expensive. Phoebe frowned at the memory. Despite Regina's assertion that she wished to fill her
new home with clean, modern lines, she nonetheless grav-
itated to more traditional designs. It seemed Miss Asquith
had endless ideas on how Regina should and shouldn't
spend her money.

And that gave Phoebe pause . . .

At long last they turned onto the drive of High Head
Lodge, and Phoebe yearned to retreat to her bedroom with
a hot cup of tea and enjoy some quarrel-free moments to
herself. As she stepped out of the Daimler, the motorcar
carrying Eva and Miss Stanley turned up the service drive,
and then a third motorcar puttered through the main gates
and headed toward the house.

"Who is this, then?" Phoebe gestured at the approaching vehicle. "Are you expecting more company, Regina?"

"No, I am not." Regina swung her feet to the ground
and daintily stepped out of the Daimler. Her exquisite
dragonfly hat pin, some three inches wide, equally long,
and studded with diamonds, caught the sunlight in sharp,
dazzling glints. Regina peered into the distance, her face
taut. Miss Asquith climbed out of her side of the Daimler
and went around to stand beside Regina. As the motorcar

drew closer, they exchanged what Phoebe would call a horrified look. They groaned, and Regina said, "Quickly, everyone into the house."

"What?" Phoebe found herself swept along with Julia and the others to the front door. "From whom are we running? Regina, what on earth is wrong? Why, that looks like . . ." She glanced again at the approaching motorcar, a prewar touring vehicle. There looked to be four passengers— two men and two women—including the driver. As they drew closer, Phoebe nodded in recognition. "Regina, that's your mother, Hastings, and Verna. I can't tell who is driving."

Regina released a labored breath. "That's Ralph Cameron, Father's solicitor. Hastings's solicitor now, I suppose. Please, everyone come inside and let's shut the door."

"Don't be absurd." Julia came down from the wide step before the front door. "Not to mention unconscionably rude. Really, Regina, what's gotten into you?"

Gravel skidded from the motorcar's thin tires as it veered around the circular drive to pull up behind the Daimler. No sooner had the vehicle lurched to a halt when the front and rear passenger doors burst open. Regina's mother, Lady Mandeville, groped her way out of the front seat in something of a lather, while Regina's younger brother, Hastings, rose unsteadily from the backseat as if exiting a boat on choppy waters.

"Regina Brockhurst, how *dare* you steal from the rest of us?" Swathed in full mourning from head to toe, Clarabelle Brockhurst, Lady Mandeville, shook a fist in the air. Regina did not favor her mother in looks at all. Though both women were tall, Regina stood in graceful, slender proportion, while her mother was stout of bosom, wide in the shoulders, and narrow through the hips, a figure reminiscent of a weight lifter's. Unlike Regina with her sleek, ebony curls, Cousin Clarabelle sported coarse red hair shot through with silver, presently braided and coiled around her head beneath her black netted hat.

"Too late," Miss Asquith murmured. "There is no running from this, Regina. You'll have to deal with them this time."

"This time?" Phoebe turned to scrutinize her cousin's suddenly florid face. At the sound of gravel crunching, she turned back to the newly arrived visitors. Cousin Clarabelle was bearing down on them with an expression as black as her bombazine dress.

"You finally managed it, didn't you, Regina? You've been manipulating your father for years, and you finally tricked him into changing his will. Why, you little conniving—"

The other two doors of the touring car opened. First out was Verna, Hastings's wife, a thin, birdlike creature with a prominent nose and too little chin to balance things out. She, too, wore black, but of a lighter, more fashionable fabric than Cousin Clarabelle's. The man who slipped out from behind the steering wheel must have been Mr. Ralph Cameron, their solicitor. He swept a bowler from his silver hair and hurried around the motor. "Clarabelle, please. Remember yourself."

Cousin Clarabelle spun about. "Don't tell *me* to remember myself, Ralph. Tell *her*." Over her shoulder, she pointed at Regina with her thumb in a most unladylike gesture. "You know I'm right. You suspected yourself—"

"Clarabelle," he interrupted tersely, "this is unproductive." He focused beyond her to where Regina stood rigid on the front step. "Can't we all go inside and discuss this calmly?"

"There is nothing to discuss," Regina fired back. She clutched Olive's hand as if, well, Phoebe thought, as if it were a weapon of sorts.

"Indeed there is, sister." Hastings Brockhurst tossed his own bowler through the open rear door onto the car seat.

His mother's red hair had asserted itself in her son, lending him thick auburn waves that flashed brightly in the sun. His currently ruddy complexion clashed unattractively, Phoebe couldn't help but notice. "You turned Father against me. Against Mother, too. You ought to be ashamed of yourself."

"I did no such thing." Regina stepped down and strode several paces toward her family, though whether she realized she pulled Olive along with her, Phoebe couldn't be sure. Olive made no attempt to free herself from Regina's grip, but remained firmly beside her like a comrade in arms. "I didn't need to, Hastings. Father saw you for what you are. A carouser and a reckless gambler. Not to mention—"

"Oh!" Verna Brockhurst scurried around to stand by her husband. When he made no move to acknowledge her, she flicked a hand at his elbow, which he then proffered in what seemed an automatic response. "How dare you speak so of my husband, Regina."

"Yes, well, I'm sorry to have to say it, Verna, but you know I'm right. Father no more trusted Hastings with his fortune than he'd trust a complete stranger. In fact, I'm quite sure he'd have trusted a stranger more."

Verna bristled. "Hastings, are you going to let her get away with that?"

Red-faced, he sputtered in an attempt to reply. Verna shook her head with a scowl.

"Even if your father didn't fully trust your brother," Cousin Clarabelle shouted, "I'm sure he didn't mean for you to abscond with the entire fortune. He would have wanted you to take care of the rest of us. He—"

"Never said a word to me about anything," Regina said more calmly. "I therefore see no reason to second-guess his intentions. Good day to you all." She pivoted on the toe of her ivory T-strap shoe and headed toward the house.

Lady Mandeville and Verna shrieked in protestation, while the solicitor held out his hands in a bid for quiet that went unheeded by the ladies. Speaking over each other as they were, Phoebe couldn't make out a word they uttered. She wondered, what had Regina been about to say when she broke off moments ago? *Not to mention*—what?

Then Hastings found his voice and raised it above the others. "You killed him, Regina. Don't deny it."

Silence fell, so thick Phoebe gasped for breath.

CHAPTER 3

Regina spun about yet again. "How dare you spew such a lie?"

"It's the truth." Hastings strode closer to her, his chin up, his body tensed as if for a fight. For a moment Phoebe worried he might actually strike his sister, even here, in front of everyone. She braced to intervene. Yet he stopped several feet away and thrust an unsteady finger toward his sister. "You killed Father, Regina," he said quietly, the false calm of an approaching tempest. "You told him . . . I don't know . . . something . . . my guess is some lie about me that caused his heart failure. You stole into his study like the spider you are and whispered some insidious falsehood that sent him to his grave. How long have you known he essentially wrote me out of his will and supplanted his heir—*his bodily heir*—with his insolent, selfish, frivolous excuse for a daughter?"

Phoebe's eyes went wide while beside her Julia inhaled sharply and pressed a hand to her lips. Miss Asquith reached out a tenuous hand to touch Regina's shoulder, perhaps to help steady her friend. Though Phoebe couldn't see Regina's face, she saw that her shoulders were shaking.

Hastings's finger again shot out, pointing not at Regina but at Miss Asquith. "And that one. I've no doubt she helped you. Probably put you up to it. Didn't you, *Olive?*" Her name dripped disdainfully from his lips.

"Indeed, Miss Asquith." Cousin Clarabelle snapped her hands to her hips, her handbag slapping against her thigh. "Regina would never have turned her back on her family if not for outside influences. Just who are you? Who are your family?" Shaking her head in rapid, tiny shakes, she looked Miss Asquith up and down with a sneer of distaste.

"I've heard quite enough. Come, Olive." Regina about-faced again and this time did not hesitate to climb the two steps to the front door. She reached out and seized the latch, which remained stubbornly in position. Of course it did; Regina had locked the door when they left this morning and there was no butler inside to open it for them.

Phoebe stepped up beside her. "You'll need your key, Regina."

"Yes, how foolish of me." She glanced down at her handbag, seeming uncertain how to access its contents. Her fingers trembled. Phoebe took the bag from her, opened the snap, and rummaged until she found the key. She slipped it into the lock.

"Don't you walk away from us, Regina." This came from her mother, followed by more footsteps crunching across the drive. "This isn't over."

Regina threw the door inward and all but leaped over the threshold. Miss Asquith followed and then glanced back at Phoebe and Julia. Behind them on the drive, Mr. Cameron called Regina's name—her given name, Phoebe didn't fail to notice.

"Do let's all talk calmly. Regina, please don't shut the door. Your family is distraught, but understandably so."

"Understandably so?" Regina took hold of the edge of

the door, ready to toss it closed. "Calling me a murderer, and in my own home, I might add? I'm sorry, Ralph, that is not my idea of understandable behavior."

"Regina, wait." Mr. Cameron closed the distance and ran up the steps to the threshold, forcing Phoebe and Julia to step aside or be knocked over. Up close, Phoebe saw that the solicitor, though middle-aged and silver-haired, was nonetheless handsome and trim of figure. His suit was of the finest quality, made to embrace his proportions. "Regina," he said more quietly, "imagine yourself in their position. What if your father had cut you off without a word of explanation, leaving you virtually penniless after a life of privilege—"

"Don't be so dramatic. They're not penniless. What's more, Hastings may deny it, but he knows precisely why our father didn't trust him with the money. He drinks like a sailor on holiday and gambles away every penny he happens to find in his pockets. If Father had bequeathed his hard-earned fortune to him, he'd be virtually penniless within a year anyway. So I ask you, what *is* the difference?"

"Oh, and what will *you* do with it all, sister?" Hastings swayed on his feet, proving Regina's words correct. He must have been drinking on the trip down from London. He flapped a hand in the general direction of the house. "Squander it on houses you don't need. Take in any rabble you happen to meet . . ."

Miss Asquith scoffed. "He thinks *I'm* rabble, does he?"

"I have plans, important ones." Regina raised her nose in the air. "Ones you could never understand, any of you. The world is changing, and—"

Miss Asquith touched Regina's shoulder, effectively silencing her.

Hastings let go a harsh burst of laughter. "A fat lot of

good your precious plans will do you when you're rotting
in a prison cell. We'll prove you killed Father. See if we
don't."

"And your so-called *friend* along with you, Regina."
Cousin Clarabelle stepped up to Hastings's side, present-
ing a united front. "Don't think we don't know how this
Miss Asquith of yours has influenced you. Changed you.
She had led you astray, Regina, all for the sake of living off
your generosity. Which, sadly, does not extend to your
family." Her lips turned down and her nostrils flared. "We
know what you're about, Miss Asquith, and we mean to
stop you cold in your greedy little tracks."

"If that is what you think, then you know nothing
about me or Regina. Money is unimportant to us. It is a
means to an end—nothing more."

"And what end is that, Miss Asquith?" Verna narrowed
her eyes and scrutinized the other woman. "Putting the
rest of us in the poorhouse? Depriving my husband of his
birthright? Pray, do enlighten us."

"If you wish to avoid the workhouse," Regina replied
smoothly, "then work, as millions of Englishmen do every
day. And if it weren't for the money, none of you would be
here now. You wouldn't give a fig what I did. Admit it."

Hastings's face darkened with ire. "Murderesses," he
mumbled. "Murderesses and thieves. Both of you."

Regina let out a cry and rushed toward her brother. Verna
screamed and sidestepped away, and Cousin Clarabelle
raised her hands to her cheeks in a show of fright.

Mr. Cameron stepped between the charging Regina and
her family and caught her in his arms. "That will be quite
enough. Come now, all of you. You're acting like children.
You're family, and surely there is a way to resolve this
civilly."

"They're accusing me of murder, Ralph."

He patted Regina's back. "No one believes you murdered your father." Before any of the others could protest, Mr. Cameron silenced them with a sharp glance before returning his attention to Regina, still wrapped in his arms. He stroked her back in a soothing rhythm. "They're upset and bewildered and lashing out. And you ... you must admit your running off as you did after the reading of the will wouldn't exactly warm their hearts toward you."

"They've accused my friend as well, and she has nothing to do with any of this." Regina laid her head on Mr. Cameron's shoulder, her hat tipping slightly askew.

"Again, they are upset. Once we've all calmed down I'm sure they'll apologize for offending you and your charming friend." He flicked a glance at Miss Asquith, but rather than kindness, Phoebe detected a shade of suspicion in his eyes. Perhaps he didn't believe his own words. Still, for the moment he had ended the Brockhursts' stinging accusations.

"I won't hold my breath," Regina said into his lapel. She turned to peer out past his shoulder and drew in a breath. "They're horrid."

"There now." Gently he set her at arm's length. "Can't we all go inside and discuss this like civilized people? We've come a long way, all the way from London."

"That's hardly my fault."

"Regina." He bent his head toward her and smiled. Phoebe could sense his charm chipping away at Regina's resolve. "Be nice. You're not someone who slams her door in her family's faces."

She took a step back, out of his hold. "Aren't I, though?" Shrugging, she started back toward the front door. "Come along, then, all of you. I suppose I'll have to serve you dinner as well in order to get rid of you. I can't vouch for what Cook will be able to scrape together for this many people on such short notice, so don't go blaming me if it's not to your liking."

"I think Julia and I should be going," Phoebe whispered when Regina reached the steps.

"Speak for yourself," Julia interjected.

"Neither of you are going anywhere." Regina grasped Phoebe's shoulder and turned her toward the open door. "Inside, both of you. You're not going to leave me alone with this lot."

"You have Miss Asquith," Phoebe reminded her.

"Call her Olive, and that's only two to four. You and Julia even out the odds."

Julia chuckled with what seemed to be genuine amusement. "Odds of what?"

"Me winning. I don't see why I owe anyone anything, and I won't be bullied." Regina stepped into the front hall. Julia offered Phoebe a delighted smile and eagerly trailed in after them. Phoebe waited on the top step until the three other Brockhursts came, somewhat tentatively, as if they suspected some sort of trap. When they reached the threshold they stopped short and regarded Phoebe.

"Hello, Hastings," she said. "Verna. Cousin Clarabelle." Though Lady Mandeville bore no relation to the Renshaws other than by marriage, Phoebe and her siblings had always addressed her as cousin, as they had her husband. She coughed awkwardly, ignoring Julia's highly amused expression. "It's . . . er . . . good to see you again. You're all looking . . ."

"Oh, don't pretend, Phoebe." Hastings stumbled over his own feet, reaching out to grip Verna's shoulder for balance. "It's not good to see us, not under these circumstances, and I'm quite sure we all look dreadful after our trip, not to mention waging battle just now."

He strode through the doorway. Phoebe followed the family inside, only to find herself once more in the middle of the fray.

"Why, that's mine, you little thief!" Lady Mandeville pointed to Regina's hat.

Regina raised a gloved hand to her hat brim. "This? No, it isn't. I bought it in London after the funeral."

"Not the hat. That!" Cousin Clarabelle's finger jabbed the air. "My hat pin. You've stolen it!"

"I have not. I borrowed it."

The hat pin holding Regina's chapeau in place glittered with the brilliance of winter stars beneath the electric chandelier. Earlier, Phoebe had admired the piece; Regina had acknowledged the compliment at the time but had said nothing of it belonging to her mother.

"You know very well that pin is a family heirloom. It belonged to my great great grandmother, and yes, you would have had it someday, but you had no right to take it now. No right, I tell you." Cousin Clarabelle paused to drag in a breath. "This only proves what we've been saying. That you are a thief, Regina."

"I'd have returned it in good time. Besides, I haven't seen you wear it in ages. But if you're so keen to have it back, here." Reaching up with both hands, Regina tugged the pin from her hat and flung it to the floor at her mother's feet. Phoebe flinched, grateful for the Persian rug that prevented the ornament from being damaged.

Regina hadn't yet finished. She pointed at the dragonfly, lying on its back as if dead. "There is your fortune, Mother. Enjoy it, such as it is."

Cousin Clarabelle pressed her hands to her mouth and cried out from between her fingers. Tears sprang to her eyes and she began to sob in earnest. Hastings and Verna appeared too shocked to react. With a sniff, Regina gave herself a shake, turned, and set off up the curving stairs. Miss Asquith was quick to follow.

"Oh, dear," Phoebe couldn't help uttering. She reached

out a hand to Cousin Clarabelle, but with a choked sob and her hands still pressed against her mouth, the woman simply ran. Several doors stood open to the hall, and she ground to a halt, peering at each one. Finally, with a shake of her head she appeared to choose a doorway at random and scurried inside.

"Damn." Hastings scrubbed a hand across his face, glanced from Phoebe to Julia to his wife, and without another word followed his mother. With a nervous twitter, Verna scampered after her husband.

Mr. Cameron regarded Phoebe and Julia with a sigh. "I'm sorry you had to witness that." He stuck out his hand. "Ralph Cameron, by the way, the Brockhursts' solicitor."

Julia tossed her head with a little laugh. "Yes, we gathered that." She grasped his offered hand. "Julia Renshaw, their cousin." She gestured with her chin over her shoulder. "My little sister, Phoebe."

"A pleasure, I'm sure." He bobbed his head with a rueful sort of smile. "Again, my apologies."

"No need." Julia's dark blue eyes sparked with humor. "You're certainly not their keeper. Or are you?" She flashed a cunning smile, and Phoebe resisted the urge to roll her eyes heavenward.

"Yes, well." He sighed again. "If you'll excuse me, I have some ruffled feathers to smooth."

"Good luck with that," Julia called to his back. She turned to Phoebe, grinning. "I haven't had this much fun in months."

"Oh, Julia. How can you call that fun?" Phoebe lowered her voice. "This family is pure poison."

"Hmm, perhaps, but please don't say that word."

Phoebe conceded Julia's point with a nod, remembering their personal brush with poison back in the spring. "We should leave at the first opportunity. I'll call home and have the car sent over."

"Oh, no, you won't. Or if you wish to leave, go ahead. I'm staying. You heard Regina, she needs us here. Are you so coldhearted you'd abandon our cousin?"

"I really don't think—"

"Goodness, after all this excitement, I need a lie down. See you after."

Julia hurried up the stairs, leaving Phoebe alone in the hall. Subdued voices droned on in the library, where Cousin Clarabelle and the others had retreated. She hoped Mr. Cameron had succeeded in smoothing some of those feathers, though she doubted his intervention would have any lasting effects, not if he couldn't quell the accusations. Good heavens—Regina, a murderer?

A little shiver traveled Phoebe's length. What *had* precipitated Cousin Basil's heart failure? It wasn't impossible that shocking news could have brought it on. She wondered, had Regina known beforehand of her father's changes to his will? Did the prospect of an inheritance send her into his study with an insidious message, as Hastings implied?

Stop it this instant. If the past months had taught her anything, it was to view uncertainties with suspicion and immediately turn her mind to questions of means, motive, and opportunity. But this was different. This was a family at one another's throats following the death of their patriarch, nothing more. It had become a common enough story, especially with how the war had depleted so many family fortunes.

A lie down sounded like a capital idea. But as she moved toward the staircase, the dragonfly beckoned with a flash of its many diamonds. In all the commotion, no one had remembered to pick it up off the floor. Phoebe did so now, the skillfully crafted piece heavy in her hand. She touched the tip of the pin and nearly pricked her finger. Yes, this dragonfly had a sting. But where to leave it? Cousin Clarabelle's quiet sobbing drew her to the library.

Phoebe knocked at the open door and poked her head in. Verna, Cousin Clarabelle, and Mr. Cameron sat near the fireplace. Hastings occupied the seat at the writing desk. He was smoking a cigarette and exhaling a long stream of gray toward a nearby open window.

"You left this in the hall." She held up the hat pin.

A tearful Cousin Clarabelle waved a dismissive hand in the air. "Just leave it on the table. I don't even wish to see the thing right now. She can have it, for all I care."

"Yes, all right." Feeling a need to tiptoe, Phoebe entered the room and carefully placed the glittering dragonfly on the library table in the center of the room.

"I agree with you, my lady. I don't think you and Lady Julia should be here." Eva neatened up the toiletries on Lady Phoebe's dressing table. Her mistress had apprised her of this afternoon's ruckus, and if Eva could pack up Lady Phoebe's things right now and whisk her home, she would. "Lord only knows what skirmishes might erupt during dinner. I half wish you wouldn't go down."

"You're not the only one. Based on what occurred earlier, this promises to be the grimmest affair I've ever witnessed. I don't know how Mr. Cameron convinced my cousin to allow her family to stay on. I hate to say it, but I almost believe Regina finds a perverse pleasure in having them here." Lady Phoebe made an adjustment to the beaded necklace hanging down the front of her gown. "Eva, do you think there can be anything to it? That someone upset Cousin Basil with the notion of hastening his demise, I mean. Is it even possible?"

Eva ran her finger lightly over the back of Lady Phoebe's

silver hand mirror as she gave the question the consideration it deserved. "Well, if you mean did someone intend murdering him that way, as Miss Brockhurst's family charges, it would be a rather unreliable means of doing so."

"That's true."

"However, someone may have found roguish pleasure in taunting the old gentleman. That would make him or her guilty in his death, even if only by happenstance."

"Then there could be some truth in the accusation. But the question remains, who is the guilty party, and what did he or she say to Cousin Basil that so distressed him?"

"I'm afraid that's something we may never know, my lady. And if you ask me, it's not for you or Lady Julia to know. It's ugly business, from start to finish."

"Yes, well. Julia won't be budged, and I can't see going home without her. Grams would have all kinds of fits. Besides, Julia reminded me that Regina insisted we stay as . . . oh, I don't know . . . reinforcements, I suppose. She wants to keep her side even with her family's."

"This solicitor you mentioned." Eva gathered up the extra hairpins lying on the tabletop. "He's on the family's side in all this mess?"

"Good question. He seems to be taking a neutral position in the interest of restoring familial harmony, but as you and I well know, appearances can be deceiving." She surveyed herself in the full-length mirror and gave a brisk nod. "I should be going down now."

"What wouldn't I give to be a fly on the wall in that dining room." Eva opened the bedroom door and stood aside for Lady Phoebe to pass.

"Why, Eva, are you developing a taste for gossip?" She treated Eva to a teasing grin.

"Not gossip, my lady. But I'll say it again. This house is no place for you. I should like to be on hand in the event violence breaks out."

"Don't worry. If I see any fists flying, I'll run for cover."

Lady Phoebe met her sister in the corridor and they fell into step together. Lady Julia chuckled. "Are you ready for the next round?"

Eva would have been a lot happier if they could all stop referring to this visit in terms of war and fighting. She closed Lady Phoebe's bedroom door and watched the Renshaw sisters turn a corner and disappear from sight, remarking inwardly what lovely women they had become, but better still, how well they had been getting on since the spring. They would likely never share the kind of closeness Eva enjoyed with her sister, Alice; they had been inseparable growing up and never kept a single secret from each other. But to see Phoebe and Julia simply being cordial, even joking together, warmed Eva's heart.

A noise from inside Lady Julia's room drew Eva to the threshold. She cracked open the door and peeked in to find Myra Stanley sitting at the dressing table.

Sitting! And gazing at herself in the mirror as though she were the mistress of a great house.

"What on earth are you doing?"

Miss Stanley turned her head only slightly and shrugged. "Can't a girl rest her feet a moment?"

"At your mistress's dressing table? Leaning on your elbows like that?"

Miss Stanley sat up straighter. "I'm not hurting anything." She fingered the filigreed back of Lady Julia's silver hairbrush, then picked it up and lightly skimmed it over her frazzled bangs.

Eva stepped into the room. "Miss Stanley, remember yourself."

"Oh, pish." Next she picked up Julia's crystal perfume atomizer and gave the tasseled, velvet-covered ball a squeeze. A cloud of fragrance encompassed her neck.

"Miss Stanley, you quite shock me. That is Quelques Fleurs by Houbigant."

"I know what it is. She'll never miss that tiny bit. And she'll never notice it on me, either. I usually smell like her perfume because I handle her clothes." She pushed back the little chair and came to her feet. At the foot of the bed lay a pile of dresses. Miss Stanley scooped them up and bunched them into a ball she hugged against her, only to drop them on the floor in front of the armoire. One by one she bent to retrieve them and place them on hangers.

"Is that any way to treat your mistress's fine things?"

Miss Stanley let out a huff. "Miss Huntford—may I call you Eva?" Eva flattened her lips in response, but that didn't deter Miss Stanley. "Eva, Lady Julia couldn't make up her mind what to wear down to dinner. As a result, I'm left to clean up after her. I'm doing the best I can. If I were you, I'd mind my own business, or you and I will not get on very well at all."

Holding a hanger in one hand and one of Julia's gowns in the other, Miss Stanley regarded Eva with no small amount of censure. Eva sensed an implied threat, and that didn't sit well with her. Not well at all. Who was this woman? Surely not a run-of-the-mill lady's maid.

CHAPTER 4

When Phoebe and Julia entered the drawing room, Regina excused herself from Olive Asquith and hurried over to them. "Julia, darling, won't you play for us until dinner is ready?"

Julia scrunched up her nose and demurred. "I hardly think the occasion calls for music, Regina."

"On the contrary. Music will soothe the family beasts. You don't wish a repetition of this afternoon, do you?"

Phoebe shuddered at the thought. Julia asked in an undertone, but nonetheless bluntly, "Whatever induced you to let them stay? A sudden desire for sainthood?"

"Hardly, darling. It's entirely due to Ralph that I didn't toss them all out hours ago." Her face softened as she mentioned Mr. Cameron, but her expression hardened again just as quickly. "Goodness knows they deserve a good tossing out, calling me a thief and a murderer." She clasped Julia's forearm and turned her toward the grand piano. "Please, do play something calm, and should tensions rise, play louder. Drown out any and all unpleasantness."

Julia emitted a sigh and a laugh simultaneously. "Very well. A bit of Beethoven, perhaps."

"Yes, yes, that'll suit." Regina gave her a nudge toward the instrument. Then to Phoebe she said, "Thank goodness you're both here. I don't think I could weather my family's visit alone."

"I do give you credit for your forbearance," Phoebe said candidly, but on second thought, she wondered about the power of Mr. Cameron's influence over each member of this family. They needed a skilled mediator, she supposed. His calm demeanor had shown him to be a man of even temper and cool diplomacy. But this temporary truce seemed . . . far too easy.

Did Mr. Cameron share the family's views on how Cousin Basil met his death? Did he blame Regina, believe her somehow responsible?

Was Regina somehow responsible?

She followed her cousin to one of the graceful French settees. As they sat, she asked, "Did you know how ill your father had become in the end?"

Regina's gaze flashed before lowering to her lap. "No, not really. Oh, we knew of Father's heart condition, of course. His physician never let us forget it." Did Phoebe hear resentment in those words? Regina looked up with a frown. "Why? Do you think I deliberately brought on his heart failure, as my family charges?"

"Of course I don't," Phoebe replied smoothly, if not with full certainty. "But if you knew about his health, others did as well. Do you think there could be any truth in the notion that disturbing news struck the final blow?"

Regina's eyebrows rose. "Oh, I do see what you're saying." She paused while Julia began playing a sonata. "Anyone might have goaded him into a fit of agitation. For instance, Hastings . . ."

"I don't mean to accuse anyone," Phoebe said quickly. "If it happened, it might very well have been unintentional.

And it could have been anyone from any*where*, with a telephone call, a letter, perhaps a telegram."

"Again, in all likelihood, it had to do with Hastings. They were forever arguing, and Father was forever receiving unpaid bills in Hastings's name, not to mention reports of my brother's indiscretions." Suddenly her expression cleared, and she turned to Phoebe. "But none of this is why I asked you here, you realize."

"I know." Irony tinged Phoebe's soft laugh. "You wished help with decorating the house."

Regina shook her head. "That's why I asked Julia. But not you, Phoebe. We both know you're hopeless when it comes to such matters. No, we'll leave colors and fabrics to your sister."

"Then why *am* I here? Other than that you were kind enough to invite me, of course."

Regina uncharacteristically reached for her hand. "I have some new ideas I wish to share with you, cousin."

"Oh?" Phoebe was intrigued. "Such as?"

"I won't go into it in detail, not here, but suffice it to say that clearing away the old in favor of the new and modern doesn't apply only to houses. It applies to life. To ways of bettering our world, and word has it you're interested in such things."

"Well, yes, indeed I am. You know I'm involved in the running of the Haverleigh School for Young Ladies, and there's the charitable organization I started for veterans residing in the area. I'm also pleased with the new voting rights for women—"

"Which don't go far enough," Regina said.

"No, I agree that they don't. The laws should be the same for men and women."

"Exactly. Too many of us are left disenfranchised. Until we're thirty, we'll have no say. I have only a year and a half to wait, but you—my goodness—it'll be ages before you may cast your first vote. Parliament should represent all people, and not pick and choose as they continue to do."

"I couldn't agree more. Do you . . ." Phoebe hesitated. As a rule, politics was rarely discussed at home. Grams and Grampapa were staunch Conservatives and assumed the same of their grandchildren as a matter of course. Phoebe never dared confess her more liberal leanings in their hearing. She turned to Regina and lowered her voice. "Do you support the Labor Party, then?"

Regina's gaze darted to where Miss Asquith stood talking to Mr. Cameron. Miss Asquith looked uncomfortable, Mr. Cameron his usual composed self. "That's what I wish to share with you," Regina murmured, "but not here, not just now. Perhaps later, after dinner. Or tomorrow, you and I might sneak off somewhere we're not likely to be followed by the others. Along one of the woodland trails, perhaps."

"I understand it's somewhat frowned upon for people of our class to support liberal ideas. I never discuss such things with my grandparents." Phoebe smiled. "But you're almost beginning to scare me. What could be so secretive that we must sneak off?"

"Phoebe, I'm sure you're aware times are changing. New ideas are making their way into our society . . ." Regina glanced up at the same time Phoebe heard footsteps. She, too, looked up to find Miss Asquith standing near their settee, glaring down at them. For half a moment Regina looked perplexed, only to sport a grin an instant later. She released Phoebe's hand. "Olive, dearest, join us. We were speaking of hopping up to London one of these days soon."

Olive primly sat at Regina's other side, or rather perched, as if ready to spring up at any moment. "We only just came from London. Why would you wish to return so soon?"

And why lie about our conversation? Did Miss Asquith not share Regina's political philosophies? Would she disapprove? Phoebe surveyed the young woman from her austere chignon to her plain white shirtwaist and pleated skirt. Why, Phoebe realized, not only did Miss Asquith not dress for dinner, she hadn't changed at all since their shopping excursion to Bristol. She had merely removed the jacket of her suit. A plain gold chain peeked out from the cuff of one sleeve, Miss Asquith's only adornment.

In her other hand Miss Asquith held a crystal tumbler, and as she raised it for a sip Phoebe realized with a bit of a shock that the glass contained whiskey. At first she thought *surely not*, but as Miss Asquith lowered the tumbler, Phoebe caught a sharp whiff that could not be anything else. *How very odd.* She herself drank wine, but only with dinner. She had once taken a sip of Grampapa's whiskey and, coughing, vowed never to do so again.

"Well, well, don't we make a domestic scene?"

Miss Asquith and Regina broke off from whatever they were saying, and Phoebe, startled from her musings, watched the rest of the Brockhurst family file into the drawing room. It was Hastings who had spoken. He sauntered in none too steadily, a tumbler similar to Miss Asquith's clutched in his hand. Verna, his wife, quickly caught up with him and slipped her arm through his. She stood close to his side, yet that didn't stop him from swaying.

Julia had stopped playing—when, Phoebe couldn't say, but she sensed it had been before the family appeared, and before Hastings had made his sarcastic observation. He made another one presently.

"Aren't we the picture of family harmony? Verna, dearest, wouldn't you say we are the happiest of families?"

"Hastings, please stop it," his wife whispered loud enough for all to hear. "Don't be difficult."

"Difficult?" Hastings drank from his glass, the crystal facets twinkling in the light of the chandeliers. "When am I ever?"

"Do sit down, and do be quiet." His mother stepped around him, while at the same time pointing to an armchair. "Verna, sit him down."

Regina released a long breath. "God help us."

Miss Asquith's lips were pinched. Mr. Cameron moved to the piano. "Do continue, Lady Julia. Your playing is very good. Quite good, in fact."

"High praise," Julia mumbled with a half smile as she tapped out the opening notes of another sonata.

"I cannot believe it. I tell you, I simply cannot believe it." Myra Stanley had just finished speaking with Lady Julia through one of the speaking tubes that ran throughout the house. She and Eva were below stairs, having their supper in the servants' hall. Myra plunked down into her chair at the table and glowered at her plate. "They're staying tonight, all of them."

Mrs. Dayton, the cook, and Margaret, her assistant, sat across from them. Mrs. Dayton snorted, a sound suspiciously akin to muffled laughter. Margaret, a spindling girl of seventeen, hid a smile behind her hand.

"What are you two tittering at?" Myra treated them to a defiant tilt of her head.

"We could have told you the whole lot would be staying on," Mrs. Dayton replied, reaching for another slice of roasted pork.

"Psychic, are you? Oh, but that's not the whole of it." Myra plucked up her fork, then set it down again with a clank against her plate. "Eva, I'll have you know that we—you and I—are now expected to wait on old Lady Mandeville *and* her daughter-in-law. They came without their maids. Without! Who on earth travels that way?"

Eva calmly sliced into a layered portion of potatoes and onions. "Your Welsh onion cake is delicious, Mrs. Dayton."

"Thank you. I hope they like it upstairs. Queer thing. That Miss Olive is in charge of the menu, and she says I'm to serve plain, hearty food, above stairs and below."

Eva nodded her appreciation, though she wondered how the Brockhursts, not to mention Lady Julia, would feel about that. Phoebe, of course, would take the menu in stride.

"Did you not hear what I said?" Myra tossed up her hands in a show of frustration.

"I certainly did." Eva chewed, savoring the baked, buttery mixture of flavors. "Did Lady Julia say which of us is to attend which lady, or did she leave it up to us?"

"Is that all you have to say about the matter?"

Mrs. Dayton shot Myra a quizzical look from across the table. "What else is there to say? You've got your orders. Now eat up. You'll need your energy." She chuckled. Margaret lowered her face to hide a grin.

"Vile woman," Myra said under her breath.

"Attending two women isn't nearly so daunting as you might think," Eva said brightly. She knew her optimism would irritate Myra. "Last spring I had six young ladies to care for."

Myra paled. "Good grief, how *did* you survive it? You must have taken leave of your senses to ever agree to such a thing."

"I did what was necessary at the time." Eva didn't add that the Renshaws had rewarded her handsomely afterward in the form of a bonus and time off to visit her parents. She would have attended those six young women either way, and she prided herself on the fine job she had made of it.

"Rather a chump, aren't you?" Myra shook her head with impatience before turning to Mrs. Dayton. "What *is* your mistress thinking, turning this house into a lunatic asylum? Or is she thinking at all?"

"Myra," Eva murmured in a cautioning tone. She cast a peek at Mrs. Dayton, then at Margaret. So far the girl had said little, even on uncontroversial matters. She did her job with efficiency and seemed skilled in the tasks Mrs. Dayton set her to. But quiet though she may be, she undoubtedly had her own opinions on the present conversation. Eva could see it in the tightening of her brow, the compression of her lips. Mrs. Dayton, too, was not impervious to Myra's chattering. Her last question brought a ruddy sheen to the cook's complexion, one that spoke of a simmering temper. Eva repeated, "Myra," and was about to add a gentle chastisement when the woman interrupted.

"Do not *Myra* me. Miss Brockhurst must be mad to allow that family of hers to stay, after the fuss they made earlier. Oh, yes," she snapped at Mrs. Dayton and Margaret, though neither had shown any particular inclination to speak up, "we heard it all. Putting away our mistress's things upstairs we were, and their voices traveled through the open windows. Calling Miss Brockhurst a murderer. A thief. And then she allows them to stay?"

"It's none of our affair, is it?" Her plate clean, Mrs. Dayton rose. With a stern expression she began collecting the dishes from the table. "Come, Margaret, let's start on the pots and pans."

Their hands full, the two marched off to the kitchen, leaving Myra and Eva alone. Eva suppressed a sigh. Myra hadn't finished saying her piece, apparently. "They won't leave, you know. That family will stay and sponge off Miss Brockhurst indefinitely, see if they don't."

"As Mrs. Dayton said, it's none of our affair."

"I'm only saying."

"I suggest you don't, if you value your position."

"What's that supposed to mean? Is it a threat?"

"Only that Lady Julia won't countenance such talk from her lady's maid, and as for the countess—well, Lady Wroxly would send you packing at the first hint of insolence." Eva pushed back her chair and stood, and leaned to retrieve her plate and utensils. Straightening, she said, "So which will it be? Do you want the new Lady Mandeville or the Dowager Lady Mandeville?"

"Bah. If you ask me, we should leave High Head Lodge, and soon."

On that point, Eva couldn't agree more.

In the drawing room following dinner, Phoebe kept close watch on Hastings. There being only the two men in the house, they had dispensed with remaining in the dining room for brandy and cigars, yet Hastings hadn't initally come to the drawing room with everyone else. He had made a detour, to where Phoebe didn't know. Now, as earlier, he wobbled a bit before settling heavily into an armchair, and his head lolled back and forth, side to side, as if he couldn't keep from dozing. At the sound of his wife's voice, his eyes popped open and he gazed about the room until he spotted her sitting at the card table shuffling a deck of cards.

"No one wants to play, Verna. Give it a rest," he said to her. Except that he hadn't spoken quite so clearly, but slurred each word into the next. Phoebe frowned, studying him. A detail in the dining room hadn't escaped her notice. He had drunk no wine and barely touched his tumbler of whiskey. A sip now and again, nothing more, not even enough to lower the level of the spirits by any significant amount.

Mr. Cameron poured two snifters of brandy and set one on the small table beside Hastings's chair.

"Here you are, Hastings. An after-dinner cordial," Mr. Cameron said pleasantly.

Cousin Clarabelle, slowly making a circuit of the long room as people used to do in the old days, harrumphed. "I hardly think he needs more, Ralph."

Hastings shrugged. Without a sideways glance, he reached out to drape his open hand around the cut crystal, but he didn't raise the snifter to his lips.

Phoebe's own gaze traced the front of Hastings's suit coat. She searched for a telltale outline of a flask in his inner pocket. Had he been nipping on the sly? The garment lay flat, except where it bulged slightly around his hips to accommodate his slouching posture.

Verna continued shuffling cards. "Anyone for bridge? Mother Mandeville? Ralph? We'll need a fourth. Julia, how about you?"

"Not me, thanks." Julia sat alone at nearly the opposite end of the room, almost as if she wished to be as far away from Phoebe as possible. When Phoebe had patted the spot on the settee beside her, her sister patently ignored the gesture and kept walking. The old Julia might have behaved that way, no question. But since the spring . . . Phoebe wondered if perhaps something at dinner had upset her.

"Regina, then," Verna suggested next, her voice as light as if the ugly scene this afternoon had never taken place. "Come play."

Regina, however, had forgotten nothing. "You expect me to play bridge as if we're all one happy family?"

Mr. Cameron quietly crossed the room to her. He moved like a cat sometimes, with hardly a sound, and so smooth one barely noticed him until he was there, at one's shoulder. Regina winced as he touched her arm. "Regina, do come and play cards. It's time to make peace."

Phoebe braced for a sharp retort from her cousin, but none came. "I've already made as much peace as I'm able, Ralph. I've taken them in, haven't I?" She turned her attention to the others. "One night, mind you, and then you must all return to London."

Verna dropped the cards, scattering them over the felt surface of the table. Hastings laughed once, a grunt that abruptly broke off. Cousin Clarabelle stopped walking. Her hand rose to press her lips as she stared down at the Aubusson rug.

Regina regarded them all in turn. "What?"

"Nothing." Verna began gathering up the cards.

Frowning, Regina appealed to Mr. Cameron. "What aren't they telling me?"

Looking pained, he slipped a hand to the small of her back, bared daringly by the plunge of her dinner gown. "Come, let's sit." He drew her to the settee closest to the hearth and waited until she had settled. With the back of his fingers he traced a lock of her black hair, pinned back in a swoop from her brow. With the same hand, he grazed her chin in an intimate gesture that made Phoebe want to look away, yet ensnared her gaze at the same time. Gently he said, "They can't go back to Mandeville House, Regina. They've let it."

"Let it . . . to whom? And why?"

"To whom doesn't matter. An American with lots of cash. The why is simple, so simple I doubt you truly need to ask. Without sufficient funds, they can no longer afford to keep the house themselves. They've nowhere to go, Regina. Nowhere but here."

The other Brockhursts looked everywhere but at Regina and Mr. Cameron. Cousin Clarabelle turned her back to them. Hastings squirmed in his chair.

Regina's mouth opened slowly, but no sound came out. Her frown deepened. "Then you're saying . . ."

"Yes. At the moment, your family is wholly dependent on your generosity." He spoke those last words softly, like a caress that filled Phoebe with a sense of observing something she oughtn't. If she didn't know better, if she hadn't heard the conversation, she would have thought she was witnessing a seduction.

Mr. Cameron and Regina?

But in the next moment Regina sprang to her feet, whisking her hand out of his reach when he tried to grasp it. "You all need my generosity, yet you arrive here, at my home, flinging ridiculous accusations as if, as if . . ."

An uproar of blame and protestation broke out. Phoebe quickly heard enough—more than she wanted, for this latest skirmish promised to be nothing more than a rehashing of the preceding hours. She pointed her feet toward the hall with every intention of climbing the stairs to her room, but out of the corner of her eye she spied Julia, still sitting alone at the far end of the room. She changed direction.

"Are you quite certain you don't wish to leave first thing in the morning?" she said as she reached her sister. She expected one of Julia's typical shrugs and another avowal of enjoying herself too much to leave. She did not expect the abrasive glower her sister leveled on her.

"Go away, Phoebe."

"What?" She hesitated, studying Julia's face. Was there a grin hiding somewhere within those lines of disregard? Search as she might, Phoebe couldn't find one. "Did I do something? Or say something?"

"Goodness, no." Julia uncrossed her ankles and crossed them again, sitting primly with her back iron-bar straight. "You never do anything wrong, do you, Phoebe? You're a saint in leather pumps."

Even in her shock at her sister's censure, from the corner of her eye she saw that Mr. Cameron had stood in an attempt to calm Regina, and now Cousin Clarabelle insinuated herself between them.

What was *that* about?

Refusing to be daunted, Phoebe sat beside Julia, who stiffened even more as she did. "What's got into you all of a sudden?"

"It's this house," a third voice declared.

Startled, Phoebe looked up to discover that Olive Asquith had joined them. She dragged a chair closer to the settee. "This house is as oppressive as a tomb in its current state."

"Oh, spare me any more talk about redecorating," Julia scoffed. "I had enough of that topic this afternoon. And if you're still determined to leave, Phoebe, I believe you should do so at the first opportunity."

"Will you come with me, or are you still determined to stay?"

"I'll stay. Or perhaps I'll go up to London." *Anywhere not with you.*

Phoebe winced. Those last words had slipped from Julia's lips on a mere breath, less than a whisper. Or had they? Julia had turned her face away as well, and Phoebe couldn't be sure if she had merely imagined what she heard. Why would Julia suddenly abhor her as if . . . as if last spring hadn't happened?

If Miss Asquith noticed the rift between them, she pretended not to. She said to Phoebe, "Won't you merely be going from one gloomy old house to another? Isn't your Foxwood Hall just a larger version of this place? I'll wager it hasn't been done over . . . well, ever." Her eyebrows surged. "I'll wager a place that size could house several large families. Perhaps a dozen."

Julia stared at her, obviously uncomprehending. Phoebe wasn't sure she understood, either. "Whatever do you mean?"

"Only that such large houses are no longer quite the thing, are they? Such a waste. It could be put to so much better use, don't you think?"

"No, I don't think." Julia pushed to her feet and without another word strode away.

"I don't suppose she does, much," Miss Asquith mused as she watched Julia go. "Think, I mean."

Phoebe bristled. "I beg your pardon. That is my sister you're talking about."

Miss Asquith shrugged in so cavalier a manner that, for a moment, she appeared more like Julia than she would have wished. "I'm sure your sister is quite talented in the way wealthy ladies usually are. But what about you, Phoebe? *May* I call you Phoebe?"

Phoebe might have mentioned that Miss Asquith had shown no inclination to be on familiar terms earlier that day, or that if she wished to be friends, she might refrain from insulting members of the Renshaw family. She might also leave off the condescending tone, for that was how Phoebe perceived that last question—as if Miss Asquith, or Olive, she supposed, doubted very much that Phoebe's talents were any more impressive than those she assigned to other women of her class. She instinctively raised her chin. "My interests take me quite out of the drawing room, I assure you. I am interested in helping England's heroes, the veterans of the Great War, as well as in seeing that every citizen of this country has access to an education."

"Do you indeed?"

"Why do you sound as if you doubt my word?"

"I simply wonder how far you are willing to go, and how hard you are willing to work, for the sake of your convictions."

"I am willing to work as hard as I must."

Olive pursed her thin lips in a little smile. "Are you? Are you *really*? And what are you willing to give up to see your goals achieved?"

"I don't understand you."

"No, Phoebe. And that, you see, is precisely the problem with this country nowadays." The young woman stood, her compressed little smile persisting as she gazed down at Phoebe with an imperious air. "My advice to you is to go home, where it is safe, before matters become too out of hand for you."

"What *are* you going on about?"

Without answering, Olive turned on her heel and strode away. She left Phoebe with a sudden determination to remain at High Head Lodge and puzzle out what exactly was going on there. In fact, she very nearly forgot that only minutes ago, she had declared her intention of fleeing first thing in the morning.

CHAPTER 5

Phoebe's eyes opened. Her dreams had been troubled ones, and now, waking in the bedroom assigned to her at High Head Lodge, she thought she understood why. Sounds penetrated her closed door, coming at her in the darkness—thumps, creaks, and voices. Muffled, and yet barbed with contention. Apparently, the walls in this house were far thinner than those at home.

She slid out of bed, finding her slippers and shoving her feet into them. Then she pressed her ear to the door. The sounds persisted. People were awake, and it seemed the day's trials had not released their grip on this household.

Shrugging into her wrapper, she opened her door and peeked out. The corridor seemed deserted, but somewhere a door thudded closed. Who was up? Where had they been? The argumentative voices surged from behind one of the doors. She ventured over her threshold, treading lightly over the plush hall runner. She came to the suite shared by Hastings and Verna.

"Stand up to her, blast you." Each word Verna spoke rang with disdain.

"How? She holds everything now, or nearly. What can I do?"

"Be a man. Not a weakling."

"That's unfair." As before, Hastings spoke in a slurred voice. "I can do nothing to change Father's will. You know that."

Behind the paneled door, Verna sniggered. "A real man would find a way."

"You never wanted me. Only the money."

"Oh, do stop whining. I'm so tired of it. So unutterably weary."

Phoebe's stomach twisted. She regretted leaving her room, hearing these hurtful words. She couldn't imagine her own parents speaking to each other like this. Mama and Papa had loved each other, hadn't they? She had been so young when her mother died, her memories were vague—but no, surely they could not have despised each other or found fault in each other like Hastings and Verna. Papa had never looked at another woman again, and he spoke of Mama often to Phoebe and her siblings, taking special care to keep her memory alive. And then there were Grams and Grampapa. She had never heard either of them speak an unkind word, or raise a voice, or make accusations one to the other.

She had said it to Julia earlier: The Brockhursts were poison. Slowly poisoning one another, and yes, the people around them. If Regina needed her, wished to confide something in her, then she could come to Foxwood Hall, because with or without Julia, she intended going home tomorrow.

Before she could move another step, a soft click drifted along the corridor; then another came, softly, like a kiss. The sound drew her attention to an open door, that of the billiard room located near the first floor landing, just like the one at home. She heard a third light click, ivory against ivory as balls slowly collided. No voices came, no sound at all but that of the balls. Well, if someone wished to while away the night hours in such a way, it was no business of hers, though she couldn't help wondering who it was. If she were to guess, she'd say Ralph Cameron. With his cool patience and smooth aplomb, he struck her as the type of man who played billiards.

Turning away from Hastings and Verna's room, she started back to her own, when another of the doors opened, this one on the other side of the corridor. She instinctively went still, held her breath, and then pulled tighter against the shadows. Someone poked her head out of Regina's room, but it wasn't Regina. The figure was too small and slight, and as she tiptoed into the corridor, Phoebe recognized Olive. Her hair was down, falling as straight and sharp as rain down the middle of her back. She started to her own room, but then something stopped her. Had Phoebe made a noise? She didn't think so, but Olive abruptly turned, craning her neck and peering into the darkness.

"Is—is someone there?"

Phoebe stepped away from the wall. "It's only me. You startled me when you opened the door. I didn't think anyone else was up." That last was a lie, of course.

"Oh, I . . . Regina was having trouble sleeping. I went in to . . . to . . . read to her. We do that sometimes. Read—at night."

"Is she all right? And you, Olive. You seem a bit upset."

"I didn't expect to meet anyone in the hall. You startled me. Anyway, Regina's finally asleep."

Phoebe expected Olive to question her as to what she was doing up, but the young woman only bade her a hasty good night and scurried off to her own room. In an instant she disappeared behind the closed door.

Phoebe hesitated. The argument between Hastings and

Verna had quieted, though murmurs of unrest continued behind their door. She crossed the hall to Regina's bedroom. Her hand descended on the knob, but she lingered, uncertain. Did she want to insinuate herself any further into this family's strife? It would only make leaving tomorrow that much more difficult. What if Regina appealed to her to stay? How could she refuse, especially now, in the simmering unhappiness of this place? And anyway, Olive had said Regina was sleeping, and Phoebe didn't wish to wake her.

She removed her hand from the cool knob and walked determinedly back to her room.

Eva set one of Lady Phoebe's portmanteaus on the bed and flipped the latches open. Morning sunlight gilded the rug and parquet floor, while the soft summer breeze stirred the window curtains. She hummed a light tune as she went to the dresser and began taking Lady Phoebe's things out of the drawers. "I can't say I'm disappointed to be going home, my lady. There is something about this house . . ." She didn't say more. It wasn't her place to openly criticize, but there was little about High Head Lodge that met with her approval. "I do wonder how the elder Lady Mandeville will manage without anyone to help her dress and all, though."

Lady Phoebe finished the last of her tea. She moved the tray table aside as she stood. "Miss Stanley will have to help Julia and both Lady Mandevilles, I suppose."

"I'm sure you didn't notice, but Myra Stanley was frightfully jumpy last night as she helped Lady Julia and the Dowager Lady Mandeville to bed. She especially didn't seem to like crossing the hall from one bedroom to another." Eva gently placed a stack of camisoles into the suitcase and smoothed her fingertips over the top one, a sheer cotton embellished with pale blue silk ribbon and eyelet lace. "She's been acting so strangely since we arrived."

"As a matter of fact, I did notice her darting across the corridor as if her heels were on fire." Lady Phoebe went to the dressing table and began opening the drawers, gathering up the items within. She made neat little piles on the tabletop. "What do you suppose is the problem?"

"I've been puzzling over that very thing." Eva laid several folded pairs of silk stockings beside the camisoles, then turned to face Lady Phoebe. "Yesterday, when we all left on the shopping trip, and Myra and Miss Brockhurst encountered each other for the first time, I could have sworn they knew each other."

"Hmm. I suppose it's possible." Lady Phoebe shrugged in an unconcerned manner. "I wouldn't be surprised to learn Regina and Diana Manners were acquainted. It's no secret that Regina tends to run in fast circles. But why would that make Miss Stanley uneasy?"

"Not just Miss Stanley, my lady." Eva leaned around Lady Phoebe to pick up the hairbrush. She ran it through Lady Phoebe's reddish-gold waves. "Miss Brockhurst seemed taken aback as well. As if she took no pleasure in finding Myra Stanley right here in her own home."

Phoebe frowned at her image in the mirror. "Interesting. I wonder why . . ." She shook her head. "Well, never mind. It's between Regina and Miss Stanley, and I suppose Julia, since Miss Stanley is her maid. If Miss Stanley wishes to leave, or if Regina wants her to go, either or both of them will have to take it up with Julia. My sister is determined to stay on. I, on the other hand, am telephoning home just as soon as I'm dressed."

As Eva arranged Lady Phoebe's hair to frame her face and pinned its length in a French twist, she studied her mistress in the mirror. Twice now Lady Phoebe had spoken her sister's name with telling emphasis, one Eva had grown accustomed to in recent years but hadn't heard in the past few months.

"Is there something wrong between you and Lady Julia?" she ventured.

Lady Phoebe hesitated before replying. She glanced down at her lap, then back up into the mirror. "I'm truly at a loss to understand it, Eva. Yesterday morning everything was fine, or as fine as it has been between us for a very long time. And then, last night after dinner . . . well . . . it was as if last spring never happened. As if we hadn't reached that unspoken understanding and decided to be civil to each other."

Hearing the distress in her tone, Eva patted her shoulder. "Did something happen during dinner? Was something said?"

"Nothing I can think of. I've gone over it in my mind a dozen times. There was nothing. We didn't even sit together. We were at opposite ends of the table. Julia and Regina seemed to be happily discussing the redecorating plans."

"And who did you sit with, and what did you discuss?"

"I sat between Hastings and Olive Asquith. What a pair. Hastings was drunk, of course . . ." She trailed off, tilting her head. "Which was odd because he seemed to drink so little, at least that I saw."

"Perhaps he's been drinking on the sly, in his room."

"Yes, probably."

"And what about you and Miss Asquith? What did you talk about with her?"

Phoebe wrinkled her nose. "She's an odd one. I tried to learn more about her. Don't people like to talk about themselves?" Eva nodded, and Phoebe went on. "She would tell me nothing—not where she was from, who her people are, only that she attended the North London Collegiate School. Lucky, wasn't she?"

A wistful note entered her voice. Lady Phoebe aspired to someday obtain a higher degree of some sort. She had attended the Haverleigh School for Young Ladies near Foxwood Hall, but until quite recently the school had focused primarily on the social graces and the running of great households or, for their scholarship students, subjects that would enable them to find employment.

"Olive issued something of a warning to me last night, after dinner."

"A warning?" The blood surged in Eva's veins. "Did she threaten you?"

"No, not quite that. But she said I should go home before things here became overwhelming for me. I haven't the first notion what she could mean. She was going on about large houses no longer being the *thing,* as she put it, and then suddenly switched to the very personal question of what I would be willing to give up to achieve my goals. I found her rather impertinent, really."

"As well you should. Miss Asquith doesn't know you, yet it sounds as though she felt free to judge you." The very notion raised Eva's hackles.

Phoebe nodded at her assessment of Miss Asquith's behavior. Eva went to the armoire and tossed its double doors wide to reveal Lady Phoebe's suits, dresses, and dinner gowns. "Would you like anything specific for today?"

"It doesn't much matter. Something simple and comfortable for the ride home, please."

"Very good, my lady." Eva was just reaching in to select Lady Phoebe's dark green silk motoring outfit, but nearly dropped the ensemble when a scream echoed from the corridor. Another shriek raised goose bumps on her arms and sent shivers up her back. She met her mistress's startled gaze.

"What on earth," they blurted at once, and hurried to the door.

Like dominoes, the doors along the corridor opened one after another. Lady Julia, Lord and Lady Mandeville, the dowager, Ralph Cameron, and even Myra Stanley poked their heads out, their eyes wide with alarm. "What is it?" the dowager asked in a shrill voice.

In the middle of the commotion, Olive Asquith stood outside Miss Brockhurst's bedroom door. The door was open, and Miss Asquith pointed inside with a rigidly extended arm. Her cheeks, devoid of color, gleamed with tears.

No one moved. Neither of the gentlemen seemed inclined to investigate any farther than their thresholds. Even Lady Phoebe stood motionless, no doubt gripped by the same apprehension that closed around Eva, making her feel detached and dizzy. Surely this could not be . . .

With a deep breath she stepped around her mistress and strode down the corridor to where Miss Asquith continued to point and shake and weep. Eva expected to have to rouse her from her stupor, but as she reached the other woman, Miss Asquith's trembling lips moved.

"Regina," she whispered. "She's . . . Oh, she can't be . . ."

Eva's stomach turned over and her throat fought each breath she attempted to draw. She peered through Miss Brockhurst's doorway. The room appeared undisturbed, tranquil, a typical morning scene, much like Lady Phoebe's, with sunshine spilling across the floor and gentle breezes rippling the curtains and bed canopy. Miss Brockhurst lay on her side in the middle of the bed, the covers loosely drawn up to her shoulders.

"Did you check on her?"

Miss Asquith nodded shakily. "I nudged her. She didn't respond. Do something. Someone needs to *do* something."

Instinctively, Eva darted glances at Lord Mandeville and

his solicitor, Mr. Cameron. Both stood framed in their doorways—literally, as if an artist had painted both men in place with their dressing gowns and mussed hair. Beyond color and form and figure, both appeared flat and lifeless.

Eva forced her feet to move, as images from the past several months flashed garishly behind her eyes. Surely this could not be happening again. Surely Miss Asquith had made a mistake. Surely Miss Brockhurst slept too deeply to be awakened by a nudge.

She reached the foot of the bed, then circled to the side where she could see Miss Brockhurst's face.

And she knew.

A blue cast tinged the corners of Miss Brockhurst's lips, and her eyes . . . her eyes stared through the slits of her eyelids to some point in midair. Eva's lungs emptied of their own accord, a heaving exhalation that drained her body of strength, of feeling. As numbness spread through her, she wanted to sink to her knees, rest her head on the side of the mattress, and let oblivion take her.

"Eva? Is she all right?" Lady Phoebe stood in the doorway, her face pinched and pale. She crossed the threshold, moving closer, and Eva found the renewed strength to lean down closer to Miss Brockhurst's prone form.

"What's this?" She leaned lower still. Tiny flecks marred the pillow on the other side of Miss Brockhurst's head. Reddish-brown flecks. Quickly, Eva went around to that side of the bed. Miss Brockhurst's black hair covered part of the pillow, with those rusty flecks marching out from beneath the tangled forest of curls. An acrid scent drifted from the bed linens to sting her nose. Her gaze flicked to the bedside table, to the crystal tumbler that sat near the corner of it, a trace of brownish liquid staining the bottom. Whiskey? Perhaps, but that was not the source of those tiny stains on the pillow. Those were different. She knew exactly what they were, knew even without seeing whatever wound had caused them.

But see she must. She reached a tentative hand beneath the curls, lifted them away from the pillow and from the back of Miss Brockhurst's neck.

Her other hand flew to her mouth, and she blinked—blinked in the glare of the morning sun playing upon an untold number of diamonds studding the wings and body of a dragonfly.

The dowager's hat pin protruded from the base of Miss Brockhurst's skull.

"Well, yes, it's true that no one in the family gets on particularly well," Phoebe told Chief Inspector Isaac Perkins an hour later. They sat in the dining room, she and the inspector and his assistant, Constable Miles Brannock. The Brockhursts had been interviewed first; Phoebe hadn't been privy to their statements. Julia had come next and had returned to the drawing room, where everyone had gathered, with a shaken look. Did the chief inspector consider her a suspect?

Now it was Phoebe's turn, and Chief Inspector Perkins had asked about the Brockhurst family's relationships. He had phrased his question almost as a statement. "Not much love is lost between them, is there?" Short of lying she could only but admit theirs had never, to her knowledge, been a close family.

The room swirled slowly around her. The chief inspector's voice wafted in and out of her ears as if water filled them, and her stomach churned like the swill in the bottom of a ship's hold.

Regina was dead. Vibrant, headstrong Regina, who had always done as she pleased, who took orders from no one, who had wished to share some secret excitement with Phoebe on this very day. Never again would she dazzle a roomful of people with her larger-than-life presence. Some people had considered her simply too much—too ostentatious, too garrulous, too overbearing. Her family, Phoebe supposed, agreed. But how could such a life be snuffed out so abruptly, so unceremoniously?

"Can you explain why that was, Lady Phoebe?"

Phoebe snapped out of her reverie. How long had her mind drifted? She couldn't say. She refocused on Chief Inspector Perkins. He sat a good distance from the edge of the table to accommodate his paunch, though that did nothing to relieve his straining suit buttons. He tipped his head back and in turn scrutinized Phoebe from down the length of his pocked nose. Beside him, Constable Brannock, an Irishman with thick red hair and keen blue eyes that missed little, waited patiently to record her answer. She took comfort in his presence; Constable Brannock had become rather well known to her in past months, and she knew him to be a fair and honest man.

What had the chief inspector asked her? Oh, yes. She drew a breath. "Several factors, I would say. There has always been strife in the family. Their personalities are all quite different, you see. Regina . . . Miss Brockhurst . . . was a particularly independent and strong-willed woman and—"

"So you're saying she caused the rifts in her family."

"What? No. I'm not saying that at all. My cousin simply wasn't one to keep her opinions to herself. If she saw behavior she didn't approve of, she said so. And she didn't approve of her brother's behavior. Neither did their father. But that's hardly for me to explain, Inspector. Did you ask the family these questions?"

"Whether I did or didn't isn't your concern, Lady Phoebe."

Miles Brannock flashed her a look from beneath a shock of his bright auburn hair. His mouth made the tiniest of twitches before he pursed his lips in an official manner and scribbled in his notepad. Phoebe and the constable were both accustomed to the chief inspector's brand of questioning as well as his condescension. Both had learned to let Chief Inspector Perkins have his way during his interrogations. The real work would come later, and Miles Brannock would perform the bulk of it—with Phoebe's help, and Eva's as well.

She turned her attention back to the inspector, who seemed to be waiting for her to say something. So far he hadn't asked any questions relating to Julia, and Phoebe restrained a sigh of relief. "I'd much prefer to relate to you what I witnessed with my own eyes, sir."

He harrumphed. "All right then, Lady Phoebe, had you ever witnessed your cousin stealing anything?"

"No, never. Of course not."

"What about the dragonfly?" he shot back at her so sharply she flinched.

"Oh, that. Regina said she borrowed it from her mother. She planned to return it."

"Hmm. They all do," the man muttered. "What happened next? Tell me about last night. You said people were awake in the house when they should have been sleeping? Your sister said the same." Ah, finally, a reference to Julia, but nothing incriminating.

"Well, I heard Lord and Lady Mandeville arguing in their suite."

"Which Lady Mandeville?"

"The younger. I did say they were in *their* suite."

Miles Brannock compressed his lips, no doubt to hide another twitch.

"Did they exit the room at all?"

"Not that I saw. I heard someone in the billiard room, although I can't tell you who it was."

"In the billiard room, you say? In the middle of the night?"

Phoebe shrugged and nodded. Then her eyes went wide. "Do you suppose whoever was in there might have . . . ?"

"I am not supposing anything, Lady Phoebe." The chief inspector raised a half-closed fist to his mouth and, to Phoebe's disgust, belched. "And don't you go supposing either. Are you sure you don't know who it was?"

"I didn't think to check, although it's safe to say it wasn't Hastings or Verna, nor Olive or Regina—"

"How do you know it wasn't your cousin or Miss Asquith?"

She blinked. "Oh, well, because . . ." Here Phoebe paused. She was only about to tell the inspector what she saw, but at the same time what she saw could possibly incriminate Olive Asquith. Yet she couldn't *not* tell the inspector. After all, Olive might have been the last person to have seen Regina alive. She might even have . . .

Phoebe shut her eyes against last night's memory. If only she had gone into Regina's bedroom. She had come so close to doing so. *Why* hadn't she?

Selfish reasons, ones for which she might never forgive herself. She hadn't wished to become embroiled any further in the tribulations of this house. She wanted morning to come, and with it the motorcar that would take her home. She had wanted to get away from everyone here, even Julia. Especially Julia, with her caustic disregard last night. Now, however, she wished only to undo whatever had damaged their rapport; she wished to return to the accord they had reached in the spring.

But . . . if she'd only gone into that bedroom last night, would she have found Regina alive? Dying? Could she have helped her? If she had found her cousin dead, would it have meant that Olive murdered her? Perhaps Olive found Regina dead, but then why hadn't she said something last night?

"Lady Phoebe, if you please," the inspector prompted.

"Miss Asquith," she said quickly, before she could change her mind. "I saw her exiting my cousin's bedroom. It was quite late at the time."

"And what were *you* doing up?"

She very nearly gasped at his implied suspicion. "Something woke me, the arguing coming through the walls, I suppose. And I heard other noises, doors opening and closing, so I got up to investigate." Even to herself, she sounded defensive, almost defiant. She breathed in deeply, searching for her composure.

"And?"

Phoebe frowned.

He held out his hand in a gesture of impatience. "Did Miss Asquith say anything?"

"She said Miss Brockhurst was having trouble sleeping, and she, Miss Asquith, had been reading to her. Then she went straight back to her room."

"And what did you do?"

"I . . . er . . ." She swallowed a bitter taste of guilt. "I also returned to my room."

"You went nowhere else?"

"No. Just to my room."

Moments stretched while Inspector Perkins studied her. She began to notice how stuffy the room had become. Despite the temperate weather, the windows had all been shut, and with the door to the hall closed as well, not a breath of air stirred. Perspiration dotted her forehead; a drop trickled down her back. The inspector, too, was sweating, but then he typically did. She couldn't remember seeing his florid complexion without a sheen from the slightest exertion. Perhaps he deliberately made the room uncomfortable to discompose, even agitate those he questioned. He wouldn't want a potential suspect to feel too comfortable, would he?

"May I go now?" she asked when the ticking of the mantel clock seemed to become deafening.

"Tell me about your relationship to the deceased," he asked bluntly. "Had the two of you argued recently?"

"No, not at all," she said quickly, loudly. The inspector raised a bushy eyebrow. Phoebe's heart thumped, and she realized how her hasty reply had sounded. She swallowed to calm her nerves. "Regina invited my sister and me here to help her redecorate the house, to help her with ideas for each room. We were having a lovely time until . . ."

"Yes?"

Why should he make her feel so exposed all of a sudden, and as if she had something to hide? Why couldn't she simply answer his questions without her pulse bucking and heat flooding her face? "Until the rest of her family arrived. As I've already told you."

"Your cousin had recently come into a great deal of money. Were you jealous of her?"

"Good heavens, no!" She swallowed again. "Certainly not. Why would I be?"

"You tell me, Lady Phoebe."

He suspected her. Her—after all the help she had provided in two previous murder cases. She darted a glance at Constable Brannock, one he returned with sympathy and, yes, exasperation in his eyes. At least *he* knew she could never commit a violent act against another individual, unless that individual threatened her life or the life of someone she cared about.

"Inspector, my cousin and I got on quite well. In fact, she had something special to confide in me today, something I'll never learn now . . ." Her throat closed around a threat of tears, and she bowed her head as she once more attempted to collect herself.

"So then, Lady Phoebe, if someone were to tell me there

had been some friction between you and Miss Brockhurst, they would be lying?"

Her mouth falling open on a gasp, she swung her head upward. "Who said that? Yes, of course it would be a lie. Regina and I never argued . . ."

"Never?"

"Well . . ." Now he was confusing her, trying to catch her up in a lie of her own, not that she had anything to lie about. Once again, he made her almost *feel* guilty, and that only served to make her *appear* guilty. She drew herself up and squared her shoulders. "Not since we were children, at any rate. And since she was several years older than I, it's not as though we played together or spent a lot of time in each other's company."

For several moments the only sound in the room was the scratching of Constable Brannock's pencil. Phoebe tried to sit calmly, her eyes focused on the mantel clock across the way from her. Chief Inspector Perkins drummed his sausagelike fingers against the tabletop and regarded her as if waiting for her to sprout wings or . . . or make a confession, perhaps.

At long last, he said, "All right, that will be all for now."

She was on her feet in an instant, yet to her chagrin, her legs trembled.

"For the time being you're not to leave this house," he admonished. "I might need to question you again." Gripping the edge of the table, he struggled to his feet, having to wiggle his bottom off the seat cushion first. He walked with her back to the drawing room, where the others waited. They had all been ordered to wait there, except the cook and her assistant, Margaret, who had been questioned first off. Eva and Myra Stanley sat at the card table, Eva at attention, Miss Stanley looking relaxed and as if she hadn't a care in the world. After the past two days of

Miss Stanley behaving like a goose counting the days before Christmas, she seemed awfully content now.

In contrast, Verna and Cousin Clarabelle, sitting on the closer of the settees, leaned against each other with their arms linked in a show of solidarity rather atypical of them. But then, of course, tragedy had a way of negating petty concerns. Their eyes were red and swollen, their faces leeched of color. Hastings slouched in a chair across from them, his chin in his hand, his gaze focused somewhere on the floor. Ralph Cameron hovered beside the fireplace, looking inappropriately dashing in a tan tweed sack suit, as if he were attending a picnic or going motoring in the countryside. His ready stance and observant air gave Phoebe the impression he had taken on the task of overseeing the others, of being ready to intervene should anyone fly to pieces.

Julia stood with her back to the room, gazing out one of the French windows to the garden beyond. And Olive Asquith . . . Olive sat alone some distance from the family. The inspector made his way over to her. Before speaking he looked her over from head to toe and back. She met his gaze only briefly, glancing away as if she found him beneath her notice. Finally, he said, "You are Olive Asquith?"

She tilted her face up at him and raised an eyebrow high above the other. "I am." Phoebe searched her features for signs of grief. Her eyes were not red like Verna's and Cousin Clarabelle's, nor vacant like Hastings's, but did that mean anything? People registered sorrow in different ways, and she doubted a stoic, serious woman like Olive Asquith would wear her heart on her sleeve.

He sniffed. "And your relation to the deceased?"

"I am—was—her friend. Perhaps her only true friend," she added in a murmur.

An objection rose up in Phoebe, but she kept her silence.

It might have been true. Hadn't she herself been intent on abandoning her cousin today? She could find no other word for it. For convenience's sake, English civility could be blamed; Phoebe had not wished to continue witnessing the very personal discord between Regina and her family. A very British thing, to claim her leaving would have been out of deference to the Brockhursts, when all along she had simply wished to avoid the unpleasantness.

Even Julia hadn't been guilty of that.

"Friend, eh?" The inspector again scrutinized Olive up and down. He pushed out his lips and scratched at his chin. "I find that claim rather difficult to believe, Miss Asquith."

Miss Asquith said nothing, but her nostrils flared and her jaw beaded with tension.

"You don't strike me as the sort of woman someone like Miss Brockhurst would deign to spend her time with."

Miss Asquith spoke from between her clenched jaws. "What sort of woman am I, then?"

"The sort who *works* for people like the Brockhursts. The sort who might, if she were very clever, wheedle her way into a rich person's life and see how far it takes her."

Phoebe went rigid. She waited for Olive's retort, for her to spring up from her chair and deliver to the inspector a thorough dressing-down. Yet Olive remained seated, breathing heavily but otherwise showing no other outward sign of anger.

But was he right about her? Just what did Olive Asquith *do* to support herself? Or had that been Regina's role?

"Well, come along, my girl. I've got questions for you." The inspector curled his fingers in an insolent gesture meant to bring Olive to her feet. She complied, but in no great hurry. In fact, she gathered herself slowly and determinedly, with a good deal of dignity, and silently led the way out of the room without once looking back to see if the inspector followed.

Would the young woman's haughtiness survive the inspector's questions and the uncomfortable heat of the dining room? Phoebe supposed that depended on whether or not Olive Asquith had something to hide.

CHAPTER 6

As soon as the drawing room door closed behind Olive and the inspector, Cousin Clarabelle let out a cry. "He thinks I did it because it was my hat pin! Not that anyone couldn't have snatched that pin. I never retrieved it from the library table."

This brought Hastings out of his stupor. "You? He thinks *I* did it."

"Well, if the truth be told, he said the same of me." Verna's birdlike features sharpened. "He can't think we *all* did it."

"Maybe we all *did* do it," Hastings mumbled. He sank lower in his chair, his head dipping between his shoulders. "Maybe we're *all* guilty."

"Don't be stupid." Verna turned to glance up at Ralph Cameron. "What did he say to you? Does he think *you* had a hand in Regina's demise?"

One hand in his trouser pocket, the solicitor shuffled his feet in an uncharacteristic show of embarrassment. "He, er, asked me what I knew about the family, and the money, of course. Asked me about when Lord Mandeville changed his will."

Cousin Clarabelle released Verna and came to her feet, obviously alarmed. "And what did you tell him?"

"The facts," he said in a placating voice. "Only the facts."

"And you, Phoebe?" Cousin Clarabelle's attention swerved to her with disconcerting swiftness.

"Oh, ah, the same, basically, as Mr. Cameron," she replied evasively. If the inspector had wished everyone to know the details of each interview, he would have questioned them together. In truth, she felt calmer now with the realization that the inspector had used the same tactic with everyone, unnerving them all in hope someone might break down and come clean.

What did it mean that, so far, no one had? That Olive was guilty? Or that the guilty party had a firm hold on his or her emotions?

"I suppose he'll tell Miss Asquith she's guilty next," Verna murmured. Her upper lip curled. "Not that he came out and said he thinks I did it, mind you. But his questions implied he did."

"The same with me," Hastings said with a nod. He peered over to the card table, where Eva and Miss Stanley looked on. "What about the two of you?"

Myra Stanley pressed a hand to her breastbone. "Me? He asked me what I had observed the past two days, that's all. I told him precious little. I'd *seen* precious little, after all, being Lady Julia's maid."

Eva dropped her gaze to her lap, waiting, Phoebe supposed, to be asked about her interview. No one bothered. They seemed content enough with Miss Stanley's reply, as if she spoke for both of them.

Cousin Clarabelle resumed her seat with a fretful sigh.

"I can't help but wonder who was in the billiard room last night." Phoebe glanced at each of the room's occupants in turn.

"In the billiard room?" Cousin Clarabelle sounded as if she had made an outlandish accusation. "At what time?"

Phoebe regarded her before replying. She already knew it couldn't have been Hastings or Verna, for they had been arguing in their room. It couldn't have been Olive or Regina, unless Olive had been lying. Her gaze drifted to Mr. Cameron, standing tall, unruffled, a study in elegance. "Was it you, Mr. Cameron?"

He stepped forward slightly with a little bob of his head. "It *was* me, Lady Phoebe. I wasn't sleeping well and decided to get up. I found myself in the billiard room."

"Rolling balls, one into another?"

"Yes, it helps me think."

Cousin Clarabelle tilted her chin to look up at him. "And what were you thinking about, Ralph?"

"How to mend the rifts in this family. What else?" He turned his attention back to Phoebe. "Does that satisfy your curiosity? Or do you think I might have crept into Regina's bedroom and—"

Cousin Clarabelle gasped. "Oh, Ralph, don't even say such a thing. No one here believes you had anything to do with Regina's . . . Regina's . . ." The words melted into tears, and Verna's thin arms encircled her.

Phoebe sighed. No, she didn't think Ralph Cameron murdered Regina. What would he have to gain, especially given the rapport that had obviously existed between them? If he had wished to continue tending the family fortune, Phoebe had little doubt Regina would have allowed him.

"And what were you doing up, Phoebe?" Verna's thin lips curled into a smile of mock sweetness. "If I may be so bold as to ask."

Phoebe's gaze didn't waver. "I heard arguing and got up to investigate. It was coming from your room, actually. The walls here are much thinner than one might suspect."

Verna paled, and her smile wilted like week-old flowers.

"You were arguing about Regina," Phoebe persisted. "You were both furious with her."

It was Verna's turn to push to her feet. She came at Phoebe in a rush, stopping a few feet short. "And why shouldn't we have been? She took the fortune—"

"She *inherited* the fortune," Phoebe corrected her. "She cannot be blamed for that."

Verna shook her head. "It doesn't matter. She took the money and left the rest of us with nothing. So yes, we were angry. That doesn't mean we—" She shut her mouth, pinching her lips tightly together.

No, it didn't necessarily make either Verna or Hastings a murderer, Phoebe could not but agree. But it certainly shed suspicion in their direction.

Across the room, Julia seemed to have ignored the discussion, continuing to contemplate the view outside, the flowers overgrowing their beds, the shrubbery fast losing its shape. With a pang Phoebe realized Regina would be hiring no gardeners, nor anyone else to care for her new estate. She turned away from Verna and the others and on still shaky legs crossed the room to her sister. Julia acknowledged her with a slight turn of her head, but just as quickly went back to staring outside.

"What did the inspector say to you?"

Julia hesitated before answering, releasing a breath laden with obvious impatience. "Probably the same thing he said to you."

"He wasn't very kind."

"It's not his job to be kind." The words were tight, terse. "Get over it."

Phoebe studied her sister's uncompromising profile. "Why are you angry with me?"

Julia turned to face her full on. "Really, with everything that's happened, that's what you're worried about?"

"I only meant—"

Julia shook her head, her mouth tightening. "Honestly, must everything be about you? Poor, poor Phoebe. Our cousin is dead, you realize, and in case you hadn't noticed, you're standing in a room full of suspects. Ourselves included."

"Julia, please, I don't understand . . ."

With an impatient gesture, her sister walked off, leaving Phoebe standing with her mouth open, the words fading away. Approaching footsteps made her turn quickly, hoping Julia had relented, but it was Eva who came to stand beside her.

"Did the chief inspector upset you very much, my lady?"

Phoebe smiled. "Dearest Eva, always concerned about me." But then Julia's parting words came back to mock her. "Does it matter if he did? It's not about me, is it? Poor Regina."

Quite unexpectedly, tears burned her eyes, and her throat closed around the sob she had held back in the dining room. She found herself just as suddenly in Eva's arms, quietly weeping. "She didn't deserve this, Eva. Such a beastly end to a short but vibrant life."

"Of course she didn't deserve it. No one does. You must be strong, my lady."

"Must I be? Why?"

"For your cousin. You've been strong before, strong enough to see justice done. Your cousin deserves that same justice."

The words penetrated the grief that enclosed her, and she lifted her head from Eva's shoulder. "Why must we be the ones to see she gets it? Can't the inspector, for once . . ." She let the thought go unfinished, for she knew the answer. Chief Inspector Perkins had enjoyed more than a decade as the local head of law enforcement with nary a crime to disturb his daily perusal of the newspapers. Whatever devilish force had invaded their sleepy corner of the Cotswolds to provoke three murders in less than a year had not managed to rouse the man to action. And he would not be roused now, not in any worthwhile manner. Constable Brannock had implied as much with those twitches of his lips.

Eva handed her a handkerchief. "It's clean. Dry your tears, my lady."

Phoebe dabbed at her cheeks. "You do realize someone in this very room is probably to blame for my cousin's death."

"Miles hasn't yet ruled out an intruder, my lady." No longer demurring about her growing affection for the constable, Eva openly referred to him by his given name these days.

"But the dragonfly. Why would an intruder use it to—" Her stomach tightened at the memory of the hat pin protruding from Regina's skull. She drew a fortifying breath. "All right. Here's what I've noticed so far. Cousin Clarabelle and Verna are distraught, believably so. Hastings is dazed and irreverent. Mr. Cameron remains the cool, detached self we met yesterday. As does Julia, though something is eating at her. She's still angry with me."

"It could merely be the strain of this house, the circumstances."

"I wish I could believe that, Eva, but I don't." Once again, her preoccupation with what her sister thought of her produced a pang of guilt. "Never mind. It's nothing compared to Regina's life. And the fact that one of her family members quite possibly killed her."

When Olive Asquith reentered the drawing room, she looked at no one and without a word settled back into the chair she had occupied before the inspector came for her. Eva tried to read her expression. It was plain to see the inspector's questions had left Miss Asquith unsettled . . . and angry. Yes, anger seethed in her eyes and glared out from her white-knuckled hold on the arms of the chair.

"Well," the dowager called to her, "what happened? What did the inspector say to you?"

Miss Asquith raised a defiant expression. "That is hardly any of your business."

"Hardly my business? Hardly my business?" The dowager rose and practically charged down the room. "How dare you, you insolent baggage? It's my daughter lying dead, isn't it? And you—living off her money as you have been doing—"

"As *you* wished to do, Lady Mandeville. You, your son, and his wife. You accuse me, but you wanted Regina for one reason only, once you learned she'd inherited most of your husband's fortune."

"That's not true. I loved my daughter. Yes, I was angry with her, we all were and had every right to be, but . . . but Regina would have come around. In time. That is, if she hadn't had *you* misguiding her every step."

"*Angry* with her? Is that what you call it?" Miss Asquith made an inelegant sound.

"Ladies, please." Ralph Cameron hurried over to them. "This isn't helping. You don't mean a word of it, either of you. You're both understandably upset. Please, Clarabelle, come sit, and let's all calm down."

Eva frowned. For Lady Phoebe's ears alone she said, "When he says 'let's all calm down,' my lady, I can't help but wonder who *all* he means. At the moment, only the dowager and Miss Asquith are upset. Everyone else is composed, at least outwardly. Even the new Lady Mandeville." Indeed, Verna Brockhurst sat watching the contention between the other two women with an expression approaching amusement. She had looked amused, too, when she had asked Lady Phoebe what she had been doing up the night before. Apparently, the woman enjoyed watching suspicion shift to anyone but herself.

The dowager slid her arm through Mr. Cameron's and pressed up against his side. "Oh, Ralph, you know how much I loved her. How much I wished she would come home to us."

"Yes, Clarabelle, I do know. And Regina knew it as well."

"I loved her, too, you know." The younger Lady Mandeville's assertion sounded more defensive than affectionate.

"I find Verna's claim rather hard to believe, based on what I overheard last night," Phoebe whispered to Eva.

"Well, don't all of you look at *me*." Lord Mandeville started to rise but fell back heavily in his chair. Eva wondered, could he have been drinking this early in the morning? When had he had the chance? "I loved my sister, you know, and despite what that bulbous-nosed inspector might think, I certainly didn't kill her."

"No one is looking at you," his wife said in a low, cautioning murmur.

"Yet you *were* out of your room, last night, Hastings." All eyes turned to Lady Julia as she made this pronouncement.

"What's this?" Lady Phoebe whispered, at the same time the dowager rounded on her sister.

"Whatever do you mean?"

"Just what I said. He was up, roaming about. I saw him prowling the corridor last night. He stopped and put his ear to Regina's door."

"That's a lie," Hastings Brockhurst said weakly.

His wife ignored him and said, with a thrust of her finger at Lady Julia, "That means *you* were up as well." Her angry strides made short work of the distance between them. "What were you doing?"

"Nothing. I heard noises, just as Phoebe had, and peeked out my door. I didn't set foot out of my room."

The younger Lady Mandeville didn't look convinced. "Humph. And what did you tell the chief inspector? That you think Hastings . . ."

"I didn't say any such thing." Lady Julia assumed a bored air. "And as a matter of fact, I don't believe Hastings did anything to Regina, nor any of the rest of us."

"Then who?" Verna Brockhurst cocked an angular hip and set a hand on it.

"If she saw me in the corridor, I must have been sleepwalking." Lord Mandeville attempted to smile, a failed effort. "I do sometimes, you know. Ask Verna."

"No one is worried about that, Hastings." His wife's tone took on an unmistakable edge of scorn. "So do be quiet." She turned back to Julia. "We all know who did it. *That* one." She pointed at Miss Asquith. "We need look no farther."

"And why would I kill my friend?" Miss Asquith appeared genuinely curious.

The dowager supplied the answer. "Because Regina had decided to return to her family, that's why. She decided to abandon you in favor of her own blood."

Miss Asquith laughed without mirth. "That certainly is rich. You all arrive here yesterday accusing Regina of murder and theft, and now you accuse *me* of murdering *her*? What had I to gain? Not nearly as much as you, Lady Mandeville, nor you, Verna Brockhurst, and most especially not as much as your husband. If I benefited in any way from my friendship with Regina, it's nothing compared to the boon you all awakened to this morning. Tell me, how does it feel to control the fortune again? Relieved, aren't you?"

Phoebe watched Miss Asquith closely, then whispered to Eva, "When I came upon Miss Asquith last night, she said Regina was having trouble sleeping. She didn't say why, and I didn't ask, since at the time it seemed of small consequence. Now I wish I had asked. Perhaps she had argued with one of her guests and was upset by it. It seems everyone was awake, even Julia."

"And from what we're hearing, almost everyone seemed to have had reason to resent her, didn't they, my lady?" Eva whispered back. "And now they're all attempting to put the blame on someone else."

Lady Phoebe raised a hand in a subtle gesture, guiding Eva's line of vision. "All except Ralph Cameron, despite having admitted he was also out of his room last night. Look how calm he remains."

"Yes, but that's probably because of all of them, he had the least reason to wish ill on your cousin, and now he's trying to remain the rational one in the bunch."

"Perhaps . . ." Lady Phoebe's gaze wandered to the card table. "Miss Stanley is frightfully calm as well."

Eva had it on her tongue to repeat what she had said about Mr. Cameron, that Myra had no reason to involve herself in the family's discord. And then she remembered Myra's behavior ever since they had arrived at High Head Lodge. A word Miss Asquith had just used popped into her head. "Relieved."

"What's that?" Lady Phoebe asked her.

"My lady, I need to speak with Miles right away."

"I tell you, Myra Stanley knew Regina Brockhurst, and there was no love lost between them." Eva and Miles Brannock went from window to door to window along the outside of the house. Presently, they climbed the steps to a side terrace outside the library. A gusty breeze stirred Miles's red hair, which hung in waves below his policeman's helmet and curled about his collar. At times, Eva longed to reach out and tuck one of those unruly locks behind his ear. She might have done, if they had been somewhere else, where they wouldn't have been visible to anyone in the house.

"But it's not unusual that a woman might be acquainted with the lady's maid of a friend," he said as he jiggled the door latch and then leaned over to inspect the mechanism. He passed his hand along the hinges of the casement windows as well, looking for signs of forced entry. Thus far, they had found none. With his faint brogue, he said, "You say Myra Stanley used to work for Lady Diana Manners? I've heard of the woman. Who hasn't?"

He referred, of course, to Lady Diana's reputation for keeping fast company and being rather loose with her morals. Until her recent marriage, she had often been featured in the scandal sheets and gossip columns.

"I'm talking about more than a casual acquaintance during the course of her duties. Myra has been acting strangely since we arrived. I didn't realize it at first, but it began as we drove up to the house with Myra complaining that no servants had lined up to greet Ladies Phoebe and Julia. She said the failure of Miss Brockhurst to assemble her staff was a slapdash way to welcome guests."

"Isn't that how toffs think and, by association, their servants?"

"Well, yes, sometimes, but taken with the rest of her behavior, I think what she found objectionable was the lack of other staff among whom she could blend. From the first, she wished to avoid having Miss Brockhurst recognize her. The next morning, when we were to accompany the ladies shopping, she came out of her room in what I can only describe as a disguise. She had cut her hair and applied layers of ridiculous cosmetics. I had her turn an about-face and wash it off. Her next antic was to complain about how Miss Brockhurst housed her guests in the main portion of the house, rather than in a separate guest wing. Again, because she feared coming face to face with Miss Brockhurst. When it finally did happen outside on the drive, the two of them looked like they'd just experienced an electrical shock. Miss Brockhurst recognized her—I know she did—but a moment later denied it and dismissed the matter."

Miles had finally turned away from the windows, and Eva had his full attention. "You're sure Miss Brockhurst recognized Miss Stanley?"

"I have no doubt, and neither would you if you had been there." She drew a breath; the air smelled like rain and rotting foliage, old dead leaves and flowers that had not been removed from the gardens. "But here's the clincher," she continued. "Having grown tired of her complaining, I suggested she should have remained in Lady Diana's employ. Myra became incensed and insisted she would have done if not for Lady Diana's marriage last month. She claimed there was no room for her in the new household, and that Lady Diana was loath to lose her."

His blue eyes twinkled with a mixture of amusement and interest. "I'm going to guess you find fault with that statement."

"I most certainly do. There is no reason a bride wouldn't bring her maid with her to her new home. This excuse of there being no room for Myra is absurd. The only explanation is that Lady Diana found fault in how Myra performed her duties and let her go."

They walked down the terrace steps together and continued to the rear of the house. "So how does Miss Brockhurst figure into this theory?" he asked.

"Isn't it obvious? At some point, Miss Brockhurst must have visited Lady Diana, or vice versa, and something happened involving Myra." Eva considered while Miles continued checking the integrity of the windows and doors. "We need to discover why Myra stopped working for Lady Diana and verify whether Miss Brockhurst actually did spend time with Lady Diana at some point, where she might have had some sort of to-do with Myra."

"Resulting in Myra murdering Miss Brockhurst."

"I believe it's highly possible."

He nodded slowly, raising his face to the gust that swirled across the terrace to billow against the house. His unkempt waves danced about his coat collar. Once again, Eva's fingers itched to comb them into submission, but she held her hands at her sides. His gaze lingered on her face, and a small smile curled his lips. Self-conscious heat crept into her cheeks. She laughed to cover her discomfiture.

"Why are you staring?"

His smile widened, and a wicked gleam flashed in his eyes. "You're lovely when you're cunning."

"Don't be absurd." She laughed again, turning her face to the wind as he had, letting it pluck fine hairs from her coif.

"I wish you weren't here," he said suddenly, solemnly. "And yet I'm *glad* you're here."

"I'll be all right." She met his gaze, and all humor between them faded like sunlight behind a cloud. She saw the concern in his eyes, the regret that once again, her life might be at risk. "I won't take chances, but I can help you solve this. I have to."

"And why is that?" He reached out, catching a few of those fine hairs on his fingertips and brushing them back from her face.

"Have you forgotten Myra is now Lady Julia's maid? If she is guilty of anything—anything at all, no matter how small—I can't allow her to remain in the Renshaws' employ."

His hand fell away, as if he suddenly remembered they were not simply strolling along a terrace together, but engaged in important police business. He continued on to the next set of windows, Eva keeping pace with him. Then they descended the steps and circled the hedges to the kitchen wing. "Julia should be safe enough," he said. "If Myra did kill Miss Brockhurst, I believe you're correct that it had something to do with their past history. It's not likely she would kill again. And I agree, we need to investigate her time with Lady Diana. And I think I know just the person to help us."

"Who is that?" Eva believed she already knew.

"Owen Seabright, of course. The man has limitless contacts, and he's not hesitant to use them. Do you think we can enlist Lady Phoebe's help?"

Inspector Perkins finally released everyone from the drawing room, with the admonishment that no one was to leave the estate until further notice. While Phoebe waited for her call to go through to the main offices of Seabright Textiles in Bradford, Yorkshire, she sought out Ralph Cameron, hoping to speak with him alone. She was in luck, for Cousin Clarabelle had pleaded a migraine from the shock and upset and gone upstairs to lie down. Otherwise Phoebe could not have hoped to pry Mr. Cameron from her side.

She found him in the library. He sat at the mahogany library table—the very one where Phoebe had placed the dragonfly yesterday—with a stack of books beside him and one open beneath his nose. Several papers also lay fanned out before him. His index finger lay atop one of them while he perused the open book. A frown of perplexity etched deep ridges across his brow.

He glanced up when she entered the room, eyeing her above a pair of gold-rimmed reading spectacles. They lent him a scholarly air, like a professor, a kindly one. Given this and his steady temperament, she could see how Cousin Clarabelle might come to depend on him; how Regina, too, might have leaned on him. Briefly she pondered his relationship with both women. Had he been toying with them? Playing them one against the other?

He closed his book, shuffled the papers into a neat pile, and removed his glasses. "Lady Phoebe, can I do something for you?"

"It's just Phoebe, and yes, perhaps you might. Although if you're terribly busy—"

"I was just going over a technicality to do with . . . well . . . to put it bluntly, Hastings's new inheritance."

"I see." She approached the table. "You looked terribly puzzled as I entered the room."

He gestured at the papers. "It can be grueling sometimes, the legal technicalities."

When she attempted to make out the top page, he abruptly turned the whole stack over. Phoebe pretended not to be taken aback by the action. "So much has changed since yesterday, hasn't it?"

"Indeed it has." Standing, he came around the table and pulled out a chair for her. Then he resumed his own seat. "I'm glad to see you aren't afraid of being alone with me." At her puzzled look, he explained, "Someone in this house is possibly a murderer, and I was out of my room last night, wasn't I?" He smiled sadly. "I take it the reason you're here has something to do with Regina?"

"I—ah—yes, it does." His comment about one of them being a murderer took her aback. Was it an odd attempt at humor or merely a statement of fact? She didn't know him well enough to distinguish his meaning. At any rate, she had left the door ajar, should she suddenly need to call for assistance.

She glanced again at the books he had been perusing. The topmost one referred to inheritance law; was he verifying what the law said about an heir who murdered his benefactor? Did he believe Hastings had murdered his own sister in cold blood? That would certainly account for his perplexity.

Clearing her throat, she said, "You might consider this none of my business, but Regina *was* my cousin."

"Second cousin," he corrected her. When she raised her eyebrows at him, he smiled ruefully. "Forgive me. My profession compels me to an almost obsessive degree of accuracy."

"Yes, it would, wouldn't it?" She returned his smile and noticed the raw nick that scored the underside of his chin. A shaving cut? Understandable. She would not wish to use a straight razor on her face on a good day, much less immediately after a murder had been discovered. "You are correct. My mother and Regina's father were first cousins, making me Regina's second cousin. And I'll confess we were not particularly close. Always cordial, but not confidantes. It had to do with the difference in our ages, I suppose, but I regret it now," she added softly.

He let a moment stretch, then spoke gently. "Do you have a question about Regina, or the family?"

"No, Mr. Cameron—"

"Ralph, please." He slid a hand across the table toward her. It stopped several inches away. She stared down at it, puzzled. It was a strong hand, the fingers long and sturdy, but unmarred by the traces of physical labor. Was she supposed to grasp it? The gesture seemed rather too familiar . . .

He calmly slid it back to his side of the table. "Call me Ralph," he repeated. "Regina always did. The rest of the family as well. I may be their solicitor, but I'm also a family friend. I worked for Basil Brockhurst for nearly a decade, but I also considered him a mentor and something of a father figure when I was younger." He paused, his gaze dropping to the closed book in front of him.

Perplexed by his talent for deflecting the conversation, Phoebe drew a breath and came to the point. "It's about

Olive Asquith. I'm assuming you've looked into her background."

"A good deduction. Of course I did. At Clarabelle's request, as soon as it became apparent how much influence Miss Asquith held over her daughter."

"And what did you learn about her?"

"It's interesting. She's not the product of a drab, lower-middle-class background, as she pretends to be. Her family is quite well off. Banking and real estate. She's distantly related to Herbert Henry Asquith, our former prime minister."

"Why, my sister asked her if there was any relation, and she flat-out denied it."

"Yes, she would. As I said, it's a distant connection, and I doubt very much she has even met the man. But apparently Miss Asquith had a falling out with her family a few years ago. She was involved with the suffragettes, arrested several times, and when her parents finally ordered her home or else, she took the 'or else.' "

"Did they follow through on their threat?"

"They did. Cut off. At least until she comes around."

"So a need for money could be behind her friendship with Regina."

"Yes and no. Her father apparently relented and set up an account where she could draw limited funds on a monthly basis. Far from a fortune at her disposal, but still generous enough to keep her from resorting to desperate measures, which would further tarnish her reputation. One supposes her father was anxious to prevent that."

Phoebe digested this information. "And yet she pretends to be of quite ordinary origins. I wonder why. Is she ashamed of her family's wealth? I witnessed her attitude toward money firsthand yesterday when my sister and I went shopping with her and Regina. She constantly urged frugality and utility. To the point she and Regina argued over purchases."

She searched her memory of the previous day for any other clues into Olive's beliefs and values. "Or is she afraid people will take advantage of her for her money? But that's the very thing Cousin Clarabelle accused *her* of. It's very confusing."

"I wish I could make sense of it. I'd dig a bit deeper, but being trapped here in this house for the time being makes it rather difficult." He tipped his chin at her. "Fancy yourself a sleuth, do you, Phoebe? Are you thinking Miss Asquith is our guilty party?"

"I'm only trying to make sense of who Olive Asquith is, how she found her way to Regina, and what sort of hold she had on her."

"You're sure it was Miss Asquith with a hold on Regina, and not the other way around?"

The question jolted her with surprise. "I hadn't considered that. Do you think so?" A second jolt went through her. If it *was* Regina who held some claim over Olive, would Olive have taken action against her? Killed Regina to be free of her?

Ralph had mentioned Olive being active in the suffragette movement. With women thirty and over having achieved the vote last year, much of the roar had been taken out of the crusade. So to what, she wondered, did a woman like Olive turn her energy now? Olive and Regina had made plans for this house, secretive ones, at least where Olive was concerned, for she had more than once stopped Regina from sharing too much. Why? What could those plans have entailed that required concealment?

"Phoebe? Are you all right?"

"Sorry, I was just thinking." She stood. Several theories had taken shape, some directly concerning Olive Asquith, others about Regina's family, none of which she intended to share with Ralph Cameron. As he had said, someone in this house possibly committed murder. Though she thought it unlikely, that someone could be him. "Thank you for speaking with me. It's important, for my family's sake, that we understand what happened to Regina." At that moment the telephone in the rear hallway rang, echoing its way to the library. "That'll be my call finally going through. If you'll excuse me."

Chapter 7

Eva avoided looking at the bed where Regina Brockhurst lay earlier that morning. The coroner had been, making his initial examination and taking scrupulous notes before instructing his assistants to carry the body away.

Now she once again stood in that room, only this time with Miles while he, too, examined the furniture and contents and filled his writing tablet with his illegible scribbles. Presently, he held a magnifying glass and was searching the sheets and pillowcases for stray hairs that might not have been Miss Brockhurst's. Eva took special care to touch nothing, disturb nothing, but Miles had wanted an extra pair of eyes to help scan the room.

Her eyes. He had wanted her specifically, she thought with a twinge of pride. They had shared such circumstances twice before, and though resistant at first, he had learned to trust her instincts and skills of observation. Perhaps someday, when and if Lady Phoebe no longer needed her, she might have a future in law enforcement—she and Miles together. The notion made her chuckle out loud.

"What's so funny?"

She compressed her lips, startled to have been caught in her fanciful musing. Then she assumed her most serious expression. "Nothing. Why do you ask?"

He held her gaze another moment before gesturing at the bed. "There's not much here to go on, other than that faint odor. You were right, it's whiskey. On the pillow and in that glass." He wrinkled his nose. "Stale whiskey. Was Regina a habitual drinker of strong spirits?"

"I wouldn't know. We could try asking Lady Phoebe. Do you think she might have been too drunk to fight off her attacker?"

"That's one possibility. The other is that the glass contained something other than whiskey."

"You mean she was drugged?"

"It's a distinct possibility." He went to the chaise, where he had set down his evidence bag. From it he drew a small envelope and opened the seal.

Eva craned her neck to see. "What is that?"

"Lycopodium powder. It's made from dried clubmoss. For detecting fingerprints."

She had not seen him do this before and ventured closer to watch. Tipping the envelope, he scattered a fine covering of the yellowish powder across the night table. Then he slid his fingers and thumb into the glass Eva had first noticed when they found Miss Brockhurst that morning, spread them wide, and lifted the glass from the table without touching the cut crystal on the outside. Onto this, too, he sprinkled the powder, blowing away the excess. He did the same with the powder on the table.

He raised his magnifying glass and peered closely at the dusty surfaces.

"Do you see anything?"

He continued searching another moment. "I do. Of course I do, but I've a hunch they're all going to turn out to be Miss Brockhurst's. There's nothing conclusive on the glass at all, thanks to the pattern of the crystal. There's no surface large enough to get a good print."

"I suppose you'll have to take fingerprints of everyone in the house?"

He made a disparaging sound. "With this bunch, that'll be pleasant, won't it?"

Eva didn't reply; she didn't have to. They both knew the Brockhursts would be incensed at having to suffer the indignity of having their fingers inked and pressed onto paper. He continued examining the bed table, and she resumed studying her surroundings. Something that had escaped her notice previously caught it now, and she moved to the fireplace. "Miles, look at the screen." She pointed to the embroidered square of silk stretched across a carved, gold-leafed frame set before the fireplace opening. One of its legs had been knocked askew from the hearthstone and onto the hardwood floor. "It's crooked."

He straightened and regarded the piece. "So it is. Someone might have bumped into it."

"Or moved it purposely." Eva set the screen aside. The firebox was both tall and deep, and fitted with an iron grill. Against the charred brickwork, she detected a pile of a lighter gray substance lying in the back corner. "There are ashes inside, a heap of them." She crouched and reached for the fire poker beside her. "Yet there is no kindling or other sign of a fire having been laid, not to mention it's summer and unlikely that Miss Brockhurst would have wanted a fire."

Miles came and looked in over her shoulder. "It looks like something has been deliberately burnt. Documents, or letters, perhaps."

"It does appear to have been paper," she agreed as she probed with the poker. She leaned farther in. "I don't see any bits of anything to suggest wood or another solid object."

"Be careful," he cautioned. She could feel his closeness as he leaned over her. "Both of your head and of anything you find. You don't want to destroy evidence with that poker."

"What's this?" Setting the poker aside, she reached in with her arm, but lost her balance and started to fall forward. She would have hit her head on the brick firebox wall, but from behind Miles wrapped his arms around her waist and held her steady.

"Are you all right?" He started to draw her out.

"I'm fine. Don't pull me out. There's something behind the grate and I can almost . . ." Having squeezed her hand between two iron slats of the grate, she brushed her fingertips against a scrap of paper that had apparently escaped the flames. "If I just lean a bit more . . ."

"I could have moved the grate, you know." With his torso against her bottom and his arms around her waist in a way Eva dared not dwell on—not now, at any rate—he leaned her farther forward. After a little wiggling and stretching, she managed to latch on.

"Got it. Help me out."

He gave a tug that propelled her backward, and the next thing she knew he was sitting on the floor, his arms still around her, and she on his lap. A scrap of paper, charred about the edges, hung from between her fingers. She should have scrambled off him immediately. But he smelled rather nice and felt so lovely and warm beneath her, and his arms—his arms were solid and fit so snugly around her waist. And really, falling backward had quite disoriented her; she needed a moment to collect herself. Except that his face was so close to hers she could feel the fan of his breath and the heat of his cheek against her own. So tempting. So *very* tempting.

"Are you all right?" he murmured.

"Oh, yes. Heavenly." Goodness, had she really said *that*? "What I mean is . . ." It was too late. His look of concern transformed to one of endless amusement, raising a bubble of glee inside her. Laughter spilled from her lips and from his as well, but of course they couldn't remain in this undignified posture all day, so she pressed a hand to the hearth surround to steady herself as she lifted up from his lap.

A throat-clearing from the doorway—good heavens, the *open* doorway—stopped her cold.

"My lady, ah . . . we had a . . . er . . . mishap—slipped and fell . . ."

With a smile to rival one of Miles's in its cheekiness, Lady Phoebe crossed the room and stretched out a hand to Eva. "You look as though you could use a bit of help."

"Indeed, my lady." Her face scorching, she ducked her head, swallowed her mortification, and somehow managed to lever her feet beneath her. A little grunt of discomfort sounded in Miles's chest, but Eva didn't stop to evaluate its origin, merely hoped whatever appendage of hers had made contact with whatever part of him didn't hurt too badly.

In a moment she was on her feet, wishing Lady Phoebe would stop looking at her with such speculative delight. In another instant Miles pushed to his feet as well, the scrap of paper in his grasp.

"Did you speak with Owen Seabright, Lady Phoebe?" he asked in a level tone, as if the last moments hadn't occurred. Eva silently thanked him for his ability to brush off the incident, though her face continued to tingle with heat and she would have liked to dive beneath the bed.

Lady Phoebe assumed a more serious air. "I did. He'll look into the matter of Myra Stanley's departure from Diana Manners's employ." She frowned. "He's rather having a difficult time of his own presently. His workers are unionizing. He says that in itself isn't a bad thing, but there is a militant faction making unreasonable demands. Not just at Seabright Textiles, mind you, but all over industrial towns in the north."

"Seabright's a fair man," Miles said. "He'll find a solution."

Lady Phoebe nodded. "I just hope it's before violence breaks out. Have you found something?" She gestured at the scrap in Miles's hand.

"Ah, yes, this." He brought it to the dressing table and switched on the lamp. He angled the lampshade to direct the light and flattened the fragment on the tabletop.

"It looks like a bit of newspaper." Eva turned to Lady Phoebe. "I'd noticed ashes in the fireplace and took a closer look. We found this piece had escaped the flames."

"It must have floated away from the rest," Lady Phoebe observed. "Or just barely, by the look of it. What does it say? Can you read it?"

Miles leaned closer, holding the singed wisp down with his thumb and forefinger. "It's from a newspaper, but there isn't enough here to trace it. All I can make out is 'list labor.' That's 'list' with a small L, and 'labor' with a capital. And below, it says Edinburgh."

"List Labor?" Eva took the paper from him and studied it. "What could that mean?"

"Let me see." Lady Phoebe reached out, and Eva placed

the scrap in her hand. "There was something that came after, but I can only make out the very edge of the first letter. It looks to be another L, perhaps. Or I don't know, it could be a D or any letter that's fashioned with a straight vertical line on the left side. But above those words, I can make out the bottom edge of more letters, perhaps the publication's title?"

"This could be a fragment of a front page," Eva guessed, sidling up to Lady Phoebe to view the charred portion. She retrieved the poker from where she had leaned it and sifted through the ashes again. "If only there were more bits that escaped the flame."

"But why would someone burn a newspaper?" Lady Phoebe asked.

Miles shrugged. "A very good question."

"I suspect I know." Eva leaned the poker in its stand with the rest of the fireplace tools, having discovered nothing else of use. Having spent many years in service, she understood exactly what would make someone dispose of reading material. The publications deemed contraband for house staff by butlers and housekeepers were too innumerable to name. Most of those books, magazines, and newspapers had found their clandestine way into servants' quarters all the same, only to be secreted to the furnace once the pages had been thoroughly perused. "It seems Miss Brockhurst was in possession of reading material whose nature she didn't wish discovered by anyone else."

"Her secret plans for this house," Lady Phoebe blurted. "I think she might have intended to hold political meetings here. She expressed to me her unhappiness about the Qualification of Women Act passed last year. It left too many women without a say in government. Perhaps she was involved in renewing suffragist efforts."

Miles nodded slowly. "Then this might have been one of their newsletters. But why burn it? It's no secret most women don't believe Parliament went far enough with the act, and more and more men are in agreement. Not exactly a controversial notion."

"No, you're right." Eva smiled at a recent memory. "Even my mum, who never supported the suffragettes before, says in for a penny, in for a pound. Parliament should stop prevaricating—her word, mind you—and let all adults in this country vote."

"We're obviously missing something." Miles drummed his fingertips on the mantel, then began pacing. "Someone murders Miss Brockhurst, not simply to dispatch her, but to convey a message. Thus the hat pin . . . the Dowager Lady Mandeville's hat pin."

"Surely you don't think my cousin Clarabelle killed her own daughter?" Lady Phoebe looked incredulous. "It would be too obvious for her to use her own hat pin—the very same one they argued over only hours earlier."

"Stranger things have happened, my lady," Eva reminded her.

"There is the hat pin that killed her," Miles continued as if Eva and Phoebe hadn't spoken. She could all but see the wheels turning in his head. "A glass with a trace of whiskey is left on her bedside table, more whiskey spilled on the bed linens." He pivoted to regard Lady Phoebe. "Did Miss Brockhurst, to your knowledge, drink whiskey?"

"She might have done . . . I couldn't say with any certainty. But I've actually never seen her drink it. Hastings and Miss Asquith are another matter. They were both drinking whiskey last night."

"Were they now?"

"Miss Asquith definitely was. Hastings only seemed to hold his. I never actually saw him drink it, and that made me curious." She shook her head. "I'm afraid I'm not being very helpful."

"On the contrary, Lady Phoebe." Miles turned back to the bed. "Someone might have made it appear as if Miss Brockhurst had been drinking . . ." He drew up, his shoulders tightening. "Or forced her to drink, in order to incapacitate her."

"My lady, before you came in Miles was theorizing that perhaps this whiskey contained some kind of drug," Eva explained. "Or how else could someone have killed her in such a barbarian fashion without creating signs of a struggle?"

"They might have taken the time to straighten the room again, though, mightn't they?" Lady Phoebe suggested. "And perhaps it wasn't Regina who burned that newspaper, but her murderer. What if that newspaper contained something incriminating that pointed directly to that person?"

Miles stopped pacing and addressed Lady Phoebe. "You said Miss Asquith seemed upset when you saw her leave this room last night."

" 'Upset' might not be the right word. Disconcerted best describes her state when I saw her."

"They could be the same thing," Eva said. "Especially with a woman like Miss Asquith."

Lady Phoebe nodded her agreement. Miles returned to the bedside table, this time with his evidence bag, and slipped the crystal tumbler inside. "We might not learn anything conclusive, but I'll have this sent to the police laboratory in Gloucester just in case. In the meantime, let's all be on the lookout for any other suspicious reading material lying about the house."

Phoebe wasted no time in complying with Constable Brannock's request. She began with the post, left lying on the post salver in the hall. Sorting through, she saw a London *Times*, a Gloucester *Gazette*, and what looked to be several bills from shops both in London and the local area. Nothing appeared to be out of the ordinary—surely nothing worth burning. Should she open one of the invoices? She held one up and slid her finger beneath the corner of the flap . . .

"What are you doing? Isn't that addressed to my daughter?"

Phoebe whisked the letter to her side. Cousin Clarabelle stood halfway down the staircase, scowling. "I'm only seeing what's arrived. There may be items that need to be tended to."

Cousin Clarabelle descended the remaining stairs and approached Phoebe with her hand extended. "Then I shall tend to them."

"I mean no harm. I was only trying to help." It wasn't a complete lie; after all, discovering insight into Regina's life might help determine who had killed her. Phoebe placed the missive in Cousin Clarabelle's palm.

The woman heaved a sigh. "Yes, I know, Phoebe. Do forgive me. This has been so . . . so distressing." She raised a fingertip to the corner of her eye, but dabbed at dry skin. "I'll have Ralph go through these and make the necessary payments, if any are due. You needn't worry about them. Do you suppose Regina owed a great deal of money to people?"

"I couldn't say," Phoebe replied in an almost apologetic way, at the same time wondering why that should be Cousin Clarabelle's primary concern. "She was in the middle of refurbishing this house and had placed orders for furnishings."

Cousin Clarabelle's gaze passed over the hall and traced the curve of the staircase. "What was she thinking, buying this place? She didn't need it. She could have lived in the London house with the rest of us, and then we would not have had to rent it out. Oh, Phoebe, do you know how humiliating it is to be forced to rent out one's home?" Tears gathered in her eyes in earnest now. Phoebe opened her arms, and Cousin Clarabelle stepped into them, allowing her cheek to fall against Phoebe's shoulder.

She had no answer to the woman's question. That Regina had specific plans for this house she had no doubt, but what those plans were—they might never know. The way Regina had spoken last night of her interest in bettering society, Phoebe might have suspected her cousin wished to transform the house into a school or perhaps a rehabilitation hospital. That was what *she* would have done with High Head Lodge had it belonged to her. But if that had been Regina's plan, why hadn't she come out and said as much? Her request to meet with Phoebe in private suggested something altogether less benevolent.

Did it have anything to do with the burned newspaper?

Cousin Clarabelle lifted her head suddenly, her expression alarmed. "We'll need to cancel those orders she placed. We can't have things suddenly showing up and workmen expecting to be paid. As soon as all is resolved, we'll be selling the house. Where is Ralph? Ralph . . ."

Calling the solicitor's name, Cousin Clarabelle bustled off, leaving Phoebe alone in the hall. She crossed to the library, which she was glad to discover empty. Her search for controversial reading matter continuing, she went through the cabinets, the drawers in the library table, and perused the shelves. She doubted very much any of the books had belonged to Regina, but instead had been left behind by whomever lived there previously.

When nothing interesting presented itself, Phoebe considered the other rooms in the house. She doubted she would find anything in either the drawing or dining rooms. Why would Regina hide anything of importance in furnishings she intended disposing of? The same went for most of the other rooms on the ground floor. In fact, the house held a transient air, for Regina had added scant few personal effects.

No, if any further clandestine materials were to be found, Phoebe felt sure they would be upstairs, in one of the bedrooms. Eva and Constable Brannock had already gone through Regina's bedroom. What about Olive's? Since the murder weapon had been left in plain sight for all to see, the inspector had deemed a search of the house unnecessary.

But Olive wasn't the only person awake last night. It seemed everyone had been up and moving about. Julia had seen Hastings in the corridor. She hadn't been able to pinpoint the exact time, however, and Phoebe wondered who had actually seen Regina last.

The telephone rang again, echoing throughout the ground floor. Thinking Owen might be ringing back with information, Phoebe hurried along to the rear corridor where the telephone was located. Whoever had installed it apparently hadn't liked the idea of the device being a visible part of everyday life.

She reached the telephone desk at about the fifth ring and seized the ear trumpet from its cradle before the other party could disconnect. "Yes, High Head Lodge. Owen, is that you?"

"What? To whom am I speaking? Phoebe, is that you?"

"Grams? Is anything wrong at home?" She could think of no reason why her grandmother would be persuaded to use the telephone at home unless some trouble had arisen. Then it occurred to her that her grandparents didn't yet know about Regina.

"Where is your sister?"

"Julia?"

"Are you there with any other sister?"

"Em . . . no. I . . . She might be upstairs, if you'd like to hold while I check."

"Yes, please do. I must have a word with Julia—this instant."

Phoebe hesitated. Should she inform Grams of Regina's fate? Beyond a doubt the Countess of Wroxly would order them both home immediately, but would Inspector Perkins allow them to leave before his investigation had been completed? Phoebe thought not. What was more, she didn't wish to leave until Regina's death had been resolved. She and Eva had proven their usefulness to Constable Brannock on two dire occasions, contributing in ways the average policeman could not.

She was just laying the receiver alongside the candlestick base when Grams's voice once again rang out. "Phoebe, are you still there?"

She raised the device back to her ear. "Yes, Grams."

"While I have you . . ." Uncharacteristically, Grams hesitated. The line crackled and Phoebe wondered if the connection had been broken. Then Grams spoke again. "What do you know about Julia and Theo Leighton?"

The abruptness of the question took her aback, and she coughed and swallowed. "Julia and . . . Theo?" In truth she knew precious little. Even during the détente that had blossomed between them, Julia had avoided all talk of Theo Leighton, who had recently inherited the title of Marquess of Allerton from his deceased elder brother. Phoebe had her suspicions based on a couple of coincidences last spring that had placed the pair in the village of Little Barlow at the same time, but Julia had refused to answer any of Phoebe's half-teasing questions. That in itself was telling, but sharing mere speculation with Grams would not have been fair to Julia.

"Well? You must know something, or you wouldn't be stalling for time."

"I'm not stalling, Grams. I was thinking. Truthfully, I don't know anything about Julia and Theo. Why?"

"Humph. Never mind. Please find your sister for me."

Phoebe discovered her outside, sitting on the balustrade of the terrace, staring down at tangled rows of shrubbery and overgrown flowerbeds. "Grams is on the telephone. She wants to speak to you."

Julia turned her head slowly. Spiraling blond tendrils that had slipped free from her coif framed her face in a charming, carefree manner that contrasted with her indifferent tone of voice. "I suppose she's heard about Regina and wants us home?"

"No, it isn't that. She doesn't know yet. Besides, the inspector hasn't given any of us permission to leave."

"Then what?"

Phoebe considered lying and saying she didn't know, but she thought it wouldn't be very sporting of her to let her sister be taken off guard the way she herself had been by Grams's question. "She's curious about you and Theo."

Julia surged to her feet. "What about me and Theo?"

"I don't know. She asked if I knew anything about the two of you."

Julia's plump lips fell open on an indignant huff. Then she seized Phoebe's wrist. "What did you tell her? Have you been telling tales about me?"

"Let me go." Phoebe tugged her wrist free and rubbed it with her other hand. It throbbed slightly. "What's the matter with you?"

"I don't need you discussing my business with Grams or anyone else."

"Fine. I didn't. I told her I didn't know anything about you and Theo, which I don't."

Julia's eyes narrowed. "That's because there's nothing to tell."

"Good. Go and tell that to Grams. She's waiting, and you know how she doesn't like to be put off."

Her lips pressing together and turning down at the corners, Julia brushed by her and strode into the house.

CHAPTER 8

"Another slice?" Mrs. Dayton's serving knife hovered over the lardy cake. Miles shook his head and pushed his plate a few inches away. Eva also declined another piece of the rich concoction stuffed with raisins and currants.

"Thank you, no, Mrs. Dayton. But it *is* wonderful." She moved her cup and saucer aside as well.

"My grandmum's secret recipe," the woman said, then turned her head to call into the kitchen. "Margaret, come collect the dishes please."

While the teenage girl stacked dishes and cups as she circled the table, Lady Julia appeared in the doorway. Eva came to her feet, as did Miles, albeit more slowly. He nodded in greeting and resumed his seat, but Eva remained standing.

Since Lady Julia had her own maid now, it was unusual for her to come looking for Eva—especially below stairs. Something must surely be wrong. "My lady? Is there something I can help you with? Are you looking for Miss Stanley?"

"No, Eva," she replied quietly. Though normally of a clear, translucent complexion, she appeared too pale now, drained and peaky. "It's you I need to speak with, if you would."

Eva didn't hesitate, but came around the table. "Of course. Perhaps the old housekeeper's sitting room?" She led the way down the corridor past the kitchen and the butler's pantry, into what had once been the two-room housekeeper's suite. A bedroom lay off to one side. Eva waited for Lady Julia to choose a seat in an easy chair, though she herself remained standing.

"Please." Lady Julia gestured to the wooden, high-backed settee, and Eva sat. "I realize you aren't my maid anymore, so I really have no business imposing on you this way."

"I'm always at your service, my lady, and always will be, as long as you need me."

That produced an earnest little smile. "Thank you, Eva. Something has happened, and I can't trust Stanley. I'm afraid I never should have."

"I don't understand." But Eva did, or at least she thought she did.

"I've just got through speaking to my grandmother on the telephone. It seems Mrs. Sanders confiscated a *Daily Mirror* from one of the parlor maids at home and brought it to Grams's attention."

"But why would Mrs. Sanders bring a broadsheet known for its gossip columns to the countess's attention?" Even as Eva asked the question, her stomach clenched.

"It mentioned me." A pause ensued before Lady Julia added, "And Lord Allerton."

"Oh, dear." Eva stared down at her lap. She thought about the scrap of newspaper she found in Miss Brockhurst's fireplace. Had that been illicit reading material as well? Had it posed a threat to Miss Brockhurst, or to the person who murdered her? And what consequences would this article from the *Daily Mirror* have on Lady Julia's life?

"The author speculated on our impending engagement."

Her gaze snapped back to Lady Julia. "Are you . . ."

"No, we are not. *Of course* we are not. But it would appear someone who knows that Lord Allerton and I occasionally meet has decided to let slip a detail or two to a member of the press."

The implications quickly added up in Eva's mind. "And you think Miss Stanley is that person?"

"Who else could it be? Oh, Eva, I thought I could trust her. She came so highly recommended."

From Diana Manners, Eva thought. "I can see how this is upsetting to you. But as long as there's no scandal, no accusations that you and Lord Allerton have behaved in an unbecoming manner, there shouldn't be too much harm done. You can set the story straight with your friends and family."

Lady Julia sighed loudly and came to her feet, prompting Eva to do the same, though she remained in place when Lady Julia began pacing back and forth. "Under normal circumstances, that would be true. But Grams is . . . exceedingly vexed."

"Why? Unlike his brother, Lord Allerton seems like an honorable man."

Lady Julia ceased her strides long enough to cast an ironic look in Eva's direction. "More honorable than the scoundrel Grams practically forced me to marry last year? Goodness, yes. But also on the brink of bankruptcy, thanks to his brother. Grams never comes right out and says it, but I know the idea of my marrying Lord Allerton, or any man in his financial position, positively gives her the vapors." She paused again, hands on hips, head shaking slowly, sadly. "The war, death taxes, and workers' unrest in the past year have taken their toll, Eva. Grams is determined that my sisters and I marry financially independent men in order to keep the Foxwood estate intact for my brother."

Yes, Eva did know this, for Lady Julia had confided in her before about the family's reduced circumstances. She also knew of Lady Wroxly's fierce determination to protect her youngest grandchild's birthright. Young Fox would someday become the Earl of Wroxly, and the countess couldn't bear the thought of his inheriting an empty title and a bankrupt estate. Not that the Renshaws were no longer wealthy. Relatively speaking, they were still an affluent, noble family. But people like the Earl and Countess of Wroxly believed in maintaining the old ways, including a full host of servants to run their estate, and allowing their home farms and investments to fill their coffers while Julia and her siblings would never be expected to work a day in their lives.

As much as Eva respected the old traditions, even she knew the habits of the landed gentry were a thing of the prewar past.

"Grams was livid, not only at the thought of my entertaining a secret engagement, but at having read my name—her own granddaughter's name—in a gossip column."

"Yes, I can certainly imagine how unsettling that was for her." Eva couldn't help cringing a little. "What did you tell her?"

"I swore to her that Lord Allerton and I were merely friends, and that I was helping him find a suitable auction house for some items he wishes to dispose of." She shrugged. "That last bit is true, actually. Poor Theo. But Eva, do you think Myra Stanley would have betrayed my trust this way?"

Eva did think so, but she held her tongue. It wouldn't be fair to malign Myra Stanley before they learned why she left Lady Diana's employ. Yet at the same time, Eva couldn't help advising caution. "I think, my lady, that until you learn more, it might be a good idea not to let Myra know all of your business."

Lady Julia threw herself back into the easy chair. "That'll be blasted inconvenient, considering she's my maid, sees me every day, and goes nearly everywhere I go."

"Quite true." Eva let a moment stretch as she resumed her seat on the settee. "Do you know if perhaps Myra and Miss Brockhurst knew each other?"

Lady Julia's features tightened as she thought about this. "Didn't Regina ask the very same thing before we left on our shopping trip yesterday? I remember. It was a rather awkward moment. Regina said Stanley looked familiar—which in itself was odd, because Stanley had rendered herself practically unrecognizable yesterday. Whatever possessed her to cut her hair like that?"

Good, Eva thought. She hadn't had to share her suspicions; Lady Julia remembered the incident concerning Myra and Miss Brockhurst. Julia Renshaw was no one's fool, and Eva felt assured she would be wary of Myra Stanley from now on.

"I don't know what I'll do now," she said with a sigh.

Eva regarded her quizzically. "If Miss Stanley doesn't suit, my lady, I'm sure your grandmother will be more than willing to replace her."

"That's not what I mean, although yes, you're right about that. No, what I'm left pondering is where I'm going to go when the chief inspector releases us. Obviously we can't all stay here with a murderer on the loose. But I certainly don't want to go home and deal with Grams and all her questions about Theo." She gave her head an adamant shake. "Yet I doubt we'll be allowed to leave the area until the murderer is apprehended. We are all suspects, after all."

Eva hesitated, then asked, "Were you considering going to Lord Allerton's estate?"

"Impertinent as ever, aren't you?"

"Forgive me, my lady—"

"No, no, I'm teasing. If anyone has license to be impertinent, it's you, Eva. You've been with us through the most horrendous of times, always loyal, always such a comfort to my sisters and me." Lady Julia raised her eyebrows and blew out a breath as she grinned. "The answer to your question is yes, I *was* considering visiting Lord Allerton. I'd called him only a couple of hours earlier. But as I said, it's impossible now."

"My lady . . ." Eva trailed off and stretched out her hand to the other woman. Lady Julia hesitated, but apparently understood Eva's meaning plainly enough, for she got up from her chair and came to join Eva on the settee. She clasped Eva's outstretched hand.

"I hope I'm not overstepping my bounds in speaking to you as a friend, my lady."

Lady Julia shook her head. "Please do, Eva. I can use a friend right about now."

"My lady, if you care for Lord Allerton, don't let anyone dissuade you of the idea."

She smiled sadly, shaking her head. "Oh, Eva, such a romantic notion. But I'm afraid romance isn't for women like me."

"Why not? Why can't it be?" Miles's face flashed in Eva's mind. She, too, resisted the lure of romance, but for reasons having to do with this very moment—with the conversation she was having with the eldest Renshaw sibling. All three of the sisters needed her. Eva wouldn't abandon them—*couldn't*—until she knew of a certainty that they were happy and safe and . . . and whole individuals before she would even think of leaving them.

Lady Julia patted their clasped hands with her free one. "Women like my sisters and me live by hard and fast rules.

Duty and loyalty to one's family must come first. The future and well-being of Foxwood Hall is of the utmost importance. You see, Grampapa instilled in us the notion that we are merely custodians of the estate for future generations. If my sisters and I don't marry well—marry men who can be of benefit to Foxwood Hall—all could be lost to those who come after us."

Sadness wrapped itself around Eva. Her poor ladies were expected to labor under the yoke of their family's traditions. No one had believed in those old ideals more than she, until quite recently. Now, with the reality of such harsh choices descending upon her dearest girls, she was beginning to see how cumbersome the old conventions had become. She wanted her girls to be happy. Nothing and no one had the right to stand in the way of that.

And yet there was more than simple happiness at stake. "My lady, have you ever considered the possibility of marrying a self-made man? Or becoming a self-made woman yourself?"

Lady Julia slid her hands free and leaned back against the settee. "A self-made woman—listen to you. Next you'll tell me I should go to university and study law or medicine or . . ." She touched the backs of her fingers to her brow. "You've been spending too much time with Phoebe, I'm afraid. The war might have changed some things, but certainly not in ways she'd like to believe."

Phoebe *had* lately opened Eva's eyes to a world of new possibilities. "But if we don't believe, my lady, who will make those changes happen?"

Lady Julia shifted, looking distinctly uncomfortable. "That's enough of that talk. My immediate problem is where I'm going to go after Chief Inspector Perkins decides we may leave High Head Lodge, and how I'm going to make my escape without Myra Stanley following me."

"Can't you simply tell her to go back to Foxwood Hall?"

"I doubt it. Technically, she works for Grams, and it's Grams from whom she takes her orders. I thought about simply laying the blame for that article squarely at Stanley's feet and letting Grams give her the sack, but I thought . . . well . . . one can't just go ruining someone's life without some evidence that they deserve it."

"You're very generous, my lady." And Eva wondered if Myra Stanley deserved that generosity. Perhaps she had also betrayed her former mistress's trust as well, revealing a secret she knew about Lady Diana to some gossip columnist in exchange for money. The very notion brought a bitter taste to Eva's tongue. But Lady Julia was right. Dismissal without references was no small matter. It *would* ruin Myra's life, so they mustn't be hasty.

But if Myra *had* betrayed Lady Julia, Eva would see that she received her comeuppance—and then some.

"Someone is going to hear about this, young man." Cousin Clarabelle's shrill complaint echoed off the dining room's coffered ceiling. "Where is the chief inspector? Who is his immediate superior? Never mind. I'll find out for myself. I'll go straight to the top. This only adds insult to the tragedy of my daughter's death. My family and I heartily protest being treated as suspects. It's . . . it's a *travesty*." She used her free hand to dab at her eyes, at tears Phoebe didn't see. "It's unconscionable—you hear me? Unconscionable. Mark my words, Constable. You'll both be out of a job and on the streets by the end of the week."

"Yes, ma'am. It's merely standard procedure." With an admirable show of patience, Constable Brannock held out his hand and waited for Cousin Clarabelle to place hers in it so that he might get on with the process of recording her fingerprints. "If you'll just press your fingertips to the ink pad, and then allow me to roll them onto the card . . ."

Midday sunlight threw grotesque shadows of the unkempt shrubbery through the mullioned windows, creating images across the floor and walls of hulking monsters crouching in cages. Phoebe had long since lost patience with sitting and waiting for the Brockhursts to finish being fingerprinted. Hastings had gone first, rocking in his seat, his fingers trembling, his hand jerking out from beneath Constable Brannock's before the prints were complete. It had taken several print cards to complete the job properly, without smudges. Verna had gone next, her nostrils flaring in a look of disgust, behaving as if inking her fingertips might somehow permanently stain not only her skin but her impeccable reputation as well.

Ha. Phoebe hugged her arms around her middle and drifted to the corner window. The hours since the morning had passed with interminable slowness, and she wondered how many more hours would pass before the chief inspector decided he'd collected enough evidence to allow them all to stay or leave, as they pleased. He had been holed up for nearly an hour now questioning Ralph Cameron on the particulars of the will, no doubt in the attempt to ascertain which of the Brockhursts stood to gain the most from Regina's death.

But when they were finally able to leave High Head Lodge, she wondered what Julia would choose to do. Regina's death had surely changed her thinking about staying on and witnessing the drama between the members of this contentious family. Then there was the call from Grams, concerning the matter of Julia and Theo. Was there more than friendship between the two of them?

Phoebe wished her sister would confide in her, but even during the spring thaw in their chilly rapport, Julia had never spoken about Theo. That he held a place in Julia's affections Phoebe didn't doubt, which was in itself unusual because so few people ever did feel an affinity for Theo Leighton. Being permanently disfigured during the war—at the Battle of the Somme—had left Theo reticent and guarded, a hard man to know. And the fact that Julia, who had little patience when it came to the inconvenient vagaries of individuals, had taken the time to befriend Theo Leighton certainly said something about the depth of her feelings for him.

Her thoughts broke off abruptly as, outside, movement caught her attention. From where she stood, she could see the turn in the drive just before it disappeared beneath a stand of yew trees. Two figures ambled toward the house in no particular hurry, one male as evidenced by his gray trousers, dark coat, and battered homburg hat; beside him, a woman wore a plaid skirt that flapped heavily around her booted ankles, a matching jacket, and a close-fitting cloche hat. Like his, her chapeau appeared wilted and worn.

"Who on earth can they be?" she mused aloud, straining to make out finer details. When the Brockhursts had shown up yesterday, Regina had said she wasn't expecting company. Were they from Little Barlow? They didn't appear at all familiar, although from this distance it was hard to tell. She half turned to speak over her shoulder. "Constable, there's someone coming up the drive. Two people, actually."

Cousin Clarabelle, who had continued complaining non-stop while the constable took her fingerprints, abruptly ceased chattering, and asked, "Was my daughter expecting anyone?"

"I don't think so," Phoebe said, still watching the approaching couple.

"Where is that Olive creature?" Verna slid back her chair at the table and came to her feet. "Miss Asquith?" she called out. Phoebe winced at the screech of her voice. "Miss Asquith, you are needed in here. You must come at once."

Heels clattered on the tiles in the hall. Olive, looking weary and drawn, appeared in the doorway. "What is it now?"

Just as she asked her question, the two figures came to an abrupt halt. They stood, staring toward the house. What did they see that held them immobile?

"Someone is coming. Who are they?" Verna demanded as though Olive were somehow at fault.

Olive advanced toward the window; then, like the couple outside, she went utterly still. A look of alarm drew her eyebrows tightly together. With hurried steps she continued to Phoebe's side, where she shaded her eyes from the sunlight with one hand and peered into the distance. Phoebe sensed the tension spreading through her like ice over a pond.

"Well?"

Olive flinched at Cousin Clarabelle's impatient prompting. A breath poured out of her, and she turned to face the room—rather like a convict facing a firing squad. Phoebe wondered if the others noticed her alarm.

"It's the, em, cleaning people," Olive said. Before anyone could comment, she retraced her steps. Once more her heels raised a clatter across the central hall, and then Phoebe heard the front door opening. Crunching drew her gaze back to the drive. Olive hastened over the gravel, at one point turning her ankle with a lurch but not so much as pausing. Meanwhile, the mystery couple had turned about and were rapidly retreating down the drive.

"Constable," Phoebe started to say, but he was already on his feet.

"We'll see about these cleaning people." He rushed out after Olive.

CHAPTER 9

Julia and Eva entered the main hall from behind the baize door that led into the service corridor. Phoebe barely had time to wonder where they had been or what they had been up to when Eva spoke.

"Where did Miles go rushing off to just now?"

"There's two people coming up the drive. Or, there were. They seem to have changed their minds. Olive claims they're here to clean, but the way she went running out to meet them suggests there's more to the pair than buckets and mops. It was very strange. Miles went after her . . . or them." She shrugged.

"Regina never said anything about housekeepers, did she?" Julia went to the open front door and looked out. "I for one am glad they've arrived. This old mausoleum could use a good scrub." After a brief pause she asked, "What do you mean they changed their minds?"

"I'd completely forgotten," Eva blurted. "Miss Asquith mentioned a cleaning staff when she showed Myra and me to our rooms. I believe she said they come every other day or so to clean."

"That may be, but it doesn't explain why Olive looked

as if she'd seen a pair of ghosts coming up the drive, and why she took off as if to head them off before they reached the front door. Or why they stopped in sight of the house, turned about, and hurried off." Phoebe joined Julia at the front door and looked out.

A possible answer presented itself outside on the drive: the police vehicles. The chief inspector and the constable had arrived in separate motorcars, each marked with the Gloucestershire constabulary emblems. "This grows odder and odder," she said. "Either Regina's housekeepers are as skittish as rabbits, or they have something to hide."

She stepped down to the drive. Constable Brannock and the others were no longer in sight, but the distant crunching of gravel reached her ears. Eva came out while Julia continued watching from the door. With a bored sigh, she turned away and closed the door.

"Come on," Phoebe said to Eva. She lifted her skirts and took off at a run. Eva kept pace until she suddenly stopped and called Phoebe's name.

"There, my lady." She pointed into a copse of birch trees on the east side of the lawn. Beyond were several small outbuildings built to resemble quaint, well-kept cottages. Like elsewhere on the estate, the shrubbery and flowerbeds surrounding the structures sprawled in tangles. At first Phoebe saw nothing unusual, but then a flash of plaid darted from behind an overgrown hawthorn hedge before disappearing around a corner.

Phoebe changed course, prompting Eva to do the same. At the same time, Eva called out the constable's name. He came around the bend in the drive and headed over the lawn in their direction. Olive followed several strides behind him, gasping from exertion. "Eva, Lady Phoebe! Let me handle this."

In deference to the constable, Phoebe stopped running, but gathered her breath to call out. "You there! You can neither hide nor get away. We have a policeman with us and you'll only be in deeper if you don't give it up this instant."

"My lady, I must insist you stay where you are." Constable Brannock sounded winded as he loped by her. "You too, Eva."

He needn't have bothered with that last, for the moment Phoebe ceased her pursuit, so too did Eva. It seemed the man and woman also decided to heed the constable, for they slowly sidestepped out from behind one of the outbuildings. Though the constable had procured no weapon, they held their hands in the air with the dramatic flare of a crime novel.

Olive, still gasping, came up beside Phoebe and Eva and bent over, setting her hands on her knees.

"Well, who are they?" Phoebe demanded, noting how like Verna she sounded. She attempted to soften her tone. "And please don't insult our intelligence by claiming they're merely here to clean the house."

Olive straightened, her breath still coming in ragged puffs. "It's the truth."

A surge of anger thrust Phoebe's hands to her hips. "What kind of fool do you take me for?"

"Regina hired them to clean. It's just that . . . they're new to this country and . . ." Olive pressed a hand to her bosom and made a show of struggling to catch her breath. Sincere? Or a way to stall for time while she concocted a story? Phoebe glanced at Eva and waited, sorely tempted to tap her foot. "Where they come from," Olive continued, "having police or officials of any sort showing up at one's doorstep only brings news of the very worst kind. Where they lived, such a visit could be a matter of life and death."

*   *   *

"*My ne imel vidu nikakogo vreda.*" The man, whose name they learned was Dmitry, dragged his hat off his head as Miles ushered them into the house. He tipped a bow as he spoke. Beside him, the woman, Valeria, nodded vigorously. Her eyes were large, the whites showing, the pupils dark and haunted.

Miles darted a questioning glance at Eva. She shrugged, understanding their language no better than he. It was Miss Asquith who translated, or at least provided the gist of the words.

"They were afraid. They certainly meant no harm."

"*Da.*" Dmitry nodded. "No harm." He held out his hands. "No harm," he repeated in his heavy accent.

Lady Phoebe frowned as she concentrated on his pronunciations. "Are you from Russia?"

When the couple stared uncomprehendingly, Miss Asquith again supplied an answer. "Yes. They come, I believe, from Petrograd. That's in the western part of the country, to the north, near Finland." She turned to the man. "Rossiya."

"Da, Rossiya." He held his hat up against his chest with his two hands and bowed again. "Rossiya. Petrogradskiy."

"You see?" Miss Asquith's tone implied she was attempting to explain the situation to imbeciles.

Lady Phoebe angled her chin. "Just how do you know so much about where they're from?"

"Your cousin did interview them before she hired them, after all."

"How?" Miles sounded incredulous, which was how Eva felt. "Lady Phoebe, did your cousin speak Russian?"

"Certainly not that I know of."

Once again, Miss Asquith intervened. "They speak enough English to understand basic questions and supply answers. It's just that—as I've told you multiple times now—they are frightened. A natural result of having been traumatized during the fighting in their home country. When you're frightened or upset, Constable, can you remember how to do difficult things? No, I should think not."

Miles shot her a warning look. "I'm beginning to not like your insolent tone, Miss Asquith. As it happens, when I'm frightened or upset I fall back on instincts honed during the war. I block out all else but what I must do to complete a task and stay alive."

A little shock went through Eva. Miles never spoke of his service in the Great War. She had tried asking him a time or two, but he either found ways of changing the subject or simply made no reply at all. What tasks had he completed? What dangers had threatened his life? She burned to know, to fully understand him, to empathize with him. But he wouldn't allow it. However gently, he always pushed her away from this one aspect of his life. Why? Did he not trust her? Not trust himself? Was he ashamed of something? Or were the horrors he'd witnessed simply too unbearable to speak of?

He had asked another question or two that escaped Eva's hearing. Now she turned her attention back to the present. Miles regarded the couple again, his lips skewed to one side as he obviously considered. "You saw the inspector's and my motors and did a quick turnabout. I've heard about the goings-on in your country. I can understand why the sight of official vehicles might prompt you to run. Is that it? Our police vehicles frightened you?"

Miss Asquith huffed with impatience. "Of course that's it, Constable."

He released a breath as he studied the pair. But it was to Miss Asquith that he spoke. "Are they married?"

"Yes, they are."

"And their last name?"

"Grekov, I believe. But Regina merely called them by their first names."

Miles turned to Lady Phoebe. "My lady, would you mind finding Chief Inspector Perkins and asking him to come to the morning room as soon as he's able, please." It was an instruction, not a request, and while Eva quite expected her mistress to balk, Lady Phoebe surprised her by nodding and hurrying off to the library, where the chief inspector and Mr. Cameron had been talking for some time now.

Miles held out a hand, gesturing for Dmitry and Valeria to follow him. Miss Asquith started forward as well, but Miles paused. "Not you," he said to her.

"How will you communicate with them?"

"Do you speak Russian, Miss Asquith?"

"Well, no, but—"

"Then I fail to see what good your presence will be." He dismissed her by turning abruptly away. "Eva, I'd like you to accompany us, if you would."

Eva smiled and gave a little nod. "Certainly."

"Wait a moment." Miss Asquith's cheeks ruddied. "Why her and not me?"

Dmitry and Valeria traded wary glances. Miles tipped his head. "Because I trust her intuition and her instincts. Now then."

"But—" Miss Asquith's protest died on her lips.

In the morning room, Miles shut the door and joined the others at the small table by the corner windows. Dmitry and Valeria hovered in front of the chairs looking uncertain and decidedly fearful. The poor homburg hat had already taken quite a beating between Dmitry's hands, and now his fingers convulsed around the turned-up brim. Eva's heart went out to both of them. She could only imagine the disadvantage they felt at being foreigners and unable to effectively speak the language, only to find themselves the subjects of a police investigation. Surely they feared being ejected from England. Where would they go? Back to their native country? Eva inwardly rejected the idea. The Great War might be over, but she knew a civil war raged on in Russia.

"Please sit." Miles gestured and then chose a place at the table for himself. He indicated the chair beside him. "Eva."

She settled in as the other two fumbled to scrape back chairs. Dmitry helped Valeria pull up to the table. Then he sat and placed his homburg on the table before him. He folded his hands beside it, peered guardedly over at Miles, and waited.

"I understand you are married," Miles asked. "Is that correct?"

When the pair exchanged uncomprehending glances, Eva held up her left hand and pointed to her ring finger. "Married?"

"Ahhh. *V brake.*" Dmitry nodded, yet held up his *right* hand, the ring finger encircled by a thin band. Valeria glanced down at a similar ring on her own right hand. "*Da.*"

"And your last name?" Miles thought a moment, and then pressed a hand to his coat front. "I am Miles Brannock." He repeated his name slowly, then pointed to Dmitry. "Dmitry . . . ?"

"Miss Asquith told us their last name," Eva put in.

"I must have it from them, for the record," Miles told her. He repeated his question.

"Dmitry Grekov." He pointed at his wife. "Valeria Grekova."

"Very good. Wasn't so difficult," Miles added in an undertone. He took his writing tablet and pencil from his coat pocket and jotted down their names. "Now then, how long have you been in this country? In England?"

To help facilitate his meaning, Eva again held up a hand, but this time counted off on her fingers. "How long in England? One? Two? Three . . . ?" Judging by their lack of English, she assumed it had only been a matter of months, not years, since they had arrived. Or perhaps even weeks.

The pair conversed quietly in their native language, seemed to reach an accord, and turned back to Miles. With painstaking annunciation, Dmitry said, "Four months."

"Thank you." Miles again made a notation. When he looked up again, it was with a pensive expression, his eyes keenly sharp. "How did you manage to leave Russia?"

The pair frowned in incomprehension.

"I'm afraid that's a rather more difficult question." Eva considered how best to make the query understood. An idea came to her. "I know. I'll be right back."

She passed the chief inspector on his way out of the library. He ignored her, but Mr. Cameron, the Brockhursts' solicitor, met her inside.

"Miss Huntford, I understand there has been a development in the form of new arrivals here?"

"There has indeed, Mr. Cameron. Apparently they are the cleaning people Miss Brockhurst recently hired. They're from Russia and don't speak much English." She hurried to the nearest bank of shelves and began scanning the books. This lot appeared to be mostly world histories, so she moved on to the next section.

"Cleaning people? Why haven't they been mentioned before this? They could be essential to the investigation." As the statement seemed rather obvious, Eva didn't feel the need to reply. She felt Mr. Cameron's scrutiny on her back. "What are you looking for?"

"An atlas, sir. I believe it might assist the constable in questioning the couple. He's trying to discover how they left their country and made their way here."

"Ah. Let me assist you." Mr. Cameron crossed to the opposite side of the room. "I've been looking through the books here myself, and I believe I saw . . . Yes, here are several atlases."

"I need one that would include Russia and northern Europe."

Mr. Cameron slid a heavy tome from the shelf and carried it over to the library table. A little puff of dust dispersed from the tops of its pages as he opened the front cover. Eva joined him at the table. He began leafing through until he found what he sought and tapped it with his index finger. The two open pages displayed western Russia, Scandinavia, and northern Europe. "Will this do?"

"It's perfect, Mr. Cameron, thank you." Eva snatched up the book, but before she reached the door Mr. Cameron had parting words for her.

"Has anyone thought to search these people for keys to the house? Regina might have given them a set so they could come and go without her having to be here to let them in."

That stopped her. Did they possess keys to the house? Or had they previously? The couple seemed both afraid and harmless, but they mustn't dismiss how Miss Asquith had hurried to meet up with them first. No one knew what words or deeds had passed between her and the Grekovs before Miles reached them. She would point this out to him, if he hadn't already thought of it.

The chief inspector had joined the others in the morning room, his paunch pressed up against the table by the window. The Grekovs didn't look any happier than when Eva had left minutes ago. In fact, they looked even more perturbed and befuddled.

"How long have you been working here?" the chief inspector demanded. "How did Miss Brockhurst engage your services? Did you come with letters of recommendation? Come now, we need answers from you. You don't wish to be arrested for obstructing the investigation, do you?"

"Sir, nothing has been explained to them yet," Miles put

in quietly. "To my knowledge, they don't yet know what happened to their employer."

"Well, then we must tell them, man." Chief Inspector Perkins snorted and coughed. "Your mistress is dead. Murdered. Just this morning. What do you know about it?"

The Grekovs' expressions became alarmed, and the beginnings of panic peeked out from the whites of their eyes. Without taking her gaze off the inspector across from her, Valeria fumbled for her husband's hand, found it, and squeezed. Dmitry winced, but he neither spoke nor attempted to ease his wife's hold.

"Chief Inspector, if you would allow me." Miles finally noticed Eva and the book she held in both arms. "What have you got there, Miss Huntford?"

"An atlas." With a thud she set it on the table and opened it to the place she had saved with a finger between the pages.

The chief inspector snorted again, leaning over the table to view the book. "This is hardly the time for a geography lesson, Miss Huntford."

Resisting the temptation to roll her eyes or, worse, make a retort, she moved the atlas in front of the Grekovs and pointed. "Russia. Petrograd." She moved her finger to the left. "England. How did you come?" Once again she moved her finger, tracing an imaginary line from one country to the other. Her route encompassed the countries of Estonia, Latvia, south through Poland, into Germany, then Belgium, and across the channel into England. But until nine months ago, much of that part of Europe had been torn apart by war, and the healing in many places had only recently begun. How could anyone have made their way through the scarred landscapes, the resulting poverty, and the lingering bitterness, to arrive in England only four months later?

At her pantomime, Dmitry's expression cleared and he nodded. With a faint smile, he reached out to trail his own finger over the page. His course took them not across an overland route but from Russia to Latvia, and then across the Baltic Sea into eastern Denmark, where, he implied with hand motions, they eventually boarded another ship that crossed the North Sea into England. Eva inwardly braced herself at the thought of such sea crossings. She could almost feel the deck rocking beneath her feet, her body swaying, her insides tossing. Motorcars were disquieting enough, but boats—ugh. She shuddered, wishing she were hardier.

Over the next several minutes she and Miles pieced together the Grekovs' story of fleeing Petrograd on the heels of the retreating White Army in the summer of 1918 and traveling south, and waiting in Latvia several months until the Great War ended and they were able to book passage on the first of the ships that brought them to England. Eva listened closely, their faltering story renewing the harrowing rumors she had heard during the war about the *other* war that had broken out in their country—a revolution and civil war all in one. Terror, an immeasurable death toll on both sides, and their czar murdered—brought before a firing squad like a common criminal. Some stories had it that his entire family was killed. Others denied the claim, but either way, Eva could not imagine the courage it had taken for the Grekovs to make their escape.

Then it struck her how such an escape could be managed, and the realization chased all other thoughts from her mind. Were the Grekovs omitting a key detail of their story? Were they as they appeared? She wondered.

Finally, the chief inspector determined they had learned enough from the pair for the moment. "Don't leave the

house," he told them brusquely before turning to Eva.
"Show them down to the servants' hall, would you? They
can wait there." Then, to Miles he said, "Fingerprint them."

He stood, prompting the couple to do the same. Eva
asked them to wait for her by the doorway, gesturing as she
spoke. Then she stole the opportunity to whisper to Miles,
"Have you checked them for keys to the house?"

"Of course. When you went for the atlas and before the
inspector came in." He offered her a lopsided grin. "I'm
not completely helpless without you, you know."

She smiled back, then sobered. "But that doesn't rule
out their having dropped them somewhere on the drive
when Miss Asquith went out to them."

He nodded his agreement. "No, we'll have to search.
And search Miss Asquith's room as well. She might have
taken the keys and hidden them."

"There's something else, Miles, something I gathered
from their story. Most people attempting to flee would
make their way by land to the nearest haven. But not the
Grekovs. They managed to book passages on ships. That
tells me something about them."

With a glance at the door, where the Russian couple
stood, Miles moved closer to Eva and lightly grasped her
forearms. "And what is that, my clever girl?"

Her cheeks heated and she attempted to pull away. He
wouldn't let her, but instead tugged her another step closer
until she could feel the heat of him. With an indignant
huff, she continued. "It tells me they had funds at their
disposal. The Grekovs are not what they appear. Oh, they
might be poor here in England and need to clean houses
for a living, but I'll wager other people cleaned their house
for them in Russia."

Miles's expression went from one of affection to one of

the utmost seriousness as he released Eva's arms. "Then we must discover who exactly the Grekovs are, mustn't we? You seem to have established something of a rapport with them. Give them some time to settle in, and try questioning them again, subtly."

Eva nodded. "I'll see what I can learn."

CHAPTER 10

While Constable Brannock and Eva questioned the Russian couple, the house grew quiet again. The Brockhursts retired to their respective rooms, and Olive had also disappeared somewhere; Phoebe didn't know where. She stole the opportunity to use the telephone again. This time she used the one below stairs in the butler's pantry to ensure her privacy, and she waited there until the operator put her call through.

She snatched up the receiver as soon as the phone rang. "Owen, it's me again."

"Phoebe. Has something more happened?" Concern clipped his words sharp.

"No, not exactly. But Eva and Constable Brannock found something that might be a clue. A bit of newspaper that escaped someone's attempt to burn it."

"You're in the middle of things again, aren't you? Never mind, don't answer that. Of course you are. Phoebe, I worry about you."

"I know. I can't help being in the middle of this, Owen. I'm a suspect, after all."

"Don't say that." His voice took on greater urgency, a

raw quality. A little rush of . . . oh, something . . . not pleasure exactly, not under the circumstances, but his concern
spread a deeply contented feeling all through her.

"I'm not *particularly* a suspect, mind you," she assured
him. "But technically everyone who spent last night in this
house is potentially guilty. And even two people who didn't
spend the night here."

"Yes, yes, I suppose you're right." A sigh came over the
wire. Then Owen said more severely, "What do you mean,
two people who didn't spend the night there? Who else is
involved?"

"A couple Regina hired to clean. They apparently live
nearby and come several days a week. They happened by
today, and there was a bit of a to-do because of it. Apparently they saw the police vehicles and became afraid of getting involved. You know how it is, servants are always
blamed for everything. Remember poor Vernon last Christmas, when Henry Leighton was murdered."

"How can I forget? Now, about this newspaper you
found . . ."

"Eva found, and it was just a scrap—most of it had
been burned in the fireplace in Regina's bedroom. There
are parts of words still visible, and they look like they
might have been part of a headline. 'List Labor'—that's all
we can make out. The first L is lowercase, suggesting *list* is
part of a larger word. I know it doesn't seem like much
and might not be important at all, but I thought it might
possibly ring a bell with you . . ." She trailed off, realizing
how little chance existed that Owen or anyone could iden-
tify a periodical with so little to go on.

" 'List Labor,' eh? Labor list might make more sense."

"Yes, I know, it could mean any number of things. But
its having been burned in an otherwise unlit fireplace suggests the publication meant something significant that

Regina, or someone, didn't want others to see. It could give us a hint as to who murdered her."

"Perhaps. Are you certain there wasn't more?"

"Quite. Eva poked through the ashes. There was only that one legible bit."

"All right. Let me think about this a while, see if any ideas come to me. But don't go getting your hopes up. I made a couple of calls concerning Lady Diana, by the way."

"Oh! And did you find out anything?"

"Afraid not. If Diana and Myra Stanley parted ways for any other reason besides Diana's recent marriage, no one seems to know anything about it."

Phoebe sighed. "Which only makes sense, I suppose. If Myra Stanley blackmailed Diana about some potentially ruinous secret, Diana would certainly go to great lengths to cover up any evidence of it."

"Right. But chin up. Something might turn up. In the meantime, I'll give this 'list Labor' some thought. I suppose you'll be remaining there."

"The chief inspector hasn't given us permission to leave yet."

"And when he does? Will you leave?"

She heard the resignation in his voice. "We'll see. Thank you for all your help."

"Don't thank me yet, not until I've discovered something useful. I'll ring back as soon as I do. Oh, and Phoebe?"

"Yes, Owen?"

"Do be careful."

"Of course I will," she replied brightly, casually, in an attempt to underplay any danger that might arise from her cousin's death.

"No, Phoebe," he said, his voice a low, grave rumble. "Be very, very careful. For me. I don't want to lose you. Ever."

With that, he rang off, leaving her with a racing heart and a flame flickering inside her.

Owen's parting words—and the sentiments behind them—filled Phoebe's thoughts as she climbed to the ground floor. Voices drew her into the drawing room, which she found empty. Puzzled, she strolled into the room and spotted the open terrace door. She approached it, wondering who had decided to come downstairs. Laughter, quickly hushed, revealed the identity of one of the speakers.

Julia.

"You mustn't make me laugh. It isn't right," she said in a voice bordering on coquettish. The sound of it made Phoebe cringe, not so much because of the inappropriateness of flirting here and now, but because of how it evoked memories of their past, of Julia commanding the attention of every man in any room she entered, while those same men barely noticed Phoebe. Or those who did notice her were quickly distracted by her more beautiful, more clever sister.

She dismissed the sibling rivalry as a second person—a man—spoke.

"You're quite right, my lady. Forgive me, I meant no disrespect to Regina's memory. But this family, Hastings in particular, well, you don't know what it's like dealing with them day after day."

Ralph Cameron. They were out of Phoebe's view, but she could hear them clearly enough. She envisioned Julia's cavalier shrug, the haughty tilt of her chin, as she laughed again and said, "I think you were sweet on her. Regina, I mean."

"Not in the least, you mustn't think so. I'm merely an employee of the family."

"Hmm . . . And yet, Regina told me once, not very long ago, that there was someone, an older man who caught her fancy." Julia practically sang the words, drawing them out in her melodious voice.

"She could have meant any number of gentlemen. I assure you it wasn't me."

"If you say so, Ralph . . ."

Obviously, Julia had her doubts about Ralph's protestations. Phoebe had wondered as well after seeing Regina and Ralph together yesterday, witnessing the influence he held over her. Using very few words, he had been instrumental in persuading Regina to let her family stay the night here, even after all their accusations.

Yet at the same time, Cousin Clarabelle maintained an almost proprietary presence beside Ralph and made no effort to be discreet about it. Once again she wondered if Ralph might have been dallying with both women.

"Tell me, Julia, is there a special gentleman in your life?"

The question snapped at Phoebe's attention. She instinctively moved closer to the open door, well aware of the dishonorable nature of eavesdropping. She'd be contrite about it later. She was too interested in Julia's answer to stop herself now. She turned her ear to the door, straining to hear. Glass thunked against glass, the sound of one of those heavy crystal tumblers being set on the glass-top garden table. What were they drinking? she wondered. Lemonade, or something stronger?

"There's no one." Julia's voice grew sad and held a note of finality. She paused—for another sip? Then, brighter, she continued. "Oh, don't misunderstand. There could be. There are those who have tried. But no, no one *I* consider special."

Phoebe's stomach plummeted. What about Theo—that impoverished, disfigured war hero about whom Grams called demanding answers such a short time ago? The very same Theo who had risked his life in an attempt to apprehend his brother's murderer last Christmas. Was he not special to Julia? Or could she be honest with no one about her feelings?

"You'd rather break hearts, wouldn't you?"

Julia laughed again, softly. "Perhaps I would at that . . ."

Oh, Julia. Surely she didn't mean that. Feeling vaguely nauseated, Phoebe regretted eavesdropping and eased away from the door.

Eva placed a camisole and slip she had hand-washed for Lady Phoebe in the top dresser drawer and then set about tidying up the room. Miles and the chief inspector had poked around each bedroom, though the greater part of their attention had been saved for Miss Asquith's room. They had not, however, found any spare keys to the house. Both he and Miles had left High Head Lodge a little while ago to bring the evidence and fingerprints to their small office in Little Barlow, and to arrange to have it all sent up to the main police station in Gloucester. The inhabitants of the house had once more been warned not to leave. It's not as though any of them would get very far if they did try to sneak away. Routes out of Little Barlow and its environs were limited and easily monitored. And Miles promised to return soon.

She left Phoebe's room, intent on slipping upstairs to her own room for a few minutes. On her way, noises in the billiard room caught her attention. The telltale shush of a ball rolling over felt was followed by the tap of two balls lightly colliding. Was Mr. Cameron in there again, thinking, as he had claimed about the night Miss Brockhurst died? She peeked in, surprised to spy Miss Asquith leaning over the billiard table, her elbow bent and her chin propped on her hand. She absently reached for a ball and sent it rolling onto another. They thumped against a bumper and began the journey back toward her.

Miss Asquith's behavior at the appearance of the Grekovs had certainly raised questions, but the chief inspector had been especially hard on the young woman, not only in his suspicions but in his general opinion. Apparently, he found Miss Asquith well beneath the status of the other guests, lower even, judging by his behavior toward her, than Myra Stanley and Eva herself. Added to that was Miss Asquith's utter lack of friends presently in this house. Not that she wasn't in part responsible for that. From what Eva understood, she had made no great overtures of friendship toward either Phoebe or Julia, and the Brockhursts were certainly not interested in forging ties with her.

Eva couldn't help feeling rather sorry for her. Yet at the same time, she knew an opportunity when she saw one.

"Miss Asquith," she said, standing in the doorway, "is there anything I can do for you?" The young woman had expressed distaste at the very idea of servants, but Eva didn't make her inquiry in the spirit of service.

She rolled another ball and straightened slowly, regarding Eva from across the width of the table. "Thank you, Miss Huntford, but I don't think there is."

"Oh. If you're sure . . ." Eva hesitated, searching for an excuse to stay and make conversation. It came from an unexpected source: Miss Asquith herself.

"Wait. Please." She dropped the ball she was holding and moved away from the billiard table. It was then Eva saw the tumbler, very much like the one found in Miss Brockhurst's bedroom this morning, sitting on the top rail, previously hidden by Miss Asquith's torso. She estimated two fingers of something strong. Had there been three fingers originally? More than that? How long had Miss Asquith been alone here, drinking spirits? "I . . . that is, if you're aren't terribly busy, would you stay a moment?"

"Of course." Eva advanced farther into the room, stopping when Miss Asquith held up a hand.

"But only if you wish to. Don't stay out of obligation, because I'm a guest and you're the servant of a guest."

"No, that's not why I'll stay." She took in the young woman's general demeanor. It was clear the chief inspector had left her shaken. Her very posture suggested she could use a spot of kindness from someone. She looked far less confident than previously, and even her demand that Eva stay only because she wished to felt drained of the vigor with which Olive Asquith had spoken to Myra Stanley only yesterday. Eva approached the billiard table, glancing at the tumbler, then looking away. She wasn't here to judge, merely to talk.

She nodded at the colorful array of balls. "Do you play?"

"A little. You?"

Eva nodded and said with a laugh, "I'm not supposed to. My dad sometimes used to take my sister and me down to the pub with him, in the afternoons when no one minded us being there. Mum would have had fits if she knew. We were very young. He stopped once we were old enough that people would talk. Then he took our younger brother, Danny—" She broke off. Every time she believed she could mention Danny's name without her throat closing and her heart aching, well, she learned different. It might have helped if he had been buried in the churchyard in Little Barlow, where she might have visited, brought flowers, kept the grave tidy, and spoken softly, when no one else was about, to let Danny know how much she missed him. But his final resting place lay far away, in a makeshift cemetery beside a battlefield in France, and Eva didn't know if she would ever go there . . .

Swallowing, she took a pool cue from the rack on the wall and chalked the tip, then returned to the table. Miss Asquith had grown quiet and watched her intently. Eva leaned over the table, lined up a shot, and sent the cue into the red ball. The shot went awry, sending the ball ricocheting wildly. Eva chuckled and leaned the cue stick against the table. "Well, it's been years, actually."

Miss Asquith picked up the tumbler and sipped, making a face as if she'd tasted lemons. Eva pretended not to notice. She watched the young woman drift away from the table, walking aimlessly, then pacing back the way she had come.

"They're awful, you know," she said at length. She used the hand holding the glass to gesture toward the door. Eva glanced over at an empty threshold. Miss Asquith didn't leave her wondering at her meaning for long. "Those Brockhursts. They didn't give a raw fig about Regina, at least not the real Regina. They didn't even know her."

"How do you mean?"

"They wanted to control her—to mold her into the kind of woman who *can* be controlled. Like your mistress and her sister, one supposes."

Eva drew up, her shoulders squaring of their own accord. Miss Asquith apparently saw her mistake and looked contrite. Hastily, she said, "Sorry. That wasn't sporting of me. But they're typical aristocrats, these Brockhursts. Think a woman can't be more than a wife, mother, and"—she shuddered—"a society hostess. They hated Regina for inheriting her father's money. Hastings most of all, but the other two as well." She scoffed, her lip curling. "The two Lady Mandevilles. Such a joke. There's nothing noble about either of them."

"Perhaps you're wrong about how they felt about Miss Brockhurst." Though Eva had her own doubts about that, she saw no reason to encourage Miss Asquith in her bitterness. It would serve no purpose and only make matters worse for everyone here. "She was a daughter and sister. Surely they loved one another despite their differences."

She half expected Miss Asquith to protest vehemently.

Instead, she said, "One would think so, but no, not in this case. Even their solicitor treated Regina like a fragile doll in an effort to control her. Always flattering her and pretending to take her side in matters, only to side with the family the moment Regina left the room. He was no friend to her, Miss Huntford, I promise you that. They argued after everyone had gone to bed last night. He told her she was being unreasonable and ungenerous, that she owed her family better than to allow them to be cut off. He upset Regina very much."

"Is that why Miss Brockhurst couldn't sleep?"

"I'd say it was one of several reasons, their names being Verna, Hastings, Clarabelle, and, yes, Ralph Cameron. Regina was very much alone within her family, with no true friends until she met—"

Before she finished the sentence, Miss Asquith took another sip of her drink. Holding up the glass, she appeared to take its measure and, apparently finding the level of its contents to be less than satisfactory, she strode to the drinks cabinet beside the hearth. A decanter sat on top of it, and Miss Asquith poured a generous amount.

Eva wanted to hear more. She allowed Miss Asquith to indulge in another swallow before asking, "Until she met whom, Miss Asquith?"

"Me. And others. True friends who allowed Regina to be herself, not some hollow ideal of what a baron's daughter should be."

"And what was Miss Brockhurst like away from her family, surrounded by her friends?"

Miss Asquith turned a brilliant smile upon Eva. "She was inspired. Full of ideas and life and generosity."

Eva tensed. Miss Brockhurst's generosity could be interpreted in more than one way. Had her open-handedness been her own idea, or had she been convinced to part with her money? However much she might sympathize with

Miss Asquith and her current circumstances in this house, she didn't know the woman. She didn't know what motives might have been behind her friendship with Miss Brockhurst. Did this argument with Ralph Cameron happen, or was the woman attempting to cast guilt on everyone but herself?

But rather than press Miss Asquith about that, she took a different tack. "I can't help but wonder who these others were."

Miss Asquith took another sip. "Others?"

"Yes, those you mentioned, who brought out such good qualities in Miss Brockhurst. Who are they? Surely they must be informed of Miss Brockhurst's fate. They'll wish to pay their respects. I'm guessing they aren't friends of the family."

"No, they are not. And yes, they will be informed in due time. I will inform them myself."

"Well, if you require any assistance with that, I'd be happy to help."

"No." For a moment Miss Asquith's expression became alarmed. Then she relaxed. "I mean, thank you, but no. I can manage. And the others will spread the word. If . . . if you'll excuse me . . ."

Eva had one more question for her and called out her name to halt her in her tracks. Miss Asquith stopped short, hesitated a moment, and turned with a wary look. "Was Lady Diana Manners among Miss Brockhurst's good friends?"

Miss Asquith's features relaxed, and she almost smiled. "Not really. Diana Manners always ran with a different set, people who amused Regina but whom she never took seriously. Why?"

"I only wondered because she seemed to know Myra Stanley." At Miss Asquith's blank expression, Eva explained, "You know, the other maid who arrived here with me. Myra used to be Lady Diana's maid, until recently.

Now she's Lady Julia's. You wouldn't know anything about her time with her former employer, would you? Or how she and Miss Brockhurst might have been acquainted?"

Another hesitation set Eva speculating that Miss Asquith did indeed know something. But she shook her head. "Sorry. If Regina knew Myra Stanley, she never mentioned it to me. And she never spoke much about Diana. Why would she?" Gripping her tumbler, the woman strode from the room, leaving Eva convinced she was lying.

CHAPTER 11

Only the basics had been set out for breakfast that morning, and no luncheon at all was served at the proper time. While Eva understood the oversight, she also knew that going without food could stretch tensions to the breaking point. To that end, after leaving the billiard room she went below stairs to help Mrs. Dayton assemble an adequate meal. She found the woman standing in the servants' hall, staring down at what appeared to be a shirt spread out on the table before her.

"Mrs. Dayton, I believe our guests could do with a spot of lunch, if you wouldn't mind. I'll help you."

The cook flinched, turning to Eva with an alarmed expression.

"I'm sorry, I didn't mean to startle you. What's that you've got there?"

Mrs. Dayton mutely gestured for Eva to come closer. "I sent Margaret up a little while ago to collect the laundry to be sent out." She spoke in hushed tones. "Well, one must maintain order, mustn't one? We discovered *this* balled up in a pile of towels left outside the linen cupboard."

Eva leaned over to inspect the garment, a man's white dress shirt. Smudges of pale brown streaked the collar and one of the cuffs. "Yes, well, no wonder. It's stained."

"Look closer, Miss Huntford. Those aren't ordinary stains." The woman's voice dropped several more notches. "That's blood, or I don't know my business."

"You're a cook, Mrs. Dayton. Not a laundress."

"Indeed, and I've nicked enough fingers in my career to know blood when I see it. Whoever this shirt belongs to tried to wash it out, but used warm water instead of cold." She held up the shirt in front of her. "Warm water sets blood hard and fast, as well you must know. It'll likely never come out now, not without a good bleaching, but bleach will ruin this fine percale. The question is, whose blood is this?"

Eva took the shirt from her, holding the fabric taut to examine the stains. "Whose indeed."

At Eva's request, Phoebe met her in her bedroom on the top floor. It was the one place they might close the door and converse without anyone interrupting. A chill went through Phoebe when Eva held up a shirt whose collar and right cuff looked as though they had been dipped in diluted brown paint.

"Mrs. Dayton is certain it's blood, my lady, and I agree."

Phoebe agreed as well. Paint aside, not much else could leave stains of that hue, especially if the wearer had attempted unsuccessfully to wash away the evidence. "Well, we know this shirt can only belong to one of two men: Hastings or Ralph Cameron." She reached for one of the sleeves and held it up. "Hastings is more heavyset than the size of this shirt would allow, so it must belong to Mr. Cameron. There's nothing for it but to simply ask him.

Not only whether this is his shirt, but how it came to have blood on it. Oh, Eva, do you suppose . . . ?

Eva's mouth flattened in a way it sometimes did when she thought especially hard about something or weighed the wisdom of speaking out about a controversial matter. Phoebe waited, but not long. "A little while ago I had the opportunity to speak with Miss Asquith. She was in the billiard room, drinking whiskey. Among other things, she mentioned Miss Brockhurst had argued with Mr. Cameron last night after everyone went to bed. It seemed he was taking the family's side in the dispute over the money. It upset Miss Brockhurst, and that's why she couldn't sleep."

Phoebe gasped. "He never said a word about it. Even after admitting he'd been in the billiard room, he never mentioned having spoken to Regina, much less arguing with her."

"I do wonder, my lady, about whether a killer would have put this shirt in the laundry rather than disposing of it where no one would find it."

Phoebe thought about that. "Yes, but disposed of it where? He might have been afraid the constable would find it in the trash. He couldn't burn it, because as you realized when you noticed the ashes in Regina's fireplace, it's summer and a hearth fire is a dead giveaway that someone is trying to hide something. Instead, he tried unsuccessfully to wash the blood away, and when that didn't work he hid the shirt in a bundle of towels waiting to go to the laundress, hoping no one would notice it."

"If so, he took an awful chance. I don't think we should do anything until Miles returns. It shouldn't be long now."

Phoebe continued turning over possibilities in her mind. "So Mr. Cameron and Regina argued over the current situation with the family. Perhaps she threatened to fire him. I'd suspect he makes a goodly salary as the family solicitor.

Or . . . it could have been an act of passion. You may not have noticed, not having spent much time around the guests, that Mr. Cameron's affections seemed divided between both my cousin and her mother."

"Is that so strange? He's also a family friend, isn't he, my lady? And especially now, with Lord Mandeville gone . . ."

"It's more than that. Perhaps Regina realized he had been leading them both on, became infuriated, and threatened to tell her mother about his machinations. He might have killed her to silence her."

"My lady, do you really think—"

At the rumble of an approaching motorcar, Eva broke off, and they both hurried to the window.

"Here's Miles now," Eva said with a note of satisfaction and, Phoebe thought, relief. "We'll bring this to his attention and see what he says, and then you and I won't have to speculate any further."

"You're really no fun at all, Eva. You do realize that, don't you?"

"It isn't my job to be fun or amusing, my lady. My job is simply to look after you."

Phoebe grinned ruefully and pointed at the shirt Eva still held. "Let's go down and show him. Oh—I just remembered something." She had started for the door but stopped, thinking back to her earlier conversation with Ralph Cameron in the library, or more specifically, to his appearance at the time. "He cut his chin."

"Who?"

"Mr. Cameron. I noticed it earlier. He must have cut himself shaving this morning. I remember thinking it was no wonder his hands were a bit unsteady after we found my cousin. Then again, a shaving cut shouldn't have done *that*, should it?"

A few minutes later downstairs, Miles Brannock concurred with her conclusion. "A man would have to have the royal disease to bleed this much from a razor cut."

"You mean hemophilia?" Phoebe said.

"I do, my lady. How big was this nick you saw?"

"Not very, really."

"Then I shall need to have a talk with Mr. Cameron."

"There wasn't much blood on Miss Brockhurst's wound or the pillow," Eva pointed out. "So how would this much blood come to be on this shirt, and why on the collar?"

Miles continued studying the shirt. "That's a very good question."

The three of them parted ways shortly after. Mrs. Dayton and Margaret delivered platters of sandwiches and a tureen of soup to the dining room, and Phoebe went in to join the others while Eva returned below stairs to partake of a similar meal with Myra Stanley and the Grekovs. Before she left, she promised Phoebe she would make another attempt to ask the couple questions about their past and their journey to England, as well as question Myra Stanley about whether she had known Regina before coming to High Head Lodge. It was time for some direct inquiries.

Ralph Cameron did not join the others for lunch. The constable had drawn him aside, and the two of them were presently talking in the morning room. As Phoebe entered the dining room, an uneasy-looking Julia approached her.

"What does Constable Brannock want with Ralph?" she murmured so the others around the table wouldn't hear.

"That's the constable's business, I'm afraid." Phoebe walked to the buffet.

"The constable's business, indeed," Julia retorted, following close behind her. "You know exactly what's going on."

"It's not my place to tell tales." With a sandwich on a

plate in one hand and a bowl of soup in the other, Phoebe went to the table.

"What tales?" Cousin Clarabelle, sitting at the head of the table, reached for a wine decanter and poured a generous measure into her goblet. At that rate, Phoebe thought, she'll be intoxicated by tea time. "Where is Ralph?"

"Seems the constable has more questions for him." Julia stared at Phoebe as she spoke. Phoebe's cheeks warmed, not because Julia was making it obvious she might know something, but because of the anger evident in her tone.

"What questions?" Cousin Clarabelle sat stiffly upright, her spine not touching the back of her chair. "Why is the constable singling out Ralph? Surely he can't believe he's guilty."

"Maybe he is." Hastings, having entered the room after Phoebe, hobbled away from the sideboard and approached the table. What had become his signature tumbler of whiskey awaited him there. With his foot he kicked a chair out several inches and managed to slide in without spilling anything, but only just, for his plate tipped and his sandwich slithered precariously to the edge, while the soup sloshed dangerously.

"Don't talk like that," his mother snapped.

"Why not? Someone killed Regina. If not Ralph, the constable will suspect me. Or Verna. Or our two charming cousins here. Or even you, Mother. Would you prefer that?"

"Don't be stupid," Verna murmured from across the table. She paused to sample her soup. "We all know who killed Regina."

As if on cue, Olive sauntered into the room, and silence fell over the table. She noticed their scrutiny and came to an abrupt halt. "What are you all staring at?"

Cousin Clarabelle's glare became piercing before she

lowered her gaze. Verna went on brazenly staring. Julia bit off a corner of her sandwich.

"We were just speculating, Miss Asquith." Hastings raised his crystal glass as if in a toast. Their gazes locked for several seconds. Then Olive proceeded to the sideboard, selected a sandwich, and turned back to them with a defiant expression.

"I'll eat in my room."

"I'm curious, what did you do in Russia?" Eva set the dishes on the table in the servants' hall. She had already put out the serviettes and silverware. How different from life at Foxwood Hall, where even the servants had underservants to wait on them.

Dmitry moved to help distribute the plain earthenware dishes. "Rossiya?"

He'd responded to the one word he understood. Eva groped for a way to make him understand. "Employment. Work."

"Ah." Dmitry nodded and glanced over at his wife, who nodded as well. "Clean. Fix."

"In Rossiya? You cleaned and performed maintenance? Where, in a house like this one?"

More nods, but Eva remained unconvinced. Russian aristocrats were arriving in England every day. But unless Russian employers were extremely generous with their servants' wages, how would the Grekovs have saved enough money to make the long trek? It simply didn't add up.

Margaret came in carrying the pot of soup and a ladle, which she placed on a trivet in the center of the table. "Who's this, then?"

Neither she nor Mrs. Dayton had seen the Grekovs since they'd arrived, for they had been too busy preparing lunch. But shouldn't Margaret have met them previously when they came here to work? This certainly puzzled Eva. "Who's who? The Grekovs?"

The teenage girl addressed them directly. "Hello, I'm Margaret."

Before Eva could reply or express her surprise, Mrs. Dayton entered with the sandwiches. "Oh, company below stairs? No one told me. Ah, well, I've made plenty. Thought I'd serve us the same for dinner if we had leftovers."

"You don't know them either, Mrs. Dayton?" Eva treated the cook to an incredulous frown.

"No, should I?" Huffing, she leaned over to set the platter of sandwiches on the table. "I'm Mrs. Dayton, the cook here at High Head Lodge. And you two are? And do the toffs above stairs know you're here?"

The Grekovs only stared back in incomprehension. Confused, Eva turned to Margaret, who had since left and returned with the teapot. "Then neither of you has met them before?"

"I've never seen them before in my life," the girl attested.

"But Miss Brockhurst hired them to clean. That's why they've come today. They had no idea about Miss Brockhurst's passing, and the sight of the police vehicles rather upset them."

Mrs. Dayton, still standing, examined the couple with a wary look. "Why don't they speak?"

"They're from Russia and have only been in this country for a few months. We were able to establish that much when they arrived, though not much else."

"Well, I'll be." Mrs. Dayton slid back a chair and sat. "Come to clean, you say?"

Eva nodded.

"Margaret's been helping out with the cleaning since Miss Brockhurst first arrived. Isn't that right, girl?"

Margaret nodded. "Mostly light housekeeping. With only the mistress and her friend to look after, there wasn't much else needed." She regarded the Grekovs and shrugged. "Maybe Miss Brockhurst hired them and never got round to telling us."

"Is that it?" Mrs. Dayton raised her voice as if talking to someone hard of hearing, enunciating each word. "Miss Brockhurst—when did she hire you?"

"Shouting doesn't help them understand," Eva said. "I could have sworn Miss Asquith said someone comes to clean several days a week. *Comes*, not *will* come. But perhaps I misunderstood. Where's Myra?"

"I'm here. Who wants to know and why?"

Leave it to Myra to arrive in time for the meal, but not to help set it out. Though still partially disguised by her raggedly cut and curled bangs, Myra had at least foregone the garish cosmetics today. But then, with Miss Brockhurst gone, she had no one to hide from, did she?

"Do you remember what Miss Asquith said the other day about the couple who comes to clean the house?" Eva asked her.

"Maybe. I suppose." The woman sat and reached for the sandwiches.

"Do you recall if she implied the couple had only recently been engaged?" Even as she asked, Eva held out little hope for insight from this woman. She was correct.

"Not particularly. Why should I care who comes to clean the house and when?" As Myra bit into a sandwich, she peeked at the Grekovs, who were observing the conversations around them with guarded expressions. "Are you the couple? If so, you might start with the third floor bath. It could use a good scrub. Isn't that so, Eva? And we can't be expected to do it."

Eva had a sudden idea as she took her seat. Why hadn't

she thought of it sooner? With a reassuring smile at the Grekovs, she tucked into her lunch, prompting them to do the same. She covertly watched them from the corner of her eye—or specifically, she studied their hands. Her idea worked, yet her observations left her puzzled.

CHAPTER 12

After lunch, Phoebe helped an astonished Margaret collect the luncheon dishes and leftover food and carry them down to the scullery. It was clear the girl had never before encountered a "toff" willing to lend a hand in such a way. Phoebe also understood that her presence below stairs not only disconcerted the staff, but would be seen as something of an intrusion, a breach of etiquette that most servants would not thank her for. However, she hadn't followed Margaret in any sort of symbolic gesture, but rather because she wished to speak with Eva without delay.

In the scullery, she encountered Mrs. Grekov, her sleeves rolled to her elbows and her hands submerged in sudsy water. Her husband manned a mop in the main kitchen, under the cook's watchful eye. After accepting Margaret's stammered thanks, Phoebe went looking for Eva, whom she found in the servants' hall.

She didn't immediately enter the room or make her presence known. Upon seeing Eva inside, a second voice prompted her to pause in the corridor.

"All right, yes. I'd met her before." Myra Stanley sounded indignant. "What of it?"

"I think something happened that made you shy away from her here."

"That's ridiculous."

"Then why did you change your hair and attempt to disguise yourself with cosmetics yesterday morning? Why were you so skittish about being in the same hallway as Miss Brockhurst? Any *why*, Myra, did Miss Brockhurst recognize you out by the car yesterday?"

After a pause, Miss Stanley cleared her throat. How Phoebe wished she could see the woman's face. "I hardly see what business it is of yours."

"You are lady's maid to Julia Renshaw now, and she is very much my business. All the sisters are. Anyone who hurts one of those girls in any way will have to answer to me. Now, what happened between you and Miss Brockhurst?"

"Nothing. She . . . she took a dislike to me, is all. Because . . . because I felt the same about Lady Diana as you do about the Renshaws. Because Miss Brockhurst thought I was being overprotective."

"Overprotective about what?"

"Well, she was trouble, wasn't she? Miss Brockhurst, I mean. There was something not right about her and her doings, something improper. Why, look how she treated her own family."

At this, angry heat surged through Phoebe. How dare Stanley speak ill of someone no longer capable of defending herself? How dare she—

"I should think a woman like Lady Diana could fend for herself," Eva said. "She isn't exactly known for being a shrinking violet. Quite the opposite."

"That's a matter of opinion. I saw Lady Diana's softer side. Just as you apparently see the softer side of the icicle I presently serve."

Phoebe's ire barely had time to renew itself before Eva snapped, "Don't you dare speak of Lady Julia in that disrespectful manner."

A long, strained silence made Phoebe wonder if the conversation had ended and whether Myra Stanley would come striding through the doorway to discover she had been listening in. Not that Phoebe cared a whit if she did; she wouldn't be apologizing for it. But then Eva spoke again.

"I know for a fact you have not been above board, not about your time with Lady Diana, nor now, with Lady Julia." Eva remained calm, her voice level, reasonable, which garnered Phoebe's admiration, for she knew Eva had no such knowledge, not definitively, and was therefore bluffing. "Don't bother to deny it, Myra. I have my sources, dependable ones."

Another silence, and then Myra cleared her throat. "Wh-who have you been talking to? Not Lady Diana, surely."

"No," Eva said, "but you know how secrets travel."

"You couldn't possibly—"

Myra bit back whatever she'd been about to say. Once again, Eva spoke calmly. "Couldn't possibly what, Myra?"

"Oh, Lady Phoebe, is there something I can do for you?" Phoebe whirled to see Mrs. Dayton standing just outside the kitchen. "Is something needed upstairs?"

Phoebe smiled through her disappointment at not hearing more of Eva and Myra Stanley's conversation. But at Mrs. Dayton's hail, the women in the servants' hall had ceased talking. Inside, a chair scraped against the floor, and a moment later Stanley appeared in the doorway. Her gaze met Phoebe's for an instant before sliding away.

"My lady," the woman murmured in greeting before turning into the corridor and heading for the service stairs.

Phoebe crossed the threshold to find Eva on her feet. "Did you hear much of that?" Eva asked.

"I did. If only Mrs. Dayton hadn't caught me lurking. But it seems Stanley has something to hide, and you convinced her you were on to her."

"True, but we're not much closer to knowing what she and your cousin were at odds about."

"What did you mean about Stanley not being above board with Julia? Has she wronged my sister in some way?"

Eva compressed her lips, a sure sign she would rather not answer, that whatever she knew she had learned in confidence.

Knowing Eva would not betray that confidence, Phoebe changed the subject. "You can try again with Stanley later. Did you learn anything from the Grekovs?"

"Let's talk in the housekeeper's parlor." Eva led the way. After closing the door behind them, she said, "It appears I was wrong about the Grekovs. After trying in vain to question them during lunch, I realized I have only to look at their hands to learn about their past."

"Their hands? How so?"

"Calluses, my lady. They've got them, and they don't look to be new. So they were used to hard work in their home country. What I don't understand is, that being the case, how did they come by the money for their journey here. Did they steal it?"

"Russia is in shambles. Perhaps they came by valuables left behind in an abandoned home. From what I understand, many people fled the warring factions with little more than the clothes on their backs."

"If that's the case, my lady, we'll have to keep a sharp eye on them. We don't want them pilfering valuables from High Head Lodge."

"Don't be too hard on them, Eva. If their traveling money came from illicit means, it only shows how desperate they were to escape the fighting."

"I suppose you're right, my lady. It's hard to imagine what it must be like. Even in the Great War, most of England remained safe from the bombings, and no enemy armies marched through our villages."

"Just so."

"Has Miles finished with Mr. Cameron?"

Phoebe shook her head. "I haven't seen either one of them yet. I'm burning to know how Mr. Cameron explained the blood on his shirt, assuming it *was* his shirt."

"It must be. As you pointed out earlier, it tapers too narrowly to accommodate your cousin's waistline, which is rather wider than Mr. Cameron's."

At a knock at the door, Eva opened it to admit Margaret, who bobbed a curtsy and held out a folded piece of paper. "My lady, when I was gathering up the last of the lunch dishes upstairs just now, one of the gentlemen asked me to give this to you."

Surprised, Phoebe took the note from her. "Thank you, Margaret." The girl nodded and turned away. Eva closed the door again as Phoebe unfolded the page. Aloud, she read, " 'Phoebe, please meet me in the billiard room at three thirty. I have something important to tell you, of a sensitive nature. Please come alone.' He signed it 'R.' " She looked up. "It must be from Ralph."

"You won't go, my lady."

"But obviously, he's got something he wishes to confide."

"Then he should have confided it to Miles. Come, we'll show Miles right now."

"Perhaps something came of his talk with the constable, and he feels a need to discuss it. Although why me, I cannot imagine. Unless . . . I wonder if it has something to do with Julia."

"Why Julia?"

"I can't be certain, but I overheard them talking earlier—"

"My lady, were you eavesdropping again?"

"Can I help it if they leave doors ajar? Anyway, they seemed rather cozy. Flirtatious. It irked me, because I know she cares for—" Phoebe stopped. Yes, this was Eva she was talking to, and they kept no secrets from each other, but Theo Leighton was Julia's secret, not hers.

Eva smiled gently. "You were about to say she cares for the new Lord Allerton. I know about it, my lady."

"Then you also know Grams would disapprove because Theo inherited a bankrupt estate from his brother. But Eva, she flirts with other men, wealthy men, and then turns them away the moment they show the slightest interest in becoming serious with her."

"My lady, why should it concern you what your sister does?"

"Because *she* concerns me, Eva. Despite our differences, I want Julia to be happy. I know she'd be happy with Theo, and I'm afraid she'll destroy herself with the games she plays with other men. She'll become bitter and cynical and alone in the end. If only Grams didn't put such pressure on her to make a lucrative match."

Eva gestured to the note caught between Phoebe's fingers. She had almost forgotten it. "What about Mr. Cameron's request?"

"It's very odd. I think I should meet him at the appointed time, but I'm not foolish. Let's find the constable and tell him about this."

*　*　*

Eva wasn't happy, not one bit. "Miles, I don't think it's at all a good idea to allow Lady Phoebe to enter that billiard room alone."

Before he could reply, Lady Phoebe said, "I'll leave the door open, and the constable will be close by."

This argument had been going on in the morning room for some ten minutes now, and Eva felt outnumbered in her objections to letting Phoebe meet with Mr. Cameron alone. She ignored Phoebe's latest, and oft repeated, reasoning. "Miles, it's too dangerous. We're talking about a man who might have lodged a spike—a *spike*—into the base of a woman's skull. That is nothing to take casually."

"It was a pin, not a spike," Phoebe pointed out, much to Eva's irritation.

"I assure you I take nothing casually, Eva." Miles bristled, but only for a moment. Well, she *had*, in a way, called his competence as a policeman into question. "But I'm hoping what Mr. Cameron wouldn't tell me, he's willing to tell Lady Phoebe."

"What did he say when you questioned him?" Lady Phoebe asked.

"He kept insisting he'd cut himself shaving and attempted to wash it out of the shirt. When I pointed out that the garment appeared to have been hidden within the linens, he said he'd merely balled everything together without a thought about it."

"And do you believe him? Did you ask him if he has a bleeding disorder?"

"I did, actually. He said he does tend to bleed rather much at the slightest cut. Then, much to his indignation, I examined the nick on his chin. It's small, though rather wide. Inconclusive, really. And that makes me wonder. If the wound was self-inflicted to make us *believe* it to be the cause of the bloodied shirt, wouldn't he have made it large enough to be more credible?"

Eva pondered this. "Is every criminal smart enough to consider such things?"

"Mr. Cameron seems particularly intelligent to me," Lady Phoebe said. "He's a solicitor, after all. Such a profession requires a certain wiliness, doesn't it?"

Eva braced for more of Phoebe's rationalizations for proceeding with Mr. Cameron's request, when Miles said, "It could be that his position as the family's solicitor prevents him from speaking freely with me. It occurs to me that he has no idea of our prior acquaintance and shared experiences. He might very well believe Lady Phoebe will keep his confidence."

"I hadn't thought of that," Eva said.

"No, nor me, either," Lady Phoebe concurred. "That must be the case. He views me as an objective bystander whom he can trust."

"And if we are to learn what he wishes to trust you with, you'll have to meet with him." Miles forestalled Eva's protest with the flat of his hand. "I will be close by, in the next room. Whose bedroom is beside the billiard room?"

Eva reviewed the upper floor in her mind. "I believe that's Miss Asquith's room, no?"

"I believe it is," Lady Phoebe confirmed. "Which may present a problem. Miss Asquith took her lunch upstairs with her. I don't believe she's come down since."

"And the room on the other side?"

"There isn't one," Eva told him. "The billiard room is the first room off the landing."

"Right. Then I'll listen in from the landing. If Lady Phoebe—"

A crash from somewhere above their heads cut off his words. The chandelier above the table swayed, the crystals clinking one against another. Eva, Miles, and Lady Phoebe went utterly still, startled expressions mirrored on each face.

Lady Phoebe spoke first. "What was that?"

Miles answered by springing into motion. Eva and Lady Phoebe hurried after him. They met no one on the stairs on the way up, nor on the landing. But doors along the corridor were opening and heads poking out. When Eva and Lady Phoebe reached the billiard room, Miles was already inside.

And so was Olive Asquith.

Eva stopped short, and someone knocked into her from behind. She turned to find Hastings, along with Lady Julia and Myra attempting to squeeze their way into the room.

"What in the world was that?" Lady Julia exclaimed.

Her answer came in a scream, a piercing, high-pitched keening as the Dowager Lady Mandeville shoved her way past the others, ran to the far side of the billiard table, and sank to the floor.

"Ralph! Oh, Ralph. Oh, heavens . . ."

Eva's ears seemed to fill with water, and her vision wavered. Suddenly Phoebe was beside her, and their hands seemed to join of their own accord, fingers clenching tightly. As together they advanced farther into the room, the scene on the other side of the table took shape.

Ralph Cameron lay sprawled his back, his usually tidy silver hair wildly mussed and sticking out about his ears. His legs were bent, his arms akimbo, as if he had tried to fight off whatever had felled him. A gash on the side of his head told the story, glistening wetly, darkly, while an andiron with its attached bracket—solid brass and weighty iron—lay on its side a foot or two from his inert form.

"Oh, my lady," Eva whispered.

The dowager knelt over him. She gripped his shoulders and shook him relentlessly, crying out his name as if to wake him. All at once voices filled the room, a crescendo of jumbled notes each fighting to be heard, until a shrill whistle from Miles brought silence. Pale and frightened faces stared back at him, and then a voice cried out, "She did it! She killed Regina and now she's killed Ralph!"

It was Verna Brockhurst who made the charge. She stood in the doorway, the last to arrive on the scene. All gazes converged on Miss Asquith.

"Well, miss?" Miles approached her, stopping inches away. He bowed his head to study her face with his keen scrutiny. "You were here before anyone else."

"I heard the noise." Her voice came as a weak and tremulous croak. She swallowed and said louder, "It was like an anvil hitting the floor. The mirror on my dressing table shook. I came to see and . . . and he was there."

Miles looked her up and down, his features unreadable. "Did you see anyone when you came out of your room?"

"No, not a soul. The corridor was completely silent. I saw and heard no one."

"Of course not," Verna Brockhurst snapped. "Because no one else was about. Only you, Miss Asquith."

Fiery color suffused Olive Asquith's face. "He was on the floor when I came in."

"You were in Regina's room last night." Phoebe spoke in a low, tight voice. "You were the last to see Regina alive, and now this."

The words, rife with speculation, startled Eva. It wasn't like Phoebe to make quick judgments, much less voice them publicly. But the shock—two deaths in a single day—it was taking its toll on all of them.

Miss Asquith rounded on Lady Phoebe. "You think I

killed Mr. Cameron?" She encompassed the entire group
in seething resentment. "How easy to blame me, the out-
sider. We wouldn't want to point fingers at any of the
Brockhursts or their illustrious cousins. No, accuse poor,
plain Olive. No one will care."

"But you're not poor, are you, Olive?" Lady Phoebe let
go of Eva's hand and stepped forward. "You pretend to
be, but we both know you're from a wealthy family." She
turned around to address the others, who looked mutely
on as if suspended in their disbelief. "Asquith—it's no coincidence that she shares a name with our former prime
minister. They're related." Once again facing Olive, she
said, "Aren't you? Julia asked you that very question, and
you denied it. Why, Olive? What have you been hiding?"

"Before she died, Regina had something to tell me."
Phoebe's heart pounded in her throat and in her ears. "And
today, so did Ralph Cameron. Perhaps their secrets were one
and the same, but they both took them to their graves. And
both times, you were the one to find their bodies. Why is
that, Olive?"

Olive's lack of reply only fueled Phoebe's bluster. She
heard the words coming from her mouth, but it was as if
someone else were speaking. She knew better than this—
better than to accuse based only on appearances. Poor
Vernon, the head footman at Foxwood Hall, had been arrested for murder last Christmas based solely on circum-
stantial evidence and easily might have been hanged, had
Phoebe, Eva, and Constable Brannock not probed deeper
for the truth.

Both Eva and Miles stared at her, the astonishment and
disbelief plain on their faces. Sudden shame spiraled
through her. No, she must not fall prey to the temptation
to cast blame on the easiest target, because if she had

learned anything, it was that the easiest target was almost never to blame.

She compressed her lips and dropped her gaze to the floor. "I'm sorry. I spoke out of turn."

"Yes, you did," Olive retorted. "And—"

Constable Brannock signaled for silence. "That's enough."

Behind him, Cousin Clarabelle leaned one hand heavily on the top rail of the billiard table and dragged herself to her feet. Tears had streaked through her face powder and rouge, leaving pale, gleaming stripes down her cheeks. "No, that is not enough. Phoebe is right to suspect this insolent baggage. Miss Asquith has been imposing on my daughter's generosity, and Ralph must have somehow learned the truth."

Phoebe still held Ralph Cameron's note in her hand. She opened and reread it, searching for some clue, some hint of what he had wished to impart. But there was nothing, only a request that she join him here. He had handed the note to Margaret to deliver to her . . .

"Margaret."

The constable had gone to stand over the body. "What's that?"

"Mr. Cameron gave the note to Margaret to deliver to me." Even as she spoke, she hadn't quite turned the possibilities over in her mind. But she kept talking, letting the logic form of its own accord—hoping it would. "Margaret carried the note. She might have opened it, might have known what it said. Who else might have known? Where did he pen the missive? Did anyone see him do it?" She looked up at the others. The urge to accuse took hold again. "Did you, any of you?"

"What note?" With her birdlike scowl, Verna shook her head. "What are you talking about?"

Phoebe heard the constable's whispered request to Eva. "Find Margaret. Bring her here."

Eve slipped from the room, but not before setting a hand on Phoebe's shoulder and giving a reassuring squeeze.

"Everyone, sit down." The constable gestured at the various seating around the room.

"Here?" Cousin Clarabelle shook her head. "With . . . with *him* here? Surely not."

"Sit, Lady Mandeville," the constable snapped. His thinning patience emanated from the tension of his shoulders. "Someone go and get something to cover him with."

"I'll go." Julia moved swiftly into the corridor. She returned only moments later with a sheet. This she calmly handed to the constable, who rounded the billiard table and draped it over the body. Phoebe shuddered.

"This is insanity." Hastings staggered to the nearest seat, a wingback in front of a window. The chair skidded an inch or two as he heaved himself unsteadily into it. "Where is the chief inspector? Why don't you take that criminal to jail where she belongs, before she kills someone else?"

"I did not—"

"Miss Asquith, please." The constable removed his policeman's helmet and ran a hand through his unruly red curls. "Do not engage with Lord Mandeville or anyone else. No one is to speak until I have asked you a direct question."

"What on earth are we to do in the meantime?" Verna demanded.

"You are to sit down, ma'am," Constable Brannock returned, "and be quiet. Need I remind you once again that everyone here is a suspect, with the exception of Lady Phoebe and Miss Huntford."

"Oh, of course." Julia, sitting on the long leather sofa,

slid to one end to make room for Verna and Cousin Clara-belle. "Saint Phoebe is never to be suspected."

"Your sister and her maid were with me when the murder occurred," the constable informed her. "Where were you, Lady Julia?"

"Me?" She let out a low chuckle. "In my room." Then, with a look of amusement, as if this were all a game for a rainy Sunday afternoon, she asked, "Stanley, where were *you*?"

"Me, my lady?" Myra Stanley looked startled. "Why, I was on my way to your bedroom to collect any laundry and to see if you needed anything."

Julia's amused look didn't fade, and she chuckled again. "Were you now, Stanley?"

"Of course, my lady."

"Well, aren't you terribly dedicated?"

Myra Stanley smiled at first; then her lips inched downward, like the tail of a dog who has been chastised. She frowned. She had obviously heard, as had Phoebe, the derisive note in Julia's comment. "My lady?"

Crossing one leg over the other, Julia turned away, effectively dismissing the other woman. Phoebe rather understood how Myra Stanley felt, having been on the receiving end of Julia's cold shoulder more times than she could count. Eva returned a few minutes later, leading Margaret into the room. The girl's eyes were large, her young face pinched. As Phoebe well knew, servants never liked being called away from their duties, for it rarely portended anything good. Margaret apparently thought likewise, for she asked, in a small voice, "Did I do something wrong?"

Constable Brannock waved her to come closer, yet he took care not to let her advance too close to the billiard table or to see around him to what lay on the other side.

"Margaret, did you deliver a note earlier from Mr. Cameron to Lady Phoebe?"

"Y-yes, sir, I did. Was that wrong of me?"

"No, Margaret. But tell me, did you read the note before handing it over?"

"No, sir! Of course not."

"You're quite certain about that?"

"Yes, sir. I would *never*."

"And you don't know what the note said?"

"No idea, sir." She sounded scandalized by the very notion.

"And it never left your hand before you gave it to Lady Phoebe?"

Here Margaret hesitated.

"Well? Did it or didn't it?" The constable tapped his foot, which Phoebe had learned he sometimes did to keep those he questioned off their guard.

"It . . . er . . . slipped from my hand, sir. When I was going below stairs. I had a tray in my hands, you see, sir, and I stumbled a bit. I caught my balance quick enough, but the note slid out from between my fingers and fluttered all the way down to the landing."

"And then what?"

"And then that nice Russian woman happened by. She picked it up and handed it back to me when I reached her. And then I brought the note to Lady Phoebe."

Everyone had been quietly listening; now a tense stillness gripped the room. The constable's mouth tightened, and he asked, "Did the Russian woman open the note?"

"Of course not, sir."

"Are you sure? *Quite* sure? Could you see her the entire time you continued down the stairs?"

"I . . . er . . . well, no, sir, I suppose not the *entire* time.

I—I was holding the tray in front of me, and it blocked a bit of my view, especially what was directly below me."

"So then Mrs. Grekov could have glanced at the note without your noticing."

"I suppose so, sir. But why would she? She doesn't speak English, does she, sir?"

"Indeed . . ." Constable Brannock chewed the corner of his lip a moment. Then, "Thank you, Margaret, that will be all for now. Miss Asquith, I'll need to confine you to your room for the time being." The woman only shrugged, as if she had expected as much. The constable turned to Eva. "And then you and I are going to speak with the Grekovs."

CHAPTER 13

Miles locked Miss Asquith in her room and then handed the key to Eva. "Here, I'll trust you with this. Should she need anything, you can provide it to her. I'm not keen on depriving a young woman of food and drink or other necessities."

"Yes, all right." Eva slipped the key into a pocket at the front of her dress. "I don't suppose Miss Asquith will attempt to overpower me and escape."

After telephoning the coroner's office to make arrangements for poor Mr. Cameron's body to be removed, Miles led the way below stairs. On the way he explained his plan to Eva, which he implemented upon finding the Grekovs in the main kitchen. Mrs. Dayton had apparently set them to work. Mrs. Grekov, or Grekova, Eva supposed it should be, was scrubbing the work counter, while Mr. Grekov stood high on a ladder cleaning the windows that looked out onto the kitchen garden.

"They were hired to clean," the cook said in explanation as Eva and Miles entered the room. "Might as well earn their keep while we're all waiting to see what the police have to say."

"Thank you, Mrs. Dayton," Miles said. "If you wouldn't mind, I'll ask you to wait in the servants' hall for a few moments. I have something to say to Mr. and Mrs. Grekov."

"Oh." The woman hesitated, giving Eva the distinct impression she had never before been asked to vacate her kitchen. "Where is Margaret?" she asked.

"I also sent her down to the servants' hall." Miles held out an arm in a gesture meant to usher Mrs. Dayton along. She set down the wooden spoon she had been using to stir whatever bubbled away on the stove, lowered the flame, and sauntered off with a pout.

"I think you'll owe her an apology when this is all over," Eva murmured.

Thus far the Grekovs had only briefly looked up from their toils. In his most affable tone, Miles said, "Mr. and Mrs. Grekov, you are both under arrest on suspicion of fraud."

They weren't really, but he and Eva had decided on this strategy. The couple immediately exchanged alarmed glances, proving they understood English far better than they had let on. Still, Eva wasn't prepared for what happened next. Dmitry eschewed the steps of the ladder and instead leaped down to the floor, his sopping rag in one hand and a rubber-edged tool in the other. Valeria, meanwhile, sprang away from the work counter, her scrub brush sending out a spray. The pair charged for the door. Miles attempted to block their way, but working together and tossing their sodden cleaning tools at him, they barreled past, knocking him off his feet.

No doubt his shock at their reaction had put him off his guard. Instinct sent Eva several steps in their wake, but Miles's shout stopped her short.

"Don't you dare." He was already gaining his feet, his hand on his weapon. "I take it they speak English rather well," he said ruefully and, already on the move, added,

"I'm going after them. Ring Inspector Perkins and tell him what's happened. Tell him we'll need reinforcements."

Eva ran after him, calling to his back as he made short work of the corridor to the outside door. "Should I set Miss Asquith free?"

"No." He didn't stop. "Don't do anything until you hear from me, and don't let any of the others leave." With that, he flung open the door at the end of the corridor and disappeared into the lengthening afternoon shadows.

Eva closed and secured the door behind him. When she turned, Mrs. Dayton was standing in the corridor. "What the devil just happened?"

Eva hesitated as her heart slowly stopped racing. "Apparently the Grekovs aren't who they say they are. At any rate, they were only pretending not to speak English. They understood well enough when Constable Brannock told them they were under arrest. It was a test he devised for them, and they failed miserably. Or passed, depending on your point of view."

"My heavens. Are they dangerous? Where are they now?"

"Out there, somewhere." Eva pointed at the door over her shoulder. "I just hope the constable will be all right, going after them like that."

"Don't you worry about your young man, dearie. He seems a capable sort to me."

Heat rose to Eva's cheeks at Mrs. Dayton's reference to Miles being her "young man." Were they so obvious?

But there were more important things to worry about. "If there are any other entrances down here, make sure they're locked. Tell Margaret to stay inside and not open any doors to the outside."

"Do you think they'll be back?"

"I don't know," Eva admitted. "Nor do I know if they pose a threat or if they're simply terrified of police matters because of their past experiences. But with two people dead, we mustn't take any chances. If you need anything, I'll be upstairs."

She made her telephone call to Chief Inspector Perkins and went searching for Lady Phoebe.

Phoebe paced back and forth in her bedroom while Eva watched her from an easy chair beside the hearth. It had become a familiar if unfortunate scene these past months, the two of them comparing notes and going over what each learned during the course of an investigation. It was typically Phoebe's habit to think on her feet, to work off the restless energy that came with frustrations and apparent dead ends. She often wondered how Eva maintained such outward calm, though she knew better than to believe her maid unaffected by such events.

"And to think I felt sorry for them," Eva was saying now of the Grekovs. "I went so far as to trust them."

"It was frightfully clever of the constable to trap them the way he did."

"Clever enough, perhaps, to trick them into revealing their guilty consciences and their ability to understand English, but not so clever that they didn't get away. They've acted so meekly, we never thought they would fight their way out the way they did." Eva glanced out the window. "Thank goodness the days are long now. I do hope Miles finds them and isn't hurt in the process."

"He'll be fine," Phoebe said automatically. She nearly winced at her own words, however, for she couldn't be sure of any such thing. Still, it wouldn't help to fear the worst. "At any rate, they weren't armed."

"No, that's true. Miles would have found any weapons on them when he had them turn out their pockets for a house key." She laughed without mirth. "Unless you can consider a scrub brush a weapon."

"All right," Phoebe said briskly, turning their attention

to the matter at hand as much to distract Eva from her worries about the constable as to review what they knew so far. "The Grekovs are not who—or at least not exactly *what*—they claimed to be. That means they're probably guilty of something, although of what is not yet clear. Even if they were in possession of a house key, I can't believe they sneaked in last night to kill my cousin and then returned here today."

"You're right, my lady, that doesn't make sense. Especially with how surprised they were to find the police here. Then again, they have proved to be convincing actors. Isn't it said that guilty parties often return to the scene of the crime?"

"True enough. All right, the Grekovs remain on the list of suspects. Then we have Olive Asquith, who conveniently was the first to find both Regina and Mr. Cameron. And she was most likely either living off Regina's money or persuading her to spend her resources for some cause or other. That also makes her suspect, because Regina might have decided to cut her off."

"Myra Stanley is also suspect," Eva said. "I'm quite sure Diana Manners sacked her for some kind of betrayal, and that Myra had somehow offended your cousin in the past. Myra admitted to knowing Miss Brockhurst."

Phoebe studied her, then made a guess. "There is another strike against Stanley, and it has to do with Julia, doesn't it?"

"I cannot say, my lady." Eva compressed her lips in an all too telling way. Phoebe decided not to question her further. Unlike Myra Stanley, Eva would never betray someone's trust.

Phoebe nodded and moved on. "Hastings, Verna, and Cousin Clarabelle all had reason to wish Regina dead, since they stood to gain as her legal heirs and were incensed by her inheritance. In addition to that, I do believe

Cousin Clarabelle was in love with Mr. Cameron, and might have been jealous of Regina's affections for the man and his for her."

"Do you believe the dowager would have murdered her own daughter?"

"Truly?" Phoebe stopped pacing long enough to shake her head and sigh. "No, but we can't entirely rule it out. However, Hastings and Verna are another matter. Except that . . ."

"Except what, my lady?"

"Hastings always seems too inebriated to kill anyone. Not Regina, and certainly not Mr. Cameron, who would have possessed the strength to fight him off fairly easily, one would think."

"Don't forget about that beastly andiron, my lady. Even staggering, Lord Mandeville might have been able to swing it, and obviously Mr. Cameron couldn't get out of the way."

"Yes, but with Hastings so unsteady all the time, it seems doubtful he could have managed to aim that andiron with any measure of accuracy."

"Hmm . . . I do see your point. But such a weapon would have been difficult for anyone to use, most especially one of the women. Take Miss Asquith, for instance. She's just a wisp of a thing."

"She is at that." Phoebe had been all too willing to condemn Olive when they found Ralph on the billiard room floor. It wasn't simply that Olive had found both bodies; there was more, something Phoebe didn't like to admit, something she was perhaps missing from her own life . . . "Olive and my cousin," she said and stopped.

"Yes, my lady?"

"They were very close."

"Yes, my lady, I agree. They seemed quite close friends."

"More than that. Like sisters, only yet again, more."

Eva's head tilted. "I'm not sure I understand."

Phoebe couldn't meet her gaze. "They argued fiercely at times when we went shopping, while at other times they were sullen with each other. And then the next minute they'd act as if nothing had gone awry between them. They had a bond unlike anything I've ever enjoyed with anyone." She walked several steps, stopped, and turned back to face Eva. "I believe I was . . . or am . . . jealous of that."

"Of what, my lady?" Eva shook her head in incomprehension.

"Of sharing that kind of closeness with another human being. I haven't. Not even with my sisters. Julia and I—well, I needn't explain that to you. And Amelia is still too young. Someday, perhaps, but not now. And as for friends . . . I cannot think of anyone I would feel so comfortable with. We are always so polite, we British, aren't we? It prevents . . . well . . . true friendship in many cases, I think. At least the kind of friendship Regina and Olive enjoyed."

Eva came to her, her hand rising to cup Phoebe's cheek. "My dearest lady. I am your friend. Yes, I serve you, but you must never believe that mere employment is what keeps me at your side. I . . ." Eva trailed off and looked away, blinking. When she returned her gaze to Phoebe's it was with a spark every bit as fierce as any emotion she had witnessed between Regina and Olive.

She smiled and shook her head. "You needn't say more, Eva. I'm foolish sometimes. I forgot how very much I have, how lucky I am." And then a sobering thought struck her. Twice in the past, Phoebe's life had been threatened, and Eva had responded with vehement devotion and ardent protectiveness. "Powerful emotions can produce extreme actions, can't they? Even in the name of friendship."

"Indeed they can." The intensity of Eva's reply made Phoebe believe that perhaps their thoughts had taken a similar turn. "*Especially* in the name of friendship, my lady."

"Olive was singularly possessive of my cousin. I saw it. She clearly resented Julia's and my presence here. I believe she wanted Regina all to herself, while Regina, perhaps, wished others to join their circle. This might have greatly angered Olive. She claimed Ralph Cameron argued with Regina, but maybe it was Olive who argued with her last night and . . ."

Eva placed a hand on her wrist. "That is a possibility, my lady. But you mustn't blame yourself again for not going into your cousin's room last night. You could not have known what was going to happen."

"Or what had already happened." Phoebe gulped, then swallowed her guilt. "Olive is hiding something, that much is certain. Her wealthy family has disowned her, true, but she puts on airs as if she's from a working-class background. A kind of reverse snobbery, if you will."

"Her boots," Eva said with a nod. When Phoebe didn't understand and said as much, Eva explained, "Her boots are of fine quality. The plain design is deceiving, but they're made of high grade, hand-stitched calfskin. Probably Italian. Expensive."

"Leave it to you to notice such details."

"It's my job to notice such things."

Phoebe resumed pacing. "We need to consider the facts we're sure of. Regina's room was left remarkably undisturbed by the crime, and she didn't appear to awaken during the attack. There were no bruises on her face or neck, other than the wound left by the pin."

"A glass with traces of whiskey sat on her bedside table," Eva added, "and some appeared to have been spilled on the pillow. Also, a newspaper was burned, leaving only a partially legible scrap."

"Yes, our mystifying 'list Labor.'" Phoebe tapped her

chin, trying to place each clue into a larger picture. She began reciting: "Regina spending money wildly to put her plans for this house in motion; Olive, with her pretense of being poor and her possessiveness toward Regina; the Brockhursts, who wished to be anything *but* poor; the Grekovs, who show up out of the blue—" She went still. Her mouth opened upon a jarring thought.

"What is it, my lady?" Eva looked alarmed.

"*Was* the Grekovs' arrival really so out of the blue? We've already determined they aren't what they claim to be, but I do believe they are from Russia. It would be difficult to fake that, especially without much warning, and more importantly, *why* fake being from there? You said Olive claimed they came every few days to clean, yet the story changed, didn't it, when Mrs. Dayton and Margaret didn't recognize them. Then, suddenly, Olive claimed they had been hired but hadn't yet begun their duties."

"Unless I heard Miss Asquith wrong when she first mentioned them. What are you getting at, my lady?"

"Think about it. Regina with her secret plans for this house. Olive with her utilitarian views. The Grekovs, who speak enough English to know to run when a policeman tells them they're under arrest." She set her hands on her hips, confident in the conclusion she had drawn. "Eva, what is going on in Russia as we speak?"

"A civil war."

"Precisely. A civil war between the old regime as well as opposing factions of the new Communist Party, who also call themselves socialists." Her heart began to race again, pounding hard against her ribs, as another realization struck home. "Eva, '*list* Labor'—*socialist* or *communist* labor. I'd wager my motorcar the burned publication was from the Socialist Democratic Federation, or some such group, which is actively spreading its doctrine in England. Regina and Olive spoke of new ideas for the future. *Of course*. We should have seen it sooner. I believe they were both advocates of spreading socialism right here in England. And I will bet you the Grekovs are part of it."

Eva sank into the nearest chair. "Bolsheviks here, in England? Your own cousin?"

"I'll wager the Grekovs, and a host of others, came from Russia to help disperse communist ideas throughout Europe. That is the goal, you realize. Their trip here might even have been funded by the Communist Party."

"My lady, how beastly. After what the Red Army did to the czar."

"And possibly his entire family, though no one is quite certain of their fate." Phoebe hugged her arms around her middle. "Can you imagine such a thing happening to our own royal family?"

"No wonder someone burned that publication. But who? Miss Brockhurst? Her brother? Miss Asquith? Who?"

"That's what we need to find out." Phoebe dragged a chair closer to Eva's. Sitting, she reached for Eva's hands. "We need a plan. Whatever mischief brought the Grekovs to England, I'm not convinced they murdered my cousin, although as you said, we cannot rule it out. As for the others . . ." She thought a moment, and remembered something Eva said the day before. "Being a fly on the wall would certainly come in handy now. If we could only observe the others for signs of guilt. With two victims now, there is sure to be evidence someone is desperate to conceal."

Eva's bottom lip slipped between her teeth. Then her face lit up. "I have an idea, my lady. A rather underhanded one. One that would get me the sack immediately if I ever dared use it."

"Don't keep me in suspense, Eva. What is it?"

Eva leaned closer, her fingers tightening around Phoebe's. "The speaking tubes, my lady. We'll open them from the bedrooms and any other rooms we can. By switching from room to room at my end, I'll be able to hear anyone talking below and listen in. We'll just have to devise a way to keep Myra downstairs so she doesn't overhear the voices coming from my room. Do you think your sister would help us?"

"Assuming Julia isn't guilty . . ."

"My lady!"

"I'm only joking. Yes, I think Julia can be prevailed upon to help us." She frowned in sudden doubt. "Perhaps if you asked her . . ."

"Then you'll do it, my lady? You'll keep Myra away from the third floor?" Eva held her breath while she waited for Lady Julia to consider. Lady Phoebe's parting expression earlier haunted her mind's eye. Her sadness had been unmistakable, along with her reluctant admittance that Lady Julia would not likely do her any favors. Eva didn't understand it any better than her lady. The rivalry had existed between the sisters for years now, but Eva could find no logical reason why a woman as beautiful and accomplished as Julia Renshaw would not treat her younger sister with affection and generosity.

Lady Julia rose from her perch on the chaise longue at the foot of her bed. "I suppose I can keep Stanley busy for the next couple of hours. Though honestly, I don't know what you and Phoebe hope to accomplish by listening in on people. It's not likely any of them is going to confess to murder in the privacy of their bedrooms."

"We don't expect a confession, my lady, but one never knows what people might murmur when they're alone or when speaking to someone else. Your sister will be attempting to engage the others in leading conversations."

"That's all very well and good, but you do understand, given the circumstances, what an inconvenience it will be for me to have to spend time in that woman's company."

"I do, my lady. You don't trust Myra, with good reason. I'm not asking you to take her into your confidence or even remain in the same room with her, but merely to charge her with enough tasks to keep her occupied below stairs."

"Did you tell my sister about Stanley's probable treachery?"

"No, I didn't. It's not for me to tell. If you wish to explain to Lady Phoebe—"

"I don't, Eva. It's none of Phoebe's business. She knows too much about the matter as it is."

A heavy pause ensued, one in which Eva groped for the proper words that might help alleviate some of the rancor between the sisters. "You know, my lady, you would find a very willing ally in Lady Phoebe if you wished. She would never betray your trust."

Lady Julia looked as if she had something contrary to remark, but then her expression cleared, and she shrugged a shoulder. "No, I suppose she wouldn't at that."

"Then why—?"

"I don't wish to discuss it. Please let Stanley know I wish to see her."

"Yes, my lady." Eva should not have expected anything different from the eldest Renshaw sister, a woman who rarely shared her deepest feelings with any but a select, privileged few. Occasionally, Eva had been the recipient of Lady Julia's confidence, as earlier when the Countess of Wroxly had telephoned to confront her granddaughter about her affections for the new Marquess of Allerton. That privilege would not, apparently, be extended again, not today at any rate.

It wasn't merely concern for Lady Phoebe that drove Eva to discover the root of the sisters' discord. She wished to see them reconciled—truly friends again, as they had been years ago—as much for Lady Julia's sake as Phoebe's. Siblings were a precious commodity and not to be squandered. The war had taught her that.

Below stairs, Myra Stanley grumbled at the summons Eva delivered. She had just poured a cup of tea and made herself comfortable in the housekeeper's parlor, her stockinged feet propped on a footstool. She glowered at Eva from beneath her frizzled bangs. "What on earth can she want now? I can't imagine she needs me to iron a gown for dinner, not with two dead bodies in one day. Who will care what anyone wears?"

Eva winced at the woman's bluntness. "*She* has a name. Lady Julia. And whatever she wishes you to do, it's your duty to oblige."

"Never a moment's rest." Myra blew into her tea and took a sip. She didn't look at all inclined to relinquish either the earthenware mug or her comfortable seat.

"Shall I go back and tell your mistress you're indisposed?" Eva tapped her foot impatiently.

"Oh, now that *is* an idea. Tell her I'm ill, or that these murders are quite shredding my nerves. Do you think she'd go for it?"

That response baffled Eva. "Myra, why *did* you become a lady's maid?"

"What would you have me be? A scullery maid? No, thank you. And I certainly can't cook. I was a parlor maid years ago, but, as I've a passing fair vocabulary, a sound knowledge of fashion, and no liking for dust rags and mops, lady's maid seemed a good choice. Of course, I didn't simply walk into the job, mind you."

"How *did* you come by the position?" Eva asked in spite of herself. She shouldn't have given Myra the satisfaction of showing her curiosity, but she couldn't fathom how an insolent slacker like Myra Stanley had risen so high in the hierarchy of service.

The woman chuckled unpleasantly. "By always being on hand to clean up the other girls' messes."

Eva narrowed her eyes, suspecting many of those messes were undoubtedly caused by Myra herself. She crossed to the woman and took the mug from her hand. "If I were you I'd get myself upstairs and see to my mistress's needs. At once. Or you'll find yourself *longing* to scrub floors and dust furniture, if you catch my meaning."

"Is that so? See here. You may have been in the Renshaws' employ longer than me, but need I remind you that as the eldest granddaughter's maid, I outrank you."

It was Eva's turn to chuckle. The woman obviously had no idea how precarious her position was, what with Lady Julia's suspicions. "I doubt that very much, Myra. Very much indeed."

Next, Eva and Lady Phoebe tested their plan. Eva returned to her room on the third floor. A few minutes later she heard Lady Phoebe's voice, distant and slightly muffled, a result of her speaking from the middle of her bedroom rather than directly into the tube. "Can you hear me?"

"I can, my lady."

"Good. I'll go and open the other speaking tubes, at least the ones in unoccupied rooms. I think everyone except Julia is downstairs at the moment, and she said she'd open her own tube." Her voice came in stronger and louder; she must have moved closer to the mouthpiece. "There's not much to be done about Olive's room, since she's locked in. But since she's alone it's not as if she'll be speaking out loud about committing crimes."

"One never knows," Eva replied. "Sometimes the guilty murmur in their sleep."

"Then what should we do?"

Eva thought a moment, then brightened and reached into the pocket of her dress. "In all the excitement I'd nearly forgotten. Miles left the key to Miss Asquith's room with me. In a little while, I'll use the excuse of bringing Miss Asquith something to eat. While I'm in the room, I'll try to unhook the tube."

"Brilliant. While you do that, I'll take your place upstairs. Do you think the constable will object to your visiting Olive?"

"He did give me the key for the purpose of providing her with anything she might need."

"Good. I'm going to open the other tubes now. Listen carefully."

A few minutes later, another familiar voice reached Eva's ear.

"I'd like this skirt hemmed, Stanley. About this much." Eva imagined Lady Julia holding her thumb and forefinger a short distance apart. "And this shirtwaist—look at these wrinkles. Really, Stanley, you must learn not to crowd my things in the wardrobe. Oh, and these pumps. The shine is becoming rather dull, don't you think? Please take them down and give them a thorough buffing. And while you're at it, I could really do with some strong tea and something to eat. Something sweet. Ask Mrs. Dayton, I'm sure she's got something on hand. Well, what are you waiting for?"

"Yes, my lady. Er . . . is my lady actually planning to wear the shirtwaist today? Might it wait until . . . say . . . we arrive back at home? And your skirt—"

"I don't know what I'll wear at dinner tonight, Stanley. I'll decide that later. Off with you then."

Despite the seriousness of her present task, Eva couldn't contain a grin.

Phoebe slipped out of her bedroom and moved soundlessly along the corridor. Detecting no sounds but a low hum of voices from downstairs, she went to Olive's door. All was quiet inside. Had Olive fallen asleep?

Moving away, she crossed to Cousin Clarabelle's room and again pressed her ear to the panel. She gingerly tried the knob, ready to claim she had knocked softly and was just checking to see if her cousin needed anything. The room stood empty, and she stole inside. The speaking tube apparatus occupied the wall to her right. She hurried over and pushed the button that moved the disk aside. A bell would have sounded upstairs, but she didn't linger to find out if Eva had heard. Certain she had, Phoebe exited the room and moved on to the suite shared by Hastings and Verna.

There she repeated her actions, but upon her retreat to the door, footsteps thudded along the hall runner. She peeked around the edge of the doorway. Hastings advanced in her direction.

Chapter 14

As he traveled the corridor, Hastings stared down at the floor as if he were contemplating the design in the hall runner. Panic surged through Phoebe. Should she back up and hide somewhere in the room? She'd done that once, having nearly been caught snooping through a man's bedroom. His sudden arrival had sent her diving into an armoire among his personal effects. Humiliating enough, crouching behind a man's boots, but worse had been the realization, later, that he'd known of her presence all along.

No, she couldn't risk being caught stooping behind a chair or cowering under the bed. Beside, Hastings still hadn't looked up. He staggered from side to side, his weight shifting heavily from foot to foot. He veered to his left, and his hand came up to brace against the wall with a thump that tilted a gilt-framed painting. He stumbled, then managed to right himself.

Quickly Phoebe closed the door behind her and hurried over to him. "Hastings, are you all right? Are you ill?" Her words came breathlessly as she covered her own alarm with a show of concern. A sharp odor wafted between them, prompting her to turn her face aside and hold her breath.

Good heavens, he was pissed, completely and utterly.

"Verna? Wh-what are you doing up here?" The words came in a slurring heap. "Didn't I just leave you downstairs?"

"It's Phoebe, Hastings. Come, let's get you to your room."

She slung an arm around him, and together they stumbled to his door. His weight threatened to drag her down one moment and crush her against the wall the next. His fingertips dug into her shoulder painfully as he held on. Somehow she kept him upright until they reached his room. With her balance established precariously at best, she reached out and turned the knob. Down the corridor, another door opened, and Julia stepped out.

"What's going on? I thought I heard another crash like earlier."

"Nothing like that. Our cousin is just a bit in his cups." As if to prove her point, Hastings tripped over the threshold. Phoebe nearly doubled over in her attempt to prevent him falling facedown on the floor. "Do you think you might lend us a hand?"

Julia appeared at Hastings's other side and dragged his arm around her shoulders. "Come along now, there's a good lad. Heavens, Hastings, can't you hold your brandy better than this?"

"That's not helping," Phoebe pointed out.

Their cousin coughed, letting out another bitter exhalation. "Where's Verna?"

"I'll go and get her just as soon as we've got you settled." To Julia, Phoebe said, "To the bed."

They managed to reach the edge of the bed and turned Hastings around so that his back faced it. As they lowered him, he sank heavily to the mattress and promptly fell over sideways, landing on his cheek. Phoebe used the momentum to swing his legs up as well. Hastings rolled to his stomach and immediately passed out.

Julia blew out a breath. "Good grief. That was unpleasant."

"At least he came peacefully." Phoebe rubbed her shoulder where Hastings had gripped it. "Thank you."

Julia regarded their inebriated cousin and wrinkled her nose. "Stinking drunk. He smells like a dentist's office." She turned on her heel and headed for the door.

Phoebe followed her into the hallway. "A dentist?"

"Quite." Julia spoke without slowing her pace. "The last time I accompanied Grams to have a tooth pulled, Dr. Sayers administered some sort of gas that made her so sleepy she didn't feel the pain. It smelled dreadful."

Phoebe stopped short. "You mean ether?"

Julia shrugged. "I don't remember exactly. I was more concerned with Grams breaking my knuckles, she squeezed my hand so hard before she drifted off."

"Julia, wait." Her sister stopped and turned, an eyebrow raised in query and a smidgen of impatience. "Can we . . . that is, I wish to ask you something."

"So ask."

Phoebe glanced over her shoulder down the empty corridor. Someone could appear at any time, and she didn't wish to air her thoughts in front of the others. "Can we talk in your bedroom?"

Julia's release of breath hinted at reluctance, but she turned and led the way, then closed the door behind them. "What is so important?"

Phoebe pressed the words out in a rush, before she changed her mind. "Why are you so angry with me? What did I do?"

Julia's gaze lifted toward the ceiling. "Nothing, dear sister. You're perfect as always."

"Don't make a joke of it, Julia. We've been getting on so much better since last spring. What changed?"

Julia studied her, her expression unreadable. Phoebe silently willed her to give an honest reply and not hide behind her usual shrugs and clipped witticisms. But as the moment lengthened, Julia's clear complexion darkened and her eyes sparked. Quite abruptly, she flung the door open. "This room has grown intolerably oppressive. I'm going downstairs. Good luck with your snooping. I'll send Verna up. Maybe Hastings will awaken, and they'll discuss how they plotted to kill Regina and Ralph, and Eva will overhear them from the third floor. It's a frightfully clever plan, after all."

"Julia—"

Too late, her sister had gone.

Eva hovered near the wall, the funnel-like receiver of the speaking tube pressed to her ear. Every few minutes she connected to a different room. At the moment, she was listening to a symphony of snores from Hastings Brockhurst. She was about to switch the connection again when the creaking of a door played a brief harmony with the man's snorts. Lady Mandeville the younger called her husband's name in a petulant voice. She tried twice more. When he didn't answer, Eva didn't wonder why. She had heard for herself through the tube earlier that Hastings Brockhurst had passed out cold. And then Lady Julia had said that very odd thing about visiting the dentist.

At a knock at her own door, she reluctantly pulled away from the tube, remembering to close the connection first. While she didn't wish to miss any conversation should Lord Mandeville awaken, she also didn't want Myra discovering her listening in on the guests. It wasn't Myra, however, but rather Lady Phoebe standing in the corridor.

"Hurry, let me in before Stanley comes up and sees me here."

"I feared you might be her when you knocked." Eva stepped aside. "Your sister promised to keep her busy below, but one never knows. Have you learned something?"

"I have, and I need to search Hastings and Verna's suite as soon as possible. I must discover what's been keeping my cousin intoxicated. I don't believe it's whiskey."

"Does this have anything to do with Lady Julia's curious comment? She said Lord Mandeville smelled like a dentist's office. But then I couldn't hear any more."

"Yes, at that point we went into the corridor. What you missed was my guess that what Julia smelled was ether."

"Ether . . ." A realization crept through Eva. She had heard of this. During the war, Danny had written in one of his letters home about how some of the other soldiers stole ether from the field hospitals. Some used it to escape the constant terror; others sold it for profit. He had promised their parents he had never done any such thing, nor would he, but he had seen the drug incapacitate his fellow soldiers, rendering them useless in the trenches.

Eva shivered at the bleak realities Danny had faced every day on the battlefields. "Your cousin fought in the war, yes?"

Lady Phoebe nodded. "But he was captured and held prisoner for a time. After his release he spent the remainder of the war behind the lines."

"Do you know where he was held?"

"No. The details were rather sketchy. Cousin Basil didn't seem to want to talk about it with Grampapa, and Cousin Clarabelle told Grams only that Hastings had been through a horrendous time, and that it had changed him."

"Shell shock?" Eva had encountered just such an individual last spring, a nurse who had experienced firsthand the horrific consequences of battle. She, too, had found an escape, not with ether but with potentially deadly doses of morphia.

"I don't think so, at least not in the usual sense," Lady Phoebe replied. "More of a general malaise, not of the body but of the mind, a discontent that made Hastings more sullen and languid than ever. But then, he never was one for industry or achievement. I suppose that's why his father disinherited him."

"A rather harsh thing to do, considering his tendencies were made worse by the war."

"I suppose Cousin Basil wished to ensure the survival of his estate and everything he'd worked to accomplish during his lifetime. Blameworthy or no, Hastings might have lost it all. Still might, as things have turned out. But why did you ask about the war?"

"Because I happen to know that some soldiers obtained and abused ether. It was a way to escape. To dull the terror and panic. There's nothing new in ether addiction. It was rather commonplace decades ago and had begun to fade away, but I suppose in the middle of bombs and guns and death, a man finds relief in whatever is available."

Lady Phoebe sat on the plain wooden chair beside the equally plain dresser. "I thought it odd that Hastings was forever carrying around a glass of whiskey, but never seemed to drink any. Do you suppose he uses it as a prop? You know, to pretend he's drinking when in fact he's been sneaking off to inhale ether fumes."

"A cunning ruse. Few would interfere with a man and his whiskey, but ether is another matter." Eva's bottom lip slipped between her teeth as she considered. Ether. Whiskey. Pretending . . .

With breathtaking suddenness, a few scattered pieces fell into place. "My lady, the whiskey in Miss Brockhurst's room, on her pillow—"

Lady Phoebe gasped. "To cover the scent of ether. Eva,

that's how Regina was killed without disturbing anything in the room. Whoever did it—Hastings, in my opinion—slipped in, probably covered her nose and mouth with an ether-soaked cloth, and then plunged that beastly dragonfly into her skull."

"Let's be careful not to jump to conclusions, my lady. The ether must be found first. Lady Julia could be mistaken about the odor. Word must be sent to the police laboratory in Gloucester that your cousin's pillowcase should be examined again for any traces of the chemical. And you can't accuse Lord Mandeville without more evidence that it was him. Any of the others could have found the ether in his room and used it."

"Very true. His wife, for instance. She must know he's an ether addict. How could she not . . . ?" Lady Phoebe went silent, her gaze locking with Eva's. "It easily could have been Verna who killed Regina."

"I do wish Miles would return." Eva worried her hands together. "For all we know, Miss Asquith made the very same discovery about Lord Mandeville weeks ago, when she and your cousin were staying with the family in London. She herself might have used the ether on Miss Brockhurst, hoping Lord Mandeville would be accused."

"Then why the whiskey? Why not let the smell of ether be discovered and lead the authorities directly to Hastings? No, it seems that whiskey was spilled to mask the other odor and confound the authorities."

Lady Phoebe made a good point. "Perhaps . . . perhaps the whiskey was Miss Brockhurst's, or Miss Asquith's, and its being there was merely a coincidence. But I should get back to listening." She returned to the speaking tube and opened the connection once again. Then she remembered another part of their plan. "Actually, my lady, if you care to take my place here now, I could bring Miss Asquith something to eat and attempt to open her speaking tube."

"My money is still on either Hastings or Verna, but yes, you go ahead. I doubt anyone will miss me below for twenty minutes or so. Try to linger a bit with Olive. She's talked to you before."

"She has at that."

"Good, then for now I'll stay here and listen to Hastings snore."

Balancing a tray on one hand, Eva unlocked Miss Asquith's bedroom door, but before opening it, she knocked. No answer came from within. Eva knocked again, but this time didn't wait for a response before going in.

"Miss Asquith, I've brought you something to eat."

The room was much smaller than either Phoebe's or Julia's, but nonetheless well appointed in dark, burled walnut furniture that Miss Brockhurst had undoubtedly planned to be rid of during her extensive renovations of High Head Lodge.

Eva felt slightly ashamed of that last thought, realizing she was judging the vagaries of someone no longer here to defend her actions. Miss Asquith, sitting at an escritoire with her back to Eva, continued scratching her pen across the paper in front of her. "I'm not hungry. You may take it away."

With a quick assessment, Eva located the speaking tube. As luck would have it, the device occupied the same wall as the long bureau to her left. She went to the bureau, set down the tray and, flicking a glance at Miss Asquith's back, reached out to flip aside the brass disk covering the mouthpiece.

Lowering her arm to her side, she said, "Please, Miss Asquith, it doesn't do to neglect one's health."

Miss Asquith set down her pen and slowly turned. She scrutinized Eva from head to toe and then blinked. "Where

is the constable? Why hasn't he returned to take me off
to jail?"

Eva hesitated, debating how much to divulge. She decided Miss Asquith couldn't very well interfere with the
pursuit of the Grekovs while locked in her room. "He's
not here. Earlier, he trapped Dmitry and Valeria into revealing how much English they actually understand. They
ran for it, and Miles—er, that is, Constable Brannock—
has gone after them. They were not hired to clean, were
they?"

Miss Asquith's face registered surprise and then re-
aligned into an unreadable mask.

"I'm sorry if I interrupted your writing." Eva gestured
at the escritoire and whatever Miss Asquith had been poring over when Eva knocked. "A letter to your family?"

Miss Asquith's brows drew together. "Hardly."

No, Eva hadn't really thought so, not with what she had
learned about Miss Asquith's relations with her family. Then
again, her father had relented and granted his daughter a
portion of her allowance. Perhaps . . . "If there is anyone
you would like me to contact for you, I'd be more than
happy."

"Would you now?" The woman merely went on staring
Eva down, as if she sensed Eva's ulterior motives. Perhaps
she suspected that Eva wished to loosen her tongue. Eva
only hoped Miss Asquith wouldn't deduce that Lady
Phoebe was listening in from above.

"Yes," Eva said in her most solicitous tone. "A friend, a
relative. Surely you don't wish to face this ordeal alone."

"Face what, exactly, Miss Huntford? I haven't done
anything wrong, despite what your mistress might think."

Eva shook her head. "Lady Phoebe regrets what she
said in the billiard room. It was the shock of discovering
Mr. Cameron, nothing more."

"She doesn't like me. No one here does. They want to suspect me because I'm different, because they can't understand me."

Eva took a chance at being overly familiar by perching at the edge of the bed. Leaning slightly forward, she said with a note of earnestness that was not entirely fabricated, "I would like to understand you, Miss Asquith."

"How can you? You occupy the other side of the same coin as your employer. You are part of the old ways, and as far as I can perceive, you are a willing participant. If you truly had any interest in understanding people like Regina Brockhurst and myself, you would not be in the employ of the Renshaw family. At least, not in the capacity of lady's maid."

"Service is all I've ever known, at least since I reached adulthood. As I child I helped out at home, on my parents' farm. But once my brother was old enough to help my father with the bulk of the work, I sought my own livelihood." She smiled fondly. "For a time, I attended finishing school on scholarship."

"For a time?" Miss Asquith shifted her chair to better face Eva. "What happened?"

"My father was hurt. He broke his wrist, a bad break, and I was needed at home. Since there was no telling how long I'd be away from school, my scholarship was awarded to another girl."

"That's unfair. Haven't you grown weary of having the largesse of the wealthy doled out to you as they see fit, when and *if* they see fit?"

"Miss Asquith, there have always been the rich and the poor, and there always will be. It's simply a fact of life, and there is no use grumbling about it."

Miss Asquith's features hardened, and her chin came up. "Isn't there? Perhaps you're wrong about that. Perhaps times are changing. Perhaps the wealthy will no longer control everything and everyone. Will you be ready when that happens, Miss Huntford? Will you know what to do?"

The very air in the room tensed as Eva and Miss Asquith regarded each other. Eva would swear the other woman had quite forgotten herself, had been swept up in a conviction that had left her unguarded and careless, or she would never have said so much. The time for a frank conversation had arrived.

"I won't pretend I don't know what you mean, Miss Asquith. Between things Miss Brockhurst said to Lady Phoebe and a newspaper found burned in her fireplace, and finally the Grekovs' appearance here this morning, I rather believe I have figured out what you are about."

"Then perhaps you're more clever than I gave you credit for." Miss Asquith sat back a bit, looking genuinely pleased. "The question is, are you elated or terrified at the prospect of your servitude coming to an end?"

"Neither." Eva couldn't help emitting a laugh. "For I don't think of myself in such terms. Yes, I am in service. It is how I earn my living. But I assure you, it is my choice, and I am quite content. If I were not, I would seek employment elsewhere, under different circumstances."

Miss Asquith flushed. Her eyes flashed with something bitter, resentful, but only for the merest instant. "Would you indeed, Miss Huntford? And how, exactly, would you go about doing that? Do you believe opportunities for our sex are so numerous they are there for the plucking? Do you believe the average person can travel society's ranks at will in order to better his or her lot in life?"

Eva heard the ridicule in those questions, but she refused to be unnerved. "It is possible. It's happening in ways that didn't exist before the war. Have you heard of Talbot House?"

"What is that?" The question held impatience, as if

Miss Asquith had already dismissed what Eva was about to say. She spoke nonetheless.

"It was a tavern in Belgium. During the war, English soldiers could take their ease there while on leave. The notion of rank didn't exist inside its walls. Officers and enlisted men alike ate, slept, prayed, sang, played cards, and whatever else, side by side. There was no saluting, no addressing anyone as *sir*. Inside the walls of Talbot House, all men were equal."

"Yes, well, the war is over. Surely you don't think that holds true here and now."

"It was a beginning. Gradual changes will continue, and opportunities for our sex are increasing every day." Eva almost surprised herself with her words. A year ago, she wouldn't have thought such things, much less spoken them aloud. But the past months had increased her knowledge of the world, of the people inhabiting it, with all their hopes and dreams, disappointments and foibles. Serving Lady Phoebe, a young woman of singular spirit and determination, had taught her much as well.

"If you think so, then you are a fool, Miss Huntford. As soon as the war ended women were told to leave their jobs and return home to be wives and mothers. The old ways persist. There is only one way to break their hold on this country."

A heavy pause held them in its thrall, while a word seemed to echo between them. Eva gathered her courage to speak it. "Revolution, Miss Asquith? Is that what you wish for our country, after these terrible years of war?"

Miss Asquith pinched her lips together, but her defiant expression spoke of her willingness to see exactly that sort of upheaval sweep through England.

Eva, usually so careful about her own expressions, allowed her true sentiments to reveal themselves in an equal show of defiance. "That is treason."

"By whose definition?"

"I assume not the Grekovs'." She smiled, a gesture filled with irony. "Since it's clear they were *not* hired to clean, one can only conclude their purpose here was to coach you and Miss Brockhurst, and others of your acquaintance, on how to spread socialist ideals throughout the country, and to incite revolution if necessary. That was Miss Brockhurst's plan for High Head Lodge, was it not? To serve as a headquarters for your revolution?" Miss Asquith only raised an eyebrow as if in appreciation of Eva's deductions. Eva frowned. "Tell me, who burned the newspaper? Was it you? It was a socialist publication, wasn't it?"

"Perhaps." The defiance had returned to Miss Asquith's expression, and no further explanation seemed imminent.

"And did you burn it? Did you fear someone would discover your plans?"

"Good heavens, no, it wasn't me. I certainly make no apologies nor try to hide my beliefs." She appeared to consider. "Nor Regina, I shouldn't think."

"Did she share your views? I mean, share them so entirely?" Had Miss Brockhurst wished to see England embroiled in another war, perhaps bloodier than the one fought on the continent?

"Of course she did," Miss Asquith snapped, as if Eva had made an accusation to the contrary. "It was the basis of our friendship."

"And yet the two of you argued frequently yesterday. I heard quite a bit of it firsthand during your shopping trip."

"Friends sometimes argue. What of it?"

"Did you and Miss Brockhurst argue last night, before she died?"

Miss Asquith hesitated so long Eva didn't think she would reply. Or if she did, it would be to tell Eva to mind her business, or get out. But after a moment she said, "We did. She was terribly upset about her family and their accusations, and I didn't help matters when I pointed out that she should not have allowed them to stay."

"Is that all?"

"Should there be more?"

"I simply wondered if perhaps Miss Brockhurst's ideals didn't quite match yours after all, and if she might have had second thoughts. Horrible things have happened in Russia. People have died, and continue to die. Surely the Grekovs have explained it to you."

"Indeed they have." Miss Asquith took on an almost dreamy look. "The October Revolution was a glorious triumph." Her gaze drifted to some point across the room. Then her eyebrows drew together. Slowly, she said, "Thank you for bringing the tray, Miss Huntford. If you don't mind, I should like to rest now."

She came to her feet, prompting Eva to do likewise. She had been dismissed, but she had achieved her main objective in opening the speaking tube. Had Lady Phoebe heard the conversation?

Socialism. Revolution. Treason. Those words and more raced through Phoebe's mind as Olive Asquith's story unfolded through the speaking tube. Cousin Regina a traitor? Or, as Eva insinuated, perhaps Olive's plans went too far for Regina's liking, and Olive murdered her out of spite.

Phoebe had been so sure of Hastings's guilt. The whiskey, the ether—both had left their signature at the crime scene, and both led directly back to Hastings.

Yet she only *supposed* ether had been used in Regina's death. It made perfect sense, a way to incapacitate Regina so she didn't awaken and struggle. Was Phoebe only filling in the details to support her theory? To be sure, she needed access to Hastings and Verna's bedroom.

While these thoughts distracted her, she had been only half aware of Olive asking Eva to leave her. Now the room had gone quiet. Phoebe strained her ears to detect any sound, but none came. She waited another minute. Silence prevailed. Eva should be back upstairs any moment now.

When minutes passed without an appearance from Eva, Phoebe concluded she must have gone below stairs. Perhaps she went to the kitchen to return the tray she had brought to Olive's room. Olive *had* said she wasn't hungry.

She pushed the button to connect to Hastings's room again. The snores has ceased. His and Verna's voices blended incoherently, and then Hastings's became distinct.

"I said get it for me." His diction had cleared of its earlier blurriness. He sounded awake, lucid.

"You've had enough."

"I decide when I've had enough."

"You aren't fit to decide anything." Verna's voice oozed disgust.

Was Hastings demanding his ether?

A crash exploded from the tube. Phoebe flinched, lurching away. Had one of them thrown something? A vase? An ashtray? She crept close again. The voices were once more jumbled and garbled. They were arguing, no mistake. And then Verna, sounding unaffected by the crash, said, "You'd not have been disinherited otherwise."

"I'm not disinherited." Hastings laughed, the sound sharp with mockery.

Verna's voice rose. "He'd most likely be alive, if not for you."

This seized Phoebe's attention more than anything else so far. Breath held, heart thumping, she waited.

"Don't be absurd. I had nothing to do with whatever shock killed him. I wasn't even in the house at the time. It was undoubtedly Regina. Or her little toad of a friend."

"I don't mean this last shock. That's what did him in.

But he'd been ill much longer than that. You know what I'm talking about. Your disappearance three years ago. It nearly killed him."

Verna put emphasis on "disappearance." Sarcastic, sardonic emphasis. Three years ago, Hastings had been captured by the Germans . . .

"Shut up about that. You don't know what you're talking about."

"Don't I, my love? I was with him when the news came. I saw what it did to him. And I know to what lengths he went to save his son."

How could Cousin Basil have saved Hastings? What sway could he have held with the German forces?

"Of course he went to great lengths to save me. It is what a father does, Verna. I fail to see—"

"You may tell your mother and the world what you like, but I know the truth. I know what you are. I know what it did to him."

"Shut up. You'll shut up if you know what's good for you."

Phoebe stood with both hands braced against the wall on either side of the speaking tube, utterly engrossed, almost forgetting where she was, impatient to hear the rest. Were they speaking of Hastings's addiction? Had learning of it nearly killed his father three years ago? But how could Cousin Basil have discovered such a thing while Hastings sat in a German prison? That revelation could only have come later, when Hastings finally returned home.

Disappearance . . .

Phoebe's stomach knotted. She had never questioned Hastings's war service. Had there been some incident Cousin Basil needed to cover up for his son? She longed to talk with Owen. With his extensive contacts he could probably uncover whatever secret lurked in her cousin's past.

That was, if they didn't divulge the truth now. She turned her attention back to the tube, but the voices continued in murmurs now. They must have realized how loudly they were speaking and feared being overheard through the walls.

Phoebe glanced at the clock on the dresser. It was nearly time to go down for dinner. She would go down, plead a headache and, while the others were dining, steal into Hastings and Verna's room to search. She closed the speaking tube.

CHAPTER 15

Phoebe checked her locket watch, hanging from its gold chain around her neck. Then she compared the time to that on the little figurine clock on her bedside table. Both read ten minutes after seven.

Eva should have been there by now ostensibly to help her change for dinner, but in actuality to compare notes on what each had learned while they were apart. Although Phoebe had heard most of Eva's conversation with Olive, Eva still had no idea what Phoebe had overheard between Hastings and Verna.

Both conversations had yielded incriminating details, yet neither had been conclusive. She heard doors opening in the corridor and cracked her own open enough to spy Verna proceeding toward the staircase. Hastings must already have gone down. Judging from this afternoon, she would not have expected him to be awake, much less able to negotiate his way through the house.

The prospect of an empty room tempted her to dash across the corridor now and begin her search. But it wouldn't do for someone to wonder why she hadn't appeared for dinner and come upstairs to inquire after her. Moving in front of the full-length mirror, she smoothed her dress. She wore a pale green chiffon tunic over pink satin, with a beaded sash she only just managed to fasten herself. Without Eva's help, she had swept the sides of her hair up in combs and arranged a simple twist at the back of her head. By formal dinner standards neither the dress nor the coif would have passed muster, but this was no ordinary dinner, not with a killer possibly among the company. Perhaps Eva had returned to her room, was right now listening in at the speaking tube.

Downstairs, Julia met her in the hall, and they walked together to the drawing room. "Have I kept Stanley busy long enough? I'm running out of chores for her to do."

"For now, at least, I believe so. But have you seen Eva? Is she helping Stanley with something? She didn't come in to help me dress."

Julia scanned her with an appreciative glance. "You did well enough on your own."

"That's not the point." Phoebe knew Julia hadn't issued her a compliment, for she had heard the sarcastic quality of her sister's appraisal. "It isn't at all like Eva not to send word if she's detained for some reason. You know that."

"Yes, I suppose I do. Dear Eva." They stopped outside the drawing room door, Julia's hand on the knob. "I didn't appreciate her as much as I should have done. Now I know better."

"What do you mean?" But Phoebe was not to hear the answer. Julia opened the door and stepped inside. Phoebe had no choice but to follow.

Hastings, Verna, and Cousin Clarabelle were all inside, speaking in hushed tones. How small their group had become. Two dead, and Olive locked in her room under suspicion. Phoebe joined her relatives where they stood grouped around the unlit fireplace. This being summer, a lavish floral arrangement would typically have spilled from the empty hearth in lieu of a crackling fire. Instead, nothing hid the charred stone and brickwork or the clawlike fingers of the grate.

"I don't understand why the inspector hasn't released us from this dreadful house yet," Cousin Clarabelle was saying. "How long does he intend holding us prisoner here? We all know who murdered my daughter and Ralph."

"It's not even a full day yet since Regina died," Phoebe reminded her. "And only hours since Ralph met his fate. The police have no solid evidence yet that Olive is guilty of either crime."

"Haven't they?" Verna's gaze shot venom. "What more proof do they need than finding the creature twice standing over the deceased before anyone else arrived?"

"Coincidence," Phoebe said. "Unfortunate timing on Olive's part."

"Unfortunate timing." Hastings scoffed. The tumbler in his right hand tilted; the amber contents nearly spilled over.

"And how are you feeling now, Hastings?" Julia asked brightly. She raised her eyebrows in a show of concern, but Phoebe didn't miss the amusement in the tilt of her mouth. "You were rather indisposed earlier, weren't you?"

"Was I?" He raised the glass to his lips, but if he sipped at all, he did so sparingly.

"You were indeed." In silk and tulle, Julia drifted to an armchair and, like a flower coming to rest on a tuft of grass, sank into it. "As for Olive . . . who's to say the first person on the scene killed poor Ralph? Perhaps it was the last person."

"How dare you?" Verna snapped, and Phoebe remembered that Verna had been the last to arrive, at least a full minute or more behind everyone else. Why? What had caused the delay? Or had she been there first . . . ?

"Or anyone else, for that matter," Julia continued matter-of-factly.

"How would any of the rest of us get in and out fast enough without being seen?" Cousin Clarabelle stood imperiously before Julia's chair. "Assuming Miss Asquith *is* innocent—which I do not—she would have seen the guilty person making their escape."

"Perhaps." Julia drew out the word, allowing it to linger on the air before it faded like the tone of a bell. And like a bell sounding, an idea struck Phoebe.

"What if the guilty person never left the room? What if they were inside the whole time, even when Olive came running in. Behind the door or a chair, in a corner where Olive wouldn't have noticed. Then the rest of us poured in, and that person merely blended in."

Hastings let out a harsh round of laughter. His wife shushed him. "That's quite a scenario you've invented, Phoebe. Bravo. You should be writing dramas for the West End theaters."

"Perhaps the billiard room has a secret passage." Cousin Clarabelle settled into a wing chair. She pinched her lips together, then went on. "Who knows, the house might be riddled with them. Or perhaps there's a mischievous ghost in residence. Really now, we know who murdered my daughter and Ralph, and she is under lock and key, where she should be. No, I misspoke. She belongs at the end of a rope."

But Phoebe had stopped listening after Cousin Clarabelle mentioned a secret passage. Yes, it sounded like something out of a penny dreadful. But old country houses such as this *were* riddled with them, whether they had been built to hide family fortunes during times of unrest, or to hide one's priest during the Reformation. She considered the old turret at Foxwood Hall with its hidden, unused staircase leading up to the servants' quarters on the top floor. As houses were renovated and modernized, often older sections were merely hidden behind new façades.

Her gaze drifted to her sister, who sat frowning in concentration until she met Phoebe's eye. "Perhaps it's worth a look," Phoebe said.

Julia came to her feet. "Perhaps it is."

"Perhaps *what* is," Verna demanded.

"Perhaps there *is* a passage in the billiard room." Phoebe didn't wait for further comment. She heard the others following her, but didn't stop until she reached the billiard room. She hesitated before going in, as if she would be confronted once again by Ralph Cameron's body. But the constable had called in the coroner, and he and his assistants had removed the deceased, although not all evidence of it.

Inside, Phoebe avoided looking at the dried blood that marked where Ralph Cameron had died. Instead, she studied the richly paneled walls. Julia came in behind her.

"Maybe one of the panels opens," Phoebe said to her.

"It would make more sense if this were the library, where a bookcase might swing open. Isn't that how it's done in novels and moving pictures?" The question mocked, but only slightly. Julia went to the wall opposite the door and began sliding her palms over the woodwork. Where moldings met, forming deep, coffered squares, she tried pushing. Nothing happened. Phoebe chose a wall and began doing the same, applying pressure at the seams and mitered corners.

Soon, Cousin Clarabelle and Verna were doing likewise, while Hastings looked on and told them their efforts would yield them nothing. How was he so certain?

And yet, when a quarter of an hour had passed without results, Phoebe leaned with her hands on the rail of the billiard table. Hastings grinned at her. "I told you so."

"I certainly didn't think we'd find anything, either,"

Cousin Clarabelle said. "Though I suppose it was worth checking, just to be sure."

"To be sure Olive is guilty, you mean," Verna added. She took hold of Hastings's arm. "I'm hungry. Let's stop this foolishness and go down."

As the others made for the doorway, Phoebe hesitated. If she went down now, it would look entirely strange for her to suddenly plead a headache during dinner. Slipping a hand around her back, she flicked open a hook on the sash of her dress.

Julia stopped on the threshold. "Are you coming?"

"Oh, I . . . I must have caught my dress on something. I think it tore. I'll just go change and be down in a few minutes."

"Come here, I'll check it for you."

"No, that's all right. I can feel it's torn. You go down. I won't be long."

With a shrug, Julia turned away.

Phoebe waited until the last footsteps faded in the hall below, then sped into action.

The surface beneath Eva's cheek shifted, spinning like a boat without a rudder on heaving seas. Her eyes were closed, the lids thick and heavy. She tried to blink them open but they resisted, as her hand resisted when she attempted to move it. Easier to fall back into oblivion . . .

No. She dragged in a breath, then another in an effort to steady herself and gather her strength. She blinked and this time forced her weighted eyelids to open sufficiently to let the light in, to let a field of gold fill her vision. What was it, gleaming in front of her like late afternoon sunlight, except without any semblance of warmth?

Not sunlight, for as her eyes remained open a pattern slowly took shape, a diamondlike design. She forced her cheek to lift from the woven rug beneath it, gritting her teeth against the dizziness, breathing through her nose, and leveraging her hands beneath her. A bed took shape beside her, draped in gold silk damask.

Miss Asquith's bed, in the room in which Miss Asquith had been locked. Only she wasn't here now, and the person locked in, Eva deduced, was herself. It took her some moments, leaning against the bed, her cheek now resting against the cool sheen of the silk, before snippets of what happened began to filter through her mind. Miss Asquith had been so calm, had dismissed Eva without so much as a blink.

I'd like to rest now . . .

Eva hadn't realized what Miss Asquith had noticed right before she spoke those words. Nor did she notice that, as she approached the door, Miss Asquith bore down on her. How quiet she had been, a model of stealth. A resounding pain had seized the back of Eva's head. Then . . . nothing, until just now.

Again, she drew in breath after deep breath, blowing them out slowly, letting everything inside her find its normal balance. She couldn't rush it . . . except she *must* rush. Where had Miss Asquith gone? Where were Ladies Phoebe and Julia?

Were they in danger?

She closed her fists around the counterpane and dragged herself up along the side of the bed until she could place the flats of her hands on the mattress and push upright. Or nearly upright. The room turned, first one way, then the other, while a tiny drummer inside her skull kept an uneven rhythm. Eva breathed through it, dredging up the patience to wait rather than stumble blindly and risk passing out again.

There. Better. Her head ached but only vaguely. She planned her course. To the end of the bed, then across to the dresser, where she leaned a moment or two, her head down, until steadiness returned, however briefly. Releasing her hold on the beaded edge, she pushed away, moved her feet, and with outstretched arms found the door. Closed both hands around the knob. Tried to turn it.

She had been correct. Miss Asquith had found the key and locked her in. Try the speaking tube? By now, Lady Phoebe would have gone down to dinner, surely. They would all be downstairs now, and if they heard Eva pounding on the door, wouldn't they dismiss it as Miss Asquith trying to gain their attention?

She had no choice, she must try. Every passing moment gave Miss Asquith that much more time to get away. She had to alert Miles.

"Help me," she cried out and beat her fists against the door. "Someone let me out. Miss Asquith has escaped . . ."

Phoebe hurriedly changed into a fresh frock and hadn't finished doing up the buttons in the back before she darted out of her room and across the corridor to Hastings and Verna's suite. Before she could step inside, a pounding held her frozen.

Had she been caught? That made no sense, for if Hastings or Verna had returned upstairs, they would have called out to her, not pounded on the wall. Yet the clamor continued. Phoebe identified the source: Olive Asquith's room. Phoebe closed the door of the suite and moved down the corridor.

"Olive?"

"Lady Phoebe? No, it's me, Eva. I'm locked in. I . . ."

Phoebe jiggled the knob, but to no avail. "I can't open it. Are you all right?"

"Yes, I . . . I'm fine. But Miss Asquith has escaped." Even through the door, her voice sounded shaky, even frail.

"You've been in there all this time? Oh, Eva, what did she do to you? I should have searched for you. I'm so sorry—"

"Phoebe." Eva's voice came stronger, firmer. "Please check with Mrs. Dayton for extra keys. There are sure to be some somewhere. The housekeeper's parlor or the butler's pantry."

"Yes, I'll go now." Phoebe started to hurry away, but Eva called her back.

"Telephone the chief inspector's office first. He and Miles need to know that Miss Asquith has escaped."

"Yes, all right." She pressed her hand against the door, wishing she could see Eva, touch her, to reassure herself that her dear friend was truly all right. "I'll be back soon."

CHAPTER 16

As Phoebe reached the downstairs hall, the sounds of a motorcar pulling up to the house sent her detouring to the front door. She opened it without stopping to consider it might be someone other than the constable and earned a scowl from him as he climbed out of his sedan.

"I thought I gave orders that no one was to admit anyone without first checking to see who it was."

"I'm sorry, Constable. But I guessed it was you."

He climbed the two steps to the front door. "You knew no such thing, Lady Phoebe. That was reckless, especially since the Grekovs have not yet been found."

Unable to argue his point, she changed the subject as she closed the door behind him. "It doesn't matter. It *is* you, and Olive Asquith has escaped. She somehow overpowered Eva and locked her in her bedroom."

"In Miss Asquith's bedroom?" He had moved ahead of her into the hall. Now he swung back around, reaching out but not quite grasping her shoulders. He spoke with urgency. "How did this happen? Never mind. Is Eva hurt?"

"No. At least she said she wasn't. But I've got to find an

extra key to let her out. Go up to her, Constable, and I'll come as soon as I can."

He had already reached the first step as he said, "Hurry."

Phoebe made her way past the dining room, keeping well away from the doorway to avoid anyone inside seeing her. She didn't quite know why she chose furtiveness, but somehow it seemed the most prudent course, for now. Reaching the baize door, she pushed her way through and hurried down the staircase.

Myra Stanley occupied the first room she passed. With a sour cast to her face, the woman stood before an ironing board and hefted a non-electric iron over what looked like one of Julia's shirtwaist blouses. She glanced up briefly at Phoebe but didn't speak. Phoebe moved on, finding the cook and her assistant in the servants' hall.

"Mrs. Dayton, do you know where extra keys to the bedrooms might be?"

Both women came to their feet at the sound of her voice. Mrs. Dayton hastily wiped her napkin across her lips. "We haven't had to use them, my lady, but I believe there are extra sets somewhere."

"Yes, Mrs. Dayton, but where?"

"Hmm . . . Margaret, do you know?"

"I surely don't, ma'am. It's not my place to go looking for the extra keys."

Her impatience rising, Phoebe about-faced and found her way to the housekeeper's parlor. The room housed a wooden settee and a couple of chairs, a writing table, a small bookcase, and a cupboard. Phoebe went to the writing table first and pulled open the drawers. But for some scraps of paper and a few half-used pencils, they were empty. The cupboard came next. She hoped to find key hooks on the back of the door, but only unpainted wood met her scrutiny. The shelves inside didn't yield anything, either. The bookcase? Nothing but a few tomes on house-keeping, a collection of cookbooks, and not much else of interest.

She sprinted to the end of the hall to the butler's pantry. She had not entered this room before and found it soared two stories above her head, the first floor comprising glass-encased cupboards that wrapped around three walls, filled with china dinner service in various patterns. The cupboards above appeared mostly empty, the contents having been cleared out, ostensibly by the house's previous owner. A dumbwaiter and a walk-in safe dominated the fourth wall. Beside them sat a rolltop desk.

Phoebe began searching the desk, opening drawer after drawer, her sense of futility rising. The rolltop loomed before her, but a tug confirmed what she had feared: It was locked.

"And where would the key to *this* be?"

She no longer cared. Doubling back to the kitchen, she scanned the equipment. Pots and pans, some copper, some steel, others of iron, hung from hooks above the center work table. She chose a cast iron skillet, lifted it from its hook, and returned to the butler's pantry.

Unbidden, images of Ralph Cameron's final moments flashed in her mind as she gripped the pan's handle with two hands and raised the heavy object above her right shoulder as though it were a bat. Was this how the murderer raised the andiron before swinging it into poor Ralph's head?

The thought and the accompanying image forced her eyes shut as she swung the pan and smashed it edgewise into the desk's curving tambour. The wooden slats splintered against the weight of the cast iron. Opening her eyes, Phoebe set the pan aside and with her hands broke off the remaining wood and ripped aside the canvas of the rolltop.

"What on earth was that?" Mrs. Dayton scurried into the room with Margaret at her heels. "Lady Phoebe, what are you doing?"

Phoebe reached in, grinning. "Finding keys. The only question is, which are which?" She held several rings in each hand and appealed to Mrs. Dayton. "Any ideas?"

The woman shook her head. Behind her, Margaret did the same.

Myra Stanley appeared in the doorway. "What do you need the keys for, Lady Phoebe? Is it anything to do with Lady Julia?"

Once again, an inner caution advised Phoebe not to reveal the truth. "No, nothing to do with my sister." She almost added the excuse that she had lost the key to her own room, but then remembered that she needn't justify her actions at all. Despite her beliefs to the contrary, there *were* times the privileges of her station came in handy.

She tightened her fingers around the bundles of keys and headed for the door, prompting the other three women to step out of her way. Their curious stares followed her down the corridor.

She wasted no time in returning to the first floor, arriving in time to witness Constable Brannock, helmet and coat removed, heaving his shoulder against the door that separated him from Eva. Phoebe called to him.

"Constable, I've brought keys." She held them out and hastened to him.

Quickly he retrieved his coat and shoved his arms into its sleeves. "Sorry to be out of uniform, Lady Phoebe . . ."

"Nonsense," she replied. "I simply wouldn't want you to break your shoulder. Here. The keys weren't labeled. I can only assume the former butler knew one bunch from another, but I'm afraid we'll have to try them until we find the right one." She moved closer to the door. "Eva, are you all right in there?"

"Quite, my lady. Just eager to be out. I told Miles he should be searching for Miss Asquith, not worrying about me."

"First things first," he murmured, and snatched a random ring of keys from Phoebe. The first few he tried didn't work, and he murmured again, this time incoherently beneath his breath. Meanwhile, Phoebe fell to studying the other sets of keys and devised a theory.

"Here, try these. They're less worn than the others and must not be used as much. That to me suggests they could be the extras for the bedrooms, used only in emergencies."

The constable hesitated a moment, surveying the keys she held out. With a nod he took them from her. On the third try, the latch clicked and the door opened. Eva stepped out into his arms.

Eva found herself crushed to Miles's torso, her cheek nestled in his coat collar—infinitely smoother and more comforting than the rug on the floor had been. For several moments she relished his steadiness, a pillar of protection, and breathed in the deeply earthy scent of his shaving soap.

Something soft and moist grazed her forehead in the gentlest fashion. His lips. They nudged her face to his, until their brows met, and he traced tiny kisses down her nose until he found her mouth and prodded, tempted, and coaxed her response.

A quiet footfall penetrated the enfolding bliss, and Eva lifted her head suddenly. "Oh, my lady, forgive me . . ."

Lady Phoebe was already turning, backing away, but stopped. "No need. I'm just happy you're free and not harmed worse than you were. You are all right, aren't you? You didn't just say that? What did Olive do to you?"

"Yes, what did she do?" Miles repeated, rather more fiercely.

Eva reached around to finger the back of her head. Through her hair, she found a lump that was tender to the touch. But her headache had subsided, and she judged herself to be sound enough. "Miss Asquith hit me with something, I don't know what, but I promise you, I'm all right."

They all peered into the bedroom. There, lying not far from where Eva had lain, a solid glass paperweight reflected the light from the desk lamp. Miles swore beneath his breath. His arms went around her again.

"Miles, I'm all right." With a shift of her gaze she indicated Lady Phoebe.

"Don't mind me," her lady said. "I'll just . . . actually, there is something I must do." She started away along the corridor, increasing her pace as she went.

"Are you quite sure you're all right?" Miles spoke no endearment, yet Eva almost could have sworn she heard one— are you all right, *my darling*—in his tender tone. He cupped her cheeks. "Perhaps we should get you to the doctor?"

She raised her own hands to his, pressing them where they framed her face. "I'm fine, Miles. You needn't fuss."

"Needn't fuss? Needn't *fuss*? The woman attacked you, Eva. She might have *killed* you." His hands left her cheeks, and his arms again enfolded her.

"I'm sure she had no such intention. She merely wanted out of her confinement."

He pulled away, holding her at arm's length. "I don't see how you can be so calm about it. But what exactly happened? I see the tray." Eva looked over her shoulder to follow his gaze to where the dinner tray she had brought still sat on the dresser, the food untouched. "You brought her a tray, and when you turned to leave, she attacked?"

She turned back to him but was unable to meet his eye. "Yes, well, generally speaking."

"What do you mean, 'generally speaking'?" He tipped her chin upward. "Eva, what did you do?"

"I merely went in and talked to her a bit. And learned a great deal, I'll have you know. She's a socialist, or a communist, I'm not quite sure which, and so was Miss Brockhurst. *And* the Grekovs. That's why they were all here, and I expect others would have joined them eventually, and together they would plan how to bring communism to England. I think that's why Miss Asquith decided to escape—because she realized she had revealed too much to me, and then she noticed the speaking tube and—"

Here Miles's frown of disapproval became one of bafflement. "What speaking tube? What are you talking about?"

Eva raised a hand to point into the room. "There, on the wall. The tubes lead to the servants' quarters on the upper floor. Lady Phoebe and I opened them to the bedrooms so I could listen in on conversations and—" She left off, suddenly not quite as proud of their plan as she had hitherto been. Speaking of it out loud now, she heard how underhanded it sounded. As she had initially told Lady Phoebe, if she had been caught in such a scheme at home, she'd have been given the sack immediately.

Judging by Miles's expression, he didn't think much of their spying, either.

She spoke again before he could. "I know, it was most inelegant of us, most deceitful and—"

He raised a finger to her lips to silence her. "It was an ingenious idea. I'm only peeved with you for putting yourself in danger."

His touch left behind a tingle and a trace of warmth. Eve savored the sensation, before saying, "You haven't said if you found the Grekovs."

"No, not yet, I'm afraid. But I have constables in the surrounding villages on the alert. The Grekovs are on foot, so they can hardly go far without being found out." He blew out a breath. "But I must leave again and spread the word about Olive Asquith. It could very well be that wherever the Grekovs are headed, she's going there, too."

"You mean they might have a prearranged meeting place?"

"Let's hope so." His russet eyebrows brows drew inward. "If they're all part of the communist movement and planned to use this house as a headquarters, it's likely there are others holed up somewhere close by, waiting until High Head Lodge was ready for them. Which could make the job of finding them easier. I have to let my associates know about this."

"Miles, is it illegal, what they're doing?"

"It depends on how they go about it. There are no laws against sharing ideas, even ideas that go against our traditions. It's when people start disrupting daily life that they stray into trouble with the law."

Eva nodded, considering. "Then it's possible that Miss Asquith and the Grekovs haven't actually done anything wrong. If they aren't responsible for Miss Brockhurst and Mr. Cameron, that is."

"Running away seems to me an admission of guilt—of something."

Before she could reply, Lady Phoebe's urgent whisper reached them from down the corridor. She stood outside Lord and Lady Mandeville's suite, holding what appeared to be a pint-sized bottle in each hand. "Eva, Constable, come here."

When they reached her, she held out the bottles so they could read the labels.

"Shaving cologne," Eva said, puzzled. "And hair tonic."

Lady Phoebe shook her head and handed the bottle marked "hair tonic" to Miles. "Open it and take a whiff."

He complied, bringing the open bottle close to his nose and then whisking it away. "Ether."

"I thought so," Lady Phoebe said with a nod. At the puzzled look Miles flashed her, she explained, "While you were gone, Hastings became inebriated, or so I believed until my sister said he smelled like a dentist's office." She looked ruefully down at the bottle in her hand. "Sure enough, he hasn't been drinking. He's been drugging himself."

Eva reached for the other bottle and smelled the contents. The odor raised a shiver of repugnance. "Awful."

Miles held the bottle up to eye level. "These were in Lord Mandeville's things?"

"They were among his toiletries in the bathroom. I believe he must have a smaller bottle or other container that he keeps with him."

"Some kind of inhaler, is my guess." Miles tightened the cap on the bottle. "Something that would allow him enough of a dose to produce euphoria without risking unconsciousness."

"Where would he get such a thing?" Eva asked him.

"Any number of places, especially in London. Or it could be homemade," he replied. "It wouldn't be difficult. A vial, with a piece of rubber or metal tubing attached, and a cap to close it off."

"Yes, well, I believe whoever killed Regina used a common handkerchief soaked in ether to drug her so she wouldn't wake up while she was being murdered." Lady Phoebe's expression challenged them to question her theory.

"Incapacitated Miss Brockhurst to make killing her easier." Miles almost sounded impressed. "And quieter. This would explain the lack of signs of a struggle."

"And the whiskey could possibly have been used to mask the odor of the ether," Eva added.

"Yes, but that's not all." Lady Phoebe cast a glance down the corridor and lowered her voice even more. "Hastings has something to hide. I overheard him speaking of it with Verna. Or, rather, she spoke of it. She actually accused Hastings of causing, if not his father's death, his illness. It was something that happened during the war. The timing of it would have been after he was captured by the Germans. Verna said she knew the truth, and knew what the incident did to his father and to what lengths Cousin Basil went to save his son."

"Save him from a prison camp?" Miles narrowed his eyes. "I can scarce believe any amount of English money could have released his son from a German prison camp."

"Then what could they have been talking about?"

"My lady, you said Lord and Lady Mandeville senior didn't seem particularly eager to discuss the details of their son's imprisonment with your grandparents."

"No, they claimed it was too painful."

"Too painful," Miles said with a canny look, "or too shameful?"

Lady Phoebe flashed a puzzled frown. "What do you mean?"

"I mean, Lady Phoebe, that perhaps your cousin wasn't taken prisoner at all." Miles gritted his teeth until a muscle in his cheek bounced with tension, and his lips pulled back in disgust. "It wouldn't be the first time a family paid to have reports changed and certain incidents covered up."

Lady Phoebe shook her head. "I'm afraid I don't understand."

Eva placed a hand on her shoulder and spoke gently. "I believe what Miles is saying, my lady, is that rather than having been taken prisoner, your cousin might have . . ." She hesitated, searching for the least brutal way to term it. "Might have turned his back on his duties."

Lady Phoebe's mouth dropped open, and her eyes widened in horror. "Desertion?"

"I'm sorry, Lady Phoebe, but yes, quite possibly." Miles spoke gruffly. He fisted a hand and pressed it, unconsciously, it seemed to Eva, against his thigh. "This certainly changes things. Makes me wonder if Miss Brockhurst knew the truth about her brother and threatened to use it against him. Had he been caught during the war, he would have been court-martialed and shot. He could still be prosecuted."

Lady Phoebe blanched. "And shot?"

"I doubt that, but he'd be ruined, wouldn't he?" Miles held the bottle up to the light of a wall sconce and studied its contents. "Still three quarters full. I don't suppose it takes much to produce the desired effects."

Even as he seemed to dismiss Lord Mandeville's war service, Eva sensed his lingering rancor in the jut of his jaw and the harsh, seething light in his eyes. Patriotic fervor? Or something more personal? Miles rarely spoke of his time in the war, and his reticence had once been a source of contention between them, a barrier that prevented her from truly knowing him. She had believed the barrier gone, dissolved, but clearly there existed a side to him that remained a stranger.

For now, she let the matter go but with a vow to revisit the subject soon. She said, "Lady Phoebe and I talked earlier about who might know of Lord Mandeville's addiction. His wife and his mother, and even Miss Asquith might have known, for she stayed at their London house weeks ago with Miss Brockhurst. Any of them might have used the ether against her."

"Up until this moment, Olive's escape made her look guilty." Lady Phoebe's comment seemed to quiver in the air. Surely they were all thinking the same thing, that Hastings

Brockhurst, the disgraced son and disinherited brother, harbored enough bitterness and resentment to compel him to commit murder.

Lady Phoebe raised her chin. "Olive is a communist and a radical, to be sure, and that may be why she ran away, because she fears her politics will be held against her, and she'll be wrongfully charged with murder. But as I listened in through the speaking tube earlier, she didn't *sound* like someone who murdered two people." She paused, sighing. "Eva, I'm sorry I didn't listen more closely. I might have heard what she did to you, might have realized . . ."

"No, my lady, you couldn't have. I was in the room with her, and I didn't hear her sneak up behind me." Eva raised a hand to her head, once again feeling the tender lump.

"Still and all, I'm very sorry."

Miles cleared his throat. "You should both be sorry. Neither one of you should have been in that room with Miss Asquith without someone else, namely me, nearby to make sure she didn't do exactly as she did."

Lady Phoebe looked stricken, and Eva experienced a stab of guilt. "We're responsible for her getting away, aren't we?"

Miles took the other bottle from her. "Don't worry, she'll be found. For now, I'm putting these back. Let's pretend we never found them, that we don't know what Lord Mandeville is up to, or that anyone else might know his little secret." Then, to Lady Phoebe he said, "Tell me where you found them."

"Why don't I just go and put them back?"

"Because you're to go down and prevent anyone from coming up until these are safely stowed away and I've prepared my next step. Does anyone else know about Miss Asquith's escape?"

Lady Phoebe shook her head. "I don't believe they have any idea, actually. Not even that you're back."

"Good, let's keep it that way. I'm going to relock Miss Asquith's bedroom door as well. As far as anyone is to know, she's still safely under lock and key."

When Phoebe returned to the ground floor, she found the others had left the dining room and adjourned to the drawing room.

"What kept you so long? We were growing worried about you," Verna said as she entered the room. Her tone expressed more boredom than concern.

"I wished to get that dress to Eva immediately." She joined them where they sat grouped near the south-facing windows. The evening twilight hovered in gray shadows over the gardens, and Phoebe marveled that they had discovered Regina only that morning, and Ralph that afternoon. Mere hours ago, yet it seemed like days.

"Is a tear in a dress worth missing dinner?" Cousin Clarabelle obviously didn't believe so, not the way she presently eyed Phoebe up and down.

"It's a favorite dress, and I wasn't very hungry anyway." She shrugged despite her rumbling stomach. "I'll have something later."

"Well, while you were tracking down your maid, we came to a decision," Cousin Clarabelle announced. "We are going to ring up the chief inspector and inform him we are not going to spend another night in this house."

"But he hasn't given us permission to leave," Phoebe pointed out.

Cousin Clarabelle's nostrils flared. "Are we going to be ordered about by a civil servant?"

"I should think not." Hastings, his legs stretched out before him, crossed his ankles and slouched in a slovenly manner.

"We aren't safe being in the same house with a killer," Verna said. "Even if she is locked in her room. How do we know she won't figure a way out? Why, she might even know how to pick locks. Her kind typically do."

Hastings agreed with a halfhearted nod. "She's probably waiting for the right moment."

"And how do we know those odd foreigners aren't in on it with her?" Cousin Clarabelle, becoming animated, sat up straighter. "They've run off, but what's to keep them from returning to slit our throats?"

She went on, with Hastings and Verna chiming in every now and again with their agreement and their own theories. Phoebe watched them all closely. How much did they really know about Regina's activities? And which, if any of them, might be the most alarmed to discover a member of their own family aiding the spread of communism?

Cousin Clarabelle, to her credit, had never been an ardent social climber. Phoebe supposed that, as the wife of a peer, she had been secure enough in her place in the social pecking order not to worry overmuch about scratching her way higher. Still, she had always been scrupulous in maintaining the family's dignity, so much so that at first, she had opposed Hastings's marriage to Verna, whom she had deemed beneath them. How would Cousin Clarabelle feel about her own daughter's joining the ranks of the Marxist reformers and compromising the family's long-held Tory stance?

Phoebe shifted her attention. Slender, angular Verna, with her prominent nose and weak chin, hailed from gentry whose lands near Birmingham had been chipped away during the last half century until they owned little more than the original house with a few outbuildings and truncated gardens. Still respectable, yes. But from the upstairs rooms of the house, one could look out over the roads, rowhouses, and railroad depot where once had been forest and farmland. Verna had come into the Brockhurst family with a long list of desires, chief among them living in a style to which she longed to become accustomed and taking what she perceived as her rightful place in society. Phoebe had once overheard Grams remarking such to Grampapa. Having a communist in the family would surely stem the tide of invitations during the London season, and Verna would have been horrified by the thought. Not to mention, doing away with Regina brought Hastings back into his inheritance.

Hastings . . . She contemplated her cousin while he grunted half-intelligible responses to his mother's and Verna's debate over who would likely slit their throats first, Olive or the Grekovs. Hastings, an ether addict . . . and a deserter? She wished she could dismiss the possibility, wished the queasiness the word evoked would go away, but considering the latest argument she had overheard, well, the facts seemed to fall into place. Then she thought back on last night, on the other argument she'd overheard between them. Verna had goaded Hastings, all but accusing him of not being a man. Had she pushed him to his limit? Struck some chord deep inside him that spurred him to action?

Yet there was still one person to consider who was not presently in the room: Myra Stanley. Phoebe still believed Miss Stanley had reason to either fear or resent Regina; perhaps both. And since Regina's death, Miss Stanley had become much more relaxed.

Of course, they couldn't entirely rule out Olive Asquith or even the Grekovs. A piece of information, or perhaps several, continued to elude them. If only she had been able to meet with Ralph Cameron. She felt positive he had died knowing the identity of Regina's murderer and had himself died for his pains. What had he learned? How had he learned it?

She turned her attention back to the conversation, focusing on what Cousin Clarabelle was presently saying. "We've been waiting for that inept constable to return, but since he shows no likelihood of doing so before morning, we've no choice but to take matters into our own hands by telephoning the chief inspector. Now." She clapped her hands together. "Who wants the honor?"

The three Brockhursts eyed one another. No one spoke up. Cousin Clarabelle's gaze drifted to Julia. "What about you? You're a local resident, you must know the man. And he'll heed the demands of the Earl of Wroxly's granddaughter."

With a huff, Julia pulled back in her chair. "I'm not telephoning anyone. Chief Inspector Perkins is hardly likely to listen to me. If anything, he'll tell me to mind my business and stay put until he says otherwise. Which I think perhaps is the wise course in this instance."

"The wise course?" Cousin Clarabelle reddened with outrage. "*Wise* course? Are you mad?"

While the others fell to expressing their opinions, Phoebe thought, *Good for Julia.* She wholeheartedly agreed with her sister that they should remain at High Head Lodge until the killer was identified, whether it be Olive or Hastings or someone else. The easiest way to do that was to keep everyone together, where they could all be observed. If they were to scatter now, Constable Brannock's job would become that much more difficult.

"But if you're all set on leaving," Julia went on as if her last comment hadn't created verbal chaos, "perhaps Phoebe would achieve better results with the inspector than I would."

What? Phoebe did a double take as the others ceased their banter to listen. She pointed to herself. "Me?"

Julia smiled sweetly at her.

"Oh, yes, Phoebe, do ring up the inspector for us. Surely you don't want to remain here in this awful house." Cousin Clarabelle gave a dramatic shudder.

"I really don't think the inspector will listen to me any more than he would Julia."

Cousin Clarabelle didn't bother to hide her annoyance as she turned her attention to Hastings. "Then you do it. You're Lord Mandeville now. He'll have to listen to you."

He started as though just awakening from a nap. "Who are we talking about?"

"The chief inspector," Verna said between her clenched teeth, then added in a whisper, "Idiot."

A sudden idea brought Phoebe to her feet. "All right, I'll go. Perhaps he'll allow us to go to Foxwood Hall."

"Oh, do you think so?" Cousin Clarabelle's entire demeanor changed. The irritation smoothed away, leaving her the picture of hope and reason. "Foxwood Hall would be lovely. I should very much enjoy visiting with your grandparents. Do convince him, Phoebe, dear."

Phoebe crossed to the doorway. "I'll see what I can do."

CHAPTER 17

Miles slipped out of Lord and Lady Mandeville's suite after replacing the containers of ether in their rightful places and quietly closed the door. With a hand at Eva's elbow, he escorted her to the end of the corridor, to the door that opened onto the service staircase. They stepped in onto the landing and spoke in hushed tones, both of them well aware of how sound traveled in stairwells.

"I want you go back to listening in, please, Eva."

Without stopping to think of the wisdom of her action, she reached out, grasping his wrist and tugging up his sleeve a bit. Months ago, she had noticed the aviator's watch he wore, but when she asked him about it, his answer had been terse at best and not really an answer at all.

His gaze followed hers, and they both regarded the large dial with its prominent numbers and faint green glow. His lips compressed, and the breath that went out of him murmured of resignation.

She released him. "Miles, please tell me."

He didn't at first meet her gaze, but stood with his head down, his shoulders hunched. She feared he wouldn't answer and half wished she had said nothing, or at least left the matter for some later date. She had once believed Miles hadn't served in the war at all. Irishmen hadn't been compelled by law to fight, and she had considered him too whole, too unaffected to have seen battle. Yet, with time, she had realized his wounds were not physical, but buried inside him, deeply, in a place he kept protected at all times.

She started to apologize. He spoke at the same time. "I flew with the Royal Flying Corps throughout the war. I flew bombers across enemy lines, targeting strategic sites." He looked up, finally, and smiled, a tight gesture so filled with pain she nearly stepped back. As it was, she held her ground, waiting silently for him to continue. "Do you know that in the early years, there were no guns mounted on our planes?"

She shook her head. She hadn't known that, hadn't thought about it before.

"We'd fly back and forth, we and the Germans, each dropping his load on some target far below, and then, on the way back to the airfields, as we'd pass one another in the air, we'd wave." He let out a laugh. "Wave. Can you imagine it? Time after time, bombing factories and towns, only to wave hello to the enemy afterward. As though passing a friend on the street."

He pressed his fingertips to his brow. "I counted myself lucky. What an easy time of it I had. A gentleman's war, or so it seemed from the sky. Until . . . well. Finally, they fitted out the aircraft with guns, and that ended our friendly encounters with the enemy. After one mission . . ." He fell silent, exhaling. Eva didn't dare speak a word as she waited. "After one mission, I sustained some damage and was forced into an emergency landing behind enemy lines, close to my last target. Quite close. Too close. And for the first time, I saw."

"Saw what?" Eva whispered back.

"The village I'd destroyed," he said softly. "I'd been told I was targeting a munitions factory. What I hadn't been told was that this factory was in fact surrounded by a village. A village I destroyed. I don't believe a soul was left alive."

"Miles . . ."

"The worst of it is, I continued flying missions. Knowing what I knew, I continued dropping my loads—on villages, on human beings. On children."

"It was war," she whispered urgently. "You had no choice."

He nodded, his face filled with bitterness. "I did my duty."

"You did."

"And now you know." He gave himself a visible shake and squared his shoulders. "I have my duty now. Come."

And with that, he drew back into himself, shutting the door on that protected place inside himself. He became the policeman once more: brisk, efficient, focused.

She should not have distracted him; should not have succumbed to her own need to know his secrets. Yes, she had pondered these matters for months, had wondered and devised theory after theory about what he so obviously kept hidden, what he had not wished to discuss. As he had said, now she knew. But did her knowing serve any good purpose for him? She feared that, in her quest to know him better, she had opened a wound in his soul. A sense of shame filled her, but, like him, she set it aside for now. She too had her duty to perform. "What are you going to do?"

"Is there a telephone below stairs?"

"Yes, in the housekeeper's parlor."

"Good. I need to let the chief inspector and others know that Miss Asquith is on the run. Then I'm going to double around to the front door and pretend I've only just arrived. My plan is to claim the coroner found traces of anesthetic in Miss Brockhurst's system, along with prints pointing to a suspect."

"Fingerprints?"

"I'll be vague. It could also mean bruising in the size and shape of someone's hands."

"Won't they guess you're bluffing?"

"Perhaps, perhaps not. Typically, the guilty party won't wish to take chances. I'm hoping whoever it is will go running upstairs to do away with any incriminating evidence— the handkerchief or whatever was used in administering the ether to Miss Brockhurst, and whatever small vessel was used to steal some of Lord Mandeville's stash."

"Unless Lord Mandeville himself did the deed."

"Unless. In which case, it'll be his lordship who scurries upstairs."

Eva thought of something. "Myra Stanley is below stairs, and you mustn't let her see you. Remember, she's a suspect, too."

"Could she have known about the ether?"

"Yes, easily. If Miss Brockhurst knew about her brother's habit and discussed it with Lady Diana, Myra could have overheard and saved the knowledge for when it presented an opportunity for her. And there is little doubt she felt threatened by Miss Brockhurst."

"All right, then." Miles paused, tight ridges forming between his eyes. He grasped her shoulders. "How certain are you that Olive Asquith did not kill Miss Brockhurst? I know you can't be entirely sure, but what do your instincts tell you?"

He held her gaze with such intensity she was taken aback, and for a moment she couldn't form an answer. After she had just forced him to speak of an unspeakable horror, he still trusted her—so much so the responsibility of what he was asking overwhelmed her, even frightened her. What if she was wrong about Olive? What if the woman was such a good actress she had fooled Eva completely?

But no, Miss Asquith hadn't acted, hadn't put on any pretense, had she? While she had maintained her innocence, she hadn't pleaded or cajoled. She had merely stated her case. And though Miss Asquith had revealed rather more about her political plans than perhaps she meant to, she had made no apologies for her convictions. Surely, if she had sought Eva's sympathies in order to convince her of her innocence, she would have guarded her tongue more carefully.

She compressed her lips, and then said with as much assurance as she dared, "I believe she is innocent of murder, Miles. You are right in that I can't be entirely certain, but my heart of hearts tells me she did not kill Miss Brockhurst or Mr. Cameron."

"All right, then." His confidence in her left her humbled, grateful, and rather awed. He seemed not to notice her bewilderment as he continued planning out loud. "I'll hold off going below stairs to use the telephone. Perhaps I'll have you go downstairs, so that when I 'arrive,' you can go below and have Miss Stanley come up and join the others. I'll make my announcement, and then see who scatters and where they go. That's when I'll need you back in your room, listening in."

"Yes, all right. How will you leave without being seen?"

"Don't worry, I'll get out. You just wait about ten minutes and find some excuse to go downstairs. A question for Lady Phoebe, perhaps. I know it's unusual for lady's maids to be in the main section of the house, but under these circumstances I doubt anyone will think twice about it."

She nodded. "I daresay you're right."

"Are you ready?" He gave her hand a squeeze, and she smiled.

"Ready."

Phoebe hurried to the telephone in the rear hallway before any of the others decided to follow her. Actually, she hoped one of them would, and quite expected it, just not until she put her plan in motion. To that end, she didn't waste a moment in picking up the candlestick telephone, while keeping a finger on the receiver cradle to prevent the operator from being summoned.

"Yes, please connect me to the Little Barton Police Station." She waited, listening to the sound of approaching footsteps, female ones, indicated by the clatter of heels. When she judged them close enough, she said, "Chief Inspector Perkins? This is Phoebe Renshaw. Yes, I'm still here at High Head Lodge. Yes, we are all still here, just as you ordered." She pretended to listen, peeking down the corridor. A moving shadow appeared around from the corner, growing larger as the footsteps became louder. Phoebe turned her attention back to the telephone. "What we are wondering, Inspector, is whether we might leave High Head and go, all of us, to Foxwood Hall. Yes, I understand, Inspector, but—" She pretended to be interrupted, tapped her foot, sighed, and then continued, "But we'd all be in one place should you need to question anyone . . ."

The approaching figure turned the corner with a swirl of plum tulle. Julia. With an ironic expression, she slowed but continued toward Phoebe.

Phoebe debated whether to end her pretense, but then remembered she had no ally in her sister. "Yes, Inspector, I understand. I'll let the others know. They won't like it . . . Yes, Inspector." Carefully, she released her finger from the receiver cradle and set the earpiece onto it.

"The others sent me to check up on you. Or rather, when they squabbled over who should do it, I volunteered." Julia halted, her arms crossed her chin at a tilt. "It's no good, is it?"

"I'm afraid not. The inspector won't be budged."

"Did you try offering him a bribe?"

Phoebe chuckled. "No." She moved away from the telephone table. Julia reached out to stop her.

"You didn't ring him, did you?"

Phoebe's pulse jumped. She schooled her features not to show her surprise. "You just heard me speaking to him."

"I heard you speaking. I heard you being very polite and oh so reasonable."

"So . . . ?"

"So you don't speak to Chief Inspector Perkins in that way. You don't take pains to hide your impatience with the man's inanities. Rather, you talk to him as a teacher speaks to a particularly difficult student." Julia smiled sweetly. "What are you planning now?"

Did Phoebe dare take her sister into her confidence? She had helped with the speaking tube plan, but beyond that she hadn't offered much in the way of assistance. And how would she react to the possibility of Hastings having committed treason? Would she lash out at him? Make cutting remarks? Now wasn't the time for that.

She settled on revealing the least possible information. "If I *had* called the inspector, do you think he would have allowed us to leave?" She shook her head. "I thought pretending to call the best way to prevent the others from dashing upstairs to pack their things."

"Is that all?"

"Yes, that's all."

Still smiling, Julia declared, "I don't believe you. I believe you and Eva have something new up your sleeves, and I want to know what it is."

"Julia, leave it alone, please. Once this is over, I'll tell you everything. But right now . . . even I don't know the full plan. You see . . ." She obviously had to tell Julia something to placate her, to prevent her from causing trouble with the others. With a glance behind her down the hallway, she leaned closer and lowered her voice. "Constable Brannock returned a little while ago. Whatever the plan is, it's his to implement."

"What about Olive? Why doesn't he take her to the police station?"

Phoebe swallowed, once again schooling her features not to give anything away. No one knew yet that Olive had escaped her room. "He's not convinced Olive killed anyone. He has a plan to test that theory."

Julia's smile flattened, her lips thinning to a line of displeasure. "And I suppose he eagerly took you and Eva into his confidence."

"No. I just told you I don't know the full extent of what he intends to do."

"Oh, you know more than you're willing to admit. Saint Phoebe, always around to save the day. To save us mere mortals from the pitfalls of our own mistakes."

Julia turned to retreat down the hallway. Phoebe reached

out and caught her elbow, and Julia spun around, her face filled with anger.

"What is it?" Phoebe demanded. "What on earth have I ever done to you to make you treat me this way?"

For several endless seconds Julia said nothing. Would she answer? Or would she turn back around and walk away? Phoebe regarded those deep, dark blue eyes, filled with a storm of emotion; she scanned her sister's beautiful features, contorted, almost twisted with something approaching rage, yet surrounded, as always, by the halo of bright golden hair so like that of a Renaissance angel.

"What is it, Julia?" she repeated in a whisper. "What wrong have I done you?"

Julia's nose flared; her eyes narrowed. "You are who you are."

Disappointment surged even as her heart plummeted. "Yes, I'm who I am. As you are you. What does that mean?"

"It means . . ." To Phoebe's astonishment, Julia's chin quivered. She turned her face aside, swallowed, and drew in a breath. When she again faced Phoebe, her composure was back in place. " 'We'll leave colors and fabrics to your sister. I have some new ideas I wish to share with you, cousin.' "

"What?"

"I heard you and Regina talking last night. You didn't realize I'd stopped playing the piano, did you?"

Baffled, Phoebe said, "Actually, I did notice. But why be angry at me for something Regina said?"

"Because it's always the way of it, isn't it? Oh, we'll trust Phoebe with the important things. Running the school. Catching the killers. Meanwhile, we'll let Julia decorate the house. We'll give her lots of lovely clothes to keep her quiet and marry her off at the earliest opportunity."

Phoebe stepped back, shocked. "It's not that way. Grams expects all of us girls to marry, Amelia and I as much as you. You're not the only one. And as for running the school, if you had taken an interest last spring . . ."

"You don't understand."

"No, I don't." Phoebe raised her hands, as if Julia could fill them with answers. "Please help me to."

"Perfect Phoebe," Julia scoffed, her lips curling.

"Me? *You've* always been the perfect one. I've always lived in your shadow. Why, the two of us could enter a room at the same time, wearing identical gowns, decked out in identical jewels, and no one would notice me. Only you. It's always been that way."

"Yes, pretty Julia."

"Beautiful Julia," Phoebe said fiercely. "Clever, smart, witty Julia. No one ever says such things about me. Never. Yet . . ." Earnestness softened her voice. "I don't hold it against you. I never have. I never would."

Julia turned away again, and her voice came hard and coarse, as if it were ripped from her innermost self. "I heard him that day."

Phoebe blinked. "Heard who? What day?"

"Papa," her sister said without meeting her gaze. "Before he went off to the war. By the willow tree. You and he were walking together, talking. I was beneath the tree, and I was about to come out and let you both know I was there. But then he said it."

"Said what, Julia?" Phoebe spoke very softly, as if, like a timid deer, Julia might bolt at any moment.

"He said—" She turned back to Phoebe with a stricken look. "He said you must watch over everyone. The family, the servants, even the villagers. You, he said. Because there was no one else. Fox was too young, Amelia too soft-hearted, and Julia, he said . . ." Her lips stretched, quivered, pulled tight. "Julia is, well . . . *Julia*, he said. As if that single word, my name, summed up all that is useless and frivolous and *undependable*. Oh, but not you. Not his Phoebe. He would leave you in charge because he trusted his Phoebe."

She remembered that day. How could she not? It was her last deeply personal conversation with her father before he left Foxwood Hall—and their lives—forever. She remembered the pride that spread through her at his words. Yes, he had said those very things, just as Julia repeated them—except without the resentment. Without the judgment. He had loved Fox and Amelia, and he had loved Julia. Oh, how he had loved his beautiful, eldest daughter. Phoebe knew it. He had loved them each for who and what they were. If Phoebe had been his dependable child, Julia had been, as her name implied, his treasured jewel, his star in the night sky. Beside her, Phoebe had always known she paled.

And yet, Phoebe *had* felt singled out that day for possessing qualities that perhaps her siblings lacked. Perhaps Papa's confidence in her *had* swelled her head, led her to believe she was somehow better than the others, and perhaps Julia had sensed this and had sought a way to shield herself from feeling inferior by one-upping Phoebe at every turn.

It explained so much of the past several years . . .

"Julia, I'm sorry if—"

"Never mind." Julia's tone had lightened, sounded carefree, or almost. "It's my problem, not yours. One I must learn to live with."

"How can you say that when—"

Julia's back was already to her as she retreated down the hallway, leaving Phoebe with her words unspoken, but resounding loudly in her heart.

We are sisters and the problem is ours, to be solved together.

*   *   *

Eva was just coming down the stairs when Lady Julia clattered her way across the front hall and entered the drawing room. A moment later, Lady Phoebe came from the same direction from which her sister had come, but while Julia's expression had been unreadable, Eva plainly saw the unhappiness in her mistress's eyes. She hurried down the remaining steps.

"My lady, what's wrong?"

Lady Phoebe said nothing at first but clutched at Eva's hand. Eva thought she saw tears welling, but Phoebe blinked adamantly and said, "I know why she hates me."

The resignation, the sheer acceptance in Lady Phoebe's voice, gripped Eva's heart. "Lady Julia doesn't hate you. I'm sure she doesn't."

"No, I believe she does. In part, anyway. A part of her loathes a part of me, the part my father valued most."

"No, you mustn't think so."

"She just told me, spelled it out for me as clearly as you please."

Before Eva could respond to that, the door knocker sounded outside, three clangs that sent echoes bouncing through the hall. Lady Phoebe jolted. Eva hastened to reassure her.

"It's Miles," she whispered. "Part of his plan. Just play along."

Lady Phoebe nodded. Eva went to answer the door, unbolting it from the inside. The others filed out of the drawing room, the dowager first, followed by her son and his wife, then Lady Julia.

"What is that racket?" the dowager demanded.

Miles answered her question by stepping inside.

"Well, it's about time you returned," the dowager declared in a voice that resounded through the hall nearly as loudly as the door knocker had. "Have you come to tell us we may all finally leave this horrid place?"

"No, Lady Mandeville." Miles removed his police helmet. "No one may leave just yet."

"Why not?" The dowager's gaze found Lady Phoebe. "Didn't you call the chief inspector?"

Eva noticed Lady Phoebe's hesitation, the glance she darted at her sister, as if waiting for Lady Julia to speak up. Finally, she said, "I did. I was just coming to tell you all that his orders are for us to remain here for now."

"Oh, that insolent man. How dare he—"

"Lady Mandeville," Miles broke in. "There have been developments."

"Well then, out with it." Lord Mandeville gripped the door frame beside him.

Miles strode toward the drawing room. "If you will all please come inside and have a seat, I'll explain. But first . . ." He turned to Eva with an air of authority. "Miss Huntford, will you please have Miss Stanley join us?"

"Yes, sir." As soon as Eva had pushed through the baize door into the service hallway, she proceeded at a run. She didn't want to miss any more of the conversation in the drawing room than necessary.

Downstairs, Myra Stanley stood in front of the range, watching the flames dance beneath a kettle. A porcelain teapot and mug sat on the work counter beside her.

"Myra, we're both needed upstairs."

A weary face turned in Eva's direction. "I'm worn out. Can I not have my tea first?"

"No, Myra. The constable has returned and wants to see everyone in the drawing room. Now."

"You've no idea what I've been through these past hours. Lady Tyrant seems eager to put me in my grave. Just a half cup of tea is all I ask."

Eva went to the stove, extinguished the flame, and took a firm hold of Myra's wrist. "Don't ever let me hear you speak of Lady Julia with such disrespect again. Now come."

Back upstairs, the tension in the drawing room lay as thick as cold butter. Miles had everyone grouped near the hearth. Eva and Myra took seats a little behind the others. They did so out of deference to their stations, but Eva longed to be where she could see everyone's faces when Miles presented his "new evidence."

Verna Brockhurst said, "May we get on with it?"

"Whatever *it* is." The dowager fanned a hand in front of her face.

"The cook and her little assistant aren't here," Hastings Brockhurst mumbled. "Cute little thing, the assistant."

His wife, sitting beside him, swatted his arm. "Do keep quiet, Hastings."

"Now then." Miles stood tall in front of the fireplace. "I'll get right to the point." With a look at the dowager, he said, "I'll try to be as gentle as I can, my lady. I do understand how distressing this is for you and your family."

"Thank you." The dowager drew herself up and crossed her arms before her.

"The coroner has discovered traces of an anesthetic in Miss Brockhurst's system. Enough to have rendered her incapacitated, making the killer's job easier."

No one said anything. A strained silence filled the room, seeming to hold the Brockhurst family immobile. A telling sign? It was Lady Phoebe who finally spoke.

"What kind of anesthetic?" She made a good job of sounding puzzled.

"We believe it might be ether, although further tests will be necessary to confirm that. However, there is more. Bruises were found that, again with further tests, may be matched to an individual."

Verna Brockhurst coughed. "Yes. Olive Asquith."

"Perhaps." Miles paused. "But perhaps not."

Silence prevailed once again. What Eva wouldn't have given to be standing beside Miles, where she could read expressions. He seemed to be studying his audience one after another, and she also wished she could read his thoughts. She did, however, steal a sideways glance at Myra, who didn't look particularly alarmed. Did that make her innocent, or a good actress?

"Is that everything?" the dowager asked with a sniff.

Miles nodded. "At the moment, my lady, yes. You're all free to move about the house again. I'll be conducting another search of the bedrooms, however, so I'll have to ask you all to stay out of them."

The dowager, on her feet now, turned to him with a scowl. "For what reason?"

"To search for the anesthetic used against your daughter, ma'am."

The woman's mouth moved, at first no sound coming out. Then she uttered a single word. "Oh."

As soon as Miles formally dismissed everyone, Myra Stanley hurried back to the baize door. Eva followed, pretending to have an errand below stairs, but in fact she only wished to confirm Myra's destination. Myra noticed her following and paused briefly on the stairs.

"I intend to finally have my tea. Please, if Lady Julia asks for me, tell her you don't know where I've gone." A hint of desperation shone in her eyes. "Please, Eva. I've done everything she's asked me to do. Is a cup of tea too much to ask in return?"

"I don't suppose so." Perhaps Eva should have taken pity on Myra and allowed her to enjoy her tea without further incident, but she had questions for the woman that burned to be answered. It was lady's maid to lady's maid, and Myra had her own insolence to thank for it. Eva continued down, meeting Myra at the bottom. "Tell me the truth. Did you sell secrets about Lady Diana to the press? And have you done the same to Lady Julia?"

A tide of scarlet engulfed Myra's face from neck to hairline. "I, er, what makes you ask such a thing?"

Eva pulled back slightly to better view her. "I believe your complexion has answered my question. It's true, then. How much did they pay you?"

"It is not true. I will not stand here and be accused of betraying my employers." She turned and walked briskly toward the kitchen. Knowing she had limited time, for Miles wanted her back up on the third floor listening at the speaking tube, Eva followed her.

"The countess telephoned earlier, Myra. She asked to speak to Lady Julia."

Myra stopped short. She kept her back to Eva and said nothing, staring down at the floor.

"That's right. Mrs. Sanders found a gossip rag with Lady Julia's name in it. Tell me, how do you think it got there?"

Myra peeked around at Eva, her face still aflame. "What . . . what did it say?"

"I'm not going to repeat what it said, but it did put Lady Julia in an awkward position with her grandmother."

"And Lady Julia believes it was me who blabbed about . . . whatever it is?"

"Let's just say she is hard put to imagine who else might have done so."

"Oh, but that isn't fair. It could have been anyone at Foxwood Hall. It could have been—"

Eve strode so close to the woman she could almost feel the heat emanating off her. "It wasn't *anyone*, was it? No one has as intimate knowledge of a woman as her lady's maid." Eva took on an almost bullying tone. She loathed doing it, but would put off feeling remorseful, or perhaps even apologizing to Myra, until later. Lady Julia's well-being was as stake, and if Myra had betrayed her, Eva wouldn't let it happen again, not if she had the power to prevent it. With her hands perched on her hips, she said, rather than asked, "It was you, Myra, wasn't it."

"I . . . You don't understand. You don't know what I've gone through."

"Then perhaps you should tell me."

"Have you ever been poor, Eva? Truly poor?"

Eva frowned as a surge of indignant anger swamped her. "Yes, in fact I have. My father is a farmer, and we have known good years and bad, and very bad. Calves lost, blights that destroyed grazing land and cattle with it, severe drops in prices—oh, yes, Myra, I've been poor. But that never prompted me to cheat or betray or sacrifice someone else for my benefit."

Myra's face became a mask of rage. "I didn't hear tell of the workhouse in that little tale, Eva. Didn't hear how you, your mother, and your four brothers and sisters—the ones that lived out of the original seven, mind you—were tossed out of your cellar flat and forced into the work-house for the next five years. You talk about sacrifice. You don't have the first idea. Have I cheated and betrayed to make sure that never happens to me again?" Her voice had lost its lady's maid refinement, tumbling headlong into the guttural inflections of East London. She closed the space between them until her chin nearly touched Eva's as she thrust it forward. "Yes, I have, and I've a tidy nest egg laid by, so if Lady Julia gives me the sack, at least I won't go hungry."

Eva stared back into Myra's stormy gaze, unable to gather a reply. Myra laughed, a single bitter note. "Go ahead, run and tell Lady Julia. I'll get by. But first I'll have my cuppa."

She continued to the kitchen. As she rounded the corner of the doorway, the cook stuck her head out from the servants' hall. "What was that about?"

Eva gripped the banister and climbed the stairs.

CHAPTER 18

Phoebe stood beside Eva in her attic bedroom. Through the speaking tube, scuffling sounds came from Hastings and Verna's bedroom, familiar ones, for Phoebe recognized the sounds of someone rummaging through Hastings's toiletries case, as she had done earlier. The only question was who—Hastings or his wife?

They couldn't tell by the footsteps which of them had entered the room, for the individual had taken pains to walk softly. Her gaze connected with Eva's. They both shrugged.

"Miles should be in Olive's bedroom by now," Eva whispered.

"I hope he managed to slip in without anyone realizing Olive is gone." Phoebe whispered as well, though there was no one overhear them. According to Eva, Miss Stanley was safely below stairs, enjoying a cup of tea. She nodded to Eva, who pushed the button to connect with Olive's room.

"Miles, are you there?"

A moment passed, and he replied, "Yes, I'm here. Thought

I'd have a good look through Miss Asquith's things. No sign of pilfered ether or any fabric carrying the smell."

Phoebe leaned in to speak. "Good. There is someone in my cousin Hastings's room. We can't tell who."

"Thank you," was all the constable said before breaking the connection.

Phoebe nodded again, and Eva switched the connection back to the suite shared by the married couple. They heard a muffled knock on the door, then a creak as it opened.

The constable's voice burst from the speaking tube. "Lord Mandeville, you shouldn't be here."

It was Hastings—Hastings who had murdered his own sister. This didn't surprise Phoebe. In fact, she mouthed to Eva, "I knew it."

No, she was not surprised, but dismayed, to be sure. Had it been the money alone that drove him to it? Or Verna's goading, and the need to appear a man in her eyes? Was Verna entirely innocent of the crime, or had she known? Had she encouraged her husband to cross the hall last night?

Phoebe had little doubt the truth would come out soon enough.

The talking from below continued.

"Do you always simply walk in on people, Constable?"

"What have you got there, Lord Mandeville?"

"This? It's nothing. Merely my shaving cologne." Hastings spoke as a man of his station typically addressed those he considered beneath him: with undisguised disdain and an air of superiority.

Eva clutched the mouthpiece with such force, Phoebe feared she might break it. She touched Eva's hand, bringing her attention to the undue pressure.

"Sorry," Eva murmured. They both hovered closer over the device, each with an ear tilted toward the receiver.

"And what were you doing with it," the constable asked. "You don't appear to need a shave."

"Don't be daft. Of course I don't need a shave. I'm merely organizing my things. As you know, we hope to leave this house as soon as possible."

"But I asked all of you to remain downstairs while I searched the bedrooms." The constable maintained perfect calm. "Had you forgotten, Lord Mandeville?"

"Search all you like, Constable." The laugh Hastings emitted sounded forced, artificial. "You shan't bother me."

"May I see that bottle, my lord?"

"No. Er, I mean to say, why would you wish to see my shaving cologne?"

"To verify that it *is* shaving cologne, my lord."

"Are you calling me a liar?"

"Lord Mandeville, if you please . . ."

There were footsteps, steady ones followed by stumbling ones, and something falling over and hitting the floor. Eva gasped and pressed a hand to her mouth. Her eyes widened in alarm, and before Phoebe could stop her, she darted from the room.

"Eva, wait." But she knew Eva would not. Had it been Owen Seabright confronting a murderer, and Phoebe heard the sounds of struggle, she'd have run to help, too. For half a moment she stood poised to follow, but the voices at the other end of the tube held her still.

"Please put that down, my lord."

"Leave my room, and I will put it down."

"Lord Mandeville, what you're doing is exceedingly ill advised."

Phoebe held her breath. What was Hastings holding? Some kind of weapon? A makeshift one like the andiron he used to kill Ralph Cameron?

Eva . . .

This time Phoebe didn't hesitate but set off running downstairs, neither slowing on the steps nor when she burst through the door separating the service stairwell from the main portion of the first floor. Her heart surged to her throat when she saw that the door to Hastings's room stood open. Eva had already gone inside. What had Hastings done? Had he swung his weapon, fired a gun—no, she would have heard the report. Thrown a knife?

Panting, she reached the doorway, catching herself by gripping the frame. The scene inside astonished her. On the floor lay Hastings, with the constable sitting on his chest, leaning to pin his arms to the rug. Eva stood some several feet inside the room, and as Phoebe looked on, she stooped to pick up a bronze figurine, about a foot long, of a man in Roman garb holding a sword. A weapon within a weapon.

"Are you both all right?" she cried.

"Yes, thanks to Eva." The constable didn't look up or release his hold on Hastings. "If she hadn't opened the door and distracted his lordship here, I might be the one sprawled on my back." He eased off slightly. "Has the fight quite left you, my lord? If I let you up, will you promise to behave?"

"Yes, yes, now get off me, you swine."

"If I were you, Lord Mandeville, I'd hold my tongue." The constable slowly removed his hands from Hastings's shoulders, keenly observing his quarry as he did so.

"I'm still holding this." Eva held the figurine up with two hands. "If pressed, I will not hesitate to use it."

As the constable assisted Hastings to sit up, he turned his face aside. "Phew. How much have you had recently?"

Phoebe crossed the threshold. "You're talking about the ether, aren't you, Constable? Oh, Hastings, what did you think all this would bring you?"

Hastings took the constable's offered hand and slowly came to his feet. "I've done nothing, Phoebe. This buffoon is mistaken."

The constable spoke, echoing her exact thoughts. "How can any of us possibly believe you when you came running up here at the first opportunity to hide your bottles of ether?"

"Obviously, I didn't wish them to be found." Hastings rubbed the back of his hand across his chin. "I knew they would make me appear guilty—and they have."

"Only because you tried to hide them before the constable could conduct his search." Phoebe shook her head with a grim smile. "Actually, you fell right into his plans. Didn't he, Constable Brannock?"

"He certainly did. I knew someone would race upstairs the moment my back was turned, so I pretended to search Miss Asquith's room until someone did. Until *you* did, Lord Mandeville. Now turn around. I have to cuff your wrists."

Hastings made no move to turn. "I didn't kill my sister. Or Ralph. I may need my ether from time to time—"

Phoebe snorted. Hastings scowled at her.

"From time to time," he continued, "but I'm no murderer. I swear it."

"Then who did kill them, cousin?" Phoebe raised her eyebrows in genuine curiosity as to whom he would accuse. "Your wife? Your mother? There is no one left."

"Yes, there is. There is still that dreadful little Olive person."

"Could she have gotten hold of your ether?" the constable asked.

"She might have done. Who knows? Why don't you go ask her?"

Why, indeed. Phoebe wondered how far Olive had gotten, and if she had been apprehended yet.

The constable regarded her cousin. At first Hastings returned his gaze with a defiant one of his own, but then he blinked and looked away. Telling? He was acting awfully composed for a man accused of murder. That raised a niggling doubt about their conclusion. Perhaps it had been Olive after all. Both she and Hastings had behaved in incriminating ways. Did guilt guide their actions or fear of being wrongfully accused?

Phoebe moved before her cousin, looking up to meet his eye. "I'd like nothing more than to believe you, Hastings. Truly. But I think this isn't the first time you've lied, or failed to take responsibility for your actions."

His eyes narrowed. "What the devil do you mean?"

She drew in a breath and continued before she changed her mind. "Your war service."

"What about it? What are you implying?"

"You say you were captured, but is that the truth?"

"Why, you little . . ." His hand snaked out. Eva cried out a warning, and Phoebe jumped back. At the same time, Constable Brannock seized Hastings's wrist, and then the other one, and yanked both behind her cousin's back.

"You're in enough trouble, my lord, without adding assault to the list."

Hastings made a snarling sound in his throat, but the fight drained from his limbs. The constable released him but remained close. Hastings said, "I don't know where you got that abominable notion, Phoebe. Of course I was captured. I was held for months."

"Then why did Verna speak not of your capture but of your *disappearance*, and how it nearly killed your father three years ago? She said you may call it what you wish, but she knew the truth. What truth did she mean, Hastings?"

As feverish color suffused his face, Phoebe watched his expression plummet into shame, then confusion, and finally sheer rage. "You were listening in," he charged. "How? Where were you? Were you hiding somewhere in this room?" He began looking all around him, his gaze encompassing chairs, alcoves, the doorway into the bath. And then his searching eyes lighted on the speaking tube apparatus on the wall. His mouth slowly opened. "Why, you . . ."

Constable Brannock took hold of him again, his hands wrapping around Hastings's elbows from behind. "You are under arrest, my lord. Come willingly, and this will go much easier for everyone. Think of your mother, sir. She is downstairs, oblivious to what is happening here."

Once again, the resistance drained from Hastings's figure until he practically sagged against the constable. With a sigh that ended in a groan, he put his hands behind his back and allowed the constable to secure the cuffs on his wrists.

As the constable walked Hastings into the corridor, Phoebe went to Eva's side. She still held the figurine, cradling it like a baby in her arms. "He might have killed Miles with this."

Phoebe studied the piece, realizing the damage it might have inflicted. Hastings might indeed have killed the constable, just as the andiron had killed Ralph Cameron. "What exactly happened? Constable Brannock said you distracted Hastings."

"That's right. I opened the door, and your cousin looked away from Miles long enough for Miles to shove him and wrestle this out of his hands." She placed the Roman swordsman on the nearest bureau. "But it wasn't all that difficult for Miles, I don't think. His lordship seemed to move sluggishly, without any true vigor. I believe even if I hadn't come along, Miles would have overpowered him."

"The ether in his system slowed him down."

"Which would explain, my lady, why he would have

used the ether to subdue Miss Brockhurst before murdering her. If she had fought back, he might not have been able to carry out his plan."

Phoebe ran her hand over the statuette, the etchings cold beneath her fingertips. "How could Hastings, rendered slow and uncoordinated by his addiction, have swung that andiron at Ralph Cameron, a man who was for all appearances the picture of robust health?"

"Surprise, my lady. Mr. Cameron hadn't been expecting it."

"Yes . . . But had the constable been expecting Hastings to wield that figurine?"

"I'm not sure I follow. Miles is a trained officer of the law. His instincts are honed. Mr. Cameron's would not have been." Eva's eyebrows went up suddenly. "I nearly forgot. I had a brief conversation with Myra Stanley before meeting you upstairs in my room a little while ago. It quite convinced me she had no hand in Miss Brockhurst's death. Not that she is an innocent—quite the contrary. But her offenses aren't so much illegal as immoral. Of course, it's a moot point now that Lord Mandeville has been arrested."

High-pitched wailing traveled up the stairs. Phoebe and Eva both went still, and then Phoebe said, "Verna and Cousin Clarabelle will have just learned of Hastings's arrest. Let's go down, or Constable Brannock might not make it out of the house unscathed."

Lady Julia stood at the half landing, one hand on the bannister while she gazed down at the fray taking place in the front hall. Her mouth slanted ironically. She and Phoebe traded bemused looks, at which Lady Julia shrugged. Phoebe continued down and Eva followed her, directly into the sort of family battlefield ladies' maids avoided at all costs. Verna

Brockhurst had plastered herself to the front door, stance wide, arms outstretched, with an expression that defied Miles to attempt to move past her.

The dowager, on the other hand, had both hands wrapped around her son's upper arm, even as Miles maintained his hold on the man's other arm. Hastings Brockhurst stood between them like the rope in a tug of war. Each time his mother yanked, Lord Mandeville swayed precariously, threatening to take all three of them to the floor.

"My lady, if your son is innocent, he will be set free," Miles assured her.

"Of course I'm innocent, you dolt."

"He's done nothing." His mother kept tugging, and Lord Mandeville kept wobbling. "Let him go. Release him at once."

"You've got the wrong man," his wife shrieked for good measure.

If only Eva could slip away to her sewing and ironing and jewelry polishing. She had little experience in witnessing the crumbling of upper-crust English dignity and stood with her hands folded at her waist and her gaze focused on the far wall. Really, since she could do little to help Miles in his present dilemma, perhaps she might simply slip away, either back up the stairs or through the baize door.

Coward. The least she could do was remain and bear it and provide a bit of moral support to Miles, albeit in silence. Lady Phoebe, however, attempted to put her diplomatic skills to good use.

"Cousin Clarabelle, please listen to reason. The constable has good cause for his suspicions." Phoebe put an arm around the dowager and attempted to ease her away from her son. "But as he said, if Hastings is innocent, he'll go free. Better to allow him to go for questioning than worsen matters by making . . . well . . . a scene."

"A scene? A *scene*?" The dowager stood firm, her hands remaining locked as tightly around Lord Mandeville's arm as the handcuffs around his wrists. Perhaps more so, for he winced as she applied pressure. "I'll give you a scene. If Hastings must be questioned, let him be questioned here. And where is that little guttersnipe, Olive Asquith? *She's* the guilty one. Constable, I insist you bring her down here, snap the cuffs on her, and remove her at once."

Eva, Phoebe, and Miles exchanged glances. The dowager noticed.

"What are you three hiding? Where is Olive? Why isn't she being arrested instead of my son?"

"Olive is . . ." Lady Phoebe hesitated for the briefest instant. ". . . No longer here, Cousin Clarabelle."

The dowager's grip on her son visibly eased, if only a fraction. "You mean she's already been arrested?" The question met with silence, which the woman interpreted incorrectly. "Then why is my son also being arrested? Surely you cannot believe them to have conspired together. Hastings wouldn't deign to speak to the likes of Olive Asquith, much less form a diabolical plan with her."

Lord Mandeville's wife came away from the front door. "Yes. If the guttersnipe is already in custody, why are you treating my husband in this abominable manner?"

Miles responded swiftly. "Because there are questions he needs to answer. And because after learning that the coroner discovered an anesthetic in Miss Brockhurst's system, Lord Mandeville scurried upstairs to hide the ether in his possession." He raised in eyebrow in silent question to both women.

The younger Lady Mandeville gazed at her feet and shuffled them for good measure. The dowager coughed. That left no doubt in Eva's mind they had both known of Lord Mandeville's addiction.

"In effect," Miles went on, "the use of your son's ether in the crime makes him either guilty or a possible accessory."

"Ridiculous." Lady Mandeville's frown belied the bravado in her voice. "Hastings, did you have anything to do with Regina's death?"

"Of course not. As I keep telling the constable, I had nothing to do with it. She was my sister, for heaven's sake."

"There." Lady Mandeville made it sound as though the case had been solved. "He didn't do it. He's a gentleman. A peer. You may take his word for it."

Eva detected Miles's effort to contain a laugh. "I'm afraid not, my lady. Now, I'm very sorry, but you'll have to excuse us."

The younger Lady Mandeville burst into tears as Miles walked her husband out the front door, but something in her manner reminded Eva of the tears of a toddler pitching a tantrum, rather than those of a distraught and loving wife. The dowager, arguing with each step, kept hold of her son all the way out to the motorcar, where Miles had to physically pry her free. Even the revving engine failed to drown out her threats to have Miles fired from his position and brought up on charges.

As the motor faded into the distance, the dowager dragged herself back into the house. She closed the door behind her and sagged against it, sliding all the way down to the floor. Lady Phoebe went to her, crouching to put an arm around her. "There, there, Cousin Clarabelle. It'll be . . . well . . . it will work out. You'll see."

"I fail to see how," the woman wailed.

Verna Brockhurst moved like a sleepwalker to the stairs and sank onto the first step. Wrapping her arms around her knees, she hugged them and stared vacantly into space.

"We'll be ruined. *I'll* be ruined. No one in society will ever speak to me again."

Eva stared at the woman in disbelief. *That* was Lady Mandeville's foremost concern? Then her gaze drifted away, only to land on the baize door as someone pushed it open from the other side. Myra Stanley stepped through. How long had she been there, listening? An uneasy sensation crept through Eva, and she started toward the other lady's maid.

CHAPTER 19

Eva took Myra by the arm and drew her into the shadows beside the baize door. "What are you doing in this part of the house? You know you have no business here unless you've been sent for."

"And how do you know Lady Julia didn't send for me?"

"Did she?"

Myra's smirk was all the answer Eva needed. "You were listening in, weren't you? More fodder for the scandal sheets?"

Myra raised her nose in the air and started to turn away, but Eva, still holding her arm, gave a little squeeze. Myra turned back with a glower. "And why shouldn't I? These Brockhursts aren't innocent victims. They're horrible people, the worst kind, and they don't deserve respect."

"That's not for you to judge."

"Isn't it? They're the sort that takes advantage of everyone, especially those less well off. People like you and me, Miss high and mighty Eva Huntford."

Eva wanted to disagree, vehemently, but couldn't gather the words or the energy. Myra was right about the Brockhursts, but that didn't justify her plans to air their private troubles publicly. Soon, not only the scandal sheets but respectable publications as well would splash the Brockhursts' shame across their front pages.

"And anyway," Myra went on, "you as good as told me I'll be getting the sack. I might as well go with my pockets well lined."

"It's wrong, and someday it will catch up with you."

"You needn't worry about me, Eva. I shall be more than fine."

"You foolish woman. You could have had a very secure future at Foxwood Hall." Eva and Myra both flinched at the voice, and turned to find Lady Julia standing within feet of them, a scowl attempting but not quite succeeding in marring her lovely features. "You could have become a valued member of the household, and when I marry, you would have come with me to my new home as part of the senior staff, second only to the housekeeper. Now where will you go?" She ended on an almost amiable note, her held tilted, her perfectly groomed eyebrows raised in a show of concern.

"My lady," Eva whispered. She should not have confronted Myra here, where they could be overheard. Where they *had* been overheard. It was as much a breach of a lady's maid's honor as Myra's betrayal of secrets. "I'm so sorry."

"For what, Eva? For revealing Stanley's true nature to me? Not that I didn't already have ample notion of her treachery. Oh, yes, Stanley, when my grandmother called to tell me she read my name in a magazine, it didn't take long for me to guess where the story originated. And to think you came so highly recommended. What won't I say to Lady Diana next time I see her . . . Well." She turned on her heel and made her way into the drawing room. Myra retreated through the baize door as fast as her feet could take her.

"What shall we do?" Cousin Clarabelle clutched at Phoebe's shoulders with shaky hands. "If only Ralph were here. Ralph would fix this. He'd know exactly what to do. He'd have that constable out on the street by morning."

Not if it was Hastings who murdered Ralph, Phoebe thought. She attempted to disentangle herself from Cousin Clarabelle's grip. "Come now, why don't we go into the drawing room and have a bit of brandy. It will help steady you."

"I know what to do. Call your grandfather. He'll know what is to be done. Oh, Phoebe, would you?"

"Yes, I will. Let's just get you up off this chilly floor. Come, Cousin Clarabelle. This isn't doing you any good, and certainly doing no good for Hastings."

Cousin Clarabelle allowed Phoebe to help her to her feet. "I suppose you're right. You're such a dear, Phoebe. And so sensible. You always were the steady one."

Even with all that happened, Phoebe winced slightly at the praise and hoped Julia hadn't heard, for it would only chafe the wound that lay between them. As she and Cousin Clarabelle crossed the hall, Phoebe noticed Verna sitting and crying at the bottom of the stairs. She reached out a hand to her. "You come, too, Verna. Please. You can't stay there all alone."

Where *had* Julia gone? She had been standing at the half landing when Phoebe and Eva came down. Back to her room? She was surprised to find her in the drawing room, where Phoebe brought the other two women, one on each arm.

"Julia, help me, please."

Her sister regarded her blankly. "What can I do?"

"Help Verna onto the sofa and pour her a brandy while I tend to Cousin Clarabelle. I fear they are both in shock." As she spoke, Eva appeared at Cousin Clarabelle's other side and slung an arm around the woman's waist.

"I'll help, my lady. Come, ma'am, we'll make you comfortable here on the settee."

Moments later both women sipped brandies while staring into the empty hearth. Eva left for a few minutes and returned with a blanket for each of them. Phoebe tucked the blankets around them, wishing she knew what to say to soothe them. Her gaze kept straying to Eva, standing off to one side, as if Eva could somehow silently transmit advice on how to handle the situation. Suddenly, Cousin Clarabelle sat up straighter.

"Phoebe, you said you'd call your grandfather."

Julia stood. "I'll go. It's about time Grams and Grampapa learned what happened here. And I can't imagine we're still required to stay on. The police have made their arrest."

Cousin Clarabelle raised a hand to her mouth and sobbed. Verna gaped at Julia, obviously aghast at her insensitivity.

"I'm sorry." For once Julia sounded earnest. "I'll . . . er . . . go make that call."

"Oh, my son. My darling son." Cousin Clarabelle placed a palm against her cheek, which gleamed with perspiration. "I'm feeling faint. Phoebe, dearest, help me upstairs. I need to lie down."

"Are you sure you can make it?" Phoebe asked.

"Yes, please help me up."

Phoebe offered both hands to help Cousin Clarabelle to her feet. Eva came around the settee to offer her assistance, but Cousin Clarabelle waved her away. "No, you stay with Verna until Julia returns. When she does, go below and have Mrs. Dayton make tea. Phoebe will be sufficient to help me upstairs."

Each with an arm around the other, Phoebe helped Cousin Clarabelle up the stairs and to her room. She expected to stay with her, but as soon as Cousin Clarabelle had stretched out on the bed and Phoebe pulled the bedclothes up over her, she waved Phoebe away.

"I'm exhausted. I wish to sleep now. Perhaps I'll wake up to find this has all been a horrid nightmare, and my child—my *dear* child—will still be here with me . . . will still be my sweet boy . . ."

"Are you sure you don't want me to stay with you?"

"No, I'll be all right now. Wake me when your grandparents arrive. I'm quite sure they'll rush right over once they've talked with Julia."

"Yes, you're probably right."

"Oh, Phoebe?" Cousin Clarabelle already sounded drowsy.

"Yes, Cousin Clarabelle?"

"Olive hasn't been arrested, has she?"

Phoebe sighed. "No, she hasn't. The truth is, she managed to escape her locked room. But I'm sure she'll be found soon."

Cousin Clarabelle, her eyes closed, nodded. "And then my Hastings will come home."

Phoebe leaned over to kiss the other woman's cheek, then left the room and closed the door behind her.

As the latch clicked, so too did something in her mind. Cousin Clarabelle had said she hoped to awaken and find her dearest child still here . . . her sweet boy . . .

Not her *children*. Her *child*. All her concerns centered around Hastings. What about Regina? Didn't she yearn to awaken and find her daughter still alive? And what of Ralph Cameron, on whom Cousin Clarabelle had leaned for both legal and emotional support?

She stopped dead center in the corridor, thinking. Regina—Clarabelle—Ralph. The three had seemed intricately linked, a trio of affections and resentments and, between Regina and her mother, a power play of sorts.

She continued to her own bedroom, wondering, as she had yesterday, what had been going on between the three of them. *Had* Ralph divided his affections between mother and daughter, not as a loyal family friend, but as a lover? Had Cousin Clarabelle truly been as incensed as she had seemed about Regina taking her dragonfly hat pin? Or had Ralph's obvious regard for Regina and his influence over her been what sent Cousin Clarabelle into a rage?

Of course, these were questions that would likely never be answered. Still, Phoebe couldn't banish them from her mind. She paused at her door but didn't go in. Instead, she kept walking, her feet taking her as if of their own accord to the billiard room. Good heavens, so much—so very much—had happened since her arrival here. Years from now she would look back on these events and hardly believe they took place in just over twenty-four hours. Surely days had passed. Just this afternoon Ralph Cameron had asked to meet her here . . .

Why? *What* had he wished to tell her? That he knew Hastings had murdered Regina? How had he reached that conclusion? The last time Phoebe had seen Ralph alive, he'd been poring over books and papers in the library. Documents to do with the inheritance, he had said. Or had she assumed? She couldn't quite remember. But . . .

What if one of those documents had revealed something about Hastings—perhaps a document concerning his disappearance during the war. Desertion? Based on his reaction to Phoebe's accusation, it certainly seemed so. Perhaps Ralph had come upon some documentation from the army hidden among Cousin Basil's papers, and this had led him to—to what? Believe Hastings killed his sister? Or had Ralph discovered Hastings's ether addiction? But no, she didn't believe Ralph hadn't known about it previously.

These thoughts ran through her mind as she did a circuit of the room. She stopped beside the billiard table, arrested by the sight of the stains on the parquet flooring. She had refused to look this way earlier, when they had searched the room for a secret door, but now she found her gaze drawn to the spot. A shiver rippled through her. Ralph's blood. The andiron had been removed, probably when the coroner's men carried out the body. The roman statuette flashed in her mind. Yes, Hastings proved his ability to snatch things and attempt to use them as weapons. But how had Hastings known that Ralph had discovered his guilt? He had written the note to Phoebe, to be delivered via Margaret, the kitchen maid. She had dropped the note, and possibly Valeria Grekov had read it. The Grekovs, both still missing. But what link could possibly have existed between the Russian couple and Hastings?

She turned to face the doorway and tried to remember who had already been in the room and who had entered behind her when they discovered Ralph. Olive had been inside, that much had been obvious. Miles entered next, followed by Phoebe and Eva. Then, she remembered, Hastings appeared, with Julia and Myra Stanley running in behind him.

That left Cousin Clarabelle and Verna. Which had entered next? She paced, thinking, while the awful memory of Cousin Clarabelle lamenting over Ralph rang out in her mind.

When had Verna come? Yes, Phoebe remembered now. It

had been a few moments later. That accounted for everyone. But it didn't explain how Hastings had gotten in and out of the room quickly enough to avoid being seen by Olive Asquith. They had all heard the thud of the andiron and come running.

All except Verna, who had lagged behind the rest. Had Verna been somehow involved? But that still wouldn't explain how Hastings had managed to slip in and out without being seen . . .

Unless he had never left the room. Phoebe studied the room again. When she admitted to having overheard the argument between Hastings and Verna, Hastings had assumed at first that she had been hiding in their bedroom. His scrutiny had darted to the various chairs, alcoves, and doorways that might have concealed her—because he had done exactly that after killing Ralph. They had searched the room for hidden passages. How silly. It was not nearly as complicated as that. He must have ducked behind a piece of furniture, perhaps one of the wing chairs, or even behind the open door, and then simply stepped out as the others began arriving. In the confusion, who would notice that he hadn't rushed down the corridor like everyone else?

But how to discover what Ralph had wished to reveal to her? An idea spurred her into the corridor.

Lady Mandeville the younger had spoken nary a word since the dowager and Lady Phoebe left the room. Adhering to the rule of speaking only when spoken to, Eva had taken up position to the side of the settee where her ladyship sat staring into space, on hand if needed but otherwise inconspicuous. That suited her, for she wouldn't have had any notion how to comfort Verna Brockhurst, especially when it seemed the woman's social prospects concerned her more than her husband's heinous actions or his likely fate.

The muffled ringing of the telephone interrupted her musings. Moments later Lady Julia returned. "Eva, that's the constable on the line. He'd like to speak with you." When Eva hesitated with a glance at Lady Mandeville, Julia nodded. "You go. I'll stay with her." To Lady Mandeville, she repeated, "I'll stay with you now, Verna."

Eva lingered another moment. "Did you speak with your grandfather?"

A change came over Lady Julia's expression, one that raised a vague sense of apprehension in Eva. "No, I didn't. I spoke to Grams and explained what has happened here. Grams was horrified, of course, but—" She broke off and nipped at her bottom lip. She lowered her voice, as if to spare Verna Brockhurst unpleasant details. "Oh, Eva, Grampapa's physician is there. He's been having chest pains. Grams can't possibly tell him about Regina's murder, nor anything else about this dreadful day. She wants us home immediately and is sending the cars to collect all of us."

"Yes, of course we must go, my lady." Eva spared a glance at Lady Mandeville, who continued staring into space and gave no sign she'd heard any of Lady Julia's news from home. "I'll go speak with Miles, and I'll tell him—*tell* him, my lady, not ask—that we are leaving High Head Lodge."

Lady Julia nodded and took a seat beside Lady Mandeville on the settee. Long strides brought Eva to the rear hallway, where she seized the ear trumpet in one hand and the candlestick base in the other.

"Miles, we are all leaving immediately for Foxwood Hall. Lord Wroxly is ill. We'll take the two Ladies Mandeville with us."

There was a brief pause, and then Miles said, "That's

fine, Eva. You're all free to leave. I only called to tell you the Grekovs were apprehended in the next village. In Bradford. They're being questioned as we speak."

"That's good news. What about Olive Asquith?"

She could almost see him shaking his head. "There is still no sign of her."

"Well, I'm sure she'll turn up soon."

"No, when I say no sign, I mean absolutely no sign. Nothing. People saw the Grekovs fleeing through the fields and the outskirts of town there. They left enough of a trail that could be followed. Miss Asquith seems to have vanished into thin air."

"That's impossible. It's dark now. Something will turn up in the morning."

"I hope you're right. I'm coming back there soon. I want to poke through Lord Mandeville's possessions again. Will you still be there when I arrive?"

"If you come soon, then yes. Lady Wroxly is sending the cars for us, but we still need to pack and prepare to leave." She was about to hang up, but a thought held her still. Once she returned to Foxwood Hall, she would once more be swept up in the day-to-day duties of caring for Ladies Phoebe and Amelia, not to mention Lady Julia again, until she found a new maid. It might be some time before she found the liberty to see Miles again. "Do hurry back," she said. "I'd like to see you again before we go home."

Pausing to listen and hearing nothing to indicate either someone coming up the stairs or Cousin Clarabelle exiting her room, Phoebe let herself into the bedroom and closed the door behind her. Rich greens and blues surrounded her, dark hues made deeper by the evening gloom. She forewent switching on the overhead light. It would be too easily seen beneath the door outside. Instead, she went to one of the bedside lamps, turned the shade to angle the light against the wall, and flipped the switch.

The sight of Ralph Cameron's dressing gown hanging over a chair nearly drew a gasp. As more of the room took shape in the dim light, she spied his shaving kit on the silent butler, a leather-bound journal on the nightstand, a pair of house shoes on the floor near the armoire. It was as if he had just stepped out and would return at any moment: a life brutally interrupted, cut off in the middle, with so much left undone. The breath left her, and she leaned against the bed as she groped for equilibrium.

When she could breathe normally again, she picked up the journal. As she had expected, here were no secrets divulged to the creamy pages, but merely lists of appointments and tasks to be completed. There were so many of them . . . so very many to which he would never attend.

She went to the desk, but this too proved unenlightening. No, what she sought would not have been left out in the open for anyone's eyes to happen upon. Ralph Cameron would have been more careful than that. She tried the armoire next, opening its doors and shoving aside suits and shirts. A leather-covered portmanteau sat against the back wall. Phoebe lifted it by its handle, having to use two hands due to its heft.

She set the case on the bed and tried the clasps. They were locked, as she had expected. Ralph Cameron would do no less with his clients' personal affairs. She studied the locks and wondered if a hairpin would do the trick. Eva had taught her how to unlock doors this way. Sometimes it worked, sometimes it didn't. But hairpins were for discretion's sake, and here, Phoebe felt little need for discretion. She wanted only answers.

Glancing around the room, her gaze lighted once more on the shaving kit. A chilling memory from last Christmas nearly arrested her intensions. Still, she crossed the room, opened the kit, and extracted the straight razor. Thank goodness Ralph hadn't opted for a safety razor, for that would have made her job more difficult. With the straight razor clutched in her right hand, she returned to the portmanteau and one by one slashed through its leather straps. When the case opened, she reached in and drew out several thick cardboard folders stuffed with papers.

Good heavens, she hadn't counted on having to pore through so much. With little other choice, she carried the stack to the desk and switched on a second lamp.

She didn't know how long she hunched over page after page, hoping she would find whatever she sought before her grandparents arrived or before Cousin Clarabelle rose from her bed. Some folders bore no relevance to the Brockhurst family. Those she set aside. But each member of the family had a folder of his or her own, including Cousin Basil. She opened Hastings's first. Her frustrations mounted with each page that offered no new information. She found no mention of his military service during the war. Had she expected to? If Cousin Basil had taken such pains to convince everyone that Hastings had been captured by the Germans, he'd hardly have supplied his solicitor with details to the contrary.

Who next? Her fingertips glided over the front of the folder marked "Clarabelle Brockhurst," then slid past onto the one marked for Regina. Phoebe picked it up and opened the cover. Nothing at first caught her eye as being significant.

And then her breath caught. Hands trembling, she held up a letter written in Cousin Basil's own hand, which she recognized from letters he had sent to Foxwood Hall. As she scanned the contents, her heart pulsed wildly beneath her breastbone.

Cousin Basil had feared for Regina's welfare, indeed had predicted an attempt on her life. Had Ralph known? Or had he only discovered this letter, perhaps today? Is this the thing he had wished to tell her?

She needed Eva. She needed the constable. She needed to get downstairs without delay.

CHAPTER 20

Cousin Basil's letter in hand, Phoebe slipped back out into the hallway—and nearly walked into Cousin Clarabelle. Startled, she whisked the hand holding the letter behind her.

"Cousin Clarabelle. Er . . . what are you doing up?"

"I couldn't sleep and thought I'd go down." She eyed Phoebe as she moved closer, making her feel pinned to the door behind her. The letter felt cold and stiff in her fingers, a message from the grave. She willed Cousin Clarabelle not to notice, to continue to the stairs. But she made no move to go. "What have you got there, Phoebe? And what were you doing in Ralph's bedroom?"

She tried to back away, hitting the door with her spine. "I . . . nothing . . ."

Cousin Clarabelle, her features impassive, seized her arm and yanked it forward, hurting her, jarring her elbow and shoulder. She ripped the letter from her grasp. At the same time, a bitter odor surrounded Phoebe. Cousin Clarabelle raised an ether-soaked cloth to her face, pressing cruelly. She tried not to breathe it in, but a sickly taste filled her mouth, her nose, her lungs. The chemical swirled about her brain with dreamlike insistence. Phoebe tried to pry Cousin Clarabelle off, but her limbs grew heavy, her hands dull and clumsy.

Before the darkness enveloped her, Cousin Clarabelle lifted the handkerchief away. Reaching around her, she opened the door to Ralph's bedroom and pushed Phoebe inside. She stumbled, sprawling headlong across the carpet. She landed facedown, her nose in the woolen pile. The fibers tickled her nose. The door clicked softly shut, and the beginnings of relief tingled along Phoebe's extremities. But then Cousin Clarabelle yanked her by the arm again, flipping her onto her back. Phoebe opened her mouth to cry out from the pain; Cousin Clarabelle slapped a hand over her mouth.

"Shhhh. One word and this goes into you." Something in her free hand gleamed slightly, catching a beam of moonlight through the undrawn curtains. No more than a pinpoint, the light danced along the object, long and thin, with something perched at its end—something metallic, a silver bird, with outstretched wings. Realization bore a lethal rent in Phoebe's courage, just as a similar object had born a lethal rent in Regina's skull. She stared down the length of the hat pin in Cousin Clarabelle's hand; such an ordinary thing, so innocent, with the power to kill. "You know I'll do it, Phoebe. I've done it before, haven't I?" Clarabelle made an ugly sound, a grunt. No, a laugh, but to Phoebe it sounded feral, guttural.

She nodded. Yes, she knew Cousin Clarabelle would do it. The hand against her mouth slowly withdrew. Her lips felt bruised, cracked where they had struck her teeth. She stared up into Cousin Clarabelle's calm eyes. How can she be so composed? Had she been so when she pressed an ether-soaked rag against Regina's face and plunged the dragonfly deep into her skull?

"Why?" Phoebe managed after a croak.

"I think you know why." She waved the letter over Phoebe's face. "My husband told me he wrote this, and that at the right moment, Ralph would find it, and any claim I tried to make on the inheritance—on *Regina's* inheritance—would immediately be deemed null and void." She swore under her breath, words Phoebe had never in her life heard a lady utter.

"He hated me, you know. Not at first, but as time went on. Because I hated *her*. Hated her from the first moment they put her in my arms. She wasn't mine, could *never* be mine. She belonged to Basil's whore, you see. But we were in India at the time, and it was easy for me to remain secluded on our estate until she was born. Even the servants didn't know she wasn't mine. But from the first, she was willful, stubborn, contrary—everything a daughter of mine would never have been." She paused, gritting her teeth. Light sparked along the hat pin, inches above Phoebe's face. The smell of ether continued to permeate the air, making her wonder, in an offhand way, if perhaps she was dreaming.

"We'd tried for years, you understand." Cousin Clarabelle spoke as if to a friend over tea. "He blamed me, of course, especially after he proved himself by getting his whore pregnant. Surprise on him when, upon returning to England, I had Hastings. It wasn't me, it was that putrid, unhealthy Indian climate. No decent woman can bear it. So I gave him a son, an heir, but was he grateful?"

Was Phoebe supposed to answer? She tried to move instead, and realized the intolerable weight she'd been feeling, but distantly, was in fact Cousin Clarabelle sitting on her stomach. Crushing, squeezing the breath out of her. She parted her lips, but no sound came out.

Cousin Clarabelle didn't seem to notice or care. Disdain

oozed from every word she spoke. "Basil preferred Regina. Oh, how perfect she was, his clever, beautiful daughter. And how his son never measured up. He wasn't strong enough, smart enough, not quick enough with his lessons. Didn't ride well or shoot straight . . ." She made another grunting sound, one Phoebe did not mistake this time for a laugh. "Everything was about Regina, *for* Regina. So, surely you can see, Phoebe, you can understand, why I could not let my son be snubbed this final time by his father. I could *not*. Nor could I let Regina simply take everything away from us. And then—oh!—then I learned what she was up to. She was a communist. Did you know that?"

Phoebe only shook her head.

"Oh, yes. Just like one of those violent, beastly Bolsheviks. She wished to spread their filth here, in England, and surely I couldn't allow her to do that, could I? I couldn't let her smear the family name, while at the same time taking everything away from us. I had no choice. None. You do understand, don't you, dear, darling Phoebe?"

"Y-yes, Cousin Cl-Clarabelle." Her tongue felt dry, fuzzy; it stuck to the roof of her mouth. She attempted to swallow and succeeded only in causing her throat to convulse. She stifled an urge to burst out coughing. "I . . . understand. You . . . had to."

"Yes, of course I did. And then Ralph told me he knew, that he had found the proof. That Basil had left him a letter, this letter you found. He said no one would believe a mother murdered her own daughter, but I wasn't her mother, was I? I wanted to find that letter first but it's been impossible to move about this house today without being seen. So I waited. I was coming in just now, you see, to find it. Oh, but my lovely Ralph. I didn't wish to lose him, Phoebe, surely you see that. But he forced my hand, just like Regina did. It was all Regina's fault. All of it."

"Yes," Phoebe managed, as bile rose in her throat.

"Good. I so wanted you to understand. I didn't want you to hate me, darling Phoebe."

"I don't."

"Good," she repeated. "Now, as soon as we're done here I'm going to go back to my room and have that nap. When your grandparents arrive and someone comes to wake me, it'll appear as if I've been tucked into bed all along, because someone drugged *me* with ether." She held up the cloth. "And when they find *you*, well . . . they'll believe that horrid Olive sneaked back into the house and killed you. Because this isn't *my* hat pin. It's *hers*. I stole it from her room." A triumphant grin accompanied those last words; it penetrated the fog surrounding Phoebe's brain and spurred her to action.

With a shout, Phoebe shoved with all her strength, rolling and taking Cousin Clarabelle with her. The hat pin flew from the woman's fingers, but it didn't go far. Phoebe groped to reach it, but their skirts had tangled and she couldn't move freely. The handkerchief hovered over her, and then descended before she could react.

Blackness rose up to swallow her. Within the vast whirling emptiness, a voice rang out. It called to her, and she swam toward it, struggling against a current that dragged at her body. She longed to succumb to the tide— how easy, how restful. But the voice called again, louder, more urgent, and she fought the shadows until her eyes once more opened.

Cousin Clarabelle was on her feet now, grappling with another figure, swathed in darkness like a creature of the dead. No, not a creature. Merely someone dressed in dark clothing. The small figure broke away, then hurled itself at Cousin Clarabelle. They stumbled closer and closer to Phoebe. She tried to command her limbs to move. She must clear her head first. *Breathe.* Take in air and breathe out the ether. She gulped in a huge draft, filling her lungs. Then she swung her legs at the two writhing forms. She struck the backs of Cousin Clarabelle's legs, and then rolled away as Cousin Clarabelle's feet came out from under her and she hit the floor, hard, on her back.

The other—Phoebe could make her out now, it was *Olive*—launched herself onto Cousin Clarabelle. "Phoebe, grab something, anything, and hit her if you must."

Phoebe tried to stand but couldn't. Grab—what? She glanced wildly about the dark room. Then she crawled to the fireplace, remembering how another fireplace had yielded a weapon. She seized not an andiron but the poker, the long brass rod cold and solid in her grasp.

She used the poker to rise to her knees, was maneuvering her feet beneath her when the electric lights burst on, nearly blinding her, and voices filled her ears.

Eva didn't at first see Lady Phoebe. But what she did see made her question her sanity. From downstairs they had heard thumping and bumping, then shouts. She had just opened the front door to Miles, and they had both gone still, listening. Verna Brockhurst and Lady Julia had stepped out of the drawing room to listen as well.

"Is that my mother-in-law I hear?" the younger Lady Mandeville had asked. That question, and another shout from upstairs, had sent them running up the steps.

The sounds had led them to an unexpected place: the bedroom formerly occupied by Ralph Cameron. How could that be? Eva hadn't wasted any time, for she heard someone call out her mistress's name. She rushed forward even ahead of Miles and pushed her way through the door.

With a flick of the switch, the lights flooded the room to reveal . . . Olive Asquith? She was on the floor scuffling with the dowager, kicking and landing blows. The young woman had surely lost her mind. Horrified at the thought of the dowager being hurt, Eva hurried to them and grasped Miss Asquith by the back of her shirtwaist collar. A now familiar odor wafted in the air, drawing her attention to a rumpled cloth lying on the floor not far from the women. Yanking Miss Asquith's collar, Eva crouched to reach the cloth. Her fingers closed around it. She managed to haul Miss Asquith away from the dowager and thrust the cloth beneath the young woman's nose.

"Eva, no. Not Olive. It's Cousin Clarabelle."

From the corner of her eye Eva spotted Lady Phoebe pushing to her feet. She held a fire poker as one might a spear. What had she said? That her cousin . . . ?

"Eva, step away." Miles grasped her hand and drew it from Miss Asquith's collar. The young woman nearly fell forward onto the dowager, but Miles caught her by the shoulder. He steadied her and helped her stand. The dowager lay on her side, panting heavily.

"Mother Mandeville." Verna Brockhurst rushed to her mother-in-law's side and sank to her knees. "Are you all right? Are you harmed? This is all too much. My nerves can't take anymore. First Hastings is carted off, and now this . . ."

What about Miss Brockhurst and Mr. Cameron? Did their fates not strain the woman's nerves as well? Eva dismissed her and met Lady Phoebe's gaze, filled with both fear and relief. Eva dropped the ether-soaked cloth and hurried to her. Their arms encircled each other, and Lady Phoebe half fell against her, her legs sagging.

"The ether," she said. "I was nearly unconscious more than once. I'm still . . . so dizzy."

Eva helped her to the nearest chair and lowered her into it. "What happened here, my lady?"

Before she could reply, the dowager groped to a sitting position with her daughter-in-law's help. She shoved a finger toward Miss Asquith. "She attacked us."

Miss Asquith glared back at her, unflinching. "I did no such thing. *She* was attacking Phoebe. I heard her through the speaking tubes." She aimed a particularly significant look at Eva.

"She's lying, obviously," Verna Brockhurst declared, as if it settled the matter. No one but the dowager paid her any mind.

"Have you been here in the house this whole time?" Lady Phoebe asked.

Miles stepped back slightly, keeping both Miss Asquith and the dowager in his sights. "A good question. Where have you been, Miss Asquith?"

"Hiding," she replied. "In the storage area of the attic. I knew everyone would think I took the opportunity to escape. And I almost did. Only one thing kept me here."

"And what is that?" Miles demanded.

"My innocence. There's a speaking tube up there, in the main storage room. I discovered it while exploring the house when Regina and I first arrived. I've been listening in on all of your conversations." She gestured with her chin at the dowager. "I heard what she was about to do to Phoebe. Kill her, and then pretend to have been asleep—drugged with ether—in her bed all the while, so that you would all think I'd done the deed." She frowned, glaring down at the dowager. "I half believed you had guessed I never left the house."

The dowager scowled back. "Had I known where you were, I'd have dispatched you without further ado."

Her daughter-in-law tried putting an arm around her, but the dowager slapped it away.

Miles turned to Lady Phoebe. "Is this true?"

"It is. I'd be dead now if not for Olive." She paused, seeming to search the carpet. Then she left her chair, took several steps, and bent down, retrieving something from the floor. "With this. Olive, I believe this is your hat pin?" She held it up, several inches of silver topped by the figure of a bird.

"Yes, that's mine."

"She's a communist," the dowager blurted. "Arrest her, Constable. She led my daughter astray, and they were going to help the Bolsheviks gain a foothold here in England."

"That may be," Miles said calmly, "but it's not against the law."

"It's treason," the dowager insisted. "How can she be allowed to get away with it? The court will agree with me. They'll never convict me. I was defending our country."

"You committed murder, and you will more than likely be convicted." Miles reached out a hand to help her to her feet. "Come, Lady Mandeville, it's time to go. And time to free your son."

"Wait, Constable. I still have a question or two." Lady Phoebe eased away from Eva to approach her cousin. Yet when she spoke, it was to Lady Mandeville *and* Olive Asquith. "What happened to Cousin Basil? Did one of you tell him about Regina's communist sympathies, thus upsetting him beyond what he could bear?"

After hesitating, the dowager admitted, "I'd suspected he was making changes to his will. The barmy gaffer. I thought enlightening him to his daughter's mischief would secure the fortune for Hastings." She shot a glance at Miles. "It was an accident, hardly my fault. Who knew he'd keel over dead?"

"But you came here accusing Regina of killing him," Lady Phoebe reminded her.

"She did kill him. If not for her political duplicity, he'd still be alive. And so would my poor, dear Ralph. It's *her* fault they're both dead now."

Lady Phoebe drew in several deep breaths, an obvious effort to maintain her patience. "All right, then, my second question. We found a burned periodical in Regina's fireplace. It must have been torn up first, and a scrap of it floated away from the flames. On it were two words: 'list Labor.' "

"*The Socialist Labor Review.*" Miss Asquith raised her chin defensively. "I brought that to Regina myself. There were several articles highlighting the inequities of English labor laws, specifically the lack of protections for women in the workplace. We can be dismissed without cause, you know, simply because a man seeks the position."

The dowager's lip curled. "Revolting rubbish. Of course I burned it, you stupid girl." The dowager's voice grated with disdain. "Hadn't Regina done enough harm to this family without it getting out that we harbored among us a social miscreant?"

"My mother-in-law is right about that." Verna Brock-hurst's fingers curled like claws around the collar of her frock; her nose was pinched, her lips thin and chapped. Had she been biting them? "Regina has ruined us utterly. How *shall* we survive the scandal? She's hateful and cruel."

Lady Phoebe rounded on her. "*Was*, not *is*, Verna. Regina is dead. She is the victim here, not you. How can you care more about your reputation than a person's life, your own sister-in-law—"

Seeing her mistress so distraught, Eva moved to go to her, but an unexpected voice interceded. "Phoebe," Lady Julia said, and went to her sister's side. "Never mind. There is no use in arguing with someone who plainly doesn't see beyond her own needs." The younger Lady Mandeville let out an indignant snort, but Lady Julia ignored her. "Come. Let's prepare to leave this dismal place. Let's allow the constable to do his job, while you and I go home. Grams has sent the car for us, and it should be here at any moment now." Putting an arm around Lady Phoebe, she glanced over her shoulder at Eva. They shared a moment's conspiratorial knowledge that the news from home wasn't good, that Lord Wroxly was not well, but Lady Phoebe didn't need to know that yet. "Eva? Shall we?"

"I'll start packing our things, my lady." Warmth filled Eva to see that small overture of friendship between the sisters. She started to the door, but stopped as her gaze met Miles's. He smiled, only slightly, but enough to let her know she would be seeing him soon enough. Her heart rejoiced, for she had feared she had crossed an unforgivable line when she forced him to speak of the war.

Miles gripped the dowager's elbow and with a nudge set her walking. The woman let out a protest, and Eva expected Miles to resort to the handcuffs. To her surprise, he did not. He weathered her verbal abuses bravely and kept her moving steadily on. Her remonstrations echoed from the stairs, then the front hall, finally to fade away as Miles removed her from the house.

Eva set her feet in motion to begin the task of packing, but Lady Phoebe called to her.

"I'll pack my own things, Eva, and then I'll help Olive with hers." She turned to the young woman. "You'll come to Foxwood Hall with us, yes?"

Miss Asquith stared back at her, her lips parting, a look of disbelief knitting her brows together. "You're inviting me to your home?"

"Yes, until you decide what you wish to do now." Phoebe looked to her sister for consensus. "Isn't that right, Julia?"

Lady Julia appeared as skeptical as Miss Asquith. "I . . . er . . . yes, if that's what you wish."

"But after everything that's happened, and everything you know about me, you'd still welcome me into your home? Even knowing I'd scorn a place like your Foxwood Hall and the kind of life you live there?"

Lady Phoebe laughed, a sound that never failed to work itself into Eva's heart. That a young woman who had been through as much as Phoebe Renshaw could still find laughter within her seemed a remarkable thing, and a precious one, too. "If you could perhaps not share your political views with our grandparents and promise not to rouse the servants to revolution, I think all will be well."

When Miss Asquith failed to laugh or even smile at the joke, Lady Phoebe sobered. "Forgive me, Olive, I shouldn't jest at your expense, for I do believe you are sincere. I fear I shall never agree with your beliefs, not entirely, though I do find merit in some of what you prescribe. But they are your beliefs and should be respected."

"Thank you, Phoebe." Miss Asquith stepped forward and took Lady Phoebe's hand. "That is more than I would have expected from someone of your station."

Eva thought that rather thin gratitude on Miss Asquith's part, but all things considered, a heartening development.

But Miss Asquith hadn't finished. Next, she approached Eva. "I'm dreadfully sorry I hit you. I'm not someone who typically resorts to violence. I'm afraid I was rather desperate, thinking I might be arrested for murder. Are you all right, and can you forgive me? I'd understand if you wished to have me charged with assault."

"Quite forgiven." Eva touched Miss Asquith's wrist. "And as things have turned out, I'm quite happy to consider the matter forgotten."

"Thank you, Miss Huntford," the other woman said. "I've been wrong about you. There is much in you to admire."

"Well, then," Lady Julia said briskly, "there's no use in standing around. Let's all get busy so we can be gone from here just as quick as may be."

"What about me?"

Eva, Ladies Phoebe and Julia, and Miss Asquith had all crossed to the doorway, but at Verna Brockhurst's petulant query, they stopped and turned. At first no one spoke, as if Lady Mandeville had posed a particularly puzzling riddle no one could solve.

Finally, the woman replied to her own question. "Oh, never mind. I don't want to go to your old Foxwood Hall, anyway. Your grandmother doesn't like me, I know she doesn't. I'll wait here for Hastings." She glanced about the room, and suddenly her expression brightened, though without bringing any semblance of beauty to her face. "Why, it has just occurred to me. High Head Lodge belongs to us now. It's mine. It's my home, and there's no reason for me to leave."

"And long may they be happy here," Miss Asquith murmured too quietly for Lady Mandeville to hear. Not that it would have mattered, for her attention was now focused on the room as she flitted from the carved headboard to the mahogany dresser to the marble-faced fireplace.

"Yes," Lady Julia whispered for their ears alone, "and I know a lady's maid I'll be more than happy to recommend to her."

Julia and Miss Asquith continued down the corridor to their bedrooms, but Lady Phoebe lagged behind with Eva.

She linked arms with her. "What a sad business this has been, from start to finish."

"I'm only happy you weren't seriously harmed, my lady. How are you feeling now? Does your head ache from the ether?"

"Hmm, only if I think about it." She touched her free hand to her brow. "So I shan't. And your head, from when Olive struck you?"

"I'm fine, my lady."

"Tell me, Eva, do you think they'll ever find happiness, Verna and Hastings?"

Eva doubted it very much, but she said, "Happiness takes different forms for different people, my lady. Perhaps in their way, they'll be happy."

"I do hope you're right. And I hope . . ."

"Yes, my lady?"

"Julia was rather kind to me just now."

"Yes, she was. She does love you, my lady."

"Sometimes I wonder. But yes, perhaps. I only hope she and I might resolve our differences someday, so that . . ." She brought them to a halt. They turned, facing each other. Sadness and a lonely, uncertain shadow of hope swam in Lady Phoebe's clear hazel eyes, making Eva's throat ache. "So that the kind of discord that has torn the Brockhurst family apart will never do the same to the Renshaws."

Eva pressed her palm to her mistress's cheek. "Have no fear of that, my lady. The Renshaw girls may snipe and tussle at times, but when you need each other, you will always pull together."

"What makes you so sure?"

Eva smiled and started them walking again. "I know my ladies. I know their hearts, and I have the utmost faith in all of you."

"Hearing it from you, Eva, I believe it must be so. Goodness, I cannot wait to be home. Do you think I can expect a telephone call from Owen Seabright when we get there?"

"I believe you should expect a *visit* from Lord Owen, my lady, and quite soon."

Lady Phoebe grinned as she opened the door to her room.

Lady Phoebe Renshaw and her lady's maid, Eva Hunt-ford, are preparing for a wedding, but it may not be the happy occasion everyone hopes for....

Since the Great War, some family fortunes have suffered, including those of the Renshaws. Despite being the granddaughter of an earl, Julia Renshaw is under pressure to marry for money—and has settled for Gilbert Townsend, a viscount and a wealthy industrialist. He is decades older than Julia, and it's clear to her sister Phoebe—and to Eva, who has been like a surrogate mother to the girls—that this is not a love match. Nevertheless, the wedding takes place—and in a hurry.

At the reception aboard the groom's yacht, there appears to be tension between Gil and several guests: his best man, a fellow veteran of the Boer War; his grouchy spinster sister; and his current heir, a nervous young cousin named Ernest. The bride is also less than pleased when she discovers that her honeymoon will be more crowded than expected—with Gil's pretty secretary, among others, coming along.

That very night, Julia pounds on her sister's door, brandishing a bandaged hand and reporting a hot-tempered outburst on her new husband's part. Julia is feeling doubt and regret about her hasty decision, but returns to the boat. Then the next morning, before the yacht can depart the harbor, Gil's body is found in the water below—and Phoebe and Eva must discover who pushed him over . . . before the Renshaws' social standing is irreparably stained by Julia's arrest for his murder. . . .

Please turn the page for an exciting sneak peek of Alyssa Maxwell's next Lady and Lady's Maid mystery

A MURDEROUS MARRIAGE

coming soon wherever print and e-books are sold!

CHAPTER 1

Cowes, Isle of Wight, April 1920

Phoebe Renshaw pressed a hand to her stomach in a futile attempt to ease the incessant gnawing inside. At a stern look from the countess, her grandmother, she remembered she shouldn't set so much as a finger against her frock, lest she wrinkle the ivory silk organza and ruin the effect of the folds and tucks and artful draping. Despite Phoebe turning twenty-one on her next birthday, her grandmother still had the ability to command her behavior with a twitch of a silvery crescent eyebrow.

Her sister, sixteen-year-old Amelia, wore the same frock, and they sported matching cloche hats covered in organza, lace, and coral silk roses, which seemed rather much for Phoebe's plain features but on Amelia looked a picture of springtime beauty, as if she had stepped off the cover of the latest edition of *La Mode*. Yet Amelia's features mirrored Phoebe's own ominous sentiments, which continued to tie her stomach into impossible knots.

Phoebe braved a glance at Eva, hoping Grams didn't notice. The lady's maid who had served the Renshaw sisters these past eight years had eschewed her dependable black today in favor of a deep blue, neatly tailored suit that accented her trim figure and whose pleated skirt swayed smartly just below her calves.

Eva's gaze collided with Phoebe's for the barest instant, but that instant told all. Eva's expression loomed as overcast as the sky outside, as steely as the choppy waters of the Solent, that wide waterway between the Isle of Wight and the mainland, spread out before the Royal Yacht Squadron clubhouse. They had borrowed a room on the upper floor, in which to ready themselves for the coming ordeal. . . .

The irony that the original tower of this building had been commissioned by Henry VIII was not lost on Phoebe. Cowes Castle hadn't been a home to kings, but rather a fortress commanding the Solent and the entrance to the river Medina to keep out invaders from France and the Holy Roman Empire. This had been intended as a place of war, and its connection to that particular monarch seemed terribly ill omened. Six wives, two of whom met horrible ends . . .

Phoebe tried to shake the morbid thoughts away. What right had she to judge Julia's actions, much less whether those actions would bring her beautiful eldest sister happiness?

"Phoebe, come here and help with this." Grams flicked a slender, long-fingered hand impatiently. Unlike Eva, Grams had adhered to basic black, her wardrobe having varied little since Papa died, though today her mourning was softened by the sheen of silk trimmed with deep lavender velvet.

Grams was determined that the next few hours would

take place with smooth precision, and for a moment resentment rose up in Phoebe. Julia wouldn't be doing this if not for Grams. An ember burned against Phoebe's heart, and the words she'd tamped down last night and all morning threatened to leap, flaming, from her tongue.

It felt awful to be so angry with someone you loved so much.

Grams beckoned again with a jerky motion of her hand. Yes, even she was feeling her nerves today, though for entirely different reasons than the rest of them. And Julia?

Phoebe didn't know what she was feeling. They had enjoyed a brief few months last year of getting along as sisters should. Then everything had changed, and Julia's manner had returned to the previous cool disregard. And her admitting—*finally*—the reason for her derision hadn't helped. If anything, it had made matters worse, for Julia seemed to go out of her way to avoid Phoebe, or at least avoid being alone with her.

She crossed the room to the small circle gathered around her sister and gingerly grasped the edges of the lace veil while Eva and Hetta, Julia's new maid, secured it to the platinum and diamond circlet that embraced her golden, upswept hair. While the circlet had been in the Renshaw family for many generations, the veil had been Grams's mother's, the Honiton lace made in Devon and designed by the same William Dyce who designed the lace for Queen Victoria's wedding gown. But that was the only harkening back to a bygone age. Julia's dress, a sleek garment of ivory satin with an overlay of beaded lace, a drop waist, and whisper-sheer sleeves, represented the very latest in bridal fashion. Phoebe's and Amelia's frocks had been designed to complement, but not overshadow, Julia's.

Julia didn't speak as they fussed around her, but gazed placidly out the wide window overlooking the Solent. In the middle of the harbor, a steamer yacht weathered the tossing waters with barely a wobble. Even from here, it appeared a small ocean liner, with its stacks and masts and tiered decks. And yet how grim a scene it made, Phoebe thought. Though newly refurbished after its service during the war, the vessel took on the dismal pallor of the sky and the waterway surrounding it and made no promise of happy sailing. Another omen? Phoebe wondered how Julia felt about spending her honeymoon on the twelve-hundred-ton, three-masted steamer named *Georgiana*, after her soon-to-be husband's first wife.

"There now." Grams smoothed her fingertips down Julia's sleeves and stepped back with a satisfied, if slightly cunning, smile. "Let's have a look at you. Oh, Julia, you're stunning."

"You are, Julia, truly," Amelia agreed. Phoebe heard her frail attempt to infuse the comment with enthusiasm. "Just beautiful."

Eva nodded her concurrence. "Indeed, my lady. There can never have been a lovelier bride."

"Oh, *ja*." Hetta Brauer had been Julia's personal maid for several months now, but her English remained barely existent. Julia preferred it that way after discovering her last lady's maid eavesdropping and selling secrets to the scandal sheets. A sturdy, good-natured girl with a hearty flush to her cheeks and thick blond braids she wore looped about her ears, she looked as though she might have been plucked only that morning from a flower-carpeted mountainside in her native Switzerland. "*Lieblich.*"

While the others gushed their approval, Phoebe struggled for words but found none she could, in good conscience, speak. Yes, Julia looked beautiful, but then with her golden hair, deep blue eyes, and classic features, she always did. That wasn't the point.

Phoebe merely smiled and hoped the gesture appeared sincere.

"Thank you," Julia said simply.

Grams made another adjustment to the veil. "A shame he's only a viscount. I had hoped for an earl at the least, perhaps a marquess. But, of course, Gil is a very *wealthy* viscount. You'll have a good life, my dear."

While the fortunes of many of the landed families had dwindled in recent years, Gil's had burgeoned, thanks to early investments in motorcar engines. During the war his factories had produced munitions and aeroplane engines, and he continued with the latter in peacetime. No one could accuse Gil Townsend of not taking advantage of opportunities when he saw them.

"Yes." A little tick contracted the skin around Julia's right eye. "And, after all, I had my chance at a marquess, Grams, and look how that turned out."

Grams pursed her lips tightly and said nothing. True, Julia had very nearly become engaged to Henry Leighton, Marquess of Allerton, the Christmas before last. That is, everyone had *believed* they were about to become engaged—all except Julia, who'd had other ideas. It turned out Julia had been right, but it was all a moot point now, anyway. Henry was no longer Marquess of Allerton. Henry was simply . . . no longer.

"What time is it?" Julia averted her face when Grams tried to adjust a pin curl framing her cheek. "Is it time to go yet?"

Eva consulted a porcelain clock ticking pleasantly on a nearby table. "Not just yet, my lady."

Julia frowned. "Then I'm ready too early. I can't very well sit and make myself comfortable until we leave."

"Don't you *dare* sit." Grams darted a scandalized glance at each sister. "None of you may sit, not even for a moment. I won't have you looking like wilted washerwomen. Eva, would you please watch for the cars and let us know when they arrive?"

Eva nodded and slipped out of the room.

"Oh, dear, how are you all going to ride in your grandfather's motorcar without wrinkling? I hadn't thought about that." Grams's expression registered something approaching horror. "What shall we do? Good *heavens* . . . Oh, I know. We could all walk up to the church."

"Arrive at my wedding on foot? Are we peasants now?" Julia aped Grams's scandalized look of a moment ago. "Shall I take off my shoes and stockings and go barefoot?"

"Oh, Julia, don't be ridiculous. I simply don't want you to wrinkle."

Julia tossed her head, but only slightly so as not to dislodge her headpiece and veil. "What would people think? No, I'm going in the Rolls-Royce, and there's an end to it."

A storm gathered between Grams's brows, and she looked about to retort. She wasn't used to being spoken to in such adamant terms by her granddaughters. By anyone, for that matter. But in this instance, she obviously agreed with Julia. An earl's granddaughter surely could not arrive at her wedding on foot. "Yes, yes, well, I suppose your grandfather mustn't walk even a short distance these days. You girls will go in his motor, and he and I, along with Fox, will ride in Gil's sedan."

This reminder of Grampapa's health sent a cold fear through Phoebe. He had suffered chest pains last summer, a symptom of his ongoing heart condition. He seemed thinner of late, paler, his zest for life on the wane. . . .

"You must try not to sit too . . ." Grams was saying. She paused, searching for words. "Rigidly."

"Perhaps you should lay us out on the seat and stack us one on the other," Julia muttered under her breath. Luckily, Grams appeared not to have heard.

Amelia went to her and sweetly said, "We'll try our best, Grams."

Grams nodded and looked about her, as if searching for something. "I'm going down to telephone the church and make sure everything there is ready. And then I'm going to make sure Fox hasn't gotten up to any of his usual nonsense." Grams left Phoebe and Amelia alone with their sister, except for Hetta, of course, but she apparently understood little of what they said.

Julia strolled to the window, her short train swishing across the area rug. A sigh came from deep within her. "Well. It won't be long now."

Phoebe had promised herself she wouldn't do this, but at the eleventh hour, she simply couldn't help herself. She practically launched herself at her sister, knowing she might have only moments before Grams returned. "Julia, are you certain—quite certain about this?"

Julia didn't bother looking around. "What are you talking about?"

"It's not too late to change your mind."

Julia chuckled. "Tell that to the church full of people and the caterer who is even now setting up the buffet on Gil's steamer."

"Never mind that. Gil is almost forty years older than you. Julia, *think*. What you do today will affect the rest of your life."

"The rest of Gil's life, perhaps."

"And what about Theo? You know you—"

Julia turned to Phoebe, her dark blue eyes sparking. "Forget about Theo. I have. A marriage between us would never work. Grams would never . . ." She let the thought go unfinished.

"No, perhaps Grams wouldn't, but isn't it time you stopped worrying about what Grams wants and do what *you* want?" The words stung of betrayal to her grandmother, for all they were justified. "This is your life, Julia. Your *life*."

"I'm marrying Gil, and there's an end to it." The same words she'd spoken to Grams about riding to church in the Rolls-Royce.

Unlike Grams, Phoebe wouldn't be put off so easily, not about this.

Light footsteps brought Amelia to Julia's other side. "Theo loves you, Julia, and you love him," she said. "Isn't that what marriage is? Gilbert Townsend is a good enough man, I suppose, but can you truly say you love him, enough to tie yourself to him for the rest of your life?"

The door opened, and Phoebe spun around, expecting to see her grandmother. But it was only a waitress, come to deliver more refreshments. Didn't she know Grams would have an apoplexy if she caught them eating in these clothes before the wedding?

"The rest of *Gil's* life," Julia said yet again in reply to Amelia's question. "He's much older than I, as you've both already pointed out countless times. He'll be gone soon enough, and then I may do as I please."

Phoebe whispered a caution. "Julia." With a flick of her gaze, she indicated the waitress setting down her tray on the low table near the sofa.

Julia remained oblivious to their audience. "If I can present him with a son before he goes, so much the better for

me. Our child will inherit, and my place as Viscountess An-
nondale will be firmly established, and my fortune fixed
for life."

"Julia!" Amelia whisked a hand to her mouth, her eyes
round and filled with the same dismay that raised the gorge
in Phoebe's throat.

"You don't mean this," Phoebe said, almost pleading.
"You don't have to do this. You—"

The door opened again, this time marking Eva's return.
She stopped short and stared across the room at them, no
doubt sensing the strangling tension. Julia seemed not to
notice her arrival as she spun fully around to face both
Phoebe and Amelia. She reached out and seized Phoebe's
wrist.

"You listen to me and listen well. Grams didn't want me
to tell you this. She said you'd each learn in your own
good time. But it's high time you both knew the truth. Our
family is no longer what it was. The money is dwindling.
If each of us doesn't marry well, Fox won't be able to support us. He won't be able to maintain the estate. We'll lose
everything."

Julia spoke of their youngest sibling, fifteen-year-old
Fletcher, whom everyone referred to as Fox or Foxwood—
the estate he would one day inherit from their grandfather.
Reminding Fox of his future inheritance and responsibili-
ties had been a way to help him cope with losing his father
in the war and having to grow up too quickly, and to
prompt him to a better understanding of the role he'd one
day assume—not that it had done much good. Fox remained an impertinent child who reveled in tormenting his
sisters behind their grandparents' backs.

But the thought of Fox inheriting an empty title, a bankrupt estate . . . Surely Julia couldn't mean things were *that*

bad. Phoebe understood that no family had emerged from the war quite as wealthy as they had been, and she knew Grams worried about that, but . . . She shook her head, unable to absorb Julia's claim. "I know the war and the death duties—"

"It's not just the war. It's everything. Most especially how far agricultural prices have fallen in the past couple of decades. Foxwood Hall doesn't support itself any longer and hasn't for some time now. We're slowly losing it. We certainly will if we girls don't do our duty."

"I know why you're doing this," Amelia whispered. Her eyes misted, and her shoulders shook beneath her ruched cap sleeves. "It's *because* you love Theo, isn't it? You think Gil will die soon, and then you can marry Theo and be happy. But, Julia, what if it doesn't work out that way?"

Julia pressed her face close to Amelia's and said in a voice she never used with her youngest sister, "Don't you dare ever say that again, to anyone. You don't know what you're talking about."

The door opened again, and this time Grams called out to them. "What are you lot doing huddled by the window? Come along. The motorcars are here. It's time to go. Amelia, are you crying? My dear, sweet child, I know you're overjoyed for your sister, but you don't wish to arrive at the church all blotchy-faced."

Phoebe and her sisters grabbed their wraps and filed from the room. Eva leveled a look of sympathetic support on Phoebe and touched her arm as she passed by. The waitress, still standing by the sofa table, also watched them go. Good heavens, Phoebe had forgotten about her, while the woman had simply stood there eavesdropping and enjoying a good bit of family drama. Well, no matter. She could gossip with her fellow servants all she liked. The Renshaws would never see her again.

Outside, she, Julia, and Amelia accepted a footman's help and slid carefully into the backseat of Grampapa's Rolls-Royce. Her grandparents were driven to the church in Gil's Mercedes-Knight tourer. The short ride along the Esplanade and up the hill to Holy Trinity Church seemed to take forever but was over all too soon.

* * *

Connect with U(s)

Visit us online at
KensingtonBooks.com
to read more from your favorite authors, see books
by series, view reading group guides, and more.

for sneak peeks, chances to win books and prize packs,
and to share your thoughts with other readers.

facebook.com/kensingtonpublishing
twitter.com/kensingtonbooks

Tell us what you think!

To share your thoughts, submit a review,
or sign up for our eNewsletters, please visit:
KensingtonBooks.com/TellUs.